R IS FOR

"A refreshing heroine."
—*The Washington Post Book World*

"If you haven't tried [Grafton] yet, you're missing a sterling example of the mystery writer's craft."
—*Entertainment Weekly*

"[A] first-class series."
—*The New York Times Book Review*

R is for Ricochet

Reba Lafferty was a daughter of privilege, the only child of an adoring father. Nord Lafferty was already in his fifties when Reba was born, and he could deny her nothing. Over the years, he quietly settled her many scrapes with the law, but wasn't there for her when she was convicted of embezzlement and sent to the California Institution for Women. Now, at thirty-two, she is about to be paroled, having served twenty-two months of a four-year sentence. Nord Lafferty wants to be sure she stays straight, stays at home and away from the drugs, the booze, the gamblers.

It seems a straightforward assignment for Kinsey: babysit Reba until she settles in, make sure she follows all the rules of her parole. Maybe all of a week's work. Nothing untoward—the woman seems remorseful and friendly. And the money is good.

But life is never that simple, and Reba is out of prison less than twenty-four hours when one of her old crowd comes circling around . . .

continued . . .

TITLES BY SUE GRAFTON

Kinsey Millhone mysteries

A is for Alibi
B is for Burglar
C is for Corpse
D is for Deadbeat
E is for Evidence
F is for Fugitive
G is for Gumshoe
H is for Homicide
I is for Innocent
J is for Judgment
K is for Killer
L is for Lawless
M is for Malice
N is for Noose
O is for Outlaw
P is for Peril
Q is for Quarry
R is for Ricochet
S is for Silence

IS FOR
Ricochet

SUE GRAFTON

BERKLEY BOOKS, NEW YORK

R

THE BERKLEY PUBLISHING GROUP
Published by the Penguin Group
Penguin Group (USA) Inc.
375 Hudson Street, New York, New York 10014, USA
Penguin Group (Canada), 10 Alcorn Avenue, Toronto, Ontario M4V 3B2, Canada
(a division of Pearson Penguin Canada Inc.)
Penguin Books Ltd., 80 Strand, London WC2R 0RL, England
Penguin Group Ireland, 25 St. Stephen's Green, Dublin 2, Ireland (a division of Penguin Books Ltd.)
Penguin Group (Australia), 250 Camberwell Road, Camberwell, Victoria 3124, Australia
(a division of Pearson Australia Group Pty. Ltd.)
Penguin Books India Pvt. Ltd., 11 Community Centre, Panchsheel Park, New Delhi – 110 017, India
Penguin Books (NZ), Cnr. Airborne and Rosedale Roads, Albany, Auckland 1310, New Zealand
(a division of Pearson New Zealand Ltd.)
Penguin Books (South Africa) (Pty.) Ltd., 24 Sturdee Avenue, Rosebank, Johannesburg 2196,
South Africa

Penguin Books Ltd., Registered Offices: 80 Strand, London WC2R 0RL, England

This is a work of fiction. Names, characters, places, and incidents either are the product of the author's imagination or are used fictitiously, and any resemblance to actual persons, living or dead, business establishments, events, or locales is entirely coincidental.

R IS FOR RICOCHET

A Berkley Book / published by arrangement with the author

PRINTING HISTORY
Marian Wood/G. P. Putnam's Sons hardcover edition / July 2004
Berkley mass-market edition / April 2005

ISBN 0-425-20386-7

BERKLEY®
Berkley Books are published by The Berkley Publishing Group,
a division of Penguin Group (USA) Inc.,
375 Hudson Street, New York, New York 10014.
BERKLEY is a registered trademark of Penguin Group (USA) Inc.
The "B" design is a trademark belonging to Penguin Group (USA) Inc.

PRINTED IN THE UNITED STATES OF AMERICA

10   9   8

For my granddaughter, Taylor,
with a heart full of love

ACKNOWLEDGMENTS

The author wishes to acknowledge the invaluable assistance of the following people: Steven Humphrey; Boris Romanowski, California State Parole Agent; Alice Sprague, Deputy District Attorney, Alameda County, California; Pat Callahan, Public Relations Officer, Valley State Prison for Women; at the California Institution for Women, Warden John Dovey, Lieutenant Larry J. Aaron, Public Information Officer, and Pam Clark, Community and Parole Relations; Bruce Correll, Chief Deputy (retired), Santa Barbara Sheriff's Department; Lorrinda Lepore, Investigator II, Ventura County District Attorney's Office; Bill Kracht, General Manager, The Players Club; Joan Francis, Francis Pacific Investigations; Julianna Flynn and Kurt Albershardt; and Gail and Harry Gelles.

And for the generous offers of support and expertise for the subplot that ended up on the cutting-room floor, thanks go to Detective Sergeant Bill Turner (retired), Santa Barbara County Sheriff's Department; Dona Cohn, Cohn Law Firm; attorneys Joseph M. Devine, Lawrence Kern, and Philip Segal of Kern Noda Devine & Segal; Daniel Trudell, President, Accident Reconstruction Specialists; James F. Lafferty, P.E., Ph.D., biomechanics and mechanical engineering; Dr. Anthony Sances, Jr., President, Biomechanics Institute; and Nancy Degger, President, Rudy Degger & Associates. Maybe next book.

R

IS FOR RICOCHET

1

The basic question is this: given human nature, are any of us really capable of change? The mistakes other people make are usually patently obvious. Our own are tougher to recognize. In most cases, our path through life reflects a fundamental truth about who we are now and who we've been since birth. We're optimists or pessimists, joyful or depressed, gullible or cynical, inclined to seek adventure or to avoid all risks. Therapy might strengthen our assets or offset our liabilities, but in the main we do what we do because we've always done it that way, even when the outcome is bad . . . perhaps *especially* when the outcome is bad.

This is a story about romance—love gone right, love gone wrong, and matters somewhere in between.

I left downtown Santa Teresa that day at 1:15 and headed for Montebello, a short ten miles south. The weather report had promised highs in the seventies. Morning cloudiness had given way to sunshine, a welcomed respite from the overcast that typically mars our June and July. I'd eaten lunch at my desk, feasting on an olive-and-pimiento-cheese sandwich on wheat bread, cut in quarters, my third-favorite sandwich in the whole wide world. So what was the problem? I had none. Life was great.

In committing the matter to paper, I can see now what should have been apparent from the first, but events seemed to unfold at such a routine pace that I was caught, metaphorically speaking, asleep at the wheel. I'm a private detective, female, age thirty-seven, working in the small Southern California town of Santa Teresa. My jobs are varied, not always lucrative, but sufficient to keep me housed and fed and ahead of my bills. I do employee background checks. I track down missing persons or locate heirs entitled to monies in the settlement of an estate. On occasion, I investigate claims involving arson, fraud, or wrongful death.

In my personal life, I've been married and divorced twice, and subsequent relationships have usually come to grief. The older I get, the less I seem to understand men, and because of that I tend to shy away from them. Granted, I have no sex life to speak of, but at least I'm not plagued by unwanted pregnancies or sexually transmitted diseases. I've learned the hard way that love and work are a questionable mix.

I was driving on a stretch of highway once known as the Montebello Parkway, built in 1927 as the result of a fundraising campaign that made possible the creation of frontage roads and landscaped center dividers still in evidence today. Because billboards and commercial structures along the roadway were banned at the same time, that section of the 101 is still attractive, except when it's jammed with rush-hour traffic.

Montebello itself underwent a similar transformation in 1948, when the Montebello Protective and Improvement Association successfully petitioned to eliminate sidewalks, concrete curbs, advertising signs, and anything else that might disrupt the rural atmosphere. Montebello is known for its two-hundred-some-odd luxury estates, many of them built by men who'd amassed their fortunes selling common household goods, salt and flour being two.

I was on my way to meet Nord Lafferty, an elderly gentleman, whose photograph appeared at intervals in the society column of the *Santa Teresa Dispatch*. This was usually occasioned by his making yet another sizable contribution to some charitable foundation. Two buildings at UCST had been named for him, as had a wing of Santa Teresa Hospital and a special collection of rare books he'd donated to the public library. He'd called me two days before and indicated he had "a modest undertaking" he wanted to discuss. I was curious how he'd come by my name and even more curious about the job itself. I've been a private investigator in Santa Teresa for the past ten years, but my office is small and, as a rule, I'm ignored by the wealthy, who seem to prefer doing business through their attorneys in New York, Chicago, or L.A.

I took the St. Isadore off-ramp and turned north toward the foothills that ran between Montebello and the Los Padres National Forest. At one time, this area boasted grand old resort hotels, citrus and avocado ranches, olive groves, a country store, and the Montebello train depot, which serviced the Southern Pacific Railroad. I'm forever reading up on local history, trying to imagine the region as it was 125 years ago. Land was selling then for seventy-five cents an acre. Montebello is still bucolic, but much of the charm has been bulldozed away. What's been erected instead—the condominiums, housing developments, and the big flashy starter castles of the nouveau riche—is poor compensation for what was lost or destroyed.

I turned right on West Glen and drove along the winding two-lane road as far as Bella Sera Place. Bella Sera is lined with olive and pepper trees, the narrow blacktop climbing gradually to a mesa that affords a sweeping view of the coast. The pungent scent of the ocean faded with my ascent, replaced by the smell of sage and the bay laurel trees. The hillsides were thick with yarrow, wild mustard, and California poppies. The afternoon sun had baked the boulders to a golden turn, and a warm chuffing wind was beginning to stir the dry grasses. The road wound upward through an alley of live oaks that terminated at the entrance to the Lafferty estate. The property was surrounded by a stone wall that was eight feet high and posted with No Trespassing signs.

I slowed to an idle when I reached the wide iron gates. I leaned out and pushed the call button on a mounted keypad. Belatedly I spotted a camera mounted atop one of two stone pillars, its hollow eye fixed on me. I must have passed inspection because the gates swung open at a measured pace. I shifted gears and sailed through, following the brick-paved drive for another quarter of a mile.

Through a picket fence of pines, I caught glimpses of a gray stone house. When the whole of the residence finally swept into view, I let out a breath. Something of the past remained after all. Four towering eucalyptus trees laid a dappled shade on the grass, and a breeze pushed a series of cloud-shaped shadows across the red tile roof. The two-story house, with matching one-story wings topped with stone balustrades at each end, dominated my visual field. A series of four arches shielded the entrance and provided a covered porch on which wicker furniture had been arranged. I counted twelve windows on the second floor, separated by paired eave brackets, largely decorative, that appeared to support the roof.

I pulled onto a parking pad sufficient to accommodate ten cars and left my pale blue VW hunched, cartoonlike, between a sleek Lincoln Continental on one side and a full-size Mercedes on the other. I didn't bother to lock up, operating on the assumption that the electronic surveillance system was watching over both me and my vehicle as I crossed to the front walk.

The lawns were wide and well tended, and the quiet was underlined by the twittering of finches. I pressed the front bell, listening to the hollow-sounding chimes inside clanging out two notes as though by a hammer on iron. The ancient woman who came to the door wore an old-fashioned black uniform with a white pinafore over it. Her opaque stockings were the color of doll flesh, her crepe-soled shoes emitting the faintest squeak as I followed her down the marble-tiled hall. She hadn't asked my name, but perhaps I was the only visitor expected that day. The corridor was paneled in oak, the white plaster ceiling embossed with chevrons and fleurs-de-lis.

She showed me into the library, which was also paneled in oak. Drab leather-bound books lined shelves that ran floor to ceiling, with a brass rail and a rolling ladder allowing access to the upper reaches. The room smelled of dry wood and paper mold. The inner hearth in the stone fireplace was tall enough to stand in, and a recent blaze had left a partially blackened oak log and the faint stench of wood smoke. Mr. Lafferty was seated in one of a pair of matching wing chairs.

I placed him in his eighties, an age I'd considered elderly once upon a time. I've since come to realize how widely the aging process varies. My landlord is eighty-seven, the baby of his family, with siblings whose ages range as high as ninety-six. All five of them are lively, intelligent, adventurous, competitive, and given to good-natured squabbling among themselves. Mr. Lafferty, on the other hand, looked as though he'd been old for a good twenty years. He was inordinately thin, with knees as bony as a pair of misplaced elbows. His once sharp features had at least been softened by the passing years. Two small clear plastic tubes had been placed discreetly in his nostrils, tethering him to a stout green oxygen tank on a cart to his left. One side of his jaw was sunken, and a savage red line running across his throat suggested extensive surgery of some vicious sort.

He studied me with eyes as dark and shiny as dots of brown sealing wax. "I appreciate your coming, Ms. Millhone. I'm Nord Lafferty," he said, holding out a hand that was knotted with veins. His voice was hoarse, barely a whisper.

"Nice to meet you," I murmured, moving forward to shake hands with him. His were pale, a tremor visible in his fingers, which were icy to the touch.

He motioned to me. "You might want to pull that chair close. I've had thyroid surgery a month ago and more recently some polyps removed from my vocal cords. I've been left with this rasping noise that passes as speech. Isn't painful, but it's irksome. I apologize if I'm difficult to understand."

"So far, I'm not having any problem."

"Good. Would you like a cup of tea? I can have my housekeeper make a pot, but I'm afraid you'll have to pour for yourself. These days, her hands aren't any steadier than mine."

"Thanks, but I'm fine." I pulled the second wing chair closer and took a seat. "When was this house built? It's really beautiful."

"1893. A man named Mueller bought a six-hundred-forty-acre section from the county of Santa Teresa. Of that, seventy acres remain. House took six years to build and the story has it Mueller died the day the workers finally set down their tools. Since then, the occupants have fared poorly . . . except for me, knock on wood. I bought the property in 1929, just after the crash. Fellow who owned the place lost everything. Drove into town, climbed up to the clock tower, and dived over the rail. Widow needed the cash and I stepped in. I was criticized, of course. Folks claimed I took advantage, but I'd loved the house from the minute I laid eyes on it. Someone would have bought it. Better me than them. I had money for the upkeep, which wasn't true of many folks back then."

"You were lucky."

"Indeed. Made my fortune in paper goods in case you're curious and too polite to inquire."

I smiled. "Polite, I don't know about. I'm always curious."

"That's fortunate, I'd say, given the business you're in. I'm assuming you're a busy woman so I'll get right to the

point. Your name was given to me by a friend of yours—
fellow I met during this recent hospital stay."

"Stacey Oliphant," I said, the name flashing im-
mediately to mind. I'd worked a case with Stacey, a retired
Sheriff's Department homicide detective, and my old pal
Lieutenant Dolan, now retired from the Santa Teresa Police
Department. Stacey was battling cancer, but the last I'd
heard, he'd been given a reprieve.

Mr. Lafferty nodded. "He asked me to tell you he's doing well, by the way. He checked in for a battery of tests,
but all of them turned out negative. As it happened, the two
of us walked the halls together in the afternoons, and I got
chatting about my daughter, Reba."

I was already thinking skip trace, missing heir, possibly
a background check on a guy if Reba were romantically involved.

He went on. "I only have the one child and I suppose
I've spoiled her unmercifully, though that wasn't my intent.
Her mother ran off when she was just a little thing, this
high. I was caught up in business and left the day-to-day
raising of her to a series of nannies. She'd been a boy I
could have sent her off to boarding school the way my parents did me, but I wanted her at home. In retrospect, I see
that might've been poor judgment on my part, but it didn't
seem so at the time." He paused and then gestured impatiently toward the floor, as though chiding a dog for leaping
up on him. "No matter. It's too late for regrets. Pointless,
anyway. What's done is done." He looked at me sharply
from under his bony brow. "You probably wonder what I'm
driving at."

I proffered a slight shrug, waiting to hear what he had
to say.

"Reba's being paroled on July twentieth. That's next
Monday morning. I need someone to pick her up and bring
her home. She'll be staying with me until she's on her feet
again."

"What facility?" I asked, hoping I didn't sound as startled as I felt.

"California Institution for Women. Are you familiar with the place?"

"It's down in Corona, couple of hundred miles south. I've never actually been there, but I know where it is."

"Good. I'm hoping you can take time out of your schedule for the trip."

"That sounds easy enough, but why me? I charge five hundred dollars a day. You don't need a private detective to make a run like that. Doesn't she have friends?"

"Not anyone I'd ask. Don't worry about the money. That's the least of it. My daughter's difficult. Willful and rebellious. I want you to see to it she keeps the appointment with her parole officer and whatever else is required once she's been released. I'll pay you your full rate even if you only work for a part of each day."

"What if she doesn't like the supervision?"

"It's not up to her. I've told her I'm hiring someone to assist her and she's agreed. If she likes you, she'll be cooperative, at least to a point."

"May I ask what she did?"

"Given the time you'll be spending in her company, you're entitled to know. She was convicted of embezzling money from the company she worked for. Alan Beckwith and Associates. He does property management, real estate investment and development, things of that type. Do you know the man?"

"I've seen his name in the paper."

Nord Lafferty shook his head. "I don't care for him myself. I've known his wife's family for years. Tracy's a lovely girl. I can't understand how she ended up with the likes of him. Alan Beckwith is an upstart. He calls himself an entrepreneur, but I've never been entirely clear what he does. Our paths have crossed in public on numerous occasions and I can't say I'm impressed. Reba seems to think the world of him. I will credit him for this—he spoke up in her behalf before her sentencing. It was a generous gesture on his part and one he didn't have to make."

"How long has she been at CIW?"

"She's served twenty-two months of a four-year sentence. She never went to trial. At her arraignment—which I'm sorry to say I missed—she claimed she was indigent, so the court appointed a public defender to handle her case. After consultation with him, she waived her right to a preliminary hearing and entered a plea of guilty."

"Just like that?"

"I'm afraid so."

"And her attorney agreed to it?"

"He argued strenuously against it, but Reba wouldn't listen."

"How much money are we talking?"

"Three hundred fifty thousand dollars over a two-year period."

"How'd they discover the theft?"

"During a routine audit. Reba was one of a handful of employees with access to the accounts. Naturally, suspicion fell on her. She's been in trouble before, but nothing of this magnitude."

I could feel a protest welling but I bit back my response.

He leaned forward. "You have something to say, feel free to say it. Stacey tells me you're outspoken so please don't hesitate on my account. It may save us a misunderstanding."

"I was just wondering why you didn't step in. A high-powered attorney might have made all the difference."

He dropped his gaze to his hands. "I should have helped her . . . I know that . . . but I'd been coming to her rescue for many, many years . . . all her life, if you want to know the truth. At least that's what I was being told by friends. They said she had to face the consequences of her behavior or she was never going to learn. They said I'd be enabling, that saving her was the worst possible action under the circumstances."

"Who's this 'they' you're referring to?"

For the first time, he faltered. "I had a lady friend. Lucinda. We'd been keeping company for years. She'd seen me intercede in Reba's behalf on countless occasions. She persuaded me to put my foot down and that's what I did."

"And now?"

"Frankly, I was shocked when Reba was sentenced to four years in state prison. I had no idea the penalty would be so stiff. I thought the judge would suspend sentence or agree to probation, as the public defender suggested. At any rate, Lucinda and I quarreled, bitterly I might add. I broke off the relationship and severed my ties with her. She was much younger than I. In hindsight, I realized she was angling for herself, hoping for marriage. Reba disliked her intensely. Lucinda knew that, of course."

"What happened to the money?"

"Reba gambled it away. She's always been attracted to card play. Roulette, the slots. She loves to bet the ponies, but she has no head for it."

"She's a problem gambler?"

"Her problem isn't the gambling, it's the losing," he remarked, with only the weakest of smiles.

"What about drugs and alcohol?"

"I'd have to answer yes on both counts. She tends to be reckless. She has a wild streak like her mother. I'm hoping this experience in prison has taught her self-restraint. As for the job itself, we'll play that by ear. We're talking two to three days, a week at the most, until she's reestablished herself. Since your responsibilities are limited, I won't be requiring a written report. Submit an invoice and I'll pay your daily rate and all the necessary expenses."

"That seems simple enough."

"One other item. If there's any suggestion that she's backsliding, I want to be informed. Perhaps with sufficient warning, I can head off disaster this time around."

"A tall order."

"I'm aware of that."

Briefly, I considered the proposition. Ordinarily I don't like serving as a babysitter and potential tattletale, but in this case, his concern didn't seem out of line. "What time will she be released?"

2

On my way back into town, I picked up my dry-cleaning and then cruised through a nearby supermarket, picking up odds and ends, which I intended to drop off at my place before I returned to work. I was hoping to touch base with my landlord before the arrival of his lady visitor later in the day. I was running the errands to provide myself with props to explain my unexpected midafternoon appearance. Henry and I confide in each other on many issues, but his love life isn't one. If I wanted information, I knew I'd do well to proceed with finesse.

My studio apartment was originally the single-car garage attached to Henry's house by way of a now glass-enclosed breezeway. In 1980 he converted the space to the snug studio I've been renting ever since. What began as a basic square fifteen feet on a side is now a fully furnished "great room," which includes a living room, a bump-out galley-style kitchen, a laundry nook and bathroom, with a sleeping loft and a second bathroom up a set of spiral stairs. The space is compact and cleverly designed to exploit every usable inch. Given the pegs and cubbyholes, walls of polished teak and oak, and the occasional porthole window, the studio has the scale and feel of a ship's interior.

I found a parking spot two doors away and hauled out my cleaning and the two grocery bags. My timing couldn't have been more perfect. As I pushed through my squeaky metal gate and followed the walkway around to the rear, Henry was just pulling into his two-car garage. He'd taken his bright yellow five-window Chevy coupe for its annual checkup and it was back now, the exterior polished to a fare-thee-well. The interior was probably not only spotless, but scented with faux pine. He bought the vehicle new in 1932 and he's taken such good care of it you'd swear it was still under warranty, assuming cars had warranties back then. He has a second vehicle, a station wagon he uses for routine errands and the occasional trip to the Los Angeles airport, ninety-five miles south. The coupe he reserves for special occasions, today being one.

I have trouble remembering that he's eighty-seven years old. I also have trouble describing him in terms that aren't embarrassingly laudatory given our fifty-year age difference. He's smart, sweet, sexy, trim, handsome, vigorous, and kind. In his working days, he made a living as a commercial baker, and though he's been retired now for twenty-five years, he still makes the best cinnamon rolls I've ever eaten. If I were forced to accord him a fault, I'd probably cite his caution when it comes to affairs of the heart. The only time I'd seen him smitten, he was not only deceived, but nearly taken for every cent he had. Since then, he's played his cards very close to his chest. Either he hadn't run into anyone of interest or he'd looked the other way. That is, until Mattie Halstead appeared.

Mattie was the artist-in-residence on a Caribbean cruise

he and his siblings had taken in April. Soon after the cruise
ended, she'd stopped in to see him on her way to Los Angeles to deliver paintings to a gallery down there. A month
later, he'd made an unprecedented trip to San Francisco,
where he spent an evening with her. He'd kept mum on the
subject of their relationship, but I noticed he'd spiffed up
his wardrobe and started lifting weights. The Pitts family
(at least on Henry's mother's side) is long-lived, and he and
his siblings enjoy remarkably good health. William's a bit
of a hypochondriac and Charlie's almost entirely deaf, but
that aside, they give the appearance of going on forever.
Lewis, Charlie, and Nell live in Michigan, but there are vis-
its back and forth, some planned and some not. William
and my friend Rosie, who owns the tavern half a block
away, would be celebrating their second wedding anniver-
sary on November 28. Now it looked like Henry might be
entertaining similar thoughts . . . or such was my hope.
Other people's romances are so much less hazardous than
one's own. I was looking forward to all the pleasures of true
love without suffering the peril.

Henry paused when he caught sight of me, allowing me
to fall into step with him as he proceeded to the house. I noticed his hair had been freshly trimmed, and he wore a blue
denim work shirt with his crisply pressed chinos. He'd even
traded in his usual flip-flops for a pair of deck shoes with
dark socks.

I said, "Hang on a second while I drop this stuff off."

He waited while I unlocked my door and dumped my
armload on the floor just inside. Nothing I'd bought would
go funky in the next thirty minutes. Rejoining him, I said,
"You had your hair trimmed. It looks great."

He ran a self-conscious hand across his head. "I was
passing the barbershop and realized I was long overdue.
You think it's too short?"

"Not at all. It shaves years off your age," I said, thinking
Mattie would have to be an idiot if she didn't understand
what a treasure he was. I held open the screen door while he

pulled out his keys and unlocked his back door. I followed him inside, watching as he set his groceries on the kitchen counter.

"Nice that Mattie's coming down. I'll bet you're looking forward to seeing her."

"It's only the one night."

"What's the occasion?"

"She did a painting on commission for a woman in La Jolla. She's delivering that one plus a couple more in case the woman doesn't care for the first."

"Well, it's nice she can manage a visit. When's she getting in?"

"She hoped to be here by four, depending on traffic. She said she'd check into the hotel and call once she's had a chance to freshen up. She agreed to supper here as long as I didn't go to any trouble. I said I'd keep it simple, but you know me."

He began to unload his sack: a packet wrapped in white butcher's paper, potatoes, cabbage, green onions, and a big jar of mayonnaise. While I watched, he opened the oven door and checked his crock of soldier beans bubbling away with molasses, mustard, and a chunk of salt pork. I could see two loaves of freshly baked bread resting on a rack on the counter. A chocolate layer cake sat in the middle of the kitchen table with a glass dome over it. There was also a bouquet of flowers from his garden—roses and lavender he'd arranged artfully in a china teapot.

"Cake looks fabulous."

"It's a twelve-layer torte. I used Nell's recipe, which was originally our mother's. We tried it for years, but none of us could duplicate her results. Nell finally managed, but she says it's a pain. I ended up tossing half a dozen layers before I mastered the thing."

"What else are you having?"

Henry took out a cast-iron skillet and set it on the stove. "Fried chicken, potato salad, coleslaw, and baked beans. I thought we'd have a little picnic on the patio, unless the temperature drops." He opened his spice cabinet and sorted through the contents, taking down a bottle of dried dill. "Why don't you join us? She'd love to see you."

"Oh please. Socializing is the last thing she needs. After six hours on the road? Give the woman a drink and let her put her feet up."

"No need to worry about her. She has energy to spare. She'd be delighted, I'm sure."

"Let's just see how it goes. I'm on my way back to the office, but I'll check in with you again as soon as I get home."

I'd already decided to decline, but I didn't want to seem rude. In my opinion, they needed time to themselves. I'd pop my head in and say hi, primarily to satisfy my curiosity about her. She was either widowed or divorced, I wasn't sure which, but during her last visit, I'd noticed she'd made a number of references to her husband. At one point, when Henry was nursing a bum knee, she'd gone hiking alone, taking her watercolors with her so she could paint a spot in the mountains she and her husband had enjoyed for years. Was she still emotionally entrenched? Whether hubby was dead or alive, I didn't like the idea. Henry, meanwhile, was busy being nonchalant, perhaps in denial of his feelings or in response to covert signals from her. Of course, there was always the possibility that I was imagining all this, but I didn't think so. At any rate, I intended to have my supper at Rosie's, resigned to my usual weekly allotment of her bullying and abuse.

I left Henry to his preparations and went back to the office, where I put a call through to Priscilla Holloway, Reba Lafferty's parole agent. Nord Lafferty had given me her name and phone number at the end of our appointment. I was already back at my car, opening the driver's side, when the elderly housekeeper had called from the front door and then hurried down the walk, a photograph in hand.

Winded, she'd said, "Mr. Lafferty forgot to give you this. It's a photograph of Reba."

"Thanks. I appreciate that. I'll return it as soon as we get back."

"Oh, no need. He said to keep it if you like."

I thanked her again and tucked the photo into my bag. Now, while I waited for Parole Agent Holloway to answer her phone, I plucked out the photo and studied it again. I'd have preferred something recent. This had been taken when the woman was in her mid- to late twenties and almost puckish in appearance. Her large dark eyes were intent on the camera, her full lips half-parted as though she were on the verge of speaking. Her hair was shoulder-length and dyed blond, but clearly at considerable expense. Her complexion was clear with a hint of blush in her cheeks. After two years of prison fare, she might have packed on a few extra pounds, but I thought I'd recognize her.

On the other end of the line, a woman said, "Holloway."

"Hi, Ms. Holloway. My name is Kinsey Millhone. I'm a local private investigator—"

"I know who you are. I had a call from Nord Lafferty, telling me he'd hired you to pick up his daughter."

"That's why I'm calling, to clear it with you."

"Fine. Have at it. It'll save me the trip. If you're back in town before three, bring her over to the office. Do you know where I am?"

I didn't, but she gave me the address.

"See you Monday," I said.

I spent the rest of the afternoon taking care of paperwork, mostly sorting and filing in a vain attempt to tidy up my desk. I also did some boning up on parole regulations from a pamphlet printed by the California Department of Corrections.

Returning to my apartment for the second time that day, I saw no sign of picnic items on the patio table. Perhaps he'd decided the meal was better served indoors. I crossed to his back door and peeked in. As it turned out, my hopes for their romantic interlude were squelched by William's presence in the kitchen. Looking aggrieved, Henry sat in his rocking chair with his usual glass of Jack Daniel's while Mattie nursed a goblet of white wine.

William, two years Henry's senior, has always looked enough like him to be his twin. His shock of white hair was thinning where Henry's was still full, but his eyes were the same hot blue and he carried himself with the same erect military bearing. He wore a dapper three-piece suit, his watch chain visible across the front of his vest. I tapped on the glass and Henry motioned me in. William rose to his feet at the sight of me, and I knew he'd remain standing unless I urged him to sit. Mattie rose to greet me, and though we didn't actually hug, we did clasp hands and exchange an air kiss.

She was in her early seventies, tall and slender, with soft silver hair she wore pulled into a knot on the top of her head. Her earrings glinted in the light—silver, oversize, and artisan-made.

I said, "Hey, Mattie. How are you? You must have arrived right on time."

"Good to see you. I did." She wore a coral silk blouse and a long gypsy skirt over flat-heel suede boots. "Will you join us in a glass of wine?"

"I don't think so, but thanks. I've got business to take care of so I have to run."

Henry's tone was morose. "Have a glass of wine. Why not? Stay for supper as well. William's invited himself so what's the difference? Rosie couldn't tolerate having him underfoot so she sent him over here."

William said, "She had a small conniption fit for no reason at all. I'd just returned from the doctor's office and I knew she'd want to hear the results of my blood work, especially my HDLs. You might want to take a look yourself." He held the paper out, pointing with significance at the long column of numbers down the right side of the page. My gaze slid past his glucose, sodium, potassium, and chloride levels before I caught the expression on Henry's face. His eyes were crossed so close to the bridge of his nose I thought they'd trade sides. William was saying, "You can see my LDL-HDL risk ratio is 1.3."

"Oh, sorry. Is that bad?"

"No, no. The doctor said it was excellent . . . in light of my medical condition." William's voice carried a hint of feebleness suggestive of a weakened state.

"Well, good for you. That's great."

"Thank you. I called our brother Lewis and told him as well. His cholesterol is 214, which I think is cause for alarm. He says he's doing what he can, but he hasn't had much success. You can pass the paper on to Mattie once you've studied it yourself."

Henry said, "William, would you sit down? You're giving me a crick in my neck." He left his rocker and took another wineglass from the kitchen cabinet. He poured wine to the brim and passed the glass to me, slopping some liquid on my hand.

William declined to sit until he'd pulled out my chair. I settled myself with a murmured "Thank you" and then I made a show of running a finger down the column of reference and unit numbers from his doctor's report. "You're in good shape," I remarked as I passed the paper to Mattie.

"Well, I still have palpitations, but the doctor's adjusting my medication. He says I'm amazing for a man my age."

"If you're in such terrific health, how come you're off to the urgent care center every other day?" Henry snapped.

William blinked placidly at Mattie. "My brother's careless with his health and won't acknowledge that some of us are proactive."

Henry made a snorting sound.

William cleared his throat. "Well now. On to a new subject since Henry's apparently unable to handle that one. I hope this is not too personal, but Henry mentioned your husband is deceased. Do you mind my asking how he was taken?"

Henry was clearly exasperated. "You call that a different

subject? It's the same one—death and disease. Can't you think of anything else?"

"I wasn't addressing you," William replied before returning his attention to Mattie. "I hope the topic isn't too painful."

"Not at this point. Barry died six years ago of heart failure. I believe cardiac ischemia is the term they used. He taught jewelry making at the San Francisco Art Institute. He was a very talented man, though a bit of an eccentric."

William was nodding. "Cardiac ischemia. I know the term well. From the Greek, *ischein,* meaning 'quench' or 'seize,' combined with *haima,* or 'blood.' A German pathology professor first introduced that term in the mid-1800s. Rudolf Virchow. A remarkable man. What age was your husband?"

"William," Henry sang.

Mattie smiled. "Really, Henry. I'm not sensitive about this. He died two days shy of his seventieth birthday."

William winced. "Pity when a man's struck down in his prime. I myself have suffered several episodes of angina, which I've miraculously survived. I was discussing my heart condition with Lewis, just two days ago by phone. You remember our brother, I'm sure."

"Of course. I hope he and Nell and Charles are all in good health."

"Excellent," William said. He shifted in his chair, lowering his voice. "What about your husband? Did he have any warning prior to his fatal attack?"

"He'd been having chest pains, but he refused to see the doctor. Barry was a fatalist. He believed you check out when your time is up regardless what precautions you take. He compared longevity to an alarm clock that God sets the moment you're born. None of us knows when the little bell will ring, but he didn't see the point in trying to second-guess the process. He enjoyed life immensely, I'll say that about him. Most folks in my family don't make it to the age of sixty, and they're miserable every minute, dreading the inevitable."

"Sixty! Is that right? That's astonishing. Is there a genetic factor in play?"

"I don't think so. It's a little bit of everything. Cancer, diabetes, kidney failure, chronic pulmonary disease . . ."

William put his hands on his chest. I hadn't seen him so happy since he'd had the flu. "COPD. Chronic obstructive pulmonary disease. The very term brings back memories. I was stricken with a lung condition in my youth—"

Henry clapped his hands. "Okay, fine. Enough said on that subject. Why don't we eat?"

He moved to the refrigerator and took out a clear glass bowl piled with coleslaw, which he plunked on the table with rather more force than was absolutely necessary. The chicken he'd fried was piled on a platter on the counter, probably still warm. He placed that in the center of the table with a pair of serving tongs. The squat little crockery pot now sat on the back of the stove, emitting the fragrance of tender beans and bay leaf. He removed serving utensils from a ceramic jug and then took down four dinner plates, which he handed to William, perhaps in hopes of distracting his attention while he brought the rest of the dinner to the table. William set a plate at each place while he quizzed Mattie at length about her mother's death from acute bacterial meningitis.

Over supper Henry steered the conversation into neutral territory. We went through ritual questions about Mattie's drive down from San Francisco, traffic, road conditions, and matters of that sort, which gave me ample opportunity to observe her. Her eyes were a clear gray and she wore very little makeup. She had strong features, with nose, cheekbones, and jaw as pronounced and well proportioned as a model's. Her skin showed signs of sun damage, and it lent her complexion a ruddy glow. I pictured her out in the fields for hours with her paint box and easel.

I could tell William was reflecting on the subject of terminal disease while I was calculating how soon I could make my excuses and depart. I intended to drag William with me so Henry and Mattie could have some time alone. I kept an eye on the clock while I worked my way through the fried chicken, potato salad, coleslaw, baked beans, and cake. The food, of course, was wonderful, and I ate with my usual speed and enthusiasm. At 8:35, just as I was formulating a plausible lie, Mattie folded her napkin and laid it on the table beside her plate.

"Well, I should be on my way. I have some phone calls to make as soon as I get back to the hotel."

"You're leaving?" I said, trying to cover my disappointment.

"She's had a long day," Henry said, getting up to remove her plate. He took it to the sink, where he rinsed it and set it in the dishwasher, talking to her all the while. "I can wrap up some chicken in case you want some later."

"Don't tempt me. I'm full but not stuffed, which is just the way I like it. This was wonderful, Henry. I can't tell you how much I appreciate the effort that went into this meal."

"Happy you enjoyed it. I'll get your wrap from the other room." He dried his hands on a kitchen towel and moved off toward the bedroom.

William folded his napkin and scraped back his chair. "I should probably run along as well. Doctor urged me to adhere to my regimen—eight full hours of sleep. I may engage in some light calisthenics before bed to aid the digestive process. Nothing strenuous, of course."

I turned to Mattie. "You have plans for tomorrow?"

"Unfortunately, I'm taking off first thing in the morning, but I'll be back in a few days."

Henry returned with a soft paisley shawl that he laid across her shoulders. She patted his hand with affection and picked up a large leather bag that she'd set beside her chair. "I hope to see you again soon," she said to me.

"I hope so, too."

Henry touched her elbow. "I'll walk you out."

William straightened his vest. "No need. I'll be happy to see her off." He offered Mattie his arm, and she tucked her hand through the crook with a brief backward look at Henry as the two went out the door.

3

Saturday morning, I slept in until 8:00, showered, dressed, made a pot of coffee, and sat at my kitchen counter, where I ate my ritual bowl of cereal. Having washed both bowl and spoon, I returned to my stool and surveyed the place. I'm inordinately tidy and I'd just done a thorough house-cleaning earlier in the week. My social calendar was un-blemished and I knew I'd spend Saturday and Sunday alone as I did most weekends. Usually this doesn't bother me, but today I felt an unsettling sensation. I was bored. I was so desperate for something to do, I thought about returning to the office to set up the files for another case I'd taken on. Unfortunately, my office bungalow is depressing and I wasn't motivated to spend another minute at my desk. Which left me to do what? Damned if I knew. In a moment of panic, I realized I didn't even have a book to read. I was on the verge of leaving for the bookstore to stock up on pa-perbacks when my telephone rang.

"Hi, Kinsey. This is Vera. I'm glad I caught you. You have a minute?"

"Of course. I was on my way out, but it's nothing pressing," I said. Vera Lipton had been a colleague of mine at California Fidelity Insurance, where I spent six years investigating arson and wrongful-death claims. She was the claims manager while I worked as an independent contractor. She had since left the business, married a doctor, and settled into life as a full-time mom. I'd seen her briefly in April with her husband, a physician named Neil Hess. Also in tow was a rowdy golden retriever pup, and her eighteen-month-old son, whose name I forgot to ask. She was massively pregnant and due to deliver her second child within days, judging by her belly. I said, "Tell me about the baby. You looked ready to drop one the day I saw you at the beach."

"No kidding. I was sway-backed as a mule. I had shooting pains in both legs, and the baby's head pressing on my bladder made me dribble in my pants. I went into labor that night and Meg was born the next afternoon. Listen, the reason I called, we'd love to have you over. We never see you these days."

"Sounds good to me. Give me a toot and we'll set something up."

There was a pause. "That's what I'm doing. I just invited you to come over and have a drink with us. We're putting some people together for a barbecue this afternoon."

"Really? What time?"

"Four o'clock. I know it's short notice, but I'm hoping you're free."

"As it happens, I am. What's the occasion?"

Vera laughed. "No occasion. I just thought it'd be nice. We've invited a few neighbors. Strictly casual and low-key. If you have a pencil handy, I'll give you the address. Why don't you plan to be here a little early and we can catch up."

I took down the information, not at all convinced. Why would she call like this out of the blue? "Vera, are you sure you're not up to something? I don't mean to sound rude, but we chatted for five minutes in April. Before that, there was a gap of four years. Don't get me wrong. I'd be happy to see you, but it does seem odd."

"Mmm."

I said, "What," not even bothering to make a question of the word.

"Okay, I'll level with you, but you have to promise you won't scream."

"I'm listening, but this is making my stomach hurt."

"Neil's younger brother, Owen, is in town for the weekend. We thought you should meet him."

"What for?"

"Kinsey, occasionally men and women are introduced to each other, or haven't you heard?"

"Like a blind *date?*"

"It's not a blind date. It's drinks and a few snacks. There'll be tons of other people so it's not like you'll be stuck with him one-on-one. We'll sit on the back deck. Cheez Whiz and crackers. If you like him, that's swell. If you don't, no big deal."

"The last time you fixed me up, it was with Neil," I said.

"My point exactly. Look how that turned out."

I was silent for a moment. "What's he like?"

"Well, aside from the fact that he walks with his knuckles barely grazing the floor, he seems to do okay. Look, I'll have him fill out an application. You can do a background check. Just be here at three-thirty. I'm wearing my only pair of jeans that haven't been split up the back."

She hung up while I was saying, "But . . ."

I listened to the dial tone in a state of despair. I could see now I was being penalized for shirking my job. I should have gone in to work. The Universe keeps track of our sins and exacts devious and repugnant punishments, like dates with unknown men. I went up the spiral staircase and opened my closet so I could stare at my clothes. Here's what I saw: My black all-purpose dress—which is the only dress I own, good for funerals and other somber occasions, not suitable for meeting guys, unless they're already dead. Three pairs of jeans, a denim vest, one short skirt, and the new tweed blazer I bought when I had lunch with my cousin, Tasha, eighteen months before. Also, an olive-green cocktail dress I'd forgotten about, given to me by a woman who was later blown to bits. In addition, there were castoffs from Vera, including a pair of black silk pants so long I had to roll 'em up at the waist. If I wore those, she'd ask to have them back, thus forcing me to drive home essentially naked below the waist. Not that I thought harem pants would be suitable for a barbecue. I knew better than that. Shrugging, I opted for my usual jeans and turtleneck.

At 3:30 promptly I was ringing Vera's doorbell. The address she'd given me was on the upper east side of town, in a neighborhood of older homes. Theirs was a ramshackle Victorian painted dark gray with white trim and an L-shaped wooden porch complete with froufrou along the rail. The front door had a stained-glass rose in the center that made Vera's face look bright pink when she peered out at me. Behind her, the dog barked with excitement, eager to jump up and slobber on someone new. She opened the door, holding the dog by its collar to prevent its escape.

She said, "Don't look so glum. You've been given a reprieve. I sent the guys out to buy Pampers and beer, so it's just us for twenty minutes. Come on in." Her hair was cropped short and streaked with blond. She still sported her glasses with wire frames and enormous pale blue lenses. Vera's the type of woman who attracts admiring glances wherever she goes. Her figure was substantial, though she'd already dropped much of the weight she gained with Meg. She was barefoot, wearing tight jeans and an oversize tunic with short sleeves and a complicated cut to the top. All the toddler and baby toting had firmed her biceps.

She held the door for me, angling her body so the dog couldn't lunge at me just yet. He'd doubled in size since I'd seen him on the beach. He didn't seem like a mean mutt, but he was exuberant. She leaned close to his face, put a hand around his muzzle, and said, "No!" in a tone that had no particular effect. He seemed to like the attention and licked her in the mouth the first chance he got.

"This is Chase. Ignore him. He'll settle down in a bit."

I made an effort to ignore the dog while he pranced around, barking happily, and then snagged the hem of my pant leg and began to tug. He emitted a puppy growl, his feet braced on the hall carpet so he could rip my jeans to shreds. I stood there, captive, and said, "Gee, this is fun, Vera. I'm so glad I came."

She gave me a look, but let the sarcasm pass. She snagged the dog by the collar and dragged him toward the kitchen while I followed. The foyer ceiling was high with a set of stairs to the right, the living room on the left. A short hall led straight to the kitchen across the back. The passage was the usual land mine of wooden blocks, plastic toy parts, and abandoned doggie bones. She shoved Chase into a kennel the size of a steamer trunk. This didn't dismay the dog, but I felt guilty nonetheless. He placed a baleful eye to one of the air vents in the kennel and stared at me with hope.

The kitchen was large and I could see a wide deck accessible through a set of French doors. The cabinets were dark cherry, the counters dark green marble, with a six-burner stove-top built into a central island. Both the baby and Vera's son, whom she introduced as Peter, were already bathed and dressed for bed. Near the kitchen sink, a woman in a pale blue uniform was piping a star of yellow filling into each of a dozen hard-boiled egg halves.

"This is Mavis," Vera said. "She and Dirk are helping, to save the wear and tear on me. I've got a babysitter on her way."

I murmured greetings and Mavis smiled in response, hardly pausing as she squeezed the filling from a pastry bag. Parsley had been tucked around the platter. On the counter nearby there were two baking sheets of canapes ready for the oven and two other serving platters, one

arranged with fresh cut vegetables and the other an
assortment of imported cheeses interspersed with grapes.
So much for Cheez Whiz—which I personally adored, being a person of low tastes. This party had clearly been in
the works for weeks. I now suspected the designated blind
date had come down with the flu and I'd been elected to
take her place . . . a B-list substitute.

Dirk, in dress pants and a short white jacket, was working near the walk-in pantry where he'd set up a temporary
bar with a variety of glasses, an ice bucket, and an impressive row of wine and liquor bottles.

"How many are you expecting?"

"Twenty-five or so. This is strictly last minute so a lot of
people couldn't make it."

"I'll bet."

"I'm still off the booze because of Twinkletoes here."

The baby, Meg, was strapped in an infant seat in the
middle of the kitchen table, looking around with a vague
expression of satisfaction. Peter, aged twenty-one months,
had been secured in a high chair. His tray was littered with
Cheerios and green peas that he captured and ate when he
wasn't squishing them instead.

Vera said, "That's not his dinner. It's just to keep him occupied until the babysitter shows. Speaking of which, Dirk
can fix you a drink while I take Peter upstairs." She removed
the tray from the high chair and set it aside, then lifted the
boy and set him on one hip. "I'll be back shortly. If Meg
cries, it's probably because she wants to be picked up."

Vera disappeared down the hall with Peter, heading for
the stairs.

Dirk said, "What can I get for you?"

"Chardonnay's fine. I'd appreciate that."

I watched while he removed a bottle of Chardonnay
from an ice tub behind him. He poured me a glass and
added a cocktail napkin as he passed the wine across the
makeshift bar.

"Thanks."

Vera had set out Brie and thinly sliced French bread, bowls of nuts and green olives. I ate one, being careful not to crack my teeth on the pit. I was curious to tour the rest of the downstairs rooms, but I didn't dare leave Meg. I had no idea what a baby her age was capable of doing while strapped in an infant seat. Could they hop in those things?

One end of the kitchen had been furnished with two sofas upholstered in a floral fabric, two coordinating chairs, a coffee table, and a television set built into an entertainment center that ran along the wall. Wineglass in hand, I circled the periphery, idly studying the silver-framed photos of family and friends. I couldn't help wondering if one of the fellows pictured was Neil's brother, Owen. I imagined him, like Neil, on the short side and probably dark-haired as well.

Behind me, Meg made a restless sound of the sort that suggested more to follow at twice the volume. I tended to my responsibilities, setting down my wineglass so I could free the child from her infant seat. I picked her up, so unprepared for how light she was I nearly flung her through the air. Her hair was dark and fine, her eyes a bright blue with lashes as delicate as feathers. She smelled like baby powder and maybe something fresh and brown in her pants. Amazingly, after staring at me briefly, she laid her face against my shoulder and began to gnaw on her fist. She squirmed and the little oinking sounds she made hinted at feeding urges I hoped wouldn't erupt before her mother returned. I jiggled her a bit and that seemed to satisfy her temporarily.

I had now exhausted my vast fund of infant-care tricks.

I heard a manly trampling outside on the wooden deck. Neil opened the back door bearing a grocery sack bulky with disposable diapers. The guy who came in behind him carried two six-packs of bottled beer. Neil and I exchanged greetings and then he turned to his brother and said, "Kinsey Millhone. This is my brother, Owen."

I said, "Hi." The babe in my arms precluded anything in the way of handshakes.

He responded with hey-how-are-you–type things, talking over his shoulder while he delivered the beer into Dirk's capable hands.

Neil set the sack on a kitchen stool and removed the package of disposable diapers. "Let me run these on up. You want me to take her?" he asked, indicating Meg.

"This is fine," I said, and surprisingly, it was. After Neil left, I peered down at her and discovered that she'd gone to asleep. "Oh, wow," I said, scarcely daring to breathe. I couldn't tell if the ticking I heard was my biological clock or the delayed timing device on a bomb.

Dirk was in the process of making a margarita for Owen, ice clattering in the blender. With his attention occupied I had an opportunity to study him. He was tall, compared with his brother, over six feet while Neil topped out closer to my height at five-feet-seven. His hair was sandy, lightly dusted with gray. He was lean, an ectomorph, where Neil's build was stocky. Blue eyes, white lashes, a good-size nose. He glanced over at me and I dropped my gaze discreetly to Meg. He wore chinos and a navy short-sleeved shirt that revealed the light downy hair along his forearms. His teeth were good and his smile seemed sincere. On a scale of 1 to 10—10 being Harrison Ford—I'd place him at 8, or maybe even 8 plus plus.

He moved to the counter where I was standing and helped himself to a canape. We chatted idly, exchanging the sort of uninspired questions and answers that tend to pass between strangers. He told me he was visiting from New York, where he worked as an architect, designing residential and commercial structures. I told him what I did and how long I'd done it. He feigned more interest than he probably felt. He told me he and Neil had three other brothers, of which he was the second from the bottom of the heap. Most of the family, he said, was scattered up and down the East Coast with Neil the lone holdout in California. I told him I was an only child and let it go at that.

Eventually, Neil and Vera came downstairs. She took the

baby and settled on the couch. Vera fiddled with her shirt, popped a boob out, and began to breast-feed while Owen and I made a point of looking somewhere else. Eventually several other couples arrived. There were introductions all around as each new twosome was incorporated. The kitchen was gradually taken up with guests, standing in small groups, some spilling into the hallway and out onto the deck. When the babysitter arrived, Vera took Meg upstairs and returned wearing a different shirt. The noise level rose. Owen and I were separated by the crowd, which was all right with me as I'd run out of things to say to him.

I made an effort to be friendly, chitchatting with any poor soul who caught my eye. Everyone seemed nice enough, but social gatherings are exhausting to someone of my introverted nature. I endured it as long as I could and then eased toward the foyer where I'd left my shoulder bag. Good manners dictated that I say thank you and good-bye to host and hostess, but neither were in sight and I thought it'd be expedient to tiptoe away without calling attention to my escape.

As I closed the front door and made my way down the wooden porch stairs, I caught sight of Cheney Phillips coming up the walk in a deep red silk shirt, cream dress pants, and highly polished Italian loafers. Cheney was a local cop, working vice last I heard. I tended to run into him at a dive called the Caliente Café—also known as CC's— off Cabana Boulevard by the bird refuge. Rumor had it he'd met a girl at CC's and the two had taken off for Vegas to get married a scant six weeks later. I remembered the pang of disappointment with which I'd greeted the news. That was three months ago.

He said, "Leaving so soon?"

"Hey, how are you? What are you doing here?"

He tilted his head. "I live next door."

I followed his gaze to the house, another two-story Victorian that appeared to be a twin of the one I'd just left. Not many cops can afford the tab on a Santa Teresa residence of that size and vintage. "I thought you lived in Perdido."

"I did. That's where I grew up. My uncle died, leaving me a great whack of dough so I decided to invest it in real estate." He was probably thirty-four, three years younger than I, with a lean face and a mop of dark curly hair, five-eight or so, and slim. He'd told me that his mother sold high-end real estate and his father was X. Phillips who owned the Bank of X. Phillips in Perdido, a town thirty miles to the south. He'd clearly been raised in an atmosphere of privilege.

"Nice house," I said.

"Thanks. I'm still getting settled or I'd offer you a tour."

"Maybe another time," I said, wondering about his wife.

"What are you up to these days?"

"Nothing much. A little this and that."

"Why don't you return to the party and have a drink with me? We should talk."

I said, "Can't. I have to be someplace and I'm late as it is."

"Rain check?"

"Of course."

I waved, walking backward for a moment before I turned and headed to my car. Now why had I said that? I could have stayed for a drink, but I couldn't face another minute in that crowd. Too many people and too much chitchat.

I was home again by 6:15, relieved to be alone but feeling let down nonetheless. Given that I hadn't wanted to meet Vera's brother-in-law in the first place, I was disappointed—the blind date had turned out to be a bland date. Nice guy, no sparks, which was probably just as well. Sort of. It was entirely possible the regrets were attached to Cheney Phillips instead of Owen Hess, but I didn't want to deal with that. What was the point?

4

I left for the prison at 6:00 Monday morning. The drive was boring and hot, my route taking me from Santa Teresa down the 101 as far as Highway 126, which cuts inland at Perdido. The road runs between the Santa Clara River on the right and a fencework of power lines on the left, skirting the southern reaches of the Los Padres National Forest. I'd seen contour maps of the area, which detailed numerous hiking trails through that bleak and mountainous terrain. Dozens of creeks are threaded along the canyon floors. There are a surprising number of public campgrounds distributed throughout the 219,700 acres that constitute the wilderness. If I weren't preternaturally opposed to bugs, black bears, rattlesnakes, coyotes, heat, stinging nettles, and dirt, I might enjoy seeing the rumored sandstone cliffs and pines growing at odd angles along the boulder-strewn hills. In years past, even from the safety of the highway, I sometimes spotted one of the last of the California condors circling in the sky, its ten-foot wingspan stretched out as gracefully as a soaring kite.

I passed countless avocado orchards and citrus groves laden with ripening oranges, with produce stands set up every two to three miles. I caught a red light in each of three small communities of newly constructed housing and lavish shopping malls. An hour and a half later, I reached the junction of the 126 and Highway 5, which I followed to the south. It took me another hour to reach Corona. The incarceration-prone family couldn't do much better than to serve their separate bids in this area, which has the California Youth Authority, the California Institution for Men, and the California Institution for Women all within shooting range of one another. The land was flat and dusty, interrupted by power lines and water towers, parcels separated by low barbed-wire fences. A thin line of trees appeared at intervals, but it was hard to see the point. They provided no shade and only the sparsest screening from the cars speeding by. The houses had flat roofs and looked shabby, with dilapidated outbuildings. There were thick, knobby trees, whose amputated branches were, if not dead, devoid of foliage. As is true of most raw acreage in California, housing developments were taking root like a slew of weeds.

By 8:30 I found myself sitting in my car in the parking lot adjacent to the Processing Center at the California Institution for Women. For years, the CIW was known as Frontera, the feminine derivative of the word frontier. The 120-acre campus (as they referred to it back then) opened in 1952, and until this year, 1987, it was the only facility in California housing female felons. I'd already been inside the building where I showed the officer my photo ID and told him I was there to pick up Reba Lafferty, whose CDC number was, by an amusing coincidence, the same as my birthdate. The officer checked his roster, found her name, and then called Receiving and Release.

He'd suggested that I wait in the parking lot, so I'd hoofed it back to my VW. So far, the community of Corona seemed a bit grim for my taste. A trail of yellow smog hung on the horizon like something a crop-dusting plane might have left in its wake. The mid-July heat was as thick as soured milk and smelled of feedlots. A buffeting wind was blowing and there were flies everywhere. My T-shirt was sticking to my back and I could feel a sheen of moisture on my face—the sort of clamminess that wakes you from a dead sleep when you've just come down with the flu.

The view through the ten-foot chain-link fences was an improvement. I could see green lawns, walkways, and hibiscus plants with showy red and yellow blossoms. Most of the buildings were dun-colored and built close to the ground. Female inmates strolled the yards in groups of two and three. I knew from reading I'd done that construction had just been completed on a 110-bed Special Housing Unit. Total staff was 500, give or take a few, while the prison population varied between 900 and 1,200. Whites were in the majority, with ages bunched in the thirty-to-forty range. The prison provided both academic and vocational programs, including computer programming. Prison industries, largely textiles, produced shirts, shorts, smocks, aprons, handkerchiefs, bandannas, and fire-fighting clothing. Frontera also served as a hub for the selection and training of firefighters, who would be assigned work in the forty-some conservation camps across the state.

For the umpteenth time, I looked at the snapshot of Reba Lafferty taken before her legal ills and her felony quarantine. If she'd abused alcohol and drugs, the excess didn't show. Restlessly, I returned the photo to my shoulder bag and fiddled with the tuner on the radio. The morning news was the usual disheartening mixture of murder, political shenanigans, and dire economic predictions. By the time the news anchor cut to the station break, I was ready to cut my own throat.

At 9:00 A.M. I glanced up and caught sight of activity near the vehicle sally port. The gates had been rolled back and an outbound sheriff's department van now idled while the driver presented his paperwork to the sally port officer.

The two of them exchanged pleasantries. I got out of my car. The van pulled through the gate, made a wide right-hand turn, and then slowed to a stop. I could see a number of women onboard, parolees headed for the real world, their faces turned to the window like a row of plants seeking light. The doors to the van hissed open and closed, and then the vehicle moved off.

Reba Lafferty stood on the pavement in prison-issue tennis shoes, blue jeans, and a plain white T-shirt without benefit of a brassiere. All inmates are obliged to surrender their personal clothing on arrival at the prison, but I was surprised her father hadn't sent her something of her own to wear home. I knew she'd been compelled to purchase the outfit she wore since the articles were considered government property. She'd apparently declined the prison-issue bra, which was probably about as flattering as an orthopedic brace. Inmates are also required to leave prison without anything in hand, except their two hundred bucks in cash. Startled, I saw that she looked exactly like the photo. Given Nord Lafferty's advanced age, I'd pictured Reba in her fifties. This girl was barely thirty.

Her hair was now cropped short and looked damp from a shower. During her incarceration, the blond had grown out and the natural dark strands were spikey, as though she'd stiffened them with mousse. I expected her to be heavy, but she was trim almost to the point of looking frail. I could see the bony hollows of her collarbones beneath the cheap fabric of her T-shirt. Her complexion was clear but faintly sallow, and her eyes were smudged with dark shadows. There was something sensual about her; a defiance in her posture, a touch of swagger in her walk.

I lifted my hand in greeting and she crossed the road, moving in my direction.

"You here for me?"

"That's right. I'm Kinsey Millhone," I said.

"Great. I'm Reba Lafferty. Let's hit the friggin' road," she said as we shook hands.

We walked to the car and for the next hour, that was the extent of our conversation.

I prefer silence to small talk so the lack of chitchat wasn't awkward. I varied my route, catching Highway 5 south until it intersected the 101. A couple of times I thought of asking her a question, but I didn't think the ones that came to mind were any of my business. *Why'd you steal the money* and *How'd you screw it up and get caught* being foremost.

It was Reba who finally broke the silence. "Pop told you why I was in?"

"He said you took money, but that's all," I said. I noticed that I'd bypassed the word 'embezzlement,' as though it might be rude to name the crime that resulted in her prison term.

She rested her head against the back of the seat. "He's a love. He deserves a lot better than me."

"May I ask how old you are?"

"Thirty-two."

"No offense, but you look about twelve. How old was your dad when you were born?"

"Fifty-six. My mother was twenty-one. There's a match made in heaven. No telling what her deal was. She dropped me like a litter of kittens and hit the road."

"Does she keep in touch?"

"Nope. I saw her once, when I was eight. We spent one day together—well, half a day. She took me to Ludlow Beach and watched me splash in the waves until my lips turned blue. We had lunch at that snack stand, you know the one near High Ridge Road?"

"Know it well."

"I had a milk shake and ate fried clams, which I haven't eaten since. I must have been hyper. I remember my stomach was full of butterflies from the minute I woke up, knowing she'd be there. We were on our way to the zoo when I got sick in the car and she ended up taking me home."

"What'd she want?"

"Who knows? Whatever it was, she hasn't wanted it since. Pop's been great, though. I'm lucky in that regard."

"He feels guilty about you."

She turned and looked at me. "How come? None of this is his fault."

"He thinks he neglected you when you were young."

"Oh. Well, he did, but what's that got to do with it? He made his choices and I made mine."

"Yeah, but generally speaking, it's better to avoid the ones that are going to land you in jail."

She smiled. "You didn't know me back then. I was either drunk or stoned and sometimes both."

"How'd you hold down a job?"

"I saved the drinking for nights and weekends. I smoked dope before and after work. I never did the hard stuff—heroin, crack, or speed. Those can really mess you up bad."

"Didn't anyone ever notice you were stoned?"

"My boss."

"How'd you manage to take the money? Seems like that would necessitate a clear head."

"Trust me, I was always clear about some things. Have you ever been in jail?"

"I did an overnight once," I said, making it sound like an outing with my Girl Scout troop.

"For what?"

"Assaulting a cop and resisting arrest."

She laughed. "Wow. Who'da thunk? You look like a real button-down type. I'll bet you cross the street with the light and never fudge the numbers on your tax return."

"Well, true. Is that bad?"

"No, it's not *bad*. It's just boring," she said. "Don't you ever want to cut loose? Take a risk and maybe blow yourself through the roof?"

"I like my life as it is."

"What a drag. I'd go nuts."

"What makes me nuts is being out of control."

"So what do you do for laughs?"

"I don't know . . . I read a lot and I jog."

She looked at me, waiting for the punch line. "That's *it?* You read a lot and you *jog?*"

I laughed. "It does sound pathetic when you think of it."

"Where do you hang out?"

"I don't do any 'hanging out' as such, but if I want dinner or a glass of wine, I usually go to a tavern in my neighborhood called Rosie's. The owner's a mama bear, which means I can eat without being hassled by guys on the make."

"You have a boyfriend?"

"Not so's you'd notice," I said, slipping into the vernacular. Better not to let her venture too far down that path. I glanced over at her. "If you don't mind my asking, have you been in trouble before?"

She turned to look out the passenger-side window. "Depends on your point of reference. I went through drug rehab twice. I did six months in county jail on a bad-check charge. By the time I got out, my finances were in the shitter so I declared bankruptcy. Here's the weird part. Once I filed? I got a ton of credit card offers in the mail and all of them were preapproved. How could I resist? Of course, I ran those up, too. Thirty thousand bucks' worth before the gates clanged shut."

"Thirty thousand for what?"

"Oh, you know. The usual. Gambling, drugs. I blew a bunch at the track and then went to Reno where I played the slots. I sat in on some high-stakes poker, but the cards were running cold. Not that I'd quit because of that. I figured I could only lose so many times before the game turned around and started working my way. Unfortunately, I never reached that point. Next thing you know, I was broke and living on the streets. That was 1982. Pop moved me into his house and then he cleaned up my debts. What about your vices? You must have *one.*"

"I drink wine and the occasional martini. I used to smoke cigarettes, but then I gave that up."

"Hey, me, too. I quit a year ago. Talk about tough."

"The *worst*," I said. "What made you quit?"

"Just to prove I could," she said. "What about other stuff? You ever do coke?"

"Nope."

"Ludes, Vicodan, Percocet?"

I turned and stared at her.

"I'm just *asking*," she said.

"I smoked dope in high school, but then I straightened up my act."

She flopped her head to one side and said, "Snore."

I laughed. "Why snore?"

"You live like a nun. Where's the friggin' joy?"

"I have *joy*. I have a lot of joy."

"Oh, don't be so defensive. I wasn't *judging* you."

"Yes, you were."

"Well, okay, maybe a little bit. I'm mostly curious."

"About what?"

"How you make it in this world if you give up living on the edge."

"Maybe you'll find out."

"I wouldn't bet on *that*, but one can always hope."

As we approached Santa Teresa, a drifting fog had curled across the landscape, wispy and pale. I drove along the beach, palms standing out darkly against the soft white of the Pacific. Reba'd been staring at the ocean since it came into view south of Perdido. As we passed the Perdido Avenue off-ramp, she turned her head, watching it recede into the mist. "You ever hear of the Double Down?"

"What's that?"

"Perdido's only poker parlor—scene of my downfall. Had some great times there, but that's over and done with. Or so I hope."

The highway angled inland and she watched the ebb and flow of citrus groves on either side of the road. Houses and businesses began to accumulate until the town itself appeared—two- and three-story white stucco buildings with red tile roofs, palm trees, evergreens, the architecture defined by the Spanish influence.

"What'd you miss most?" I asked.

"My cat. Long-haired orange tabby I've had since he was six weeks old. He looked like a little powder puff. He's seventeen now and a great old guy."

As I took the Milagro off-ramp, I glanced at my watch. It was 12:36. "Are you hungry? We have time for lunch if you want to eat before you meet your PO."

"That'd be great. I've been hungry since we hit the road."

"You should have spoken up. You have a preference?"

"McDonald's. I'd kill for a Quarter Pounder with Cheese."

"Me, too."

Over lunch, I said, "Twenty-two months. What'd you do with your time?"

"I learned computer programming. That's a hoot and a half. Also, I memorized prison stats," she said.

"Sounds like fun."

She began dunking her fries in a lake of ketchup, eating them like worms. "Well, it was. I spent a lot of time in the library reading all the studies they've done on female inmates. Used to be, I'd pick up an article like that and it had nothing to do with me. Now it's all relevant. Like in 1976? There were eleven thousand women in state and federal prisons. Last year, the number jumped to twenty-six thousand and you want to know why? Women's Liberation. Judges used to take pity on women, especially those with little kids. Now it's equal-opportunity incarceration. Thank you, Gloria Steinem. Only something like three percent of convicted felons do any prison time anyway. And here's something else. Five years ago half the killers released from prison had served less than six years. Can you believe that? Murder someone and you're back on the street after six in the can. Most parole violations, you end up doing a bullet, which is a lot if you look at it proportionately. I flunk one drug test and I'm back on the bus."

"A bullet?"

"A year. I'm telling you, the system's really screwed. I mean, what do you think parole's about? You serve your sentence on the street. What kind of punishment is that? You have no idea how many vicious guys you got walking around out here." She smiled. "Anyway, let's go meet my PO and get it over with."

5

Parole offices were housed in a low yellow brick building of a style popular during the sixties—lots of glass and aluminum and long horizontal lines. Dark green cedars grew under an overhang that ran the length of the façade. The parking lot was generous and I found a spot without difficulty. I shut down the engine. "Want me to go with you?"

"Might as well," she said. "Who knows how long I'll have to wait. I could use the company."

We crossed the parking lot and hung a right, moving toward the entrance. We pushed through the glass doors and found ourselves facing a long drab hallway lined with offices on both sides. There was no reception area that I could see, though at the far end of the corridor there were a few folding chairs where a smattering of men were seated. As we entered, a big woman with red hair and a fat file in hand peered out of an office and called to one of the guys loitering against the wall. A sorrowful-looking man in his sixties stepped forward, dressed in a shabby sport coat and pants that were none too clean. I'd seen guys like him sleeping in doorways and picking half-smoked cigarette butts out of the sand-filled ashtrays in hotel lobbies.

She glanced over at us, catching sight of Reba. "Are you Reba?"

"That's right."

"I'm Priscilla Holloway. We spoke on the phone. I'll be with you in a sec."

"Great." Reba watched them depart. "My parole officer."

"I figured as much."

Priscilla Holloway was in her forties, strong-featured, big-boned, and tan. Her dark red hair was pulled back in a French braid that extended halfway down her back. Her dark slacks were wrinkled from sitting. Over them she wore a white shirt, hem out, and a zippered red knit jacket that was open down the front, discreet concealment for the firearm she wore holstered at her side. Her build was athletic, and my guess was she played the fast, hard-sweating sports: racquetball, soccer, basketball, and tennis. When I was in grade school a girl her size would have scared the crap out of me, but I learned, in those days, that if I cultivated a friendship, I'd end up with playground protection for life.

Reba and I staked out our claim on a tiny section of the hallway where we variously leaned and slouched, trying to find a comfortable position in which to wait. There was a pay phone mounted on the wall nearby and I could see Reba's focus sharpen at the sight of it. "You have any change? I need to make a phone call. It's local."

I opened my shoulder bag and did a quick search along the bottom, fishing for stray coins. I passed her a handful of change, watching as she moved to the phone and picked up the handset. She dropped in the coins, punched in a number, and then turned her body at an angle so I couldn't read her lips while she talked. She was on the line for three minutes and when she finally put the handset back in the cradle, she was looking happier and more relaxed than I'd seen her so far.

"Everything okay?"

"Sure. I was touching base with a friend." She sank down along the wall and took a seat on the floor.

Ten minutes later, Priscilla Holloway appeared, walking her fusty-looking client to the front door. She issued him an admonition and then turned to Reba. "Why don't you come on back?"

Reba scrambled to her feet. "What about her?"

"She can join us in a bit. We've got a couple of things we need to talk about first. I'll come get you in a minute," she said to me.

The two moved down the bleak hallway, Reba looking half Holloway's size. Reconciled to the wait, I leaned against the wall, my shoulder bag on the floor. The glass doors opened and Cheney Phillips came in, passing me on his way down the hall. I saw him tap on Priscilla Holloway's open door and stick his head in. He chatted briefly with her and then turned, walking in my direction. He still hadn't recognized me, which gave me a moment to study him.

I'd known Cheney for years, but we hadn't had occasion to interact until a murder investigation two years before. Over the course of several conversations, he'd told me he'd grown up in circumstances of benign neglect and fixed his sights early on a career in law enforcement. He'd been working undercover vice the last time our paths crossed, but by now his face was probably too well-known for anything covert. He was dressed to the nines, as usual: dark slacks and a pin-stripe sport coat, wide in the shoulders and nipped at the waist. His dress shirt was midnight blue worn with a midnight blue tie with a sheen of lighter blue. His dark hair was curly, his dark gaze revealing a curious mix of cop-think and come-hither. When I heard he'd gotten married, I'd moved his name, in my mental Rolodex, from a prominent place near the front to a category I labeled "expunged without prejudice" near the back of the file.

His gaze connected briefly with mine and when he realized it was me, he stopped in his tracks. "Kinsey. I don't believe it. I was just thinking about you."

"What are you doing here?"

"Getting a bead on a parolee. What about you?"

"Babysitting a gal until she gets on her feet."

"Missionary work."

"Hardly. I'm getting paid," I said.

"When I ran into you Saturday I meant to ask why I haven't seen you at CC's. Dolan told me the two of you were working a case. I figured you'd be in."

"I don't 'do' bars at my age except for Rosie's," I said. "What about you? Last I heard, you were off in Las Vegas getting married."

"Geez, word gets around. So what else did you hear?"

"That you met her at CC's and only knew her six weeks before the two of you ran off."

Cheney's smile was pained. "Sounds so crass when you put it that way."

"What happened to your other girlfriend? I thought you'd been dating someone else for years."

"That wasn't going anywhere. She realized it before I did and dumped my sorry butt."

"So what'd you do, marry on the rebound?"

"That would cover it, I guess. What about you? How's your friend Dietz?"

"Kinsey, would you like to join us?"

I glanced up to see Priscilla Holloway approaching.

Cheney turned his head, following my gaze. His eyes flicked from the parole officer to me. "I better let you go."

"Nice seeing you again," I said.

"I'll give you a call as soon as I'm free," Priscilla said to him as he turned to go.

I glanced back, watching him as he pushed out the glass doors and turned toward the parking lot.

"How do you know Cheney?" she asked.

"Through a case I worked. Nice guy."

"He's good. Did the drive go okay?"

"Piece of cake, but it was hot down there."

"And way too many bugs," she said. "You can hardly open your mouth without swallowing one."

Her office was small and the furniture was plain. A window overlooked the parking lot, the view cut into slices by a dusty venetian blind. There was a Polaroid camera resting on the windowsill and two instant photos of Reba lay on top of a stack of thick files. I assumed Priscilla kept current photos in the file in case Reba took off without notice. There were file cabinets on her side of the desk and two metal chairs on ours. Reba sat in the one closest to the window. Priscilla took a seat in her swivel chair and looked at me. "Reba says you'll be squiring her around town."

"Just for a couple of days, until she's settled."

Priscilla leaned forward. "I've been over this with her, but I think it bears repeating so you know the score. No drugs, no alcohol, no firearms, no knife with a blade longer than two inches, except knives in her residence or in her place of employment. No crossbow of any kind." She paused to smile, directing the rest of her remarks to Reba as though for emphasis. "No consorting with known felons. Any change of residence has to be reported within seventy-two hours. No traveling more than fifty miles without authorization. You will not be out of Santa Teresa County for more than forty-eight hours and not out of California at all without my written consent. Cops pick you up and you don't have the magic piece of paper, you'll be back in the clink."

"I'm cool with that," Reba said.

"One thing I forgot to mention. If you're seeking employment, a special condition of your parole prohibits a position of trust: no handling of payroll, taxes, no access to checks—"

"What if the employer knows about my record?"

Holloway paused. "Under those circumstances, maybe, but talk to me first." She turned back to me. "Any questions?"

"Not me. I'm just along for the ride."

"I've given Reba my number if she should need me. If I'm not available, leave a message on my machine. I check four and five times a day."

"Right."

"In the meantime, I have two concerns. The first is public safety. The second is her successful reentry. Let's not screw up on either count, okay?"

"I'm with you," I said.

Priscilla stood up and leaned across her desk to shake first Reba's hand and then mine. "Good luck. Nice meeting you, Ms. Millhone."

"Make it Kinsey," I said.

"Let me know if there's any way I can be of help."

Once we were in the car again, I said, "I like Holloway. She seems nice."

"Me, too. She's says I'm the only female she handles. Every other parolee she has is a 288A or a 290."

"Which is what?"

"Registered sex offenders. 288A signifies a child molester. A couple of 'em are considered sexually violent predators. Nice company. You'd never guess just from looking at those guys," she said. She took out a folded pamphlet with "Department of Corrections" printed on the front. I could see her scanning the information as she turned the page. "At least I'm not classified as High Control. Those guys really have to jump through hoops. I see her once a week at first, but she says if I behave myself, she'll move me to once a month. I'll still have to attend AA meetings and I'll be subjected to weekly drug tests, but that's just peeing in a jar and it's really not so bad."

"What about employment? Will you be looking for a job?"

"Pop doesn't want me to work. He thinks it stresses me out. Besides, it's not a condition of parole and Holloway doesn't care as long as I keep my nose clean."

"Then let's get you home."

At 2:30 I dropped Reba off at her father's estate, making sure she had both my home and office numbers. I suggested she take a couple of days to get settled, but she said she'd been cooped up, idle, and bored for the past two years and wanted to get out. I told her to call in the morning and we'd work out a time to pick her up.

"Thanks," she said, and then opened the car door. The elderly housekeeper was already standing on the front porch, watching for her arrival. Near her sat a big long-haired orange cat. As Reba slammed the car door, the cat stepped down off the porch and strolled toward her at a dignified pace. Reba leaned down and swept the cat into her arms. She rocked him, her face buried in his fur, a display of devotion the cat seemed to accept as his due. Reba carried him to the porch. I waited until she'd hugged the housekeeper and disappeared inside, cat tucked under one arm, and then I put the car in gear and headed back to town.

I stopped by the office and put in the requisite time returning phone calls and opening the mail. At 5:00, having taken care of as much business as I intended to do, I closed up the office and retrieved my car for the short drive home. Once there, I opened my mailbox and pulled out the usual assortment of junk mail and bills. I pushed through the squeaky gate, engrossed in an ad from a Hong Kong tailor soliciting my business. I had another offer from a mortgage company suggesting ready cash with one simple call. Wasn't I the lucky one?

Henry was in the backyard hosing down the patio with a steady stream of water as fat as a broom handle. With it, he forced leaves and grit across the flat stones and into the grass beyond. The late afternoon sun had broken through the overcast and we were finally experiencing a touch of summer. He wore a T-shirt and cutoffs, his long, elegant bare feet tucked into a pair of worn flip-flops. William, in his usual natty three-piece suit, stood just behind him, carefully avoiding any spatter from the hose. He was leaning on a black malacca walking stick with a carved ivory handle. The two were arguing but paused long enough to greet me civilly.

"William, what'd you do to your foot? I've never seen you with a cane."

"The doctor thought it would help keep me steady."

"It's a prop," Henry said.

William ignored him.

I said, "Sorry to interrupt. I must've caught you in the middle of a chat."

William said, "Henry's feeling indecisive about Mattie."

"I'm not indecisive! I'm being sensible. I'm eighty-seven years old. How many good years do I have left?"

"Don't be absurd," William said. "Our side of the family has always lived to be at least a hundred and three. Did you hear what she said about *hers?* I thought she was reciting from the *Merck Manual*. Cancer, diabetes, and heart disease? Her mother died of meningitis. Of all things! Take my word for it, Mattie Halstead will go long before you."

"Why worry about that? None of us are 'going' anytime soon," Henry said.

"You're being foolish. She'd be lucky to have you."

"What in heaven's name for?"

"She'll need someone to see her through. No one wants to be ill and alone, especially toward the end."

"There's nothing wrong with her! She's healthy as a horse. She'll outlive me by a good twenty years, which is more than I can say for you."

William turned to me. "Lewis wouldn't be this stubborn—"

"What's Lewis have to do with it?" Henry asked.

"He appreciates her. If you'll remember, he was most attentive to her on the cruise."

"That was months ago."

"You tell him, Kinsey. Maybe you can get through to him."

I could feel uneasiness stir. "I don't know what to say, William. I'm the last person in the world who should give advice about love."

"Nonsense. You were married twice."

"But neither one worked out."

"At least you weren't afraid to commit. Henry's being cowardly—"

"I am not!" Henry's temper was climbing. I thought he was going to turn the hose on his brother, but he moved over to the faucet and wrenched the water off with a squawking sound. "The idea's preposterous. For one thing, Mattie's entrenched in San Francisco and my roots are down here. I'm a homebody at heart and look at the way she lives—always taking off on cruises, sailing around the world at the drop of a hat."

"She only cruises the Caribbean so it doesn't present a problem," William said.

"She's gone for weeks on end. There's no way in the world she's going to give that up."

"Why should she give it up?" William said, exasperated. "Let her do anything she wants. You can live six months up there and the other six months down. We can all benefit from a change of scene—you more than most. And don't give me that song and dance about 'roots.' She can keep her place and you can keep yours, and you can go back and forth."

"I don't want to go anywhere. I want to stay right here."

"I'll tell you your problem. You don't want to do anything that involves risk," William said.

"Neither do you."

"Not so! No sir. You're completely incorrect. By golly, I got *married* at the age of eighty-six and if you don't think that's taking a risk, then ask *her,*" he said, pointing to me.

"Really, it is," I murmured dutifully, my hand in the air as though swearing an oath. "But guys? Excuse me . . ." They both turned to stare at me. "Don't you think Mattie's feelings count? Maybe she's no more interested in him than he is in her?"

"I didn't say I wasn't *interested*. I'm discussing the situation from her point of view."

"She's interested, you dolt!" William said. "Look at this. She's coming back to town in a day. She said so herself. Didn't you hear her say that?"

"Because it's right in her *path*. She isn't stopping off to see *me*."

"Oh yes she is, or why wouldn't she drive straight on through?"

"Because she has to buy gas and stretch her legs."

"Which she could do without taking the time to see you."

"William has a point. I'm with him," I said.

Henry began to coil the hose, his hands picking up bits of grit and cut grass. "She's a wonderful person and I value our friendship. Let's just leave the subject. I'm tired of it."

William turned to me. "That's how this started. All I did was point out the obvious, that she's a wonderful person and he'd better get a move on and snap her up."

Henry said, "Nuts!" waving William off as he returned to the house. He opened the screen door and banged it shut.

William shook his head, leaning on his walking stick. "He's been like this all his life. Unreasonable. Stubborn. Having temper tantrums at the slightest hint of disagreement."

"I don't know, William. If I were you, I'd back off and let them work it out for themselves."

"I'm only trying to help."

"Henry hates to be helped."

"Because he's mulish."

"We're all mulish when it comes right down to it."

"Well, something has to be done. This may be his last chance at love. I can't bear to see him make a hash of it." There was a gentle pinging sound and William reached into his vest pocket and checked his watch. "Time for my snack." He took out a small cellophane packet of cashews that he opened with his teeth. He popped two in his mouth, chewing them like pills. "You know I'm hypoglycemic. The doctor says I shouldn't go more than two hours without eating. Otherwise I'm subject to faintness, weakness, clamminess, and palpitations. Also, tremulousness, which you've doubtless observed."

"Really. I hadn't noticed."

"Precisely. The doctor's encouraged me to instruct friends and family in recognizing the symptoms because it's imperative to render *immediate* treatment. A glass of fruit juice, a few nuts. These can make all the difference. Of course, he wants me to undergo tests, but in the meantime, a diet high in protein, that's the trick," he said. "You know, with deficient glucose production, an attack can be triggered by alcohol, salicylates, or in rare cases, by ingesting the ackee nut, which produces what's commonly known as the Jamaican vomiting sickness . . ."

I cupped a hand to my ear. "I think that's my phone. I better run."

"Certainly. I can tell you more over supper since you're interested."

"Great," I said. I began to edge toward my door.

William pointed at me with his walking stick. "As for this business with Henry, isn't it better to feel something intensely even if you're wounded in the process?"

I pointed at him. "I'll get back to you on that."

6

I had a brief debate with myself about working in a three-mile jog. I'd had to skip my morning run in the interest of reaching CIW by nine. I usually run at 6:00 when I'm still half-asleep and my resistance is down. I've discovered that as the day wears on my sense of virtue and resolve both rapidly diminish. Most days, by the time I get home from work, the last thing I want to do is change into my running clothes and drag myself out. I'm not so fanatic about exercise that I don't occasionally let myself off the hook; however, I'd noticed a growing inclination to seize any excuse to sit on my butt instead of working out. Before I thought too much about it, I went up the spiral stairs to change my clothes.

I kicked off my loafers, peeled out of my jeans, and pulled my T-shirt over my head, tugging on my sweats and my Sauconys. In circumstances like this, I make a little deal with myself. If I jog for ten minutes and really really hate it, I can turn around and come back. No shame, no blame.

Usually by the time the first ten minutes have elapsed, I'm into the swing of it and enjoying myself. I tied my house key in the laces of one shoe, locked the door behind me, and set off at a brisk walk.

Now that the marine layer had burned off, the neighbors were out in their yards, mowing lawns, watering, and pruning deadheads from the rosebushes massed along the fences. I could smell ocean brine mingled with the scent of freshly clipped grass. My block of Albinil Street is narrow. Aside from vehicles parked on either side, there's barely room for two cars to pass. Eucalyptus trees and stone pines provide shade for the assorted stucco and frame houses, most of them small, dating back to the early forties.

By the time I reached the jogging path, I was sufficiently warmed up to break into a trot. After that, I only had to cope with my protesting body parts, which gradually melded into the smooth rhythms of the run. I was home again forty minutes later, winded, sweating, but feeling virtuous. I let myself into the apartment, stripped off my sweats, and took a short hot shower. I was out and drying myself when the telephone rang. I took the call while turning the towel into a makeshift sarong.

"Kinsey? This is Reba. Did I catch you at a bad time?"

"Well, I'm standing here soaking wet, but I should be good for a minute until the chill sets in. What's up?"

"Not much. Pop was feeling bad so he's gone to bed. The housekeeper just left and the home-care nurse called to say she'd be a little late. I was just wondering if you were free for dinner?"

"Sure. I could do that. What'd you have in mind?"

"Didn't you mention a place in your neighborhood?"

"Rosie's. That's where I was headed. I wouldn't call it fancy, but at least it's close."

"I just need to get out. I'd love to join you but only if it doesn't interfere with your plans."

"What plans? I don't mind a bit. You have transportation?"

"Don't worry about that. As soon as the nurse arrives, I'll meet you down there. About seven?"

"That should work."

"Good. I'll be there as soon as I can."

"I'll grab a good table and see you there," I said, and then gave her the address.

After she hung up, I finished my routine, putting on fresh jeans, a clean black T-shirt, and a pair of sneakers. I went downstairs and spent a few minutes tidying my already tidy kitchen. Then I flipped on the lights and sat in the living room with the local paper, catching up on the obituaries and other current events.

At 6:56, I walked the half block to Rosie's through the lingering daylight. Two sets of neighbors were having cocktails outside, enjoying conversation from porch to porch. A cat crossed the street and eased its slim body through the palings in a picket fence. I could smell jasmine.

Rosie's is one of six small businesses on my block, including a laundromat, an appliance-repair shop, and an automobile mechanic, who always has clunkers lined up along his drive. I've been having supper at Rosie's three to four nights a week for the past seven years. The exterior is shabby, a building that might have served as the neighborhood market once upon a time. The windows are plate glass, but the light is obscured by sputtering neon beer signs, posters, announcements, and faded placards from the health department. As nearly as I can remember, Rosie's has never been awarded a rating higher than a C.

Inside, the space is long and narrow, with a high, darkly painted ceiling that looks like it was made of pressed tin. Crudely constructed plywood booths form an L on the right. There's a long mahogany bar on the left, with two swinging kitchen doors and a short corridor leading to the restrooms located at the rear. The remaining floor space is occupied by a number of Formica dinette tables. The accompanying chairs have chrome legs and upholstered marbleized gray plastic seats, variously split and subsequently mended with duct tape. The air always smells of spilled beer, popcorn, ancient cigarette smoke, and Pine-Sol.

Monday nights are generally quiet, allowing the day-drinkers and the usual sports rowdies to recover from their weekend excesses. My favorite booth was empty, as were most of the others, as a matter of fact. I slid in on one side so I could watch the front door for Reba's arrival. I checked the menu, a mimeographed sheet inserted in a plastic sleeve. Rosie runs these off on a machine at the back, the blurred purple lettering barely legible. Two months before, she'd in-stituted a new style of menu, closely resembling a leather-bound portfolio with a handscripted list of the Hungarian Specialties du Jour of the Day, as she referred to them. Some of these menus had been stolen and others had served as hazardous flying missiles when opposing soccer teams enjoyed a hot dispute about the last big match. Rosie had ap-parently given up her pretensions to haute cuisine and her old mimeographed sheets were back in circulation. I ran an eye down the list of dishes, though I'm not even sure why I bothered to check. Rosie makes all my food decisions for me, compelling me to dine on whatever Hungarian delica-cies come to her mind when she's taking my order.

William was now working behind the bar. I watched him pause to check his pulse, two fingers of one hand pressed to his carotid artery, the other hand holding aloft his trusty pocket watch. Henry came in and flicked a look in his di-rection. He chose a table near the front, pointedly turning his back to the bar. As I watched, Rosie moved out from be-hind the bar bearing a glass of lip-puckering white wine that she passes off as Chardonnay. I could see an inch of gray hair growing in along her part. In the past, she's claimed to be in her sixties, but now she's so quiet on the subject I suspect she's slipped over the line into her seventies. She's short, pigeon-breasted, and the red portion of her red hair is dyed to a hue somewhere between cinnabar and burnt ocher.

She placed the glass of wine in front of me. "Is new. Very

good. You sip and tell what you think. I'm saving two dollar a bottle over other brand."

I sipped and nodded. "Very nice," I said. Meanwhile, enamel was being eaten off my teeth. "I see Henry and William aren't speaking."

"I'm telling William to mind his own business, but he's no listen to me. I'm shock to see a woman can come between them two brothers."

"They'll get over it," I said. "What's your take on the situation. You think Mattie has designs on Henry?"

"What do I know? That Henry's a catch. You should hev seen little old ladies flirt with him on cruise ship. Was comical. On other hand, her husband die. Maybe she don't want to connect with some guy. Maybe she want freedom all to herself and Henry for a friend."

"That's what I've been worried about, but William's convinced there's something more going on."

"William's convince she won't be living two more years. He wants Henry to hurry in case she's dropping dead already."

"That's ridiculous. She's barely seventy."

"Very young," Rosie murmured. "I myself hope to look so good when I'm getting her age."

"I'm certain you will," I said. I picked up the menu and pretended to study. "I'm expecting a friend so I'll hold off on ordering. Actually this all sounds pretty good. What do you recommend?"

"Lucky you esk. For you and your friend, I'm fixing Krumpli Paprikas. Is stew made of boil potato, ongion, and what you call weenies cut in pieces. Is always serve with rye bread and on the side you hev choice of cucumber salad or sour pickle. Which you want? I'm think pickle," she said, scribbling a note on her pad.

"Sour pickle, my favorite. So perfect with the wine."

"I'm bring you food as soon as he come."

"It's a 'she' friend, not a 'he.' "

"Is pity," she said, shaking her head. She added an emphatic mark to her pad and then returned to the bar.

At 7:15 Reba appeared, pausing at the door to scan the room. She saw me waving from my booth and made her way toward the back. She'd changed out of her jeans and T-shirt into slacks, a red cotton sweater, and sandals. Her color had improved and her eyes looked enormous in the perfect oval of her face. The spikes were gone from her hair, strands of which she'd tucked behind her ears, causing them to protrude like an elf's. When she reached the booth, she slid in on her side, saying, "Sorry I'm late, but I ended up taking a cab. Turns out my driver's license expired while I was in the can. I was worried I'd be pulled over if I tried driving without one. I could have applied for a renewal from prison but never got around to it. Maybe tomorrow we can go to the DMV."

"Sure. No problem. Why don't I pick you up at nine and we can take care of your license and then run any other errands you have in mind."

"Maybe some clothes. I can use a few things." Reba craned her head, doing a quick survey of the room behind her where the patrons were starting to trickle in. "Would you mind switching seats? I hate sitting with my back to the room."

I slid out on my side of the booth and traded places with her, though in truth I wasn't any fonder than she was about sitting with my back to the room. "How'd you manage in prison?"

"That's where I learned to keep an eye on my ass. I trust what I can see. The rest is way too scary for my taste." She took up a menu and ran her eye down the page.

"Were you scared?"

She lifted her enormous dark eyes to my face, her smile fleeting. "At first. After a while, I wasn't scared so much as cautious. I didn't worry about the staff. It took me about two full seconds to figure out how to get along with them."

"Which was what?"

"Compliance. I was nice. Polite. I did as I was told and I obeyed all the rules. It was really no big deal and it made life easier."

"What about the other inmates?"

"Most of them were okay. Not all. Some of the girls were mean, so you didn't dare let 'em see you as weak. You backed down on anything, they'd be all over you like flies. So here's what I learned. Some bitch gets in my face? I get right back in hers. If she escalates, I do the same and keep on upping the ante until it finally dawns on her she'd better leave me alone. What made it tricky was you didn't want to be written up, especially for anything involving violence— there was hell to pay for that—so you had to find a way to stand your ground without calling attention to yourself."

"How'd you manage it?"

She smiled. "Oh, I had my little ways. The truth is I never messed with anyone who didn't mess with me first. My goal was peace and quiet. You go your way and I'll go mine. Sometimes it just didn't work out that way and then you had to move on to something else." She glanced down at the menu. "What *is* this stuff?"

"Those are all Hungarian dishes, but you don't need to fret. Rosie's already decided what we're having. You can argue with her if you like, but you'll lose."

"Hey, just like prison. What a happy thought."

I saw Rosie approach, bearing another glass of second-rate wine. Before she could put it down in front of Reba, I reached for it, saying, "Thanks. I'll take that. What about you, Reba? What would you like to drink?"

"I'll have iced tea."

Rosie made an officious note to herself like a proper journalist. "Sweet or no sweet?"

"I prefer plain."

"I'm bring lemon on the side in little diaper so you squeeze in your tea with no seeds come out."

"Thanks."

Once Rosie left, Reba said, "I would have turned that down. It really doesn't bother me to see you drink."

"I wasn't sure. I don't want to be a bad influence."

"You? Not possible. Don't worry about it." She set the menu aside and clasped her hands on the table in front of her. "You have other questions. I can tell."

"I do. What were they in for, the mean ones?"

"Murder, manslaughter. A lot for selling drugs. The lifers were the worst because what did they have to lose? They'd get thrown in detention? Whoopee-do. Big deal."

"I couldn't stand having all those people around. Didn't that drive you nuts?"

"It was terrible. Really bad. Women living in close proximity always end up on the same monthly cycle. I guess there must be primitive survival advantages—females fertile at the same time. Talk about PMS. You tack a full moon on top of that and the place turned into a loony bin. Moodiness, quarrels, crying jags, suicide attempts."

"You think being among hardened criminals corrupted you?"

"*Corrupted* me? Like how?"

"Didn't you pick up new and better ways to break the law?"

She laughed. "Are you kidding? All of us were in there because we got caught. Why would I take instruction from a bunch of fuckups? Besides which, women don't sit around trying to teach other women how to rob banks or fence stolen property. They talk about what lousy attorneys they had and how their case is going on appeal. They talk about their kids and their boyfriends and what they want to do when they get out, which usually involves food and sex—not necessarily in that order."

"Was there an upside?"

"Oh, sure. I'm clean and sober. The drunks and druggies are the ones who end up back in the can. They go out on parole and the next thing you know, they're on the bus again, coming through Reception. Half the time they can't even remember what they did while they were out."

"How'd you survive?"

"I walked the yard or read books, sometimes as many as five a week. I did tutoring. Some of the girls barely knew how to read. They weren't dumb; they'd just never been taught. I did their hair and looked at pictures of their kids. That was hard, watching them try to maintain contact. The phones were a source of conflict. You wanted to make an afternoon call, you had to get your name on a list first thing in the morning. Then when your turn came, you had twenty minutes max. The big beefy dykes took as long as they liked and if you had objections, tough patooties to you. I was a shrimp compared to most. Five-two, a hundred and four pounds. That's why I learned to be devious. Nothing sweeter than revenge, but you don't want to leave your fingerprints all over the deed. Take my advice: never do anything that points back to you."

"I'll remember that," I said.

Rosie returned with a tray bearing Reba's iced tea, the lemon swaddled in cheesecloth, and an order of Krumpli Paprikas for each of us. She set down rye bread, butter, and sour pickles, and disappeared again.

Reba leaned close to her bowl. "Oh. Caraway seeds. For a minute, I thought I saw something move."

The potato stew was tasty, served in big porcelain bowls flecked with caraway seeds. I was using my last piece of buttered rye bread to sop up the remaining traces of gravy when I saw Reba glance over my left shoulder toward the front of the restaurant, her eyes widening. "Oh my goodness! Look who's here."

I leaned left, peering around the edge of the booth so I could follow her gaze. The front door had opened and a guy had come in. "You know him?"

"That's Beck," she said as though that explained everything. She pushed herself out of the booth. "I'll be right back."

7

I waited a decent interval and then peered at the two of them standing near the door. The guy was tall, lean, and rangy in jeans and a supple black suede jacket. He had his hands in his jacket pockets and his collar turned up, which didn't look as thuglike as it sounds. His hair was a tawny mix of blond and brown, and his half-smile created a deep crease on either side of his mouth. Beside him, Reba was diminutive, a full head shorter than he, which forced him to lean toward her attentively as the two of them talked. I went back to cleaning my bowl—food, in this instance, taking precedence over idle speculation.

A moment later they appeared and Reba gestured at him. "Alan Beckwith. I used to work for him. This is Kinsey Millhone."

He held his hand out, his wrist thin, his fingers long and slim. "Nice to meet you. I'm Beck to most."

I put him in his thirties—fine lines on his face, but no

pouches anywhere. "Nice meeting you, too," I said, shaking hands with him. "Are you joining us?"

"If you don't mind. I don't want to butt in."

"We're just chatting," I said. "Have a seat."

On their side of the booth, Reba slid in first, scooting over to make room for him. He sat down, half-slouching, his long legs outstretched. He was clean shaven, but I could see the shadow of a beard. His eyes were the dark, rich brown of Hershey's Kisses. I picked up the scent of cologne, something spicy and light. I'd seen him before . . . not here, but somewhere in town, though I couldn't imagine why our paths would have crossed.

He tapped on the back of Reba's hand. "So. How've you been?"

"Fine. It feels great to be home."

I tuned them out, watching as the two exchanged pleasantries. For people who'd once worked together, both seemed ill at ease, but that might have been because he'd turned her over to the cops, a move that would put a damper on most relationships.

"You look good," he said.

"Thanks. I could use a decent haircut. I did this myself. What about you? What have you been up to?"

"Not much. Traveling a lot on business. I just got back from Panama last week and I may be heading out again. We're in the new building, part of the mall that was finished last spring. Restaurants and shops. It's really slick."

"That was in the works when I left and I know what a pain in the ass it was. Congratulations."

"Have you seen it?"

"Not yet. Must be convenient for you, working right downtown."

"Dynamite," he said.

She smiled. "How's the office gang? I hear Onni took my old job. Is she doing okay?"

"She's fine. It took her a while to learn the system,

but she's doing great. Everyone else is pretty much the same."

What did I sense? I tested the air with my little feelers, trying to identify the nature of the tension between them.

Idly, I listened while Beck continued. "I got a new deal in the works. Commercial property up near Merced. I just met with some guys who have capital to invest so we may pull something together. I stopped in here for a good-luck drink before I headed home." His attention shifted in an effort to include me in the conversation. A smooth move, I thought. He wagged a finger between Reba and me, like a windshield wiper. "How do you two know each other?"

I'd opened my mouth to speak, but Reba got in first. "We don't. We just met this morning when she picked me up and brought me home. I was going nuts, stuck at the house. Pop went to bed early and I was too hyper to sit still. The silence was really creeping me out so I called her."

His gaze settled on mine. "You live around here?"

"Half a block down. I rent a studio apartment. Matter of fact, that's my landlord over there," I said, gesturing toward Henry at his table near the front. "The bartender's his older brother William, who's married to Rosie, the gal who owns this place, just to fill you in."

Beck smiled. "A family affair." He was one of those guys who understands the power of being totally focused on the person he's talking to. No barely disguised glances at his watch, no surreptitious shift in his gaze to see who's coming in the door. Now he seemed as patient as a cat staring at a crack in a rock where a lizard has disappeared.

"You live in the area?" I asked.

He shook his head. "I'm in Montebello, right where East Glen and Cypress Lane intersect."

I rested my chin on my hand. "I've seen you someplace."

"I'm a native, Santa Teresa born and bred. My folks had a place in Horton Ravine, but they've been gone now for years. My dad owned the Clements," he said, referring to a three-story luxury hotel that folded in the late seventies. Subsequent ownerships had failed as well and the building had been converted to a retirement facility. If I remembered correctly, his father had been involved in numerous businesses around town. Major bucks.

I glanced over to see Rosie moving toward us with an empty tray, her sights fixed on Beck, her approach as direct and unwavering as a heat-seeking missile. When she reached the table, she made a point of directing all her comments to me, a minor eccentricity of hers. She seldom looks a stranger in the eye. Male or female, it doesn't matter to her. Any new acquaintance is treated like an odd appendage of mine. The effect, in this instance, was coquettish, which I thought was unbecoming in a woman her age. "Your friend would like something to drink?"

I said, "Beck?"

"You have single-malt Scotch?"

She fairly wriggled with pleasure, shooting an approving look at him out of the corner of her eye. "Special for him, I hev MaCallum's. Is twenty-four years old. You want neat or wit ice?"

"Ice. A double with a water back. Thanks."

"Of course." She cleared the table, loading our dinner plates and silverware onto her tray. "He's want supper, perhaps?"

He smiled. "No, thanks. It smells wonderful, but I just ate. Maybe next time. Are you Rosie?"

"Yes, I em."

He rose to his feet and offered his hand. "An honor to meet you. Alan Beckwith," he said. "This is quite a place."

In lieu of an actual handshake, Rosie allowed him temporary possession of her fingertips. "Next time, I'm fix something special for you. Hungarian like what you've never had until I give."

"You got a deal. I adore Hungarian cuisine," he said.

"You hev been to Hungary?"

"Budapest, once, about six years ago . . ."

Covertly, I watched the interplay between the two of them. Rosie became more girlish as the exchange went on. Beck was too slick for my taste, but I had to give him credit for making the effort. Most people find Rosie difficult, which she is.

As soon as she went off to fetch his drink, Beck turned to Reba. "How's your dad? I saw him a couple months ago and he wasn't looking good."

"He's not doing well. I really had no idea. I was shocked to see how much weight he's lost. You know he had surgery for a thyroid tumor. Then it turned out he had polyps on his vocal cords so he had to have those removed. He's still shaky on his feet."

"I'm sorry to hear that. He's always seemed so vigorous."

"Yeah, well, he's eighty-seven years old. He's bound to slow down at some point."

Rosie returned, bringing Beck a hefty glass of Scotch over ice with a small carafe of water on the side. She set his drink on a cardboard coaster and handed him a dainty paper cocktail napkin. I noticed she'd found a doily to put on her tray. If the guy had been with me, she'd have been measuring the inseam for his wedding tuxedo.

He picked up his drink and took a measured sip, sending her a smile of approval. "That's perfect. Thanks."

Rosie departed reluctantly, at a loss for any other service to perform.

Beck turned back to me. "Are you a local as well?"

"Yep."

"Where'd you go to high school?"

"S.T."

"Me, too. Maybe that's where we knew each other. What year did you graduate?"

"1967. What about you?"

"A year ahead of you—1966. Odd I don't remember you. I'm usually good about those things."

I upgraded his age to thirty-eight. "I was a low-waller," I said, indicating my association with the badass kids who sat on the low wall at the rear of the school property where the hillside sloped down to meet the street behind. We smoked cigarettes and dope and occasionally mixed vodka in our bottles of orangeade. Tame by later standards, but considered wicked in our day.

"Really," he said. He gave me a brief searching look and then reached for the menu. "How's the food?"

"Not bad. Are you really fond of Hungarian cooking, or were you making that up?"

"Why would I lie about something like that?" He delivered the line lightly, but he could have meant anything—perhaps that he'd never bother to lie about the trivial or mundane in life. "Why do you ask?"

"I'm surprised you haven't been in before."

"I've seen the place in passing, but frankly, it always looked like such a dive I never had the nerve. I had a meeting with some guys and thought I'd give it a try since I was in the neighborhood. Nicer inside than out, I'll say that."

My antennae went up with a little whining sound. That was the second time he'd explained how he happened to come in. I picked up my glass and took a sip of bad wine. Really, it tasted like a product you'd use to clean tar off your feet after a day at the beach. Reba was playing with the straw in her iced tea.

Looking from her face to his, I realized what a dunce I'd been. She'd arranged this in advance. Dinner with me was just a cover for her meeting with him, but why the subterfuge? I rearranged myself so I was sitting with my back against the side wall, my feet on the seat, keeping my demeanor casual while I watched the scenario play out. "You're in real estate?" I asked.

He downed half the whiskey remaining in his glass, adding water to the residue. He swirled the glass, rattling his ice cubes. "That's right. I have an investment company.

Development, mostly. I do property management on occasion, though not a lot these days. And you?"

"I'm a private investigator."

He smiled, bemused. "Not bad for someone who started her career loitering behind the school."

"Hey, the training was good. Hang out with a bunch of budding crooks, you get to know how they think." I made a display of looking at my watch. "Ah. I don't know about you, Reba, but it's time for me to head out. My car's just half a block down. Give me a minute to go get it and I can drive you home."

Beck looked at Reba with feigned surprise. "You don't have wheels?"

"I've got a car, but no license. Mine expired."

"Why don't I give you a lift and save her the drive?"

I said, "I don't mind doing it. I've got my car keys right here."

"No, no. I'll be happy to take her. No point in your having to go out of your way."

Reba said, "Really. It'd be easier for him than it would be for you."

"You're sure?"

Beck said, "Absolutely. It's right on my way."

"Okay with me. You two stay if you like and I'll take care of the bill. It's my treat," I said, as I slid out of the booth.

"Thanks. I'll take care of the tip."

"Nice meeting you." I shook hands with Beck again and then glanced at Reba. "I'll see you in the morning at nine. You want me to call first?"

"No need. Just come up to the house whenever you like," she said. "Actually, I ought to be heading home myself. It's been a long day and I'm bushed. You mind?"

"Anything you want." Beck finished his drink, swallowing the watered-down whiskey that remained in his glass.

I moved over to the bar and paid the bill. Glancing back, I saw that Beck was already on his feet, fishing in his pocket for his money clip. I watched him peel off two bills for the tip, probably fives since he was so eager to impress. They waited for me to join them so we could walk out together. Henry had disappeared by then, but the shank-of-the-evening drinkers were straggling in.

Outside it was dark, the moon not yet visible. The air was clear and still except for the chirping of crickets. Even the sound of the surf seemed diminished. The three of us ambled toward the intersection, chatting about nothing in particular.

"I'm down there," Beck said, pointing toward the shadowy side street to our right.

"What do you drive?" I asked.

"'87 Mercedes. The sedan. And you?"

"'74 Volkswagen. The bug. See you later."

I waved and continued walking while the two of them turned off. Fifteen seconds later, I heard the double report of their respective car doors slamming shut. I paused, waiting for the sound of an engine turning over. Nothing. Maybe they'd decided to sit and talk. When I reached my gate I pushed through, listening to the familiar squeaking of its hinges. I followed the walk around to the rear. Once I reached my front door, I hesitated, debating about Reba and Beck. Maybe I was wrong about them. Curiosity got the better of me. I left my shoulder bag on the porch and took off across the grass, crossing Henry's flagstone patio to the chicken-wire fence that ran along the rear property line. I felt my way from post to post, tracing the length until I reached his garage. I stooped and pushed the fencing aside, slipping through the gap where the fittings had come loose.

My heart was thumping merrily and I could feel my gut contract with anticipation. I love these nighttime adventures, easing in silence across darkened backyards. Fortunately, none of the neighborhood mutts caught wind of me, so my passage was completed without a chorus of shrill warning barks. At the mouth of the alley, I veered right, emerging onto the side street. I moved forward, scanning the shapes and sizes of the cars parked on either side. A single streetlight cast only the faintest illumination, but once my eyes adjusted to the dark, I had no trouble identifying Beck's Mercedes. Every other vehicle was a compact, a minivan, or a pickup truck.

I could discern his profile where he slouched in the driver's seat half-turned so that he was facing Reba. I stood there for ten minutes and when nothing transpired, I backed up with caution and retraced my steps.

I let myself into my place and set my bag on a kitchen stool. It was 8:05. I flipped on the TV and watched the front end of a movie that actually seemed amusing, despite all the annoying commercial interruptions. I kept notes so I wouldn't buy anything I saw. At 9:00 I muted the set and went into the kitchenette, where I opened a bottle of Chardonnay and poured myself a glass. On impulse, I pulled out a saucepan, the lid, and a bottle of corn oil. I turned on the front burner, set the pan in place, and added a puddle of oil to the bottom of the pan. I scrounged through my cupboard for the bag of popcorn I'd bought months before. I knew it would be stale, but it was chewier that way. I measured out a jigger of kernels and tossed them in the pan. I kept an eye on the TV screen while the sound of the popcorn accelerated like the finale to a fireworks show. Happily for me, the size of my studio is such that I can cook, watch TV, start a load of laundry, or use the john without moving more than eight or ten feet.

I returned to the couch with my wine and the bowl of hot popcorn, propped my feet on the coffee table, and watched the remainder of the movie. At 11:00, when the news came on, I left the apartment and followed the same circuitous route through the alley until I reached the shadowy street where I'd hovered before. Beck's Mercedes was still visible, parked at the curb. The rear window was fogged over with condensation as pale as gauze. Instead of Beck in silhouette, I saw Reba's legs. Her head was apparently down near the steering wheel, one foot propped on the dashboard, the other on the passenger-side door, thus providing her leverage while Beck labored in the confines of the leather-bound front seat. I went back to my place, and when I checked again at midnight, the car was gone.

8

The gates to the Lafferty estate were open, and when I cruised up the drive, I saw Reba waiting on the porch step, the cat at her feet. She had a brush in her hand and she groomed the cat while he strutted back and forth, arching his back against the bristles. When she caught sight of me, she kissed him and set the brush aside. She crossed to the front door, opened the screen, and leaned in to tell her father or the housekeeper she was on her way out. I couldn't help but smile as she bounded down the walk. She was happy, in high spirits, and I remember thinking, *That's what sex will do for you, kid.* She wore desert boots, jeans, and a nubby dark blue sweater with a large cowl neck. She looked as giddy as a young girl. Her father had said she was difficult—"reckless" was his word—but I'd seen no hint of it in my dealings with her. She possessed a natural exuberance and it was hard to picture her drunk or stoned. She opened the car door and slid onto the passenger seat, smiling and out of breath.

"What's the cat's name?"

"Rags. He's a love. Seventeen years old and he weighs in at eighteen pounds. The vet wants him on a diet, but pooh on that." She put her head back. "You don't know how good it feels to be out. Like coming back from the dead."

I pulled away from the house, shifting gears as I headed down the drive and through the gates. "Did you sleep well?"

"I did. Talk about a treat. Prison mattresses are about this thick, like lawn-chair pads, and all the sheets are gross. The pillow was so flat I had to roll it up and wad it under my head like a towel. I'd get in bed at night and my body heat would activate this strange smell in the bedding." She wrinkled her nose.

"What about the food?"

"Not too bad. I'd say the food ranged from passable to gross. What saved us was they let us have these electric coils in our cells. You know the ones you use to heat up a single cup of tea? We figured out all kinds of things to make with ours—Top Ramen, soups, stewed tomatoes in a can. I never even *liked* stewed tomatoes until I got down there. Some days, the cells stank; scorched coffee or bean sludge crusted on the bottom of the pan. Most of the time I disconnected and blocked everything out. I created this invisible force field that I kept between me and the rest of the world. Otherwise, I'd've gone bonkers."

"Did you have friends?"

"A couple and that helped. My best friend was Misty Raine, with an *e* on the end. She's a stripper—big surprise with a name like that—but she's an absolute hoot. Before California, she lived in Vegas, but after she was released and got off parole, she moved to Reno. She says the action there is better than Vegas. She's been good about keeping in touch. God, I miss her."

"What was she in for?"

"She had a boyfriend who taught her how to lift credit cards and forge checks—'hanging paper' as they say.

They'd go on these big spending sprees, stay in a bunch of fancy hotels, and charge anything they liked. Then they'd dump that card, steal another one, and mosey on down the road. Then they branched out into phony IDs. She has this artistic streak and it turns out she's a whiz at replicating passports and driver's licenses and shit like that. They made so much dough she bought herself a new set of tits. Before the boyfriend, she'd been working for one of those mobile-maid-type cleaning services for minimum wage. She said she'd've never gotten anywhere on what she made even if she worked all her life.

"My other friend, Vivian, was mixed up with this drug dealer. You don't know how many times I heard that one. He was pulling in a thousand bucks a day, and they lived like kings until the cops showed up. That was her first offense and she swears it's her last. She's got another six months to serve and then I'm hoping she'll come here. Her boyfriend's been sent up five times and he'll be in for years, which is just as well. She's still crazy about the guy."

"True love is like that."

"You really think?"

"No. That was meant to be tongue in cheek," I said. "I take it you don't have friends here in town."

"Just Onni, the woman I used to work with. I talked to her earlier, hoping I could see her this afternoon, but she was tied up."

"Isn't she the one who took your old job?"

"Right. She feels guilty about that, but I said don't be dumb. She used to do front desk, but this was an opportunity she couldn't pass up. Why would I begrudge her the chance? She said she'd have driven me around today if she didn't have to work."

I turned into the parking lot of the Department of Motor Vehicles. "If you want, you can run in and pick up a booklet and study in the car before you take the test."

"Nah. I've been driving for years so how hard can it be?"

"Well, it's your choice. I prefer to bone up myself. Cuts the flop sweat."

"I like anxiety. It keeps me awake."

I waited in the car while Reba went in. She was gone forty minutes, some portion of which I spent hanging over the seat, trying to tidy all the crap that I keep back there. I generally motor around town with an overnight case stocked with toiletries and clean underpants. This, in the event I'm presented with a pressing reason to hop on a plane. In addition, I have assorted articles of clothing that I sometimes wear while pretending to be a public servant. I can do a pretty good imitation of a postal employee or meter reader from the gas-and-electric company. It pays to look like I'm doing official business when I'm standing on a front porch, idly scanning someone's mail. I also keep several reference books in the backseat—one on crime scene investigation, *Deering's California Penal Code,* a Spanish-language dictionary left over from a class I took years ago—an empty soda can, a bottle opener, an old pair of running shoes, a pair of badly snagged panty hose, and a lightweight jacket. While my apartment is tidy, I'm a slob when it comes to my car.

I glanced up in time to catch Reba's emergence from the DMV office. She half-skipped across the lot, waving a piece of paper that turned out to be her temporary license. "Aced it," she said, as she got into the car.

"Good for you," I said. I turned the key in the ignition, shifted into reverse, and backed out of the space. "Where now?"

"I know it's only ten forty-five, but I wouldn't object to another QP with Cheese."

We ordered from the drive-through window, found a space in the parking lot, and ate in the car. We'd opted for two large Cokes, two Quarter Pounders apiece, and a large order of fries, which we doused in ketchup and ate as fast as we could. I said, "I had a friend regained his health eating shit like this."

"I'm not surprised. I like how flat the pickles are, all mooshed in there. Pop's got a personal chef who's really great, but she's never been able to duplicate this. I can't figure it out, how they do it. Doesn't matter where you are, a QP with Cheese tastes exactly the same and so does everything else. Big Macs, fries."

"Nice to have something you can count on," I said.

After lunch we drove out to the La Cuesta shopping mall, where Reba worked her way from store to store, flashing her father's credit card and trying on clothes. Like other women I've known, she seemed to have an inborn sense of what would look good on her. In most stores, I made a point of finding the nearest chair from which I watched her like a good mom while she moved from rack to rack. Sometimes she'd take out a garment, study it critically, and put it back. Other times, she'd lay the item on top of those she'd draped over her arm. At intervals, she'd head off to the dressing room and then appear twenty minutes later with her choices made. Some pieces she'd leave behind and the rest she'd pile on the counter while she looked for something else. In the course of two hours, she bought pants, skirts, jackets, underwear, knit tops, two dresses, and six pairs of shoes.

Once in the car again, she put her head back against the seat and closed her eyes. "I used to take so many things for granted, but never again. Where next?"

"Up to you. Where do you want to go?"

"The beach. Let's take our shoes off and walk in the sand."

We ended up at Ludlow Beach, not far from my house. Santa Teresa City College was perched on the bluffs above us. The sky was gray as far as the eye could see, and wind was whipping the waves, blowing spray toward the beach. We left our shoes locked in the car, along with my shoulder bag and Reba's purchases. The picnic tables in the grassy area had been abandoned except for a foursome of gulls squabbling over a bread bag that had been tied shut and left on the edge of a trash bin. Reba picked up the bag, tore through the cellophane, and tossed the crumbs across the grass. Gulls began to wheel in, shrieking, from all directions.

We trudged through a hundred yards of soft sand between the parking lot and the surf. At the water line, icy waves tumbled perilously close to our bare feet, but the sand was damp and packed hard, easier to walk on. I said, "So what's the deal with Beck?"

— She flashed me a smile. "That blew me away, running into him like that."

"Really. That's odd. I was under the impression you'd arranged it in advance."

She laughed. "No, not at all. Why would I do that?"

"Reba." I got the big brown eyes turned on me.

"Honest. He's the last person in the world I expected to see."

I shook my head. "Nope. Not honest. Lying through your teeth. That's why you sat on the far side of the booth so you could watch for him."

"That's not *true*. I had no idea he'd be there. I was totally surprised."

"Wait, wait, wait. Just hold on a second and I'll bring you up to speed. I've been telling lies for years and believe me, I know when someone's maneuvering the truth. I got a bullshit meter working 'round the clock. I watched the two of you last night and it was *ding ding ding!* I was strictly window dressing, the person, in the olden days, they referred to as a 'beard.' You called him from the parole office and told him where you'd be."

She was quiet for a moment. "Maybe. But I wasn't sure he'd come."

"Oh, he came all right, if his behavior in the car was any indication."

Her head whipped around and she looked at me in disbelief. "You were *spying* on us?"

"That's what I'm paid for. You don't want to be seen, you shouldn't do it in public."

"What a *bitch!*"

"Reba, your father cares about your welfare. He doesn't want you to end up in the shit again."

She clutched my arm, looking at me earnestly. "Don't tell Pop. Please. What purpose would it serve?"

"I haven't decided what I'm going to do. It might help if you told me what's going on."

"I don't want to talk about it."

"Oh, give it a whirl. You want me to keep quiet, you better fill me in." I could see how tempted she was. Who can resist talking about a guy that you're so smitten with?

"I'm not sure how to explain. I worked for him for years and he's always been supportive . . ."

"Not the long version, dearie, just the salient points. You're having an affair, right?"

"It's much more than that. I'm crazy about him and he's crazy about me, too."

"The crazy part I'll buy. Since when?"

"Two years. Well, four if you count the two I was gone. We've been writing back and forth and talking on the phone. We planned to get together tonight, but there's an AA meeting I'm supposed to attend. I thought I better show up in case Holloway checks. Beck called me at Pop's and said he couldn't stand the wait. I thought of Rosie's because her place is so out of the way I couldn't imagine running into anyone we know. I guess I should have told you up front, but I wasn't sure you'd approve so I just went ahead and did it."

"What'd you need me for? You're big boys and girls. Why not go to a motel and get it over with?"

"I was scared. We haven't been together for so long, I was afraid the chemistry might be gone."

"I don't get it. What's the timing on this? Were you bonking the guy while you were ripping him off?"

"It isn't 'bonking.' We make love."

"Oh, sorry. Were you 'making love' while you were making off with all his hard-earned cash?"

"I guess you could put it that way. I mean, I knew it was *wrong,* but I couldn't help myself. I felt awful. I still do. He knows I'd never do anything to hurt him."

"Losing that much money didn't hurt? I'd be cut to the quick."

"It wasn't personal. I took money from the company—"

"Which he owns."

"I know, but I didn't look at it that way. It was just *there* and nobody seemed to notice. I kept thinking I'd score big and then I'd put it all back. I never meant to keep it and I certainly wouldn't *steal.*"

"Reba, that's what stealing *is.* You pocket someone else's money without their knowledge or consent. If you use a gun, it's called robbery. Either way, it's not behavior that's designed to endear."

She shrugged uncomfortably. "I saw it as a loan. It was just a temporary thing."

"The guy must have a big heart."

"He does. He tried to help me. He did everything he could. I know he's forgiven me. He said it all again last night."

"Hey, I'll take your word for it, but it's weird. I mean, it's one thing to forgive, but then to go on with the affair? How does he rationalize *that?* Doesn't he feel used?"

"He understands I have a self-destructive streak. That doesn't mean he condones it, but he doesn't hold it against me."

"Is that why you never went to trial? Because of him?"

"Partly. When I got arrested, I knew I'd hit bottom. I was guilty as shit. I just wanted to take my licks and get it over with. A trial would've been an embarrassment for Pop. I didn't want him to suffer another public spectacle. I've caused enough trouble as it is."

"Your father tells me Beck's married. Doesn't his wife figure into the equation somewhere?"

"That's a marriage of convenience. They haven't been intimate for years."

"Oh, come *on*. Every married guy says *that*."

"I know, but in his case, it's true."

"What a crock of shit. You think he'll leave her for you? It doesn't work that way."

"Wrong. You are so wrong," she said. "He has it all set up."

"Like what?"

"This is all part of his game plan, but he has to bide his time. If she finds out about me, she'll take him for everything."

"I know *I* would."

"He told me last night he's close to pulling it off."

"Pulling what off?"

I got the double whammy—the big imploring eyes, plus the arm clutch denoting her earnest intent. "Promise you won't tell."

"I can't promise you that! What if he's planning to rob a bank?"

"Don't be dumb. He's getting his finances in shape. Once he has his assets under wraps, he'll broach the subject of divorce. By then, it'll be a done deal and what's she going to do? She'll just have to face facts and accept reality."

"Would you listen to yourself? You're telling me he's worked out a way to cheat his wife. What kind of man *is* he? First he runs around on her and then he rips her off? Oh wait. Skip that. Just occurred to me that you ripped him off first so maybe you're the perfect pair."

"You don't even know what love is. I bet you've never been in love in your life."

"Don't change the subject."

"Well, it's true, isn't it?"

I rolled my eyes, shaking my head in despair. "You are such a nincompoop."

"So what? It's not hurting anyone."

"Oh, right. What about his wife?"

"She'll come around eventually, once it's out in the open."

"Are there any kids?"

"She never wanted kids."

"That's a blessing at any rate. Look, babe. I know where you're coming from. I was once involved with a married man myself. At the time they were separated, but they were married all the same. And you know what I learned? You have no idea what goes on between a husband and wife. I don't care how he represents the relationship, you shouldn't tread on sacred turf. It's the same as walking on hot coals. Doesn't matter how much faith you have, your feet are going to *burn*."

"Tough. It's too late. It's like playing craps. Once the dice leave your hand, you can't do anything but watch."

"At least break it off until he's free," I said.

"I can't. I love him. He's everything to me."

"Oh shit, Reba. Go see a shrink and get your head on straight."

I watched her face shut down. She turned abruptly and started walking away, addressing her comments to me over her shoulder as the gap between us widened. "You don't have a clue what you're talking about. You only met the man *once* so you can keep your friggin' opinions to yourself. It's none of your business and it's none of Pop's." She walked on, heading toward the parking lot. I was left with no choice but to trot along behind.

We barely spoke during the drive to her father's house. By the time I dropped her off, I figured that was the end of the line for me. She was out of prison. She was home. She had her driver's license back and a closet full of clothes. Nothing she'd done—namely, screwing—was in violation of her parole so her actions and behavior were no concern of mine.

She got out of the car and retrieved her packages from the backseat. "I know you mean well and I appreciate your concern, but I've paid for my sins and now my life belongs to me. If I make bad choices, it's my tough luck. It has nothing to do with you."

"Okay by me. Have a good life," I said.

She closed the car door. She paused and leaned in the window briefly. I thought she meant to say more, but she decided to let it ride. I watched her until the front door closed behind her and then I headed for the office. Once there, I typed up an invoice, billing Nord Lafferty the five hundred dollars a day for the two days I'd worked. I put the bill in an envelope, which I sealed and addressed. On the way home, I drove past the post office, where I slowed to a stop and dropped it in the box at the curb.

9

For supper, I fixed myself a hot hard-boiled-egg sandwich slathered with mayo and heavy on the salt, vowing in a vague and insincere way to rectify my diet, which is woefully short of fruits, vegetables, fiber, grain, and nutrition of any sort. I'd intended to make an early night of it, but by seven I was feeling restless for reasons I couldn't name. I decided on a quick trip to Rosie's, not so much for the bad wine as a change of scene.

To my surprise, the first person I saw was Henry's older brother Lewis, who lives in Michigan. He stood behind the bar with his suit jacket off, his arms bare to his elbows and plunged in soapy water while he washed assorted glasses and beer mugs. I crossed to the bar, saying, "Well, this is a surprise. Where did you come from?"

He looked up with a smile. "I flew in this afternoon. William picked me up at the airport and put me straight to work."

"What brings you to town?"

"Nothing in particular. I needed a change. I came up with the plan on the spur of the moment. Charlie was busy and Nell wasn't in the mood, so I booked a seat and made the trip by myself. Travel's invigorating. I'm full of beans," he said.

"Well, good for you. That's great. How long will you be here?"

"Until Sunday. William and Rosie are putting me up. That's why he's teaching me to tend bar, so I can earn my keep."

"Does Henry know you're here?"

"Not yet, but I'll call him as soon as William lets me take a break."

He rinsed the last of the beer mugs and set it on a rack to drain, then dried his hands on the white towel he'd tucked in his waist. He put a cocktail napkin on the bar in front of me and shifted into bartender mode. "What are you drinking? If memory serves, you prefer Chardonnay."

"Better make that a Coke. Rosie's changed 'vintners,' though the term hardly applies. The wine she's serving has all the subtlety of solvent."

He hosed me a Coke and placed it in front of me. For a gentleman of eighty-nine, he was the picture of efficiency, his manner brisk and relaxed. Watching him, you'd have thought he'd been tending bar all his life.

"Thanks."

"You're entirely welcome. My treat."

"Well, aren't you nice! I appreciate that."

I watched him amble toward the far end of the bar to wait on somebody else. What was going on? I'd never known Lewis to fly out unannounced. Had William put him up to it? That seemed like a bad idea. I turned and glanced over my shoulder at the smattering of patrons. My favorite booth was occupied, but there were numerous other seats available. I carried my Coke and crossed to a table near the entrance. Fresh air wafted in with each opening and closing of the door, thus dispelling some of the accumulated cigarette smoke, which lay on the air like fog. Even so, I knew I'd get home smelling like soot and have to hang my clothes on the shower rod overnight to eliminate the stink. My hair was doubtless already reeking, though I wear it too short to hold a strand to my nose. Smokers listen to these prissy-ass complaints as though the charges were trumped up simply to annoy and offend.

I was scarcely settled when I sensed the welcomed shift in air current that signaled someone entering the place. Cheney Phillips stood in the doorway. I felt one of those lurches you experience on a plane that leaves you wondering if the flight will be the last you take. I watched him scan the assembled patrons, apparently looking for someone who hadn't yet arrived. His clothing was the usual mix of expensive fabrics and fine tailoring. He favored crisp white dress shirts or soft-collared silk in shades of cream or buttermilk. On occasion, he shifted to a tone-on-tone, usually in dark hues that lent him a faintly sinister air. Tonight, he wore a cinnamon sueded silk sport coat over a rust-colored cashmere turtleneck. I lifted my hand in greeting, wondering if the sweater was as soft as it looked. He sauntered over to my table and pulled out a chair. "Hey, how's by you? Mind if I sit?"

I gestured assent. "Our paths cross again. I haven't seen you for months and now I've run into you three times in the past four days."

"Not entirely accidental." He pointed to my glass. "What the hell is that?"

"Coke. A soft drink. It's been around for years."

"You need something stronger. We have to talk." Without waiting for my response, he caught Lewis's eye and gestured, indicating the need for service.

I turned in time to see Lewis hustle out from behind the bar and head toward our table. "Yes, sir."

"Two vodka martinis, straight up. Stoli if you have it, Absolut if not. And a side of olives." Glancing at me, he said, "You want ice water?"

"Oh, why not?" I said, ever the bon vivant. "This is Lewis Pitts, my landlord's brother. You've met Henry, haven't you?"

"Of course. Cheney Phillips," he said. He rose to his feet and shook hands with Lewis, who said a few pleased-to-meet-you-type things with the usual pleasantries thrown in. I found myself noting the texture of Cheney's hair, springy dark brown curls that looked as soft as a poodle's coat. I'm not a dog lover at heart. Doggies tend to bark their bad breath in my face, preparatory to jumping up and parking their cumbersome paws on my chest. Despite numerous sharp commands, most dogs behave any way they please. There's the occasional exception. The week before, in a rare moment of goodwill, I'd stopped to chat with a woman who was walking a breed I'd never seen before. She introduced me to Chandler, a Portuguese water dog who sat on command and gravely offered to shake hands. The dog was quiet and well mannered with a coat so curly and soft I could hardly keep my hands to myself. Why was I thinking about that *now?* Having missed the bulk of the conversation, I tuned in as Lewis was saying, "Be right back." It was like waking up in the middle of a TV movie. I had no clear idea what was going on.

As soon as he was gone, I turned to Cheney. "I take it you're here to meet someone."

His attention was focused on faces halfway across the room, his gaze shifting at precise intervals like a corner-mounted camera. He'd been a vice cop for years and he had a letch for hookers and dope dealers the way some guys are fixated on the size of a woman's boobs. His eyes flicked to mine. "Actually, I came in looking for you. I stopped by your apartment and when I didn't find you there, I figured you'd be here."

"I didn't realize I was so predictable."

"Your best trait," he said. His gaze caught on mine again and the effect was unnerving. I glanced at the bar, the front door, anywhere but him. Where was Lewis and what was taking him so long?

Cheney said, "Don't you want to know why I'm here?"

"Sure."

"We have an interest in common."

"Oh, really. And what would that be?"

"Reba Lafferty."

The answer was unexpected and I could feel my head tilt with curiosity. "What's your connection to her?"

"That's why I went to see Priscilla Holloway. I heard someone was driving down to CIW to bring Reba back. I didn't know it was you until I saw you that day."

Cheney glanced up at Lewis, who'd appeared with our martinis on a tray. He set them down with great care, watching the liquid tremble. The stemware was so cold I could see ice flakes sliding along the outer surface of the glass. The vodka, just out of the freezer, looked oily in the light. I hadn't drunk a martini in ages and I remembered the sharp, nearly chemical taste.

I can never decide what makes Cheney's face so appealing—wide mouth, dark brows, eyes as brown as old pennies. His hands are big and it looks like he busted his knuckles pounding someone in the chops. I studied his features and then caught myself, thinking I should slap my own face. I'd just lectured Reba on the folly of a dalliance with a married man and here I was idly entertaining the very thought myself.

Cheney said, "Thanks, Lewis. Can you run a tab for us?"

"Of course. Just let me know if you need anything else."

Once he was gone, Cheney lifted his glass and tapped its edge against mine. "Cheers."

I took a sip of my drink. The vodka was smooth, forming a column of heat that sank down my spinal cord and into my shoes. "I hope you're not saying she's in trouble."

"I'd say she's teetering on the brink."

"Oh, no."

"How well do you know her?"

"You can make that past tense. I did the job I was hired for and now I've moved on."

"As of when?"

"We parted company this afternoon. What's she done?"

"Nothing so far, but she's close."

"So you said. Meaning what?"

"She's been seeing Alan Beckwith, the guy you met in here Monday night."

"I know when I met the guy, but what's that to you?" I could hear hostility creep into my tone at the implications of what he'd said. Someone was apparently watching me the same night I was watching Reba carry on with Beck.

"Don't be crabby."

"Sorry. I didn't mean for it to come out that way." I took a deep breath, willing myself into a more sanguine place. I said, "I don't understand where you fit in. And don't make me guess. I really hate that shit."

Cheney smiled. "I'm talking to some guys who have an interest in him. Her, too, by association. You have to understand this is all highly confidential."

"I'm crossing my heart," I said, and made an X on my chest.

"You know anything about Beck?"

"I'm an innocent. Well, wait. That's not entirely true. I know his father owned the Clements, so I'm assuming the man was a major player in his day."

"The best. Alan Beckwith Senior made a shitload of money in a number of franchises, mostly real estate. Junior's been successful, but he's worked all his life in the shadow of his dad. Beck never measured up. From what I've heard, it's not like his dad made judgments about him, but Beck was conscious of the gap in their accomplishments. His old man went to Harvard and graduated fifth in his class. Beck's academic career was undistinguished. His college was good, but strictly second tier. He ended up with an MBA, but gradewise, he wasn't even in the top twenty-fifth percentile. That's just how it went. His achievements were modest compared to his dad's and I guess the older he got the worse he felt. He's the kind of guy who swore he'd be a multimillionaire by the time he was forty. At thirty, he was stalled out and getting desperate to make good. You know the saying 'Money's just a way of keeping score'? Well, Beck took that to heart. Five, six years back, he decided his prime goal was to outearn his dad. Since he couldn't manage it playing straight, he took a left-hand turn. He realized he could make a lot more money if he offered his services to people who needed to have theirs washed."

"Money laundering?"

"Right. Turns out Beck has an aptitude for financial shenanigans. Since he deals in high-end real estate, the basic infrastructure was already in place. There are half a dozen ways to fiddle funds when you buy and sell property, but the mechanism's slow and there's too much paperwork. With money laundering, you want to minimize the paper trail and put as many fire walls as possible between you and the source. His early efforts were clumsy, but he's getting better at this stuff. Now he's set up an offshore company— a Panamanian dummy corp called Clements Unlimited. Places like Panama, you can hide a lot of dough because the bank secrecy laws have been tight there since day one. 1941, they took their cue from the Swiss and went to coded accounts. Unfortunately for the bad guys, the numbered account isn't what it once was. Swiss banks don't offer the same level of protection, because they've taken so much flak for providing cover for thugs. They've finally recognized the necessity for getting along in the international banking community and that's motivated their signing treaties with a host of other countries. In effect, they've agreed to cooperate where there's proof of criminal activity. Panama isn't as eager to please. They've got lawyers who create companies in bulk and sell them off to customers who want to sidestep the IRS."

"You're talking about shell corporations, right?"

He nodded. "You can create a sham company according to your specifications or you can buy one ready-made. Once you have a shell in place, you funnel money from the U.S. by way of the shell to any financial haven you choose. Or you can set up an offshore trust. Or you do what Beck did, which was to buy himself a bank-in-a-box and start accepting deposits."

"From whom?"

"He makes a point not to inquire too closely, but his primary client is a big-time Los Angeles drug dealer, ostensibly doing business in scrap gold. Beck also dry-cleans money for a major pornography mill and a syndicate that runs a network of hookers and whorehouses down in San Diego County. Guys in the sin trades accumulate millions in cash and what can they do with it? Live lavishly and your neighbors will start to wonder about the source of your wealth. So will the IRS, the DEA, and half a dozen other government agencies. There's never a shortage of folks who need to run dirty money through the sluice and have it come up clean. The neat thing from Beck's perspective is that, until recently, what he's doing wasn't illegal in and of itself."

"You're kidding."

"Nope. Last year Congress passed the Money Laundering Control Act. Before that, the same basic transactions might have been the focus of an investigation or subject to prosecution under some other statute, but the laundering itself wasn't a crime. Sorry to be so long-winded. Bear with me on this."

"Don't worry about it. Most of this is news to me."

"Me, too. From what I'm told, the groundwork was laid in 1970 when the Bank Secrecy Act was passed. The BSA established reporting regulations for financial institutions—banks, brokerage houses, currency dealers, anybody issuing traveler's checks, money orders, shit like that. They're required to report certain transactions to the Secretary of the

Treasury within fifteen days on a form called the Currency Transaction Report—the CTR—for any transaction over ten thousand dollars. Are you following?"

"More or less. How do you know all this stuff?"

"Most of it I picked up from my IRS pal in the past couple of months. He says in addition to the CTR, there's something called a Currency and Monetary Instrument Report, the CMIR. This is for the people who physically receive or transport cash—carry it, mail it, ship it—again, that's in any amount over ten thousand dollars. There's another form for casinos, but we don't have to worry about that here. Far as we know, Beck doesn't have ties to any of the big gambling operations, though that's another nice way to scrub a load of cash and get it squeaky clean.

"The government relies on financial institutions to track the flow of cash through the system. Obviously, there's nothing illegal about dealing in large sums as long as all the proper forms get filed. Try to bypass that and you're subject to severe penalties—assuming you're caught, of course. Beck made a point of cultivating a bunch of banker pals and for a period, he was bribing one of them to look the other way. The bank officer would prepare the CTR as required and place a copy in the files, only instead of shipping the original to the IRS, he'd run it through a shredder. Problem is, the banks tend to move these executives from branch to branch, and Beck lost his co-conspirator. That's how he came to the attention of Internal Revenue. Some new VP at Santa Teresa Savings and Loan noticed a pattern of small deposits that he was pretty sure were all linked to Beck or Beck's company. He's been breaking the big deposits into a series of smaller transactions, hoping to skirt the ten-thousand-dollar requirement for a government report. This is the fundamental maneuver in any laundering operation. It's called structuring, or 'smurfing.' Beck employed a regular road crew of smurfs, who'd go from bank to bank here in town—sometimes from city to city—buying cashier's checks or money orders in the smaller dollar amounts—two grand, five, sometimes as much as nine, but never over ten. The dribbles and drabs were deposited piecemeal into a single account, and then Beck would use wire transfers to move the whole of it to a couple of off-shore banks. After that, he'd funnel it back to his clients in a more respectable form.

"Anyway, while all this was going on, the DEA was following the money from the other end, tracking funds through the system from a cartel importing marijuana and cocaine into Los Angeles. At some point, the two paths intersected and a red flag went up. I'd met the IRS investigator at a conference in D.C. about four years back. Shortly after that, he got assigned to the L.A. office to coordinate the task force. Once Beck's name surfaced, the focus shifted to him. The agent, Vince Turner, asked me to act as the local interface. His guys are keeping a low profile because the feds are trying to build a case without Beck's getting wind of it."

"Oh, good luck. In this town?"

"We're well aware," he said. "So far they've initiated mail and trash covers and they've been running surveillance, covering his movements in and out of the country. What they need now is an informant, which is where Reba Lafferty comes in."

I gestured impatiently. "You're kidding. She's in love with the man. She'd never rat him out."

"Don't be so sure . . ."

"I *am* sure. She's smitten. That's how she's managed to hold herself together for the past two years. They wrote to each other and talked on the phone a couple of times a week. That's how she survived. I got it straight from her."

"Just hear me out," he said. "You know the background on this."

"Of course. She ripped off his company for megabucks over a two-year period—"

"While she and Beck were having an affair," he said.

"I know that. So what?"

"So under the circumstances, doesn't it seem strange he'd take up with her again the minute she gets out?"

"Well, yeah. Matter of fact, I asked her about that myself. She claims he's forgiven her. She says he knew she was self-destructive and couldn't help herself. Or words to that effect."

He was shaking his head. "Nope. Don't think so. It doesn't ring true."

"I'm not defending the point. I'm just telling you what she said. I agree with you. It's hard to believe Beck would turn the other cheek. So what's the deal? I gather you know something I don't."

Cheney leaned forward, lowering his voice. I tilted my head closer and felt the whisper of his breath against my cheek as he spoke. "She took the fall for him. He had her set up accounts for a couple of phony companies. She'd invoice for bogus goods and services, then write checks out of accounts payable. He'd sign 'em and she'd send 'em off to a post office box. Later, she'd pick 'em up and deposit the money to a phony account. Sometimes, he'd wire the money offshore or she'd withdraw the cash herself and pass it on to him."

"I don't get it. Why's he stealing from himself?"

"He has people to pay off and this is how he covers his butt. He can't siphon off large sums of cash without an explanation. If he's ever audited, the IRS will want to know where the money went. He figured he'd disguise the fact he's draining off the bucks by making it look like a legitimate business expense."

"Why not use money from one of his offshore accounts?"

"Who knows the rationale? By then he'd cooked up a couple new schemes anyway and he was anxious to shift gears. He talked Reba into going down for the three hundred and fifty thou and he came out smelling like a rose. Since she claimed she'd gambled all the money away, who could prove otherwise? Truth is, she's always had a gambling problem and she was already making trips to Vegas and Reno, which suited him to a tee."

"But how'd he talk her into it?"

"Same way guys talk women into anything. He promised her the moon."

"I can't believe she went to jail for him. What an idiot."

Cheney shrugged. "My IRS buddy says there was talk of approaching her back then, offering to cut her a deal, but at the time, they were just setting up shop and couldn't afford to take the risk. Now it's crunch time. They need the inside track and she's it."

"Beck must have a company comptroller and accountants. Why not one of them?"

"They're working on that angle as a backup plan."

"Well, you better tell 'em to work hard. If Reba spent two years in prison for Beck, why turn on him now?"

"You know he's married . . ."

I could feel my impatience mount. "Of course. And Reba knows it, too. He says it's a marriage of convenience. I think it's a crock and I told her so, but couldn't get her to budge."

"She's delusional in that case. You see Beck and his wife together—her name's Tracy, by the way—there's no suggestion whatever he's anything less than devoted. Could be an act on his part, but it doesn't look that way."

"That's how guys are . . ."

"Hey, women are the same. Percentagewise, women probably screw around more than men."

"Listen to us. That's sick. How'd we get so cynical?"

Cheney smiled. "It comes with the turf."

"You think Tracy knows about Reba?"

"Hard to say. Beck's got a ton of money and he treats her like a queen. Maybe from her perspective, it's smarter to look the other way. Or maybe she knows and doesn't give a shit."

"Yeah, well, Reba's convinced he's kept his wife in the

dark, and furthermore, if Tracy finds out, she'll not only divorce his ass, but take him for everything he's got."

"How's she going to do that? He has money stashed in bank accounts all over the world. And some are banks he *owns*. She'd end up with the same nightmare we're facing, which is how to trace his assets. Reba's got that down cold. She knows where the bodies are buried if we can get to her."

"What makes you think he didn't change it all while she was gone?"

"Why would he do that? He may vary the game plan, but the accounts have been in place for years. Setting up an off-shore bank is an expensive proposition. He's not going to go back and start from scratch unless he's forced to. That's why the feds are so worried about tipping him off. They don't want him to panic before they're ready to roll."

"What do they want from her?"

"Facts and figures, banks, account numbers—whatever she can get her hands on. Some of the information they have, but they need corroboration, plus whatever she knows that they haven't come up with yet."

"But what's her motivation? You've got nothing to offer. She's a free human being. Ask her for help and she'll run straight to him."

Cheney reached into the inner pocket of his sport coat and removed a manila envelope that he pushed across the table.

"What's this?"

"Take a look."

I undid the clasp. Inside I found a series of grainy black-and-white photographs of Beck, probably taken with a telephoto lens. In two, his companion's face wasn't clear, but she appeared to be the same woman. The pictures had been taken on five different occasions, judging from the date and time recorded in the bottom right-hand corner of each print. All had been snapped within the past month. The last photo was a shot of the two of them leaving a motel I recognized on upper State Street. I slid the photos back into the envelope. "Who's the woman?"

"Her name is Onni. She's Reba's best friend. He's been bedding her ever since Reba landed at CIW."

"What a shitheel," I said. "And I'm supposed to show her those in hopes of persuading her to turn on him?"

"Yes."

I tossed the photos and they skittered across the table to him. "You have the resources of the entire United States government at your disposal. Find someone else to do your dirty work."

"Look, I understand where you're coming from, but this isn't penny-ante stuff. What Beck's doing is—"

"I know what he's doing. Don't give me this 'Money laundering is evil' bullshit. I got that already. I don't see why I should be the one who talks Reba into rolling over on him."

"We're guys. We don't know her the way you do. Just call her and chat. The woman trusts you."

"She does *not*. She doesn't even *like* me. I'm telling you, she got really pissed off when I tried telling her the truth. How can I turn around and call? She'd know I was up to something. She may be an idiot, but she isn't unaware."

"Think about it—*please*—before you make up your mind."

I stood up and pushed back my chair. "All right. I'll think about it. In the meantime, I need to go home and take a bath."

10

I did not sleep well. My encounter with Cheney Phillips had generated a gloom that seemed to permeate my dreams. I woke often and stared up through my skylight at the overcast night sky. His proposal had at least served to diminish his appeal. Reba was vulnerable by nature and only marginally stable, given to veering off course in response to her own internal tumult. So far she seemed fine (sort of) but I didn't want to trip her into a downward spiral when she'd just reached solid ground. She'd been free for two days. What would she do if she heard about this? She'd go off the deep end. On the other hand, she'd pinned her hopes on a bum and what was I to do? Sooner or later, she was going to learn the truth. Was it better to tell her now while she still had an opportunity to redeem herself?

At 5:59 A.M. I shut down my alarm and pulled on my sweats in preparation for a run. I went through my usual bathroom routine—brushing my teeth, splashing water on my face, lamenting the state of my hair, which was sticking up every which way. I looped my housekey in my shoelace, locked the apartment, and started walking at a fast pace toward the bike path that runs parallel to the beach.

Gradually I broke into a trot, my muscles protesting. My feet felt leaden, as though someone had affixed ten-pound weights to the bottoms of my shoes. The sun had already risen and for once there was no evidence of fog. The day promised to be a good one, clear and sunny. Across the rumble of the surf, I could hear the barking of a sea lion, probably some hoary old guy who'd staked out a place for himself on a marker buoy. In hopes of shaking off my depression, I picked up the pace, my sights focused on the bathhouse where I made my turnaround. By the time I started back, I wasn't exactly light of heart, but I didn't feel quite so dead.

I finished my run and walked the last couple of blocks to cool down. When I reached home, I saw Mattie's car parked in Henry's drive. *Oh goody.* I let myself into my place, showered, dressed, and ate a bowl of cereal. As I left for the office, I picked up the tantalizing scent of bacon and eggs wafting across the patio. Henry's kitchen door was open and through the screen, I heard laughter and chatting. I smiled, imagining the two of them sitting down to breakfast together. I knew better than to think she'd spent the night with him. He's entirely too proper to compromise her reputation, but an early morning get-together was well within the purview of Emily Post.

I crossed the yard and tapped on the door frame. He responded, inviting me to come in, though his tone wasn't quite as chipper as I'd hoped. I let myself in, thinking *Uh-oh.* Henry had reverted to his usual dress code—flip-flops, white T-shirt, and tan shorts. The kitchen showed all the signs of a recent meal—dirty skillets and bowls, an array of spices near the stove. Dishes and utensils were piled in the sink, and the counter was gritty with toast crumbs. Henry was at the sink, running water for a fresh pot of coffee, while Mattie sat at the kitchen table engrossed in a conversation with William and Lewis.

I caught the dynamic in a flash and I could feel myself wince. William had set this up. He'd been infuriated by Henry's attitude where Mattie was concerned. Lewis had no such qualms. I knew William had been chatting with Lewis on the phone, but I hadn't thought much of it. Now I had visions of his maneuvering Lewis onto the scene, assuming Henry's competitive instincts would kick in. Instead, Henry was reacting like a schoolboy, withdrawn and insecure in the presence of his brother's cockiness. Maybe William didn't care which of his brothers snagged Mattie as long as one of them did.

From what I knew of the family history, Lewis—two years older than Henry—had always asserted his superiority in matters of the heart. Neither Lewis nor Henry had ever married, and though I hadn't quizzed them on the subject, there was one reference I remembered. In 1926 Henry had taken Lewis's girlfriend away from him. Henry claimed Lewis had never fully recovered from the insult. Now, to all appearances, Lewis was finally mounting a retaliatory campaign. He'd made a point of dressing smartly—starched white shirt, vest, suit coat, his shoes shined, his trousers sharply creased. Like his two younger brothers, Lewis had all his hair and most of his teeth. I saw him as Mattie must—handsome, attentive, with none of Henry's reticence. The two brothers had met her on the same Caribbean cruise and Lewis had pursued her relentlessly. He'd signed up for Mattie's watercolor class, and while his efforts were crude, she'd admired his enthusiasm and his doggedness. Henry claimed he was only flirting, but Mattie didn't see it that way. Now here he was again, stepping into the picture just as Henry was making headway.

"Coffee?" Henry asked me. Even his voice sounded bruised, though he was covering as well as he could.

"Sure, I'll take a cup. Thanks."

"Mattie? Fresh pot coming up."

"Love some," she said, distracted by the anecdote Lewis was in the midst of telling. Henry wasn't listening. The story was probably one he'd heard before and he knew how it would end. I was so focused on Henry I didn't hear much of it myself. Lewis reached the punch line and both William and Mattie burst out laughing.

I sat down at the table and when the merriment subsided, I glanced at Mattie. "So what's up today? The two of you have plans?"

"Oh, no. I can't stay. I've got responsibilities at home."

Lewis slapped the table. "Nonsense! There's a show at the art museum. I read about it in the paper and I know it's one you'd love."

"What sort of show?"

"Blown glass. Extraordinary. It's a traveling exhibit the reviewer called a 'must-see.' At least stay for that. Afterward, we could have a bite of lunch at a Mexican restaurant right there in the arcade. There's an art gallery across the court you really should see. You could talk to the owner about your work. Maybe she'd agree to represent you."

William chimed in. "Fabulous idea. Don't go rushing off. Take a little time for yourself."

I felt my head swivel. William was beaming like a mother at a dance recital.

I said, "Uh, Henry? Could I see you for a minute? I've got a problem at my place."

"What sort of problem?"

"It's just something I have to show you. It won't take long."

"I'll look into it later. Can't it wait?"

"Really not," I said, hoping to signal him with my tone.

He seemed resigned or annoyed, I couldn't tell which. He turned to Mattie. "You won't mind if I slip out for a minute?"

"Not at all. I can tidy up the kitchen while you're gone."

"That's not necessary," Henry said. "I'll take care of the dishes as soon as I get back."

"Take your time," Lewis said, airily. "We'll get the place all shipshape and then take a walk on the beach. Mattie needs some fresh air. Place is like an oven in here."

Henry turned a bleak eye on Lewis. "If it's all the same to you, I'd prefer to clean the kitchen myself."

Lewis made a face. "Oh, loosen up, for Pete's sake. You're like a little old lady. We're not going to mess with your precious things. I promise we'll keep all the spices in alphabetical order. Go on. Get out of here. We're fine."

Henry's cheeks flushed with embarrassment. I tucked my arm into his and steered him toward the door. I could tell he was torn between wanting to defend himself and wanting to escape the torment. I didn't think Mattie was being mean. Her affection for both brothers was doubtless genuine. She simply wasn't tuned into the rivalry between the two.

The screen door banged shut behind us and we crossed the yard. As soon as I let him into my apartment, I could see Henry scrutinize the premises, his expression sour, looking for the problem he was there to fix. "I hope it's not the plumbing. I'm not in the mood to crawl under the house."

"There isn't any problem. I had to get you out of there. You need to chill out. You can't let Lewis get under your skin like that."

He gave me a stony look. "I don't know what you're talking about."

I couldn't tell if he was actually that obtuse or feigning ignorance to avoid addressing the point. "Yes, you do. Lewis is flirting, but he flirts with every woman he sees. It doesn't mean anything. You've got twice his charm and twice his good looks. Besides, you're the one she came to see. You can't let him swoop in like that and sweep her off her feet."

"Swoop and sweep?"

"You know what I mean. She's taking the path of least resistance. That doesn't mean she likes him any better than you."

"I wouldn't be so sure. Mattie couldn't set aside time for me. Let him propose an outing and suddenly she's got all day."

"But you could have proposed something just as easily."

"I did. I suggested breakfast."

"And she agreed. The only thing I don't understand is how Lewis and William ended up over there as well."

"A remarkable coincidence. The two were taking their morning constitutional and just 'happened' to be passing as she pulled into the drive. They stopped for a chat and naturally, she invited them to join us. Now she intends to spend the rest of the day with *him*."

"She never said that. What's the matter with you? So Lewis came up with a plan. Big deal. Think of a better one and stand your ground."

"It's not up to me. It's Mattie's call. Lewis is being pushy and competitive, vying for her attention. The way he's acting, he might as well be eight."

"Well, that's true," I said. "He is competitive with you."

"Precisely. And it's revolting—grown men scrapping over her like dogs with a bone. No gentleman should impose himself when it's a lady's right to choose."

"Mattie isn't choosing. She's being nice."

"Fine. She can be as nice as she pleases. Far be it from me to interfere."

"Oh, come on, Henry. Don't be like that."

"But that's how I am. That's exactly how I am."

"Stubborn and proud."

"I can't change my nature. I refuse."

"So don't change your *nature*. Change your attitude."

"I won't. If she's so easily swayed by his *flirtation,* as you so aptly refer to it, then perhaps I've misjudged her. I assumed she was a woman of integrity and common sense.

He's vain and superficial and if she finds that appealing, then so be it."

"Would you get off your high horse? You're only taking that position to avoid a fight. You think if you go head-to-head with him, you'll lose out, but that's just not true."

"You have no idea what I think."

"Okay. You're right. I shouldn't speak for you. Why don't you tell me how it feels."

"It doesn't 'feel' like anything. This is all beside the point. Mattie has her preferences and I have mine."

"Preferences?"

"That's right. I prefer to be accepted for myself. I prefer not to dictate the behavior of others or have them dictate to me."

"What's that got to do with Lewis?"

"She thinks he's entertaining. I do not. In addition, I find his sudden appearance highly suspect."

"Really," I said. I was reluctant to communicate my own suspicions about William unless Henry voiced them first.

Henry went on. "I believe she spoke to Lewis on the phone and he flew out in response."

"Where'd you get that?"

"He didn't seem the least bit surprised at finding her here, which means he knew in advance. And how could he have known unless she told him herself?"

"He could have heard from someone else."

"Who?"

"Rosie."

"Rosie doesn't *chat* with Lewis. Why would she talk to him? She barely talks to me."

"William, then. He could have mentioned it in passing."

"I see you're determined to protect her."

"All I'm doing is injecting a note of reality. No one's plotting behind your back. Well, Lewis, maybe, but not Mattie. You know better."

"You're implying I'm paranoid, but this is not my

imagination. Mattie's intention was to come for breakfast and then drive straight home. Lewis suggested something *off the top of his head* and now she's delaying her return. Yes or no?"

"No."

"Yes."

"Let's not argue. I don't think there's anything afoot, but you do, so let's drop the subject. My only point . . . well, I don't even know what my only point is. My only point is don't give up on her. And that's all I'm going to say."

"Good. Now if you'll excuse me, I have to get back to my kitchen and my little-old-lady ways."

I went to the office and locked myself in. Truly, it was more restful to ponder crime than human beings in love. Here I was trying to talk Henry *into* the very thing I was trying to talk Reba *out of,* and neither one would listen. Then again, why would they? I've bungled every relationship I've ever been in so it's not like my advice is worth much.

I opened the window in hopes of creating a little cross-ventilation. The thermometer outside on the window frame read 74 degrees. It felt hotter than that to me. I sat down, put my feet up on the desk, and rocked back in my swivel chair. I studied my surroundings with a sense of discontent. The windows were so dingy I could hardly see out. Grime on the windowsill. Dust on my fake plant. My desk was covered with junk and the trash can was filled to capacity. I still had boxes I hadn't unpacked since I moved in and that was five months ago. What a slattern I was.

I got up and went into my tiny kitchen, where I scrounged under the sink for a bucket, a sponge, and a quart of virulent yellow liquid that resembled toxic waste. I spent the morning scrubbing surfaces, vacuuming, dusting, shining, polishing, unpacking, and putting things away. By noon, while I was hot, tired, and sweaty, my mood had improved. But not for long.

There was a knock on the door. I opened it to find a

courier standing on my doorstep with an envelope in hand. I signed for it and opened it, pulling out a check from Nord for $1,250 in response to the invoice I'd sent him the day before. The handwritten note that accompanied the payment indicated the $250 bonus was for a job well done.

I wasn't so sure. Psychologically, the bonus put me in his debt and triggered another round of peeps from my conscience, which I'd thought to pacify with all the cleaning I'd done. I was right back in the thick of my debate. Should I tell Reba what was going on or should I not? More important, should I bring her father into the loop? His single admonition—to which I'd agreed—was to keep him informed of any backsliding on her part. This hadn't happened yet (as far as I knew), but if I told her about Beck and Onni, what would she do? She was going to crash and burn. And if I *didn't* tell her and she somehow got wind of it—which was not out of the question in a town this size—much crashing and burning would ensue anyway. She'd begged me not to tell her father about Beck, but Reba wasn't the one who was paying my bills. Witness this check.

I tried to think of an overriding principle that might apply—some moral code that would guide my decision. I couldn't think of *one*. Then I wondered if I had morals or principles of *any* kind, and that made me feel worse.

The phone rang. I picked it up and said, "What," rather more rudely than I'd intended.

Cheney laughed. "You sound stressed."

"Well, I *am*. Do you have any idea the bind you've put me in?"

"I'm sorry. I know it's tough. Would it help if we talked?"

"What's to talk about? Betraying that poor girl? Giving her the news about his screwing around?"

"I told you he's a bad man."

"But isn't it just as bad to go after her like that?"

"You have any other suggestions? Because we're open to just about anything. God knows, we don't want to pull out the big guns unless we have to. The girl's freaky enough."

"That's for sure. I notice you're using the term 'we,' so I assume you've thrown in your lot with the IRS."

"This is a law-enforcement issue. I'm a cop."

"Well, I'm not."

"Would you at least have a chat with my IRS pal?"

"So he can pile his bullshit on top of yours? That's a happy proposition. I feel like I'm going under as it is."

"Look, I'm just around the corner. You want to have lunch? He's on his way up from L.A. and said he'd join us. No hard sell. I promise. Just listen to him."

"To what end?"

"You know a place called Jay's? Hot pastrami sandwiches and the best martinis in town."

"I don't want to *drink* at lunch."

"Me neither, but we can eat together, yes?"

I said, "Hang on. There's someone at my door. I'm going to put you on hold. I'll be back in a second."

"Good deal. I'll wait."

I pushed the Hold button and laid the receiver on my desk. I got up and paced from the inner office to the outer one. What was wrong with me? Because I did want to see him. And it didn't have anything to do with Reba Lafferty. That subject was just a cover for another form of confusion I was wrestling with. I went into the bathroom and stared at myself in the mirror, noting that I looked like shit. This was ridiculous. I went back to the phone and pushed Hold, activating the line. "Give me ten minutes and I'll meet you there."

"Don't be silly. I can swing by. No point in taking two cars when we can make do with one. It's better for the environment."

"Oh, please."

I locked up the office and waited for him out on the street. There was no point worrying about my grubby jeans or my ratty tennis shoes. My hands smelled like bleach and my turtleneck was stretched out of shape. I needed a complete makeover, but I didn't think I could manage one in the next three to four minutes. Oh, to hell with it. This was business. What difference did it make if I were fresh as a daisy, wearing heels and panty hose? The more immediate problem was Cheney's IRS contact. I was already experiencing a low-level dread at the idea of meeting him. No hard sell, my ass. The man would grind me underfoot.

Cheney came around the corner in a sporty little red Mercedes convertible. He pulled in at the curb, leaned over, and opened the passenger-side door. I slid in. "I thought you drove a Mazda," I said, sounding faintly accusative.

"I left that at home. I also have a six-year-old Ford pickup that I use for surveillance. I took delivery on this baby in Los Angeles last week."

"Slick."

He turned right at the corner and headed across town. I liked his driving style. No speeding, no showing off, and no reckless moves. Out of the corner of my eye, I noted the matte finish on his red silk windbreaker—nothing shiny or vulgar—white dress shirt, the chinos, snappy Italian shoes that probably cost more than my monthly rent. Even in an open car, his aftershave smelled like spices, the scent of tiny blossoms on some night-blooming shrub. This was pitiful. I wanted to lean over and sniff deeply at the side of his face. He glanced at me, smiling, as though he knew what was going on in my head. This was not a good sign.

11

Santa Teresa has never been noted for its club scene or its wild nightlife. Most restaurants close soon after the last of the dinner orders have been plated and served. The bars are open until 2:00 A.M., but most don't provide dance floors or live music. Jay's Cocktail Lounge, downtown, is one of the few spots to offer both. In addition, from 11:30 A.M. until 2:00 P.M., lunch is served to a limited clientele who prefer the privacy and quiet for low-key business meetings and discreet liaisons. The walls are padded in gray suede, with a thick gray carpet underfoot that makes you feel you're walking across a mattress. Even by day, the place is so dark, you have to pause at the entrance until your eyes adjust. The booths are commodious, padded in black leather, and any ambient noise is dampened to a hush. Cheney gave his name to the hostess—Phillips, party of three.

He'd made reservations in advance.

I said, "God, you're cocky. What made you so sure I'd say yes?"

"I've never known you to turn down food, especially if someone else pays. Must feel like mothering."

"Well, it is, isn't it?"

"By the way, Vince called to say he's running late. He said to go ahead and order."

We spent the first part of the meal dealing with matters unrelated to Reba Lafferty. We sipped iced tea and picked at our sandwiches, unusual for me where food is concerned. I'm accustomed to eating fast and moaning aloud, but Cheney seemed to enjoy taking his sweet time. We chatted about his career and mine, the police department budget cuts, and the effects thereof. We knew a few cops in common, one being Jonah Robb, the married man I "dated" during one of his frequent separations from his wife, Camilla.

I said, "How's Jonah doing these days? Is the marriage off again or on?" I rattled the last of the ice cubes in my empty glass and, as if on cue, the busboy appeared to replenish my supply.

Cheney said, "Off, from what I hear. They had a kid. I should say, Camilla did. According to the scuttlebutt, the boy wasn't his."

"Yeah, but he's crazy about that baby all the same," I said. "I ran into him a couple of months ago and he was busting his buttons he was so proud of the kid."

"What about the two daughters? No telling what effect this is having on them."

"Camilla doesn't seem to care. I wish they'd just get back together and be done with it. How many times have they split?"

Cheney shook his head.

I studied him. "What about you? How's married life these days?"

"That's over."

"Over?"

"You know the word 'over'? As in done with."

"I'm sorry to hear that. When did this transpire?"

"Middle of May. Embarrassing to admit, but we were only married five weeks, which is one week less than we'd known each other before we eloped."

"Where is she now?"

"She's moved back to L.A."

"That was quick."

"Like ripping off a Band-Aid. Better to get it over with."

"Did you learn anything?"

"I doubt it. I was tired of feeling dead. Work we do, we take chances in the real world but not so much in here," he said, tapping on his chest. "What's love about if not risk?"

I studied my plate, which was littered with potato chip crumbs. I licked my index finger and captured a cluster that I laid on my tongue. "You're beyond my area of competence. These days, I seem to be surrounded by people who've got it wrong, Reba Lafferty being one."

He leaned forward, elbows on the table, holding his glass by the rim. "So let's talk about her."

"What's to talk about? She's fragile. It doesn't seem right to put the squeeze on her."

A flicker of irritation crossed his face. "Fragile, my ass. She's the one who elected to get involved with him. Turns out, he's a sleazebag in more ways than one. She should know what's going on."

"You're not doing this for her sake. You're doing it for yours."

"What difference does that make? She needs to be told. Or do you disagree?"

"What if the revelation pushes her over the edge?"

"If she goes off the deep end, we'll handle it." His gaze shifted to a point just over my shoulder. I turned my head and caught a glimpse of a man I assumed was Vince Turner approaching to my left. Cheney slid out of the booth and the two of them shook hands.

Vince Turner was a hefty man in his forties, round-faced, balding, wearing a tan raincoat. The wire stems on his frameless glasses had been bent at an angle that left

them slightly askew. He toted a brown leather school bag
that in sixth grade would have labeled him as hopelessly
out of it. Now the scuffed handle and the buckles on the
two exterior pockets marked him as self-assured.

Cheney introduced us. Turner peeled off his raincoat
and tossed it across the back of the banquette before he sat
down. His suit was mud brown, the jacket wrinkled across
the back. His trousers had accordion pleats radiating from
the crotch because he'd sat in them too long. He loosened
his tie and tucked the ends in the pocket of his dress shirt,
perhaps to keep them from flapping in his food.

"Have you eaten?" Cheney asked.

"I had a burger in the car coming up, but I could use a
drink."

Cheney signaled the waiter, who appeared moments
later with a menu in hand.

Turner waved it away. "Maker's on the rocks. A double."

"Would you like anything else?"

"That's fine. What about you, Cheney?"

"I'm good."

"By me," I said.

As soon as the waiter disappeared, Turner picked up his
baton of napkin-wrapped flatware, unrolled the utensils, and
set a place for himself. On his right hand he wore a heavy
gold-and-garnet class ring, but there was no way to read the
legend that encircled the stone. His face was shiny with perspiration, but his pale eyes were cold. He lined up the handles
of his knife, his spoon, and two forks, then checked his watch.
"I'm not sure how much Lieutenant Phillips has told you
about me. It's one-fifteen now. At two-fifty, I'll be on a flight
from here to LAX and then on to Washington, D.C., where I
meet with a group of IRS investigators and the DEA. That
gives us approximately one hour to conduct our business, so
I'll get straight to the point. You have questions or comments,
feel free to raise your hand. Otherwise, I'll talk until I get to
the end. Is that agreeable?" He made another minute adjust-
ment to the silverware.

"Fine with me," I said. I found it easier to watch his hands than to look him in the eye.

"I'm forty-six years old. Since 1972 I've worked in the Criminal Investigation Division of the Bureau of Internal Revenue. My first assignment was as assistant to the man who pursued the case against Braniff Airlines in the laundering of illegal corporate campaign contributions. Braniff, like American Airlines, needed the occasional government assist in those days and began to funnel money to the Nixon re-election committee by way of Maurice Stans. You remember him?"

He looked up at me long enough to see me nod.

"Having cut my teeth on Watergate, I developed an appetite for financial chicanery. I've never been blessed with a wife or children. My job is my life." He glanced down at his jacket and removed a tiny speck of lint. "A year ago, in May of 1986, Congress, in a rare moment of common sense, passed Public Law 99-570, the Money Laundering Control Act, which has provided us the hammer with which to pound the shit out of violators of the Bank Secrecy Act. The banking community is already feeling the effects. For a long time, banks in this country treated reporting requirements as a trivial matter, but that's changed. Many violations once considered misdemeanors have now been elevated to felony offenses with maximum prison sentences, fines, and civil penalties. Crocker National Bank has been fined $2,250,000; Bank of America was fined $4,750,000; and Texas Commerce Bancshares was fined $1,900,000. You can't imagine the satisfaction I've felt forcing these guys into line. And we ain't done yet."

He paused, looking up with a smile that warmed his face from within. His ice blue eyes suddenly contained a merriment impossible to resist. I think in that moment, my position shifted. I'd do what I could for Reba, but if she came up against this guy, she was in deeper shit than she knew.

The waiter arrived with his Maker's Mark, which was the color of strong iced tea. Vince Turner sucked down half without hesitation and then placed the glass carefully in front of him. He folded his hands and lifted his eyes to mine. "Which brings us to Mr. Beckwith. I've spent the past year assembling a comprehensive dossier on him. As I'm sure you know, his lifestyle looks clean and his social credentials are solid, largely because of his late father's standing in the community. He's considered by most to be an honest, law-abiding citizen, who'd never dream of trafficking in drugs, pornography, or prostitutes.

"He's what we call a market-based offender. He takes the profits from these same illegal activities, disguises their origin, and introduces them back into the system as legitimate earnings. For the past five years, he's been 'rehabilitating' funds for a man named Salustio Castillo, a Los Angeles jewelry wholesaler who also deals in scrap silver and gold. The business is just a cover for what he really does, which is to import cocaine from South America. Castillo bought a large property in Montebello through Mr. Beckwith's real estate firm. Mr. Beckwith brokered the deal, which is how they became acquainted. Mr. Castillo needed someone of Mr. Beckwith's professional reputation. His company is diverse and his financial dealings of sufficient magnitude to camouflage the funds Castillo was so eager to place. Mr. Beckwith saw the possibilities and agreed to help.

"At first, he employed the standard laundering techniques—structuring transactions, consolidating the deposits, and using wire transfers to move the money out of the country. By the time the money was routed through his company books and back to Castillo, the sources appeared to be legitimate. After six months, Mr. Beckwith got tired of paying his smurfs or maybe he got tired of keeping track of the myriad accounts he'd opened across Santa Teresa County. He began to make big deposits—two and three hundred thousand dollars at a clip, claiming these were the proceeds of commercial real estate ventures. This time he was the model of compliance, making sure all the appropriate CTRs were filed. In truth, he was counting on the fact that the IRS has to process so many millions of CTRs that his were in little or no danger of being flagged for scrutiny. Soon he was running a million a week through the system, taking one percent off the top as his service fee.

"Finally, deposits reached a level where the risks outweighed the benefits of doing business so close to home. Mr. Beckwith got nervous and decided to bypass the local banks and eliminate the paper trail. He acquired a Panamanian bank and an unrestricted banking license in Antigua, putting up the requisite one million in U.S. dollars as paid-in capital. He invested an additional five hundred thousand dollars for a second international banking license in the Netherlands Antilles, which doesn't have a tax treaty with the U.S. at this point."

I raised my hand. "A million and a half? Is it really worth that to him?"

"Absolutely. With his offshore banks, he can make deposits. He can write his own references, issue letters of credit to himself, all of this protected by complete privacy and with very little interference from the host countries. He doesn't even have to be there to handle management. Keep in mind, too, when people hear you own a bank, they tend to be impressed."

I said, "I'll bet." Cheney caught my eye fleetingly, probably thinking, as I was, about the banks his father owned.

Vince Turner paused and looked from Cheney to me.

I said, "Sorry. Go on."

He shrugged and continued as though his commentary had been recorded in advance. "By law, an American citizen is required to declare all foreign bank accounts on their yearly tax returns, but these guys aren't any more scrupulous about that than any other aspect of their business. Mr. Beckwith, under the auspices of the banks he'd bought, established an international business corporation, an IBC, in Panama, with shares being held in a Panama Private Interest Foundation, allowing him to avoid both U.S. and Panamanian taxation. With the shell company in place, he began to move currency *physically* from the States to his offshore havens. You move cash, Customs requires a CMIR—a Currency and Monetary Instrument Report—but Mr. Beckwith doesn't much care for filling out these pesky little government forms. No forms means no more violations, at least to his skewed way of thinking. Once deposited in one of his offshore banks, monies are returned to Mr. Castillo in the form of business loans with a twenty-year balloon.

"Of course, the transport of currency generates difficulties of a different sort. Bills are not only bulky, but weigh more than you'd think. The foreign markets prefer the smaller denominations—twenties and fifties. A million dollars in twenty-dollar bills tops out at over one hundred twenty-five pounds. Try toting that through an airport. Not a problem for our boy. The ever resourceful Mr. Beckwith leased a Learjet and now he flies suitcases full of cash to Panama every couple of months. Panama's currency is the U.S. dollar, so he doesn't even have to worry about the exchange rate. Between plane trips, he's been taking his wife on a series of luxury cruises, moving the cash in a steamer trunk that he keeps in his stateroom."

Turner polished off his bourbon, signaling the waiter for another round. "Anybody ever tell you how much money gets laundered every year worldwide?"

I shook my head.

"One-point-five trillion dollars—that's a one, a five, and eleven zeros—just so you get the picture. In the U.S., the figure's somewhere in the neighborhood of fifty billion, but we're talking about revenue that's never taxed, so you see how serious it gets."

Cheney spoke up. "How much can you tell her about the investigation to date?"

"Broad strokes? Four years ago the IRS, the DEA, the

FBI, Customs, and the Justice and Treasury departments put together a task force to investigate gold and precious metals dealers in Los Angeles, Detroit, and Miami, all of whom we suspect are laundering money for a Colombian drug cartel. So far they've managed to place, layer, and integrate sixteen million dollars, running the cash through four businesses, using multiple accounts, at ten different banks, one of which has a branch here in town. Alan Beckwith is responsible for processing a substantial portion of that sum.

"Ours is painstaking work. We're still sorting out the particulars, developing as much hard evidence as we can before we make our move. The trick is not to alert him until we have all our ducks in a row. A U.S. District Court judge in Los Angeles and another in Miami have recently approved electronic surveillance. That's allowed us to monitor Mr. Beckwith's phone conversations. We've also obtained authorization to seize and remove trash from his home and business premises. Right now we have our merry band of agents picking through his garbage. They've found invoices listing fictitious addresses for nonexistent businesses, assorted handwritten notes, canceled checks, discarded typewriter cartridges and adding-machine tape. Mr. Beckwith has legitimate dealings with financial institutions on a number of fronts, and he's skilled at mingling the profits from illegal activities with the mundane business he does from day to day. What he's apparently unaware of is that financial institutions are required to save signature cards, account statements, copies of checks written for any amount over a hundred dollars. The banks also retain a transaction log of wire transfers, so they can properly account for funds passing through the system. The information is all coded, but it's possible to use the sequence numbers to identify the source bank, the target bank, and the dates and times the money was sent on its way. We don't yet have access to these documents, but we're putting together the necessary paperwork to subpoena bank records."

The waiter appeared, setting down Turner's second drink. A silence fell until he'd moved away from the table and out of earshot. Turner picked up his glass of bourbon. His drinking had slowed to a sipping pace, and I could see him savoring the taste.

"What do you want from Reba? Surely you're not asking her to waltz in and lift all the pertinent files."

"Not at all. In point of fact, we can't instruct her to do anything that violates the law because we're not at liberty to do so ourselves. Even if she stole the files without our prior knowledge or approval, we couldn't even peek at them without jeopardizing our case. What we *can* ask for is an in-depth description of his records—the nature of the files he has and where they're located—which will allow us to prepare financial and document search warrants. I understand you feel protective of Ms. Lafferty, but we need her cooperation."

"Isn't there anybody else? What about his company comptroller?"

"The company comptroller's a fellow named Marty Blumberg. We've thought of him. The problem is he's so deeply implicated he might panic and run, or worse, panic and warn Mr. Beckwith. Now that she's not working for him, Reba's been removed from the line of fire and she might be more inclined to help. Lieutenant Phillips showed you the photographs?"

"Well, yeah, but I'm not sure what those are going to do for you. She finds out he's in trouble, she'll fall all over herself telling him whatever you tell her."

"I gathered as much. Do you have a suggestion about how to contain her reaction?"

"No. To me, it's like detonating a nuclear device. You risk as much destruction as you're hoping to unleash."

Turner adjusted a minute irregularity in the flatware he'd aligned. "Point taken. Unfortunately, we don't have much time. Mr. Beckwith has uncanny survival instincts. We've been discreet, but from the intelligence we've gathered, he may well suspect there's something afoot. He's consolidating his funds, picking up the pace, which we find worrisome."

"Reba mentioned that, but she's convinced he's doing it for her. He says once his assets are secure, he'll dump his wife and the two of them can hit the highway. Or that's what she hears. Who knows the truth of it?"

"There's no doubt he's preparing to make a run for it. Another week and he might succeed in placing the cash and himself beyond our reach."

"Does the money belong to him or Salustio Castillo?"

"His, in the main. If he's smart, he'll keep his hands off Salustio's cash. Last guy who crossed Castillo got turned into a concrete popsicle in a twenty-gallon garbage can."

Once it was clear Vince was finished, Cheney said, "So. Who talks to Reba? You, me, or her."

There was a silence while all three of us stared at the tabletop. Finally, I raised my hand. "I've got a better shot at it than either one of you."

"Good. Give us a couple of days. As soon as I get back from Washington, I'll set up a meeting with our FBI contact and the DOJ. Customs will want to sit in as well. As soon as we decide how we want to proceed, we'll bring you in for a briefing, probably the beginning of next week. After that, we'll hope to talk to her."

"You better make it good. I don't look forward to delivering the news."

"Don't worry about that. We'll advise you in advance."

Cheney dropped me off at my office at 2:00 P.M. The afternoon temperature was climbing, a complete contradiction of the morning weather report that promised a moderate 74 degrees. Vince Turner had called a taxi to ferry him to the airport so he could catch his flight. I was hoping Cheney would have the good grace to deliver me without reference to Reba Lafferty or Beck, but as I got out of the car, he held up a manila envelope. "I had copies made for you."

"What am I supposed to do with 'em?"

"Whatever you like. I thought you should have a set."

"Thanks so much." I took the envelope.

"Call me if you need me."

"Trust me. I will."

I waited until he'd turned the corner and the sound of his little red Mercedes had faded in the turgid afternoon air. I let myself into the office, where the air felt stuffy and dead. I passed through the reception area to my desk. I tossed my shoulder bag on the client chair and sat down with the manila envelope. I used it to fan myself and then undid the clasp and removed the prints. The photographs were just as I remembered them—Beck and Onni emerging from various motels, he with his arm around her, the two holding hands, Onni with her head on his shoulder and her arm around his waist, the two hip-to-hip walking in lock-step. Poor Reba. She was in for a rude awakening. I opened my desk drawer and tossed the envelope inside. I didn't even want to think about the sorry task of breaking the news. In hopes of distracting myself, I did something I hadn't done for ages. I walked the four blocks from my office into downtown Santa Teresa and caught two movies, back-to-back, watching one of them twice. I thus succeeded in dodging the heat and dodging reality at the same time.

12

When I reached my apartment, I saw that Mattie's car was gone and Henry's kitchen was dark. I wasn't sure what to make of that. The temperature was somewhere in the eighties, almost unheard of at this hour. It was still light out and the sidewalks shimmered with accumulated heat. The air felt sluggish, with no movement to speak of and humidity probably hovering at 95 percent. You'd think it would rain, but this was mid-July and we'd be stuck with drought conditions until late November—if the weather broke for us at all. My apartment was stifling. I sat on my porch step, flapping a breeze at my face with the folded newspaper. While most Southern California properties have sprinkler systems, few have central air conditioning. I was going to have to haul a fan out of the closet and set it up in the loft before I hit the sack.

Nights like this little kids toss aside nighties and pajamas and sleep in their underpants. My aunt Gin always swore I'd be cooler if I did a 180 turn on the bed, feet on the pillow, my head propped on the tangle of covers wadded at the foot. She was remarkably permissive, this woman who raised me, having never given birth to any children of her own. On those rare California nights when it was too hot to sleep, she'd tell me I could stay up all night even if I happened to have school the next day. We'd lie there reading our books in our respective bedrooms, the trailer so quiet I could hear her turning the pages. What I treasured was the heady sense that we were breaking the rules. I knew "real" parents probably wouldn't tolerate such license, but I saw it as one small compensation for my orphaned state. Inevitably, I'd drift off to sleep. Aunt Gin would tiptoe in, slip the book out of my hands, and douse the light. I'd wake later to find the room dark and the sheet laid over me. Odd, the memories that linger long after a life is gone.

Finally, just as the streetlights came on, I heard the telephone ring. I pulled myself to my feet and scooted into the apartment, snatching up the handset. "'Lo?"

"This is Cheney."

"Well, hi. I didn't expect to hear from you. What's up?"

There was sufficient noise in the background I had to press a hand to my ear to hear what he was saying. "What?"

"Have you had dinner yet?"

I'd eaten a box of popcorn at the movies, but I didn't think that counted. "I wouldn't call it that."

"Good. I'll be there in two minutes and we'll go out and grab a bite."

"Where *are* you?"

"Rosie's. I figured you'd be here, but I was wrong again."

"Maybe I'm not as predictable as you thought."

"I doubt that. You own a sun dress?"

"Well no, but I have a skirt."

"Wear that. I'm tired of seeing you in jeans."

He hung up and I stood there, staring at the receiver. What a weird turn of events. Dinner sounded like a *date,* unless he'd heard something from Vince Turner about the briefing coming up next week. And why would I have to wear a skirt to receive information like that?

I took my time going up the spiral stairs, trying to figure out what to wear aside from the skirt. I sat down on the bed, pulled off my tennis shoes and shed my sweaty clothes. I showered and wrapped myself in a towel. When I opened my closet door there, sure enough, was my tan poplin skirt. I removed it from the hanger and flapped the wrinkles out. I put on fresh underwear and then stepped into the skirt, noting that the hem hit me just above the knee. I crossed to the chest of drawers where I pawed through a stack of shirts and selected a red tank top that I pulled over my head and tucked in at the waist. I put on a pair of sandals, went into the bathroom, and brushed my teeth. This was all my way of stalling while I decided how I felt.

I stood at the sink and studied my reflection. Why was I compelled to stare at myself in mirrors whenever Cheney called to say he was on his way? I ran water in my hands and ruffled up my hair. Eye makeup? Nah. Lipstick? Don't think so. That would look presumptuous if this were really IRS business. I leaned closer. Well, okay, just a touch of color. No harm in that. I settled for pressed powder, a quick sweep of eye shadow, mascara, and coral lipstick that I applied and wiped off, leaving my lips faintly pink. You see? This is the downside of relationships with men—you become a narcissist, obsessed with "beauty" issues that ordinarily you couldn't care less about.

I turned off the light, trotted downstairs, and picked up my shoulder bag. I left a lamp burning in the living room, locked the door behind me, and went out to the street. Cheney was already there, his little red Mercedes idling at the curb. He leaned across the seat and opened the door for me. The man was a fashion plate. He'd changed clothes again: dark Italian loafers, sand-washed silk pants in a charcoal brown, and a white linen shirt with the sleeves rolled up. He did a quick head-to-toe appraisal. "You look good."

"Thanks. So do you."

He smiled slightly. "Glad we got that settled."

"Me, too."

He turned right at the corner, heading over to Cabana Boulevard, where he took a left. With the top down, my hair was flying every which way, but at least the air was cool. I figured we were heading to the Caliente Café. The place is a cop hangout and all-around dive—cigarette smoke, beer smell, the constant rattle and howl of blenders whipping ice cubes into margarita mix, tasty faux-Mexican cuisine, and no discernible decor unless you count the six raggedy-ass Mexican straw hats nailed to the wall.

When we reached the bird refuge, instead of turning left as I expected, we sailed right on under the freeway and up the other side. We were now in what was known as "the lower village" of Montebello. The four lanes of divided road merged and narrowed into two, lined with elegant clothing and jewelry shops, real estate offices, and the usual assortment of businesses, including beauty salons, a tennis shop, and a high-priced art gallery. By then, it was fully dark and most places, while closed, were awash with light. The trees were wrapped in strands of tiny Italian bulbs, trunks and branches sparkling as though with ice.

We continued along the frontage road as far as St. Isadore. Cheney took a left. We passed through an area dubbed the "hedgerow district" where pittosporum and eugenia shrubs grew ten to twenty feet high, shielding properties from the road. Until now, tax myself as I might, I hadn't thought of one word to say so I'd kept my mouth shut. This didn't seem to bother Cheney, and I was hopeful he disliked small talk as much as I did. On the other hand, we couldn't spend the entire evening without speaking. That would be too strange for words, as it were.

We wound along dark lanes, the little red Mercedes humming, Cheney downshifting until we reached the St. Isadore Hotel. Once a rustic working ranch that dated back to the late 1800s, the St. Isadore is now an upscale resort with luxury cottages dotted across fourteen acres of flower beds, shrubs, live oaks, and orange trees. Pets were permitted. For a mere fifty dollars per mutt, dogs were provided with doggie beds, "Pawier" mineral water, hand-painted personalized water bowls, and pet "room service" on request. I'd been here for dinner on occasion, but never as a paying guest.

Cheney pulled up at the main building and got out of the car. A parking attendant stepped forward and helped me extricate myself and then he spirited the car away. We bypassed the elegant second-floor restaurant and ducked into the Harrow and Seraph, a low-ceilinged bar located at ground level. The door stood open. Cheney stepped aside, allowing me to pass in front of him, and then he followed me in.

The walls were stone, whitewashed and cool. There were fewer than twenty tables, many empty at that hour. A small bar ran along the back wall. There was a stone fireplace on the left, the hearth dark, given that it was summer. There was banquette seating on the right with the remainder of the tables staggered across the space in between. Illumination was discreet but not so dim that you'd need a flashlight to read the menu. Cheney steered me to an upholstered bench seat backed with pillows so plump I had to push them aside. He sat across the table and then seemed to think better of it, got up and slid in beside me, saying, "No cop talk. I'm off duty here and so are you."

"I thought you wanted to chat about Reba."

"Nope. Don't want to hear a word."

I was only moderately distracted by the warmth of his thigh in proximity to mine. That's the thing about wearing poplin—the way it conducts body heat. The waiter appeared and Cheney ordered two vodka martinis, straight up, with extra olives on the side. As soon as the waiter left, Cheney said, "Quit worrying. We won't drink all the time. This is just to loosen our tongues."

I laughed. "I appreciate the reassurance. The notion did

flit across my mind." I let my gaze travel briefly—mouth, chin, shoulders. His teeth were beautiful, white and straight—always a weakness of mine. Dark hairs shaded the curve of his forearms.

He studied me, his right elbow propped on the table, his chin resting in his palm. "You never answered my question."

"Which one?"

"At lunch. I asked you about Dietz."

"Ah. Well, let's see if I can be fair about this. He tends to drop out of sight. Last time I saw him was a year ago March. Where he's been since then I have no idea. He's not big on explanations. I guess you'd call it the 'Take it or leave it' school of relationships. I've left messages on his machine, but he hasn't returned my calls. It's possible he's dumped me, but how would I know?"

"Would it matter if he had?"

"I don't think so. I might feel insulted, but I'd survive. I think it's rude to leave me hanging, but such is life."

"I thought you were nuts about the guy."

"I was, but I knew what he was."

"Which is what?"

"An emotional drifter. The point is, I chose him anyway, so it must have suited me somehow. Now things are different. I can't go back to that. It's over and done." Which was, now that I thought about it, roughly how Cheney had described his marriage.

He seemed to be considering what I'd said. "You've been married once?"

I held up two fingers. "Both ended in divorce."

"What's the story on those guys?"

"The first was a cop."

"Mickey Magruder. I heard about him. You leave him or did he leave you?"

"I was the one who pulled out. I misjudged him. I left because I thought he was guilty of something. Turns out, he wasn't. I still feel badly about that."

"Because why?"

"I didn't have a chance to tell him I was sorry before he died. I'd have liked to clear that. Husband number two was a musician, a pianist, very talented. Also, chronically unfaithful and a pathological liar with the face of an angel. It was a blow when he left. I was twenty-four years old and probably should have seen it coming. Later I found out he'd always been more interested in other men than he was in me."

"So how come I don't see you around town with other guys? Have you given up on men?"

I nearly made a smart remark, but I caught myself in time. Instead, I opened my mouth and said, "I've been waiting for you, Cheney. I thought you knew that."

He looked at me, waiting to see if I was making light of him. I returned his gaze, waiting to see what he'd do with the information. I couldn't imagine what would happen next. There were so many wrong moves, so many dumb things that might come out of his mouth. I was thinking, *Don't mess this up . . . please, please don't ruin it . . . whatever it is . . .*

Here are two things I hate to have men do:

(1) Tell me I'm beautiful, which is bullshit manipulation and has nothing to do with me.

(2) Look into my eyes and talk about my "trust" issues because they know I've been "hurt."

Here's what Cheney did: He put his arm up on the seat back and picked up a strand of hair from the top of my head. He studied it with care, his expression serious. In the split second before he spoke, I heard a muffled sound, like gas jets igniting when a match is struck. Warmth fanned up along my spine and softened all the tension in my neck. He said, "I'll give you a proper haircut. Did you know I cut hair?"

I found myself staring at his mouth. "No. I didn't know that. What else do you do?"

He smiled. "Dance. Do you dance?"

"Not very well."

"That's all right. I can teach you. You'll improve."

"I'd like that. What else?"

"I work out. I box some and lift weights."

"Do you cook?"

"No, do you?"

"Peanut butter and pickle sandwiches."

"Sandwiches don't count, except for grilled cheese."

I said, "Any other talents I should know about?"

He ran the back of his hand down along my cheek. "I'm an especially good speller. Fifth grade, I came in second in the school spelling bee."

I could feel a hum forming in my throat, the same strange mechanism that causes cats to purr. "What'd you screw up on?"

" 'Eleemosynary.' It means 'of or for charity or alms.' Should be e-l-e-e-m-o-s-y-n-a-r-y. I left out the third *e*."

"But you haven't screwed up since. So you learned."

"Yes, I did. What about you? Any skills you want to talk about upfront?"

"I know how to read upside down. I interview some guy and he has a document on his desk? I can read every word while I'm chatting away with him."

"Excellent. What else?"

"You know that party game we played in elementary school? The mom brings out a tray, twenty-five objects covered with a towel? She lifts the towel and the kids study the items for thirty seconds before she covers them again. I can recite 'em back without missing one, except sometimes the Q-tips. I tend to mess up on those."

"I'm not good at party games."

"Neither am I, except for that. I've won all kinds of prizes. Bubbles in a jar and paddles with the ball attached that goes bang-bang-bang."

The waiter brought our drinks. The connection between us faded, but the moment the waiter left, I could feel it start up again. He put his hand on my neck. I leaned toward him, tilting my head until my lips were close to his ear. "We're going to get in a lot of trouble, aren't we?"

"More than you know," he murmured in response. "Know why I brought you here?"

"Not a clue," I said.

"The macaroni and cheese."

"You're going to mother me?"

"Seduce."

"You're doing well so far."

"You ain't seen nuttin' yet," he said, and smiled. He kissed me then, but only once and not for long.

When I could speak again, I said, "You're a man of great restraint."

"And self-control. I probably should have mentioned that much earlier."

"I like surprises. Good ones," I said.

"That's all you get with me."

The waiter approached and took out his pad. We eased away from each other, both of us smiling politely as though Cheney's thigh wasn't locked against mine under the table-cloth. I hadn't taken the first sip of my drink, but I was feeling bleary-eyed, drowsy with the heat that was suffusing my limbs. I checked the other diners, but no one else seemed to notice the charged particles undulating between us.

Cheney ordered a salad for each of us and told the waiter we'd share the macaroni and cheese, which was apparently served in a ramekin the size of a bread-and-butter plate. Didn't matter to me. He'd neatly shifted me off-center, away from my usual contentious and arbitrary self. I was already hooked into him. I could feel my boundaries dissolve, desire cleaving the barricade I'd erected to keep the Mongol hordes at bay. Who cared about that? Let them swarm over the walls.

As soon as the waiter left, Cheney put his hand, palm up, on the table and I laced my fingers through his. He was staring off across the room, his gaze shifting from face to face as he checked the other patrons. I sensed he'd detached himself, but I knew he'd be back. I studied his profile, the mop of curly brown hair, mine to touch if I liked. I could see the pulse beat in his throat. He turned and looked at me. His eyes moved from mine to the shape of my mouth. He leaned into me and we kissed again. Where the first kiss had been delicate, this kiss was promissory.

I nearly hummed aloud. "We have to eat dinner, right?"

"Food as foreplay."

"I'm starving."

"I'll do right by you."

"I know."

I'm not sure how we made it through the meal. We ate a salad that was cold and crisp, pungent with vinaigrette. He fed me macaroni and cheese, hot and soft, laced with pro-sciutto, and then he kissed the taste of salt from my mouth. How had we arrived at this place? I thought of all the times I'd seen him, conversations we'd had. I'd never caught a real glimpse of this man, but here he was.

He paid the bill. While we waited for the car, he pulled me in against him with his hands on my ass. I wanted to climb his frame, shinny up his body like a monkey up a palm. The parking attendant averted his eyes, keeping his manner disinterested as he handed me into the car. Cheney tipped him, pulled his door shut, and shifted into first. As we sailed through the dark, I rubbed a hand along his thigh.

By the time we pulled into his driveway, I wasn't even sure where we were. His house, apparently. Dazed, I watched as he got out of the car on his side and came around to mine. He pulled me out of the seat and turned me until I was laid up against him, my back against his front, his lips moving along my neck. He pushed the strap of my tank top aside and kissed my shoulder, letting me feel the faintest nudge of his teeth. He said, "Let's slow down, okay? We can take as long as we want. Or do you have to be some-where?"

"No."

"Good. Then why don't we go upstairs."

"Okay." I reached back and slid my fingers into his hair, gripping, as I turned my face toward his. "Please tell me you're not so sure of yourself you changed the sheets before you left the house tonight."

"I didn't. I wouldn't do that to you. I bought new."

13

Cheney drove me home at 5:45 through the early morning light. He'd go into the gym for his morning workout and then hit the department in time for a briefing at 7:00. I intended to crawl straight into bed. We'd finally untangled ourselves at dawn, just as streaks in the sky were turning from salmon to hot pink. It had taken me less than a minute to throw on my clothes, after which I'd watched him get dressed. He was more muscular than I'd imagined, his body sleek and well defined. Good pecs, good biceps, good abs. When I'd married Mickey I was twenty-one years old to his thirty-seven, a difference of sixteen years. Daniel had been closer to my age, but soft, with a boyish body, slender and narrow-chested. Dietz, like Mickey, had been senior to me by sixteen years, a connection I'd never made before. Something to ponder later. I hadn't devoted much thought to men's bodies, but then again I'd never made the acquaintance of one quite like Cheney's. He was just so beautifully built—skin as smooth as fine leather, pulled taut over an armature of stone.

On the street in front of my place, we kissed one last time before I got out of the car and watched him rumble away. With any other man, I might already be fretting about all the dumb things women worry about—would he call, would I see him again, had he meant even one small portion of what he'd said. With Cheney, I didn't care. Whatever this was and whatever came next, it was all fine with me. If the entire relationship ended up encapsulated in the hours we'd just spent, well, wasn't I the lucky one for the experience?

I slept until ten, skipped the run, lollygagged around the house, and finally drifted into the office shortly before noon in time to break for lunch. I was just about to unwrap my cheese and pickle sandwich when I heard someone open the outer door and slam it shut. Reba appeared in the doorway, her face suffused with rage, manila envelope in hand. "Did you take these?"

I felt a spurt of fear at the sight of the envelope, given that I had its identical twin in my drawer.

She leaned across my desk and slashed the air in front of my face with the corner of the envelope, shaking it so close to my eyes she could have taken one out. "Did you?"

"Did I what? I don't even know what you're talking about." This was world-class lying, me at my best, rising to the challenge, unflinching in the heat of battle.

She undid the clasp and snatched out the prints, which she slapped down in front of me. She leaned forward again, this time supporting her weight with both hands. "Some fucking little creep came to the house and asked to speak to me. I thought it was a parole officer doing a home visit so I take him in the living room and sit him down to have a chat, cheery as all get-out just to show what a good little citizen I am. Next thing I know he's handing me these and laying out a line of shit like you wouldn't believe. That's Beck, by the way, in case the light's too grainy."

I picked up the black-and-white prints and made a display of sorting through them, trying to decide how to play this. I placed them on the desk and looked up at her. "So he picks up some hooker. What do you expect?"

"Hooker, my ass." She took one photo by the edge and pointed at the woman with such viciousness she nearly ripped the page. "Do you know who that is?"

I shook my head, my heart thudding in my chest. Of course I *knew*. I just didn't want to admit it to her.

"That's Onni. My best friend."

"Ah."

She made a face. "I don't give a shit if he had *sex,* but with her?"

"Yeah, you'd think as a courtesy, he could have screwed his wife instead of your best friend," I said.

"Exactly. I didn't expect him to be celibate. I certainly wasn't."

Ooo, what did she mean by that? With whom had she done what? In prison, the options were limited, or so one would think.

"You know what pisses me off? I'm supposed to have dinner with Onni. Tonight. Can you picture it? I'd be chatting away, happy to be with her because I missed her so much. The whole time she'd be sitting there, laughing up her ass. The friggin' bitch. She knows I'm in love with him. She *knows* that!" Her face suddenly took on that pinched look that precedes tears. She sat down abruptly. "Oh god, what am I going to do?"

I waited for a moment, listening to the tight squeezed-up sound of her weeping. This went on for a while, but once the sobs had subsided, I said, "Are you okay?"

"No, I'm not okay. Does it look like I'm okay? I'm going out of my mind. I could have gone my whole life without this."

Like a shrink, I picked up the box of tissues from the corner of my desk and pushed it over to her. She took one and blew her nose. "Hell with it. I wasn't going to do this, but I really can't help myself." She opened her bag and took out a fresh pack of cigarettes. She tugged on the thin band of red, peeling away the top of the cellophane wrapper. She tore off one half of the foil and smacked the bottom of the pack on her hand to force a cigarette forward out of the tight pack. She reached for her gold Dunhill lighter and flicked it, bending to the flame with a rapt expression on her face. She inhaled, drawing smoke into her lungs like nitrous oxide, letting it out again in a soft stream. She leaned back in the chair and closed her eyes. This was like watching someone shoot up. I could see the sedative effect as the nicotine permeated her system. She opened her eyes again. "Better. That's awesome. I hope you have an ashtray."

"Flick it on the floor. The carpet's shit anyway."

She was probably light-headed, but at least the outrage had been erased and replaced by an artificial calm. She allowed herself a thin, mocking smile. "I should have known when I bought the pack I'd crack it within a day."

"Just don't drink."

"Right. I won't. One vice at a time." She took another drag from her cigarette, tension draining from her face. "It's been a year since I smoked. Shit, and I was doing so well."

"You were doing great." I was still picking my way across what felt like a minefield, wondering if I could tell her the truth without bringing down fire on my own position.

"What's sick is the damn thing tastes so good," she said.

The subject of Beck was beside the point, now that she had her smokes. "So now what?" I asked.

"Beats the hell out of me."

"Maybe the two of us can figure it out."

"Yeah, right. What's to figure? I've been had," she said.

"I'm puzzled about the fellow who came to the house. I don't get that. Who was he?"

She shrugged. "He said he was FBI."

"Really. The FBI?"

"That's what he claimed, all superior and smarmy. As soon as I saw the first photo, I told him to get the hell off the property, but he wanted to sit there and spell it out for me, like I was too dumb to get it. I picked up the phone and told him I'd call the cops if he wasn't out the door in five seconds. That shut him up."

"Did he show you his ID? Badge, business card? Anything like that?"

"He flashed a badge when I first opened the door, but I didn't pay attention. Parole officers carry badges. I thought that's who he was so I didn't bother to check his name. I mean, what's it to me? I didn't see what choice I had so I let him in. When he pulled out the envelope, I figured he had forms to fill out, like he'd be filing some report. By the time I realized what he was up to I was so damn mad I didn't care who he was."

"What are you going to do?"

"I'm sure as hell canceling my dinner date. I wouldn't sit down with Onni if I had a gun to my head."

"Don't you think Beck's the one you should be mad at? You went to jail for the guy and this is what he does in return."

"I never went to *jail* for him. Who told you that?"

"What difference does it make? That's the word around town."

"Well, I didn't."

"Come on, Reba. You might as well come clean. I'm the only friend you have. So you're crazy in love and took the fall for him. Wouldn't be the first time. Maybe he sweet-talked you into it."

"He didn't sweet-talk me into anything. I knew what I was doing."

"I have a hard time believing *that*."

"You want to argue the point? You ask me to be honest and then you sit there and make judgments? How fucked up is that?"

I raised a hand. "Right. You're right. I apologize. I didn't mean it that way."

She stared at me, assessing my sincerity. I must have looked like an honest woman because she said, "Okay."

"Anyway, whatever the motivation, you're saying you didn't embezzle any money from him?"

"Of course not. I have money of my own, or at least I had some back then."

"That being the case, how'd you end up in jail?"

"The discrepancies showed up on an audit and he *had* to account for the missing money somehow. He thought they'd let me off easy. Suspended sentence, probation—you know, something like that."

"That seems like a stretch. You'd been in jail once before on a bad-check charge. From the judge's point of view, this was simply more of the same."

"Well, yeah, I guess it might have looked that way. Beck did everything he could to soften the blow. He told the DA he didn't want to file charges, but I guess it's like a case of domestic violence—once the system gets hold of you, you don't have much choice. There's this big gap, three hundred and fifty thousand gone and him without an explanation."

"What happened to the money?"

"Nothing. He was socking it away, shifting the money to an offshore account so his wife couldn't get her hands on it. How was he supposed to know the judge would turn out to be such a hard-ass? Four years? My god. He was more shocked than I was."

"Really."

"I'm serious. He felt like a turd. He got in this big stinking argument with the prosecuting attorney. That went nowhere. Then he wrote to the judge, begging him to be lenient, but no such luck. He promised he'd have his attorney file an appeal—"

"An appeal? What are you talking about? Beck had no standing to file an appeal. The law doesn't work that way."

"Oh. Well, maybe I misunderstood. It was something like that. He said it was his responsibility and he'd take the blame, but by then, it was too late. He had more to lose than I did. How I looked at it, as long as he was free, he could work on getting the rest of the money set aside. Besides, he was taking all the risks. If somebody had to pay, better me than him."

"So you came up with the idea," I said, trying to keep the skepticism out of my voice.

"Sure. I mean, I can't exactly remember who mentioned it first, but I was the one who insisted."

"Reba—I don't mean to sound critical so don't blow your stack—but it looks like he set you up. Doesn't it look like that to you?"

That was a stumper. "You think he'd *do* that?"

"He did this," I said, pointing to the photographs. "You're the one who toughed it out down there, day after day for the past twenty-two months. Meanwhile, Beck's up here screwing around. Doesn't that bug you? It bugs me."

"Of course it bugs me, but it's not exactly news. He's a womanizer. I've always known that about him. It doesn't mean anything. That's just the way he is. The reason I'm mad at her is she should've had more loyalty or integrity or *something*."

"You don't even know when it started. He could have been involved with her when the alleged embezzlement first came to light."

"Thank you. That's nice. Once I get done choking her to death, I'll have her verify dates and times."

"I hope that's hyperbole."

"Whatever that is," she said. "The thing I can't figure out is what this has to do with the FBI? Why's this guy chasing around town snapping pictures of Beck? And why bring 'em to me? If he wanted to make trouble, why not show Tracy?"

"I can help with that," I said, mentally cursing the bumblefuck FBI agent who jumped the gun on us. I stopped, poised on the brink. There was still time to back up. This was like standing on a ten-meter platform, looking at the drop to the water below. If you're going to jump, get it over with. It doesn't get easier the longer you wait. I felt a thin mist of anxiety settle on my skin. "The feds are interested in Beck's relationship with Salustio Castillo."

She studied me. "Where'd you get that?"

"Reba, you worked for the guy. You have to be clued in."

She veered off that topic. "Did Pop put you up to this?"

"Don't be ridiculous. I haven't spoken to him since he hired me. Besides, he's an honorable man. He'd never stoop to sleazy photos. He's got way too much class."

She took another deep drag and blew the smoke straight up. "What's your source then?"

"I have pals in law enforcement. It was one of them."

"And the FBI's involved?"

"The IRS is interested as well. Plus Customs, plus the DOJ, plus the ATF for all I know. Lieutenant Phillips is the local liaison if you want to talk to him."

"I don't get it. Why me? What do they want?"

"They need help. They're putting a case together and need the inside dope. I guess the pictures were intended to get you in the mood."

"He screws me over so I turn around and screw him?"

"Why not?"

"What else have you heard?"

"About Beck? Nothing you don't already know. He takes the illegal profits and he runs the funds through his company to make them look legitimate. He takes a percentage off the top and then he returns clean money to the thugs he works for. Right?"

She was silent. Her gaze shifted an inch.

I said, "You had to have been in on it all along. You did the books for him, bank deposits, stuff like that, right?"

"The company comptroller handled most of it, but okay, maybe some."

"The FBI can use information if you're willing to play."

She was silent, her gaze tracking the dust motes settling through the air like fairy dust. "I'll think about it."

I said, "While you're at it, think about this. Onni has your old job, which means she knows as much about his business as you do, except her information's current. If he's planning to disappear, who's he going to take with him? More to the point, who's he leaving behind? Onni? Don't think so. Not if she's in a position to blow the whistle on him."

"I'm in that position, too," she said, as though feeling competitive about her ability to squeal. She held up the last inch of her cigarette. "I have to put this out."

"Give it to me."

I reached over and took the butt end, holding it with about as much enthusiasm as I'd feel for a freshly salted slug. I left the office and carried it down the hall to my tatty toilet with the permanent rust stains. I dropped it in the john and flushed. I could feel the tension between my shoulder blades. This was *work* and I had no way to tell if the pitch would be effective. If nothing else, I hoped she'd give up her fantasy of what Beck was.

When I returned to the office, she was standing by the window. I sat down at my desk. With the light coming in, she was almost entirely in silhouette. I picked up a pencil and made a mark on my blotter. "Where's your head at this point?"

She turned and smiled at me briefly. "Not as far up my butt as it was."

And that was where we left it.

I told her to take her time thinking about the situation before she decided what to do. Vince Turner might be in a hurry, but he was asking a lot and, one way or the other, she'd better be convinced. Once she'd agreed, he couldn't afford to have her changing her mind. I watched her through the window. She got in her car and sat there long enough to light up again and then she took off. Once I knew she was gone, I put a call through to Cheney and laid out the sequence of events, including the hapless FBI agent who'd put the plan at risk.

He said, "Shit."

"That was my reaction."

"Damn. And there's no name on this crud?"

"None, and no description of him, either. I'd have pressed her for details, but I was too busy trying to act like I didn't know the whole of it in advance."

"She buy it?"

"I'd say so. In the main. Anyway, I thought you'd want to call Vince and let him know where we stand."

"Which is where?"

"I'm not sure. Reba needs time. This is a lot to digest."

"Doesn't sound like she was that surprised."

"I think she's always known more than she lets on. Now that it's out in the open, we'll see what she does with it."

"Makes me nervous."

"Me, too. Let me know what Vince says."

"Will do. See you later."

"Okey-doke," said I.

14

I closed the office at 5:00, locked the door behind me, and retrieved my car. I drove the long way home so I could stop at my favorite service station and fill the tank with gas. As I cruised down State Street past the heart of town, I spotted a familiar figure. It was William in a dark fedora and a dark three-piece suit, walking briskly toward Cabana Boulevard, swinging his black malacca stick. I slowed and honked, pulling over to the curb. I leaned over and rolled down the window on the passenger side. "You want a ride?"

William tipped his hat. "Thank you. I'd appreciate that."

He opened the car door and angled himself in, his long legs sticking up awkwardly in the cramped front seat. He kept his cane between his knees.

"You can slide that seat back and get yourself more room. The lever's right down there," I said, pointing toward his feet.

"This is fine. It's not far."

I glanced over my left shoulder, waiting for a break in

traffic before I eased into the flow. "I didn't expect to see you down here and you're all decked out. What's the occasion?"

"I attended a visitation at Wynington-Blake. Afterward, I had a cup of tea with the sole surviving family member. Lovely man."

"Oh, sorry. I didn't realize someone died. I wouldn't have sounded quite so chirpy if I'd known."

"That's all right. This was Francis Bunch. Eighty-three years old."

"Gee, that's young."

"My thought precisely. He was mowing his lawn Monday and blew an aneurysm in his brain. His second cousin Norbert is the only one left. At one count, there were twenty-six first cousins and now everybody's gone."

"That's a tough one."

"It is. Francis was quite the fellow—U.S. Army veteran, who fought in WW Two. He was a retired pipe-fitter and a Baptist. Preceded in death by his parents, his wife of sixty-two years—Mae was her name—seven children, and his brother, James. Norbert said Francis loved working in his yard so he went the way he would have wanted, except perhaps not quite so soon."

I turned the corner onto Cabana Boulevard and drove the three blocks to Castle, where I turned right again. "How long had you known him?"

William looked surprised. "Oh, I never met the man. I read about him in the paper. With so many of his family gone, I thought *someone* should be there to pay their respects. Norbert was most appreciative. We had a nice long chat."

"I thought you'd given up funerals."

"I have . . . in the main . . . but there's no harm in attending a service now and then."

I turned right onto my street, passing Rosie's. I spotted a space halfway between my apartment and the restaurant and then did a half-assed job of parallel parking. Close enough, I thought. I shut the engine down and turned to him. "Before you go, I've been wondering about something. Did you, by any chance, call Lewis in Michigan and talk him into coming?"

"Oh, he didn't require much persuasion. Once I mentioned Mattie's name, he was Johnny-on-the-Spot. I even had him thinking it was his idea. As I said to Rosie, 'This is just the ticket.' "

"William, I can't believe you did that!"

"Neither can I. In a moment of inspiration, the idea popped into my head just like that. I thought, Henry's complacent. He needs an incentive and this ought to do the trick."

"I didn't say I liked the plan. I think it stinks."

He frowned, somewhat taken aback. "Why do you say that? He and Lewis are jealous of one another. I'm surprised you weren't aware."

"Of course I'm *aware*. I'd have to be brain-dead to miss that. The problem is Henry's reaction is just the opposite. He's not going *after* her. He's backing away."

"He's a sly one, that Henry. Always has a little something hidden up his sleeve."

"That's not what I hear. He's saying he refuses to compete. He thinks it's tacky behavior so he's retiring from the field."

"Don't be fooled by that ploy. I've seen this a dozen times or more. He and Lewis set their caps for the same fair maiden and the jousting begins. It's actually working out even better than I'd hoped. You know Lewis talked Mattie into staying an extra day. You should have seen the look that came across Henry's face. That set him back on his heels, but he'll rally. It may take a bit of doing, but he'll prevail."

"Have you *talked* to him?"

"Not since yesterday. Why?"

"When I came home last night, her car was gone and his place was dark."

"He didn't come to Rosie's. I can assure you of that. You know Lewis invited Mattie to go with him to the art museum and then lunch afterward."

"William, I was sitting right there."

"Then you must have seen her response. She sparked to the idea, which Henry couldn't fail to notice. He probably came up with something special for the two of them last night."

"I don't think so. When I talked to Henry, he was adamant."

William waved the idea away. "He'll back down in the end. He'll never let Lewis get the better of him."

"I hope you're right," I said dubiously.

We opened our respective car doors and got out, taking leave of each other on the street. I wanted to say more, but it seemed wiser to let the subject drop. He seemed so sure of himself. Maybe Henry would come back fighting and William's meddling would be "just the ticket," as he'd referred to it. I watched him set off toward Rosie's, whistling and twirling his cane. As I went through the gate, I picked up Henry's afternoon paper, which was still lying on the walk.

I rounded the corner. Henry's back door was open. I went through a quick debate, then crossed the patio and tapped on the screen. "You there?"

"I'm here. Come in."

The overhead light was off and, though to all intents and purposes it was still broad daylight outside, the effect was gloomy. He sat in his rocker with his usual glass of whiskey in hand. The kitchen was spotless, appliances gleaming, the counters glossy. The oven was off and the stove top was bereft of any pots and pans. The air smelled blank. This was so unlike him. No sign of his daily baking project, no dinner preparations under way.

"I brought your paper in."

"Thank you."

I placed it on the kitchen table. "Mind if I join you?"

"Might as well. There's half a bottle of wine in the refrigerator if you're interested."

I took a wineglass from the cabinet and found the stop-
pered bottle of Chardonnay tucked in the refrigerator door.
I poured myself half a glass and looked over at him. Henry
hadn't moved. "Are you okay?"

"I'm fine."

"Ah. That's good because the kitchen looks kind of
grim. I thought I'd turn on some lights."

"Suit yourself."

I crossed to the wall and flipped the switch, which didn't
seem to help. The light seemed as dull and as flat as Henry's
demeanor. I sat down and placed my wineglass on the table.
"What happened last night? I saw Mattie's car was gone
and you were out. The two of you go somewhere?"

"She left for San Francisco. I took a walk."

"What time did she leave?"

"I didn't pay much attention. Four thirty-two," he said.

"Pretty late start for a six-hour drive. If she stopped for
supper, she probably didn't get home until close to midnight."

Silence from Henry.

"I take it she stayed for lunch. Did you go with them to
the art museum?"

"You know we don't have to discuss this. There's really
nothing to say. I'd just as soon drop the subject."

"Sure. No problem," I said. "Are you going to Rosie's for
supper? I was thinking of doing that myself."

"And risk running into Lewis? I think not."

"We could go somewhere else. Emile's-at-the-Beach is
always lovely."

He looked at me with such injury in his eyes, I couldn't
bear to see it. "She broke it off."

"She did?"

"She said I was impossible. She said she really couldn't
bear my bad behavior."

"What brought that on?"

"Nothing. It came out of a clear blue sky."

"Maybe she had a hard day."

"Not as hard as mine."

I sat staring at the floor, feeling a wave of disappointment washing over me. I had such high hopes for them. I said, "You know what I find hard? I want to believe nice things can happen to us. Not every day, maybe, but just now and then."

"Me too," he said. He got up and left the room.

I waited a minute and when it was clear he wasn't coming back, I dumped my wine in the sink, rinsed the glass, and then let myself out. I was ready to wring William's neck and I wouldn't have minded having a go at Lewis while I was at it. I could have handled pain of my own easier than Henry's. Part of my bleak mood was probably connected to my lack of sleep, but it didn't feel that way. It felt deep and permanent, a darkness being stirred up, like silt, from the very depths. Henry was a great guy and Mattie'd seemed perfect for him. He probably *had* been impossible, but so had she in her way. What would it have taken to be a little more sensitive to the situation? Unless she didn't care much to begin with, I thought. In that case, she'd cut and run the minute things got tough. As a person with cut-and-run tendencies myself, I could see her point. Life was difficult enough without having to put up with someone else's petulance.

I let myself into my apartment and checked the answering machine. I was hoping Cheney'd left a message, but the light wasn't blinking so I kissed that one off. Despite my earlier self-confidence, I wasn't keen on the idea of waiting around to see if he'd call. It was dinnertime, but I wasn't any more willing than Henry to venture into Rosie's. William would prance over, taking his own pulse and asking for the latest in the lovers' progress report. In case he was ignorant of the breakup, I didn't want to be the one to tell him. And if he'd heard it from Lewis, I didn't want to listen to him minimize the role he'd played. I suspected a run would cheer me up, but given my current mental state, I'd have had to jog all the way to Cottonwood, twenty miles round-trip.

This was one of those moments when you need a girlfriend. When you're down in the dumps, that's what you do—call your best friend—or so I've heard. You chat. You laugh. You tell her your sad tale of woe, she commiserates, and then you take off and go shopping like normal folk. But I didn't have a girlfriend, a lack I'd hardly noticed until Cheney appeared. So now, not only was I facing the fact that I didn't have him, I didn't have her either, whoever she was.

A voice said . . . *Ah, but you do have Reba.*

I thought about that one. If I made a list of desirable girlfriend traits, "convicted felon" wouldn't be one. On the other hand, I'd be a convicted felon myself if I'd ever been caught doing even half the things I'd done.

I picked up the phone and punched in the number for the Lafferty estate. When Reba answered, I said, "Reba, this is Kinsey. I need a favor. How good are you at giving fashion advice?"

Reba picked me up in her car, a two-year-old black BMW she'd acquired shortly before she'd been sent to CIW. "The DA was panting to seize the car on the premise I'd bought it with ill-gotten gains. Ha ha ha on him. My father gave it to me for my thirtieth birthday. Hopes dashed again."

"What'd you say to Onni when you canceled dinner?"

"I told her something came up and we'd make it another night."

"She was cool with that?"

"Of course. She probably hated the idea of having dinner with me. I was always pouring my heart out about Beck. There wasn't anyone else I could talk to about him. Beck said this, Beck said that. When it came to our sex life, I'd be giving her a blow by blow, so to speak."

"That was your mistake. You made him sound too good."

"You got that right. She was always jealous of me. Minute my back is turned, she walks off with my job and then she walks off with the love of my life, or so I thought at the time. I hate women who get into that competitive shit."

"What's she like?"

"You can judge for yourself as long as you end up agreeing with me. I know where she hangs out. If you're interested, we can drop by later and I'll introduce you."

"Drop by where?"

"Bubbles in Montebello."

"That's been closed for two years."

"Nuhn-uhn. The place has changed hands. Name's the same, but it's been open for a month under new management."

"Where we headed now?"

"The mall."

Passages, the newly opened shopping plaza in the heart of Santa Teresa, had been designed to resemble an old Spanish town. The architecture featured a picturesque assortment of narrow shoulder-to-shoulder buildings of varying heights, arches, loggias, courtyards, fountains, and side streets, the whole of the three-block complex capped by red tile roofs. At ground level there were restaurants, clothing stores, galleries, jewelry stores, and other retail shops. The wide central esplanade was anchored at one end by Macy's and at the other end by Nordstrom's, with a large chain bookstore occupying a prominent spot. Pepper trees and flowering shrubs were planted throughout. In the taller structures, three and four stories high, office space had been leased to lawyers, accountants, engineers, and anyone else who could afford the staggering rents.

Given Santa Teresa's resistance to new construction, the project had taken years to push through. The city-planning commission and the architectural board of review, plus the

city council, plus the county board of supervisors, plus the
building and safety commission, all at odds with one another, had to be soothed, pacified, and reassured. Citizens'
groups protested the razing of buildings five and six
decades old, though most were otherwise unremarkable.
Many were already slated for mandatory earthquake retro-
fitting, which would have cost the owners more than they
were worth. Environmental impact studies had to be approved. Numerous small merchants were evicted and dis-
placed, with only one holdout, a funky little bar called
Dale's that was still moored in the middle of the plaza like
a tugboat in a harbor full of yachts.

We ate dinner at an Italian boutique restaurant located
on one of the smaller avenues that connected the center esplanade to State Street on one side and Chapel on the other.
Temperatures were still elevated, and we elected to eat on
the patio outside. As the dark came down, the landscape
lighting began to paint walls and vegetation in colors more
vivid than their daylight shades. Details of wrought-iron
fixtures were picked out in shadow, the plaster frieze along
the roof outlined in black. If you squinted, you could almost believe you'd been transported to a foreign country.

While we waited for our salads, I said, "I appreciate
your doing this—the clothes thing."

"No problem. It's obvious you need help."

"I'm not sure the word 'obvious' should come into play."

"Trust me."

Later, while she was winding spaghetti on her fork, she
said, "You know this is Beck's project."

"What is?"

"The mall."

"He did Passages?"

"Sure. I mean, not on his own—in partnership with a
guy in Dallas, another developer. Beck moved his office to
the far end, down by Macy's. The fourth floor runs the full
block between State and Chapel."

"I didn't realize the building covered that much ground."

"Because you didn't bother to look up. If you did, you'd see that there are covered walkways that join the second and third levels in places above the esplanade. Technically, in the rainy season, you could move from one building to the other without getting wet."

"You've got a better eye than I do. I missed that."

"I have the advantage. The mall's been in development for years so I've seen the plans at just about every stage. Beck moved his office in a couple of months after I went into CIW, so I never got to see it. Turned out great, or so I hear."

I took a sip of wine, finishing the last bite of eggplant parmigiana while I watched Reba use a chunk of bread to clean up her marinara sauce. I said, "Where are you going with this?"

She popped the bread in her mouth, smiling while she chewed. "You're the kick-ass private eye. You figure it out. In the meantime, let's go buy you some clothes and then we can make the run into Montebello."

15

We shopped until the stores closed at 9:00. Reba kept up a running commentary as I tried things on. In the interests of education, she let me make my choices without reference to her opinion. At first, I tried gauging her reaction as I lifted a garment off the rack, but she looked on with the same deadpan expression she must have donned at the poker table. With no guidelines whatever, I picked out two dresses, a pantsuit, and three cotton skirts. "Okay," I said.

Her brow went up about an eighth of an inch. "That's it?"

"Isn't this enough?"

"You like that green deal, that pantsuit thing?"

"Well, yeah. You know, it's dark and it won't show spots."

"All riiiight," she said, with a tone suggesting that you have to let kids make boo-boos in order for them to learn.

She trailed behind me as far as the line of dressing cubicles in the rear. She looked on idly while I opened door after door, trying to find a room not in use. When I finally found an empty cubicle, she gave every impression of following me in.

"Hold on a sec. You're coming *in* here with me?"

"What if something doesn't fit? You can't stroll around out there in your underwear."

"I wasn't planning to. I was going to try on stuff back here and then decide."

"Deciding is my job. You try on clothes and I'll explain how misguided you are."

She sat on a plain wooden chair in a space that was six feet on a side with floor-to-ceiling mirrors on three. The fluorescent lighting guaranteed your skin would look sallow and every tiny body flaw would appear in bas relief.

I took my shoes off and began to strip down with the same enthusiasm I feel before a pelvic exam. "I can tell I have a better developed sense of modesty than you do," I said.

"Oh, please. Prison knocked that out of me. The shower stalls were a quarter this size with these skimpy canvas curtains designed to keep your head and feet in view. That was to prevent the inmates from having sex in private. Little did they know. Aside from that, you might as well forget privacy altogether. It was simpler to prance around nude like everybody else."

During these revelations, I was trying to step gracefully out of my blue jeans, but my foot caught and I nearly toppled sideways. Reba pretended not to notice. I said, "Didn't that bother you?"

"At first, but after a while, I thought, oh who gives a damn? All these naked women and pretty soon you've seen every possible body type—short, tall, skinny, fat, little tits, big ass, or big tits and no ass. Scar, moles, tattoos, birth defects. Everybody looks just about like everybody else."

I peeled my T-shirt over my head.

"Oh, bullet holes!" she said, nearly clapping her hands as she caught sight of mine.

"Do you *mind?*"

"Well, I think they're cute. Sort of like dimples."

I slid the first of two cotton dresses from the hanger and eased my arms up the interior and out the requisite armholes. I turned to the mirror. I looked about like I always did—not bad, but not that good. "What do you think?"

"What do *you* think?"

"Come on, Reba. Just tell me what's wrong with it."

"Everything. The color for starters. You should wear clear tones—red, maybe navy blue, but not that pukey shade of yellow. It makes your skin tone look orange."

"I thought that was the lighting."

"And look how loose it's cut. You've got good legs and a great set of boobs. I mean, they're not *huge,* but they're sassy so why cover them with something that looks like a pillowcase?"

"I don't like to wear stuff too tight."

"Clothes are supposed to *fit,* dear. That dress is one size too big and it looks—dare I say it—so matronly. Go ahead and try on the blue print skirt, but I can tell you right now it's another pass. You're not the big-ass Hawaiian palm-and-parrot type."

"If you already hate it, why should I try it on?"

"Because otherwise you'll never get the *point.*"

And so it went. Bossy women and I get along swimmingly as I'm a masochist at heart. I bypassed the blue print skirt and didn't bother trying on the green pantsuit, knowing she'd be right about that, too. She removed the offending garments, holding the hangers at arm's length like so many dead rats. While I waited in the dressing room, she went out to the floor and flipped through the racks. She returned with six items, which she exhibited one by one, creating the illusion that she was letting me choose. I resisted one dress and one skirt, but everything else she'd selected ended up looking great on me, even if I do say so myself.

"I don't understand how you know all this stuff," I said, getting dressed again. This is my perpetual complaint, that somehow other women have a flair for things that make me feel like a dunce. It was like thought problems in math. In high school, the minute I encountered one I'd feel like I was on the verge of blacking out.

"You'll get the hang of it eventually. It's really not that hard. At CIW, I was the resident styling maven. Hair, makeup, clothes, all of it. I could've taught a class." She paused to check her watch. "Let's get a move on. Time to party."

We sped south on the 101 with Reba at the wheel.

I said, "I'm not sure this is smart. Why go to a place where everyone's drinking?"

"I'm not going there to drink. I haven't had a drink for twenty-three months, fourteen and a half days."

"Then why put yourself in harm's way?"

"I told you. Because that's where Onni is. She goes out every Thursday night to hustle guys." I opened my mouth to protest, but she shot me a look. "You're not my mother, okay? I promise I'll call my sponsor the minute I get home. At least, I would if I had one, which I don't."

Bubbles was a Montebello wine-and-champagne bistro that had once done a lively business in concert with the Edgewater Hotel and another high-priced piano bar called Spirits. The three were in easy driving distance of one another and formed a triangle traveled by every rich, hot, single person on the market back then. All three places were heavy on atmosphere—glitz, glitter, live music, small dance floors, and low lights. Drinks were pricey, served in oversize glasses, and food was an afterthought, meant to get you home again without a fatal accident.

In the mid-seventies, for reasons unknown, Bubbles became a magnet for escort services, girls working high-end out-call and "models" from Los Angeles, who drove to Montebello cruising for love. Eventually cocaine became prevalent and the county sheriff's department stepped in

and shut the place down. I'd been there on occasion because my second husband, Daniel, was a jazz pianist who
played the three night spots in rotation. Early in the relationship, I realized if I didn't make a point of being there
with him, I might not see him until breakfast the next day.
He claimed he was out "jamming" with the guys, which
turned out to be true, in both the literal and metaphorical
senses.

We pulled up to the left of the entrance. Reba handed
her car keys to the valet and we went in. Men in suits and
sport coats stood five and six deep at the bar, checking out
our boobs and butts as we passed. Reba did a quick search
from table to table while I followed in her wake. Bubbles
hadn't changed. Illumination was achieved primarily by
way of massive fish tanks that lined the walls and separated
one seating area from the next. In the main room, there was
a bar with a U-shaped border of booths and a scattering of
tables big enough for two. In the second room, through a
wide arch, a jazz combo—piano, saxophone, and bass—was
set up on a wide deck above a dance floor the size of a tram-
poline. The music was mellow—haunting melodies from the
forties that stuck in your head for days. This was not a place
where voices were raised or raucous laughter cut through
the murmur of civilized conversation. No one got drunk and
tumbled backward into other patrons. Women didn't weep or
fling drinks on their dates. No one upchucked in the elegant
restrooms with their marble floors and baskets of tiny ter-
rycloth towels. Customers smoked, but the ventilation system
was high-tech and a roving band of busboys whisked away
dirty ashtrays and replaced them with clean ones every five
minutes or so.

Reba put a hand out and slowed me to a halt. Like a
pointer, she stood and pinned a look on Onni, who sat at a
table by herself, smoking a cigarette with an air of indif-
ference I suspected was fake. The presence of two half-
filled champagne flutes and a bottle resting in a nearby

cooler suggested a companion who'd left the table moments before. The "real" Onni bore only passing resemblance to the Onni I'd seen in the grainy black-and-white
photos. She was tall and slim, with a long thin face, wide
nose, thin lips, and small nearly lashless eyes. Her dark hair
was dead straight and spilled across her shoulders with the
high silky shine you see in ads for shampoos. Silver earrings dangled from her lobes and brushed against her neck
with every move of her head. The jacket of her black business suit had been shrugged aside, revealing a white silk
tank top that looked more like a slip than any blouse I'd
seen. Taken feature by feature, she really wasn't pretty, but
she'd managed to maximize her assets. Her makeup was
artful and her breasts looked as hard as croquet balls inserted inexplicably under the skimpy flesh on her chest.
Nonetheless, she presented herself as though she were
beautiful and that was the impression that prevailed.

Reba moved forward with trumped-up exuberance.
"Onni! How perfect. I was hoping you'd be here."

"Hello, Reba." Onni's manner was cool, but Reba didn't
seem to notice as she slid into a chair. I sat down too, fully
aware Onni wasn't at all happy to see us. Beside her, Reba
seemed childlike, animated, petite, with dark tousled hair,
the large dark eyes, perfect nose, and delicately rounded
chin, where Onni's receded slightly. What Reba lacked was
that air of self-containment that passes for breeding among
middle-class pretenders.

Reba said, "This is my friend Kinsey. I've been telling
her about you." Her gaze settled on the two champagne
flutes as though she'd just noticed. "I hope we're not cutting
in on your action. Big hot date?"

"It's actually not a date. Beck and I had to work late so
he suggested stopping off for a nightcap. I don't imagine
we'll stay long."

"Beck's here? That's great. I don't see him."

"He's chatting with a friend. I'm sorry you canceled
dinner. When you said something came up, I pictured AA."

"I did a meeting already. I'm only required to do one a week." Reba helped herself to one of Onni's cigarettes and waggled it between her teeth. "You have a light for this?"

"Of course." Onni reached into a small bag and came up with a pack of matches. Reba took the pack, struck one, and cupped a hand around the flame. She inhaled with satisfaction and returned the matches with a sly smile that Onni seemed to miss. I knew Reba well enough by now that I could see the icy rage sparkling in her eyes. She pulled the ashtray closer and then put an elbow on the table and propped her chin on her hand. "So. How are things with you? You said you'd write, but then I never heard from you."

"I *wrote*. I sent you a card. Didn't you get it?"

Reba took a drag of her cigarette, her smile still in place. "That's right. So you did. It had bunnies on it as I remember. One measly card in twenty-two months. Hey, don't put yourself out."

"I'm sorry if that bothers you, but I was busy. You left the office in bad shape. It took me months to straighten it out."

"Yeah, well, the Department of Corrections had first claim. Whisk you off to prison, you don't have the option to stop by your workplace and tidy up your desk. I'm sure you have the situation well in hand."

"Finally. No thanks to you." Onni's gaze shifted slightly.

Reba turned her head in time to see Beck approaching from the bar. He caught sight of her and his forward motion halted for a split second, like a few frames of film missing from a sequence. Reba's face brightened. She pushed out of the chair and moved toward him. When she reached him, her arms slid around his neck as though she meant to kiss him on the mouth.

He extracted himself gently. "Hey, hey, hey, gorgeous. We're in public. Remember?"

"I know, but I missed you."

"Well, I missed you, too, but suppose one of Tracy's

girlfriends is here." He steered her back to her chair, send-ing me a smile in the process. "Good to see you again."

"Nice seeing you," I said, though it wasn't nice at all. Not surprisingly, my view of him had changed radically. When I'd met him in Rosie's, I'd thought he was hand-some—long-limbed, loose-jointed, with that lazy half-smile. Even his eyes, which I'd thought were a rich chocolate brown, now looked as dark as volcanic stone. See-ing him with Onni, I could sense the trait they shared—both were opportunists.

Of the three of them, Reba currently occupied the power position. Onni knew the intimate details of Reba's relationship with Beck, but neither Beck nor Onni were aware that Reba had been tipped off about their affair. To further complicate the situation, I was reasonably sure Onni didn't know that Beck and Reba had reactivated their sexual connection. I felt a frisson of tension ripple up my spine, curious how Reba intended to play the hand she'd been dealt.

Beck sat down in the remaining chair and slouched on his spine, extending his legs as though he were entitled to more space than we were. In the geography of body lan-guage, he and Onni were lined up in parallel, their bodies tracing the same angle while Reba sat across the table from them, her body an upright that cut across the slant of their respective postures.

Onni's attention was fixed on her champagne flute.

Beck sipped champagne, watching Reba above the rim of his glass. The blond highlights in his hair must have been professionally applied. Certainly, the haphazard thatch effect was no accident. "So how's it going?" he asked.

Reba said, "Not bad. I was actually thinking of coming back to work."

Onni's expression was incredulous, as though Reba had farted in the presence of Elizabeth II.

Reba ignored her reaction, addressing her remarks to

Beck. "Yeah, I mentioned it to my parole officer and she was all for it as long as my 'prospective employer' knew about my past," she said, forming quote marks with her fingers. "I figured who better than you?"

Smoothly, he said, "Reeb, I'd love to help, but it doesn't seem smart."

"It's ridiculous," Onni snapped. "You robbed him blind."

Reba shifted her gaze. "Onni, I'm sorry, but you don't get it. Beck trusts me. He knows I'd do anything for him." She looked back at him. "Right?"

Beck rearranged his legs, pulling himself into an upright position, his tone mild. "It's not a question of trust. There's no position. It's as simple as that. I wish we had an opening, but we don't."

"You could make one, couldn't you? I remember you did that for Abner."

"Different situation. Marty was overloaded and needed the help. I had no choice in that case."

"But you have one with me, is that it? You could choose to help me, but you won't?"

He reached out and grabbed one of her fingers, giving it a shake. "Hey, babe, remember? I'm on your team."

Reba studied him with care, the lean, handsome face, the hand touching hers. "You said you'd take care of me. You owe me."

"Hey, anything you want."

"Except work."

Onni snorted and rolled her eyes. "What gall! How do you have the fucking nerve to sit there and *argue* the point after what you did?"

Beck said, "Cool it, Onni. This is between her and me."

"Well, pardon the hell out of me. I just think someone should set this girl straight. She wreaked havoc on the company and for what? So she could go on indulging herself, blowing every nickel she could get her hands on at the poker table? My god!"

I half-expected Beck to belt her in the mouth, but he

focused on Reba's face. He took her hand, placing her index finger against his lip. The effect was erotic, some intensely private communication taking place between them.
"Forget about work. Take a little time for yourself. Do
something nice, like that spa in Floral Beach. I can have Ed
set it up. You've been through tough times, I understand
that, but talk about work is premature."

"I have to do something with my life," she said, her eyes
pinned on his.

"I know, babe. I hear you. All I'm saying is you need to
take it slow. I don't want you rushing into anything you
might regret."

Reba smiled. "Like what? Coming back to work for you?"

"Like getting stressed out, upset, when there's no reason
to. You need to keep it low-key. Kick back and relax while
you have the chance."

Onni said something under her breath. She shoved her
arms into the sleeves of her jacket and shrugged herself
into it, straightening her lapels. She reached for her cigarettes and tucked them in her bag, then stood, saying,
"Night, folks. I'm out of here." Her manner seemed to be
matter-of-fact unless you knew what was going on.

"Give me five minutes and I'll drive you home," Beck
said to her.

Onni's smile was brittle. "Thanks, but no thanks. I'd
rather walk."

"You won't make it a block in those heels."

"Not your problem, champ. I'll figure it out."

"Cut the crap, Onni. Have Jack call you a cab. I'll square
the fare with him on my way out."

"Not to worry. I'm a big girl. I think I can manage to call
a cab on my own. Meantime, enjoy Panama. And thanks for
the drink. It was really swell, you fucking jerk."

Reba turned her head, watching as Onni walked away.
"What's her problem?"

"Forget it. She gets bored anytime the topic of conversation moves to something other than her," Beck said.

Reba said, "What's the deal with Panama? When did that come up?"

"It's just a quick trip. Couple of days."

"Why couldn't you take me with you? Like a minivacation. You could take care of business while I sit by the pool and get some sun. It'd be great."

"Baby, this is strictly solo. I've got wall-to-wall meetings. You'd be bored to tears."

"No, I wouldn't. I can amuse myself. Come on, Beck. We've hardly had a minute together. We could have a ball. Please, please, please?"

He smiled. "You nut. I'd do it in a heartbeat if I thought we could get it past your PO. Trust me, if you're not allowed to leave the state, you sure as hell wouldn't be allowed to leave the continental U.S.A."

Reba made a face. "Oh, shit. You're right. I forgot about that. I don't even have a passport. It expired in June."

"So get your passport renewed and I'll take you to Panama as soon as you're out from under all the rules and regs." He took a hasty look at his watch. "Speaking of which, I gotta go. The limo's picking me up in an hour to drive to LAX."

"You're flying out tonight? Why didn't you tell me?"

Beck waved the idea away. "I'm down there so often, it's not worth mentioning. Anyway, I'll call you as soon as I get back."

"Couldn't I ride down in the limo with you and come back with the driver once he drops you off?"

"It's an L.A.-based company. The driver's coming up from Santa Monica. Once he leaves me at the airport, he's on his way home."

"Shoot. I wanted to spend time with you."

"Me, too. We'll take a rain check. Meantime, let's get you out of here. It's late."

16

The three of us went out into the chill night air together as we had at Rosie's earlier in the week. I kept my distance, feigning interest in the lighted window display in the shop next door. Beck and Reba had a murmured conversation, their heads bent together like co-conspirators. Reba seemed to drink in the sight of him, her face in profile looking childlike and trusting. The revelation about Beck's relationship with Onni had apparently done nothing to mitigate his hold on her. It looked as if Cheney and Vince would have to find another source for confidential information. I only hoped she'd keep her mouth shut and not blow the whole deal.

A valet pulled up in Reba's BMW. Beck slipped the guy a tip on her behalf and then turned as a second parking valet pulled his car in behind hers. Once Reba got in the car, she took out a lipstick and applied a fresh coat, checking her reflection in the rearview mirror. She caught sight of Beck behind her and waved to him, blowing him a kiss.

She shifted into drive and turned right onto Coastal Road. I glanced back in time to see Beck pull out after we did. He made a left-hand turn, heading toward West Glen Road. As soon as he was out of sight, Reba slowed, made a U-turn, and sped after him.

"What are you doing?" I said.

"I want you to see his house."

"What do I care? At this hour? It's dark."

"It won't take long. It's just about a mile down West Glen."

"It's your car so you can do as you please, but don't put yourself out on my account."

I couldn't get a fix on her mood. At first I'd thought she was flirting with Beck purely to infuriate Onni. I was anticipating the rehash, the two of us comparing notes about Onni's reaction, especially when she walked out in such a huff. By that point in the evening, however, Beck was really pouring on the charm and she'd fallen under his spell. I found it unnerving how deftly he'd drawn her back into orbit, exerting the same invisible pull as the earth on the moon. Just when I thought we'd won her over to our side, Beck had taken her back.

We turned right on West Glen. Beck was now out of sight, several curves in the road between our car and his. Even if he noticed our headlights behind him, he probably wouldn't give the matter much thought. We reached the straightaway and caught sight of him about a quarter mile ahead. His brake lights came on as he slowed and made a right-hand turn. His car disappeared from view. Reba sped up, closing the distance, and then she slowed as well. She peered across me and out the passenger-side window as we passed a gated estate. I caught a glimpse of a massive stone mansion in a fairyland of lights.

Fifty yards beyond the entrance to his property, she pulled onto the berm. She killed the lights, shut the engine down, and got out of the car. Before she eased the door shut, she said, "You coming or not?"

"Sure. Eleven o'clock at night, I could use a walk." I emerged from the car on my side. She'd made a point of not slamming her door and I certainly knew better than to slam my own. If we were on a search-and-seizure mission of some kind, there was no point in alerting him to our presence. I joined her as she backtracked along the darkened road. Having spent half an hour in a smoke-filled bar, we must have smelled like two cigarette butts out for a breath of fresh air. This section of Montebello was dark, no streetlights, no sidewalks, and no passing cars. We were accompanied by the chirring of crickets and the scent of eucalyptus trees. She halted at the entrance to Beck's driveway.

Through iron gates, I was treated to the full panoramic view. The ivy-covered stone façade looked as stately as a monastery, mansard roof, half-timbered, a long bank of mullioned windows aglow along the front. I was guessing three to four acres with a tennis court visible on one side and a swimming pool on the other. Reba moved to the right of the gate and eased herself between the hedge and the stone pillar, where a gap permitted passage despite the solid look of the shrubs. I followed, pushing through a turnstile of branches that nearly tore off my shirt. She proceeded with an air of calm familiarity as she veered off across the lawn. I gathered she'd made the walk many times before. She seemed confident about the absence of motion-detecting floodlights and attack-trained dogs. I was worried the automatic sprinkling system (complete with toe-busting sprayer heads) would suddenly spark to life and drench us in a downpour of artificial rain.

Closer to the house, a porte cochere spanned the driveway and served as a covered walkway, sheltering residents and guests as they moved to and from their cars. Reba skirted the entrance and took up a position between two squared-off clipped shrubs on the far side. The boxwoods had been shaped to form an alcove about the size of a phone booth, easily big enough to allow the two of us to huddle. A wide slat of shadow shielded us from view.

We waited in silence. I love nighttime surveillance as long as my bladder isn't screaming for relief. Who wants to have to squat in the bushes where the high beams of any passing car can flash across the globes of your pearly hind-end? Add to that the likelihood of peeing on your own shoes and the notion of "penis envy" isn't tough to comprehend.

A set of headlights appeared at the bottom of the drive and a mechanical hum announced the slow parting of the wrought iron gates. A black stretch limousine swung into view and proceeded slowly up the drive, approaching the house with all the gravity of the lead car in a funeral procession. The driver pulled under the porte cochere and triggered the trunk lid, which seemed to pop up of its own accord.

As if on cue, the porch light went on and the front door was opened. I could hear Beck talking to someone over his shoulder as he carried out three large bags and set them on the porch. With the engine still idling, the driver got out in his tuxedo and chauffeur's cap and moved around to the rear where Beck waited with the luggage. The driver hefted the suitcases into the trunk one by one. He shut the trunk and then opened the rear limo door. Beck paused, looking toward the house as his wife stepped out onto the porch. She stopped, apparently to check the thumb lock before she pulled the door shut behind her. "Is that everything?"

"We're good. Bags are in the trunk."

She crossed to the limo and ducked into the backseat. Beck followed her in. The driver closed the limo door and then returned to the driver's seat and resumed his place at the wheel, shutting the car door. I could hear a slight pop as he released the emergency brake and then the limo glided down the drive toward the road. The lighted rear license plate read: ST LIMO-1, designating car number one of the Santa Teresa Limousine Service. The gates swung open, the limo disappeared, and the gates eased shut again.

Beside me, Reba flicked her Dunhill, the flame warming her face briefly as she took the first long drag from a fresh cigarette. She put the pack and lighter in her pocket and blew out a stream of smoke. Her eyes were remarkably large and dark, and her lips curved upward in a cynical smile. "Lying sack of shit. You know when I figured it out? Did you see the little hitch in his walk when he first caught sight of me? That said it all. I was the last person in the world he wanted to see."

"At least you managed to queer it for Onni. She was really pissed at him."

"I hope so. Anyway, let's get out of here before a sheriff's deputy decides to cruise by. Beck always notifies 'em when he's leaving town. They're quite attentive to him."

"Are you okay?"

"I feel great. How long will it take to set up the meeting with the feds?"

When I let myself into my apartment at 11:25, the light was blinking on the answering machine, a tiny red beacon in the dark. I flipped on the overhead light. I set my shoulder bag on the countertop and dumped my shopping bags on the floor. I crossed to the desk and stood there, staring at the *blink, blink, blink* as though it might be a message in Morse code. Either it was Cheney or it was not. The fact of the matter had already been entered into evidence so I might as well find out. If he hadn't called, that didn't necessarily mean anything. And if he had called, it didn't necessarily mean anything, either. The problem in the early stages of any relationship is that you don't know where you stand and you don't know how to interpret the other person's behavior.

So okay. All I had to do was push the button and I'd know.

I sat down. If he hadn't called, I sure didn't want to be the one to call him, though I was panting to tell him what had transpired between Beck and Reba. I could touch base with him for that purpose. In fact, I'd *have* to call him soon so he could set up the meeting between Reba and Vince.

But aside from business—on a personal level—he'd have to make the first move. He looked like the kind of guy women called all the time—too cute and too sexy to have to expend much effort himself. I didn't want to place myself in the same category with his other women, whoever they were. How was it, though, that after only one day I was feeling insecure? Ruefully, I remembered my cockiness of the night before.

I pushed the button and listened to the brief high-pitched squeal as the tape rewound. *Beep.* "Kinsey, this is Cheney. It's ten-fifteen and I just got off work. Give me a buzz when you get in. I'll be up." He left his number. *Click.*

I checked the clock. Over an hour ago. I made a note of his home number, then suffered a fit of indecision. He said to call, so I'd call. Nothing tricky about that . . . unless he was already in bed and asleep. I hate waking people up. Before I felt any more squirrelly, I punched in the number.

He picked up on the first ring.

I said, "If you're asleep I swear I'm going to slit my wrists with a butter knife."

He laughed. "Not at all, babe. I'm a night owl. How about you?"

"Not me. I'm an early bird. I usually get up at six for my run. How come you were working so late? I thought you got off at five."

"We spent the day cooped up in a van over on Castle, taking videos of johns going in and out of a hot new whorehouse. Heavy weekend trade coming up. We'll do a sweep as soon as we have enough little fishies in the net."

"Nothing like sitting all day to wear you down."

"I'm trashed. How about you?"

"I'm pretty trashed myself," I said. "Though I did have a productive evening. You won't believe where I've been."

"Answer can't be Rosie's. Too easy."

"I was out with Reba. First we went clothes shopping and then we went to Bubbles where we ran into Beck and Onni. I won't plague you with the details—"

"Hey, come on. Don't be like that. I love the details."

"I'll tell you next time I see you. At the moment, I'm too bushed to go into a blow-by-blow. The upshot is Reba's ready to do business."

"She's agreed to talk to Vince?"

"That's what she told me half an hour ago."

"What brought this on? I know she was waffling, but this falls into the too-good-to-be-true category, don't you think?"

"No, I'm trusting her on this. Mostly because I was right there watching when the whole thing went down. Beck laid on a bunch of BS, three or four lies in a row, and Reba nailed him on all counts. I mean, not to his face. He was stringing her along and stringing her along. I think she could have dealt with that—she's probably used to his messing with her head. The kicker was, she realized he was taking Tracy to Panama when he'd implied he was going alone."

"How'd she find out?"

I hesitated. "We did some independent research."

"I don't want to hear this."

"I thought not. Bottom line is she'll meet with the feds as soon as you can set it up."

"Shit, that's great. I'll let Vince know as soon as I can track him down. Might take a couple of days. He's hard to reach on weekends."

"The sooner the better. We don't want her changing her mind," I said.

"While we're on the subject, Vince checked on that FBI guy who went to Reba's with the photos. Turns out he'd been transferred from another office and wanted to show how good he was at taking the initiative. He got his ears boxed but good."

"Glad to hear that," I said.

"So what are you doing at the moment? Are you down for the count?"

"Meaning what, am I in bed? No, I'm up."

"Meaning, I don't want to keep you on the phone if you're about to hit the sack."

"Not a bit of it. I just walked in the door. I was worried I wouldn't catch you before you went to bed yourself."

There was a moment of quiet.

I said, "Hello?"

"I'm here. I was wondering how you'd feel about company."

"Right now?"

"Yes."

I thought about exhaustion, both his and mine. "Good. I'd feel good—assuming it's yourself we're discussing and not someone else."

"Give me ten minutes."

"Make it fifteen. That'll give me time to change."

I took the spiral stairs two at a time, whipped off my clothes, jammed everything in the hamper, showered, shaved my legs, washed my hair, flossed and brushed my teeth, all in the space of eight minutes, which gave me plenty of time to pull on clean sweats (minus underwear) and change the sheets. Downstairs again, I was in the process of refolding sections of the newspaper when I heard his tap at the door.

I tossed the *Dispatch* in the wastebasket and let him in. His hair was curly and damp and he smelled like soap. He was holding a pizza box that smelled heavenly. He closed the door behind him. "I never ate dinner. The guy just delivered this. You hungry?"

"Of course. You want to take it up with us?"

He smiled, shaking his head fondly. "Always in a hurry. We have time."

At 1:00 A.M., he gave me the promised haircut, me sitting on a stool in the loft bathroom with a towel draped across my shoulders, Cheney with a second towel wrapped around his waist.

I said, "Most of the time I do this myself with a pair of nail scissors."

"So I see." He worked with ease and concentration, taking off very little hair, but somehow making the whole of it fall together in tidy layers.

I watched his reflection in the mirror. So serious. "Where'd you learn to cut hair?"

"I have an uncle who does this for a living. Salon on Melrose, 'Hair Cutter to the Stars.' Four hundred bucks a pop. I figured if I washed out of police academy I could do this instead. I'm not sure which option was more horrifying to my parents, my becoming a cop or a guy who does women's hair. They're otherwise decent folks, barring the inherent snobbery."

"Last time I had a really good cut, you know who did it?"

"Danielle Rivers. I remember that." Cheney's attention had shifted to the nape of my neck, where he was busy snipping away, trying to even out the line.

Danielle Rivers was a seventeen-year-old hooker he'd introduced me to. He'd recently been transferred to vice, part of the regular rotation system at the police department, while I'd been hired to track down the killer of Lorna Kepler, a beautiful young woman who was caught up in porno films and sex for hire. He'd put me together with Danielle because she and the victim had been cohorts.

I said, "Danielle was appalled when she heard how little I earned—half of what she made. You should have heard her riff on investment strategies, all of which she picked up from Lorna. I wish I'd taken her advice. Maybe I'd be rich."

"Easy come, easy go."

"Remember the sandwiches you bought in the hospital cafeteria the night she was admitted?"

He smiled. "Man, those were bad. Ham and cheese from a vending machine."

"But you added all the stuff that made them edible."

He gave me a hand mirror and kissed me on the top of the head, saying, "All done."

I turned, holding the mirror so I could check the cut in the back. "Oh, wow. It looks good. Thanks." I glanced down at his towel, the two ends of which had parted in front. "I like your friend. Must be showtime and he's popped his head out to check the audience."

Cheney glanced down. "Why don't we go in the other room and see if we can catch his act?"

Eventually we slept, curled together like cats.

17

Friday morning, we dragged ourselves out of bed at 10:00. We showered and dressed, and then walked over to Cabana Boulevard, where we had breakfast at a little beachside café. Cheney didn't have to go to work until later in the day, having been scheduled for another shift in the surveillance van. Back from breakfast, we stood and chatted at the curb until we ran out of things to say. We parted company at noon. He had errands to run and I was ready to be alone. I watched until his little red Mercedes disappeared from sight and then I followed the walkway around to the back-yard.

Henry was kneeling in one of his flower beds, where nutgrass was popping up. He was barefoot, wearing cutoffs and a tank top, his flip-flops lying on the lawn nearby. Eliminating nutgrass requires patience. The weed multiplies by way of threadlike roots and tiny black rhizomes that spread underground, so simply yanking the stems free does nothing to the plant's underlying structure, which goes on mer-

rily reproducing. The small pile of weeds Henry had successfully uprooted resembled nothing so much as a cluster
of spiders with frail legs and bodies the size of blackened
match heads.

"You need help?"

"No, but you can keep me company if you like. There's
something satisfying about going after these things. Ugly-
looking little buggers, aren't they?"

"Disgusting. I thought you got rid of all the nutgrass this
spring."

"Ongoing process. You never really win." He sat back on
his heels briefly, then shifted so he could tackle the next
section.

I kicked off my tennis shoes and settled in the grass, letting the sunshine wash across my legs. Henry's dark mood
had lifted, and while he was still subdued, he seemed almost himself again.

"I see you had company last night," he remarked, without looking at me.

I laughed, feeling the blush begin to mount in my
cheeks. "That was Cheney Phillips. STPD. He's a friend of
Lieutenant Dolan's," I said, as though that were relevant.

"Nice?"

"Very. We've known each other for years."

"I thought it must be something of the sort. I've never
known you to be impulsive."

"Actually, I am. It just sometimes takes me a while to
work up to it."

There was a companionable quiet, broken only by the
sound of Henry's trowel chunking in the ground.

Finally, I said, "Is Lewis still in town?"

"He flies home tomorrow. I feel better about him, in case
you're wondering. I don't want to see him just yet, but we'll
work it out in due course."

"What about Mattie?"

"Oh, that's probably for the best. I never expected the relationship to turn into anything serious."

"But it might have."

" 'Might' doesn't count for much. I generally find it wiser to deal with what is than with what might have been. Having made it to the ripe old age of eighty-seven without a long-term romance, there's no reason to suppose I'm even capable of such a thing."

"Couldn't you at least call?"

"I could, though I'm not sure what that would accomplish. She made her feelings clear. I have nothing else to offer and nothing much to add."

"What if she called you?"

"That's up to her," he said. "I don't mean to sound like a sad sack. I'm really fine."

"Well, of course you're *fine,* Henry. It's not like you're crushed because you've dated her for years. On the other hand, I thought you were great together and I'm sorry things didn't work out."

"You were picturing . . . what? . . . a little trip down the aisle?"

"William got married at eighty-seven, why not you?"

"He's impetuous by nature. I'm a stick-in-the-mud."

I threw a handful of grass at him. "You are not."

Reba called at 5:00, interrupting what I realized in retrospect was an award-winning nap. I'd stretched out on the bed with my favorite John le Carré spy novel. The light was soft. The temperature was mild and the sheet I'd thrown over me was the perfect weight. Outside I could hear the dim buzz of a lawn mower, followed by the *pft-pft-pft* of Henry's Rain Bird, firing jets of water across the newly trimmed grass. Thanks to my sleep deprivation of the past two nights, I sank out of consciousness like a flat stone settling lazily to the bottom of a lake. I don't know how long I might have gone on like that if the phone hadn't rung. I put the handset to my ear and said, "Uh-huh."

"This is Reba. Did I wake you?"

"I greatly fear you did. What's the time?"

"Five minutes after five."

I checked the skylight, squinting in an attempt to determine if the sun was coming up or going down. "A.M. or P.M.?"

"It's Friday afternoon. I was just wondering what you'd heard from your guys."

"Nothing so far. Cheney's currently on surveillance, but I know he's trying to reach his contact in Washington, D.C. It may take a few days to set up the meeting. With so many agencies involved, the protocol's tricky to negotiate."

"I wish they'd get on with it. Beck's back Sunday night. I don't want to have to deal with him if I'm doing this."

"I can appreciate that. Unfortunately, Cheney's dependent on other people and he can only push so hard. Doesn't help we have a weekend coming up."

"I guess. You want to go someplace later? We could have dinner."

"That sounds good. What time?"

"Soon or right away, whichever one comes first."

"What'd you have in mind? You want to meet me somewhere?"

"You decide. All I know is I gotta get out before I lose my mind." I could hear her pause to light a cigarette.

"What's making you so itchy," I said.

"I don't know. I've been feeling anxious all day. Like maybe there's a drink or a poker parlor coming up real soon."

"You don't want to do that."

"Easy for you to say. I'm already back to smoking a pack a day."

"I could have told you not to start."

"I couldn't help myself."

"So you said. Personally, I don't buy it. You either take charge of your life or you might as well give up."

"I know, but I've been feeling so bad. I know Beck's a shit, but I really love the guy—"

"You *love* the guy?"

"Well, not now, but I *did*. Doesn't that count for something?"

"Not in my opinion."

"Also, you know, as odd as it sounds, I kind of miss being locked up."

"You're kidding."

"I'm not," she said. "In prison, I didn't have to make all these decisions, so that limited my chances of screwing up. Out here, what's the incentive to behave?"

I pinched the bridge of my nose in despair. "Where are you now, at your dad's?"

"Yeah, and you'll never guess who came waltzing in for a visit with him."

"Who?"

"Lucinda."

"That woman who hoped to marry him?"

"The very one," she said. "She'd love to see me violate parole. I get tossed in the can again, she'll whip back into Pop's life before the doors slam shut."

"Then you better pull yourself together."

"That'd be easier to do if I could have a drink. Or maybe I could drop in at the Double Down and just watch. No harm in that."

"Would you cut the crap? You can do anything you want, but don't kid yourself. You're just looking for an excuse to self-destruct."

"Yeah, it might be a relief."

"Look, why don't I hop in the car and come get you?"

"I don't know. Now that I think about it, maybe that's not such a hot idea. If I leave Lucinda alone with him, she'll find a way to make trouble."

"Oh, come on. What can she do? Your father told me he was done with her."

"She'll manage somehow. I've seen her do it before. Pop's like me, weak-willed and indecisive, only not as hell-bent. Besides, if he's so done with her, how come she's sitting in the other room?"

"Would you quit obsessing about her? She's the least of your worries. Look, give me a minute to throw on some clothes and I'll be up."

"Are you sure you want to go out?"

"Sure I'm sure. Why don't you start walking down the drive, and I'll meet you at the gate."

In the car on the way over, I tried to assess the situation. Reba was on the verge of coming unglued. Since the moment she'd fired up that first cigarette, I'd been waiting for signs of emotional decompression. After two years at CIW, she was unaccustomed to real-world conflicts and real-world consequences. Prison, while loathsome, apparently provided a form of containment that must have made her feel safe. Now there was too much to deal with and no way for her to assimilate the impact. Bad enough to find out Beck had hoodwinked her into taking the fall for him, worse still to discover he'd launched into an affair with the woman she'd thought of as her best friend. She was tough enough to acknowledge his deception, but perhaps not tough enough to make the break. I could see her ambivalence; she'd been dependent on him for years. What worried me was the fact she had so little tolerance for stress. If the meeting with Vince Turner had been scheduled right away, she might have sailed right on through, spilling everything she knew. With the delay of even three days, she was in danger of losing control. And while she wasn't my responsibility, I was party to the push that had her teetering on the brink.

When I arrived at the estate, she was perched on a big sandstone boulder to the right of the gate. In a navy blue windbreaker, jeans, and tennis shoes, she sat with her knees drawn up, cigarette in hand. When she saw me, she took one last drag and then scrambled to the ground. The moment she got in the car, I could feel the nervous energy pouring out of her like heat. Her movements were agitated and her eyes were too bright. "What'd you do to your hair?" she asked.

"Got it cut."

"It looks good."

"Thanks." I put the car in reverse and did a three-point turn.

She craned her neck and looked back at the gate. "I just hope she's gone by the time I get back. I couldn't believe she showed up like that unannounced."

"How do you know she didn't call him in advance?"

"That's even worse. If he agreed to see her, he's crazier than I am."

"Hey, take a deep breath and get a grip. You're all over the place."

"Sorry. I feel like there's someone inside trying to crawl out through my skin. I wish I had a guy. I'd rather have a drink, but getting laid would help."

"Call your sponsor. Isn't that what they're for?"

"I haven't found one yet."

"Then call Priscilla Holloway."

"I'm fine. Don't worry about it. I've got you," she said, and laughed.

"Yeah, right. This is way beyond me."

"Well, me too, you know? I'm just trying to muddle through the same as anybody else." She was quiet for a moment, staring out the window. "Fuck it. Never mind. I can tough it out on my own."

"As you've so amply demonstrated in the past," I said.

"Well, you're so smart, what do you suggest?"

"Find a meeting."

"Where?"

"How do I know? We'll go to my place and check the yellow pages. There's bound to be a listing for AA."

Once we reached my apartment, it took less than a minute to look up the number and make the requisite phone call. As it turned out, the closest meeting was at the city recreation center four blocks away. I drove her myself, not trusting her to make it on her own.

"I'll be back to pick you up in an hour," I said, as she got out of the car. The slamming of the door was as much as I received in the way of a reply. I made a point of waiting until I saw her walk in the door and then I waited another minute in case she intended to sneak out again. I could see how an alcoholic's family became ensnared in the game. I was already battling an urge to monitor her every move. That, or wash my hands of her altogether and be done with it. If I hadn't been intent on keeping her under wraps until she met with Vince, I might have cut her loose.

To kill time, I circled back to my neighborhood and parked outside of Rosie's. And yes, I recognized the irony of waiting for Reba in a bar while she struggled with the urge to have a drink. Lewis was there tending bar by himself, an apron tied around his waist. Two day-drinkers had taken up residence at the far end of the room. The color television mounted in the corner was tuned to a golf tournament being played someplace green. Rosie must have been back in the kitchen doing dinner prep because the place smelled like sautéed onions. She was also doing something with fried kidneys I didn't want to know about.

I perched on a bar stool and ordered a Coke. I honestly might have minded my own business, if Lewis hadn't seemed so chipper and oblivious. He gave no indication that he regretted, or even recognized, the trouble he'd caused.

He set my Coke on the bar, saying, "Where's Henry? I haven't seen him the last couple of days."

I studied him. "You really don't know."

"What? Is something wrong with him?"

I debated for half a second and then said, "Look, I know this is none of my business, but I think William was out of line when he talked you into flying out. Henry and Mattie were doing fine until you showed up."

Lewis blinked at me as though I were speaking in tongues. "I don't understand."

"You didn't have to barge in on breakfast and ask her for a date."

"I didn't ask her for a date. I suggested an art exhibit and a bite of lunch."

"Out here, we call that a date. Henry was upset and rightly so," I said.

Lewis seemed bewildered. "He was upset with *me?*"

"Sure he was. She was supposed to be spending time with him."

"Why didn't he speak up?"

"How could he? You called him a little old lady, in front of Mattie, no less. He was mortified. He couldn't speak up without looking even more foolish than he already felt."

"But that was just good-natured jostling. It was a joke."

"It's not a joke when you hustle in and try to beat him to the punch. Life's complicated enough."

"But we've always competed for the ladies. It's all in good fun. Neither of us takes it seriously. For heaven's sake, ask William if you doubt my word."

"He's never going to cop to it. He set the whole thing up. He had no business meddling, but what you did was worse. You knew Henry was interested in her."

"Of course he is and I am, too. That was obvious on the cruise. I made my pitch and he made his. If he can't handle the challenge, why complain to me?"

"Mattie broke it off. She said she didn't want to see him again."

Disconcerted, Lewis said, "Oh. Well, I'm sorry to hear that, but it's got nothing to do with me."

"Yes, it does. You flew out to California and got right in the middle of something that was none of your concern. There's nothing 'good-natured' about that. You were being hostile."

"No, no. Not a bit of it. I can't believe you're saying this. I'd cut off my right arm before I'd do such a thing."

"But you did do it, Lewis."

"You're completely wrong. That wasn't my intention. Henry's always been my favorite. He knows I'm crazy about him."

"Then you better find a way to make amends," I said.

It was close to 8:00 when Reba emerged from her AA meeting and headed toward my car. It was still light out. A massive fog bank hovered on the horizon and the breezes coming off the ocean laid a chill in the air. "Feel better?"

"Not especially, but I'm glad I went."

"You still want to have dinner?"

"Shit, we have to go back to the house. I forgot the photographs."

"Why do you need those?"

"Visual aids," she said. "There's a guy I want you to meet. He has dinner the same place every Friday night at nine. I did some reconnoitering this morning just to satisfy a hunch. We'll make a run up to Pop's for the pix, have a heart-to-heart with my pal, and then take some time to explore."

"Isn't a nine o'clock dinner kind of late?"

"I hope so. Prison, you eat at five in the afternoon. Talk about depressing. Makes you feel like a kid." She turned in her seat. "Why're you going this way? You should have taken a right back there."

"Actually, we don't need to go to your house. I have a set of pictures at my office. Cheney gave 'em to me." I wondered if she'd question my having copies of the photos, but she was sidetracked by something else and gave me a speculative look.

I said, "What."

"I notice you're dropping Cheney's name every chance you get. Is that where you got that?" She pointed.

"Got what?"

"That hickey on your neck."

I put a hand against my neck self-consciously and she laughed. "Just teasing," she said.

"Very funny."

"Well, I'd like to think you have a sex life."

"I'd like to think my sex life is private," I said. "So who's this guy you're so hot for me to meet?"

"Marty Blumberg. Beck's company comptroller."

18

I drove over to my office. I left Reba in the car, the VW idling, while I ran in and grabbed the manila envelope from my desk drawer. In the car again, I passed her the envelope and watched her out of the corner of my eye as I circled the block and headed for Passages. She removed the photographs and studied them as though viewing vermin through a microscope. She put them back in the envelope without a word, her expression impossible to read.

I found what was possibly the last space in the underground parking garage, which stretched like a low-ceilinged gray cavern that ran the length of the mall. We hiked to the escalator and went up to level one, where all the shops were located. Manila envelope in hand, Reba walked two paces ahead of me, forcing me to trot to keep up with her. She didn't seem as hyper as she had been, and for that I was glad. "Where are we going?"

"Dale's."

"Why Dale's? That's a dive."

"Not true. It's a Santa Teresa landmark."

"So's the dump," I said.

Dale's was strictly a no-frills bar. People went there to drink, pure and simple. I could feel the now familiar conflict arise: should I be protective and suggest we go somewhere else, or keep my mouth shut and let her take responsibility for the choices she made? In this instance, self-interest prevailed. I wanted to meet Marty Blumberg.

We entered the place, pausing in the open doorway to get our bearings. I hadn't been in Dale's for years, but it looked much the same—narrow room with a bar running along the left and a jukebox in back. There were six or eight small tables jammed up against the wall on the right. The lighting was primarily of the neon beer-sign variety, blue and red. There were numerous patrons on hand, occupying half of the bar stools and most of the tables. Eighty-seven percent of those present were smoking, the air as gray as morning fog. The overhead fixture made the light seem flat, very close to the quality of waning daylight outside. The jukebox, I remembered, was stocked with old 45-rpm records. At that very moment, the Hilltoppers were crooning "P.S. I Love You" while a couple danced on a narrow expanse of floor by the unisex bathroom. The sawdust underfoot and the acoustical ceiling tiles muffled the noise level so that both music and conversation seemed to be taking place in another room.

The walls were lined with black-and-white photographs, taken in the forties, to judge by the ladies' hairstyles and clothing. Each photo featured the same balding middle-aged man, perhaps the eponymous Dale. He had his arm slung around various minor sports figures—baseball players, professional wrestlers, and Roller Derby queens—their signatures scrawled across the bottom of the pictures.

At the far end of the room, a concession-sized machine produced a steady spill of popcorn that the bartender scooped into paper cups and set out for general consumption. At intervals along the bar, there were collections of assorted popcorn seasonings: garlic salt, lemon pepper, Cajun spices, curry powder, and Parmesan cheese in a green cardboard container. The popcorn wasn't sufficient to keep patrons sober, but it gave them something to fiddle with between the downing of drinks. As we were taking our seats, a peevish argument flared up, the topic being politics, about which no one present seemed to have the faintest clue.

"So where is he?" I said, looking around the room.

"What's your hurry? He'll be here in a bit."

"I thought we were having dinner. I didn't know they served food in here."

"Well, they do. Seven-way chili." She started ticking off the choices on her fingers. "Macaroni, chopped onions, cheese, oyster crackers, sour cream, or cilantro in any combination."

"That's only six."

"You can have it *plain*."

"Oh."

The next 45 selection came into play and Jerry Vale launched into his version of "It's All in the Game": *"Many a tear has to fall . . ."* I refused to think about Cheney lest I jinx the relationship.

A waitress appeared. Reba asked for iced tea and I ordered a beer. I'd have ordered iced tea myself, but only to demonstrate a virtue I didn't actually possess. In the face of her sobriety, I was acutely conscious of every sip I took. I was also worried the minute I turned my head, she'd snatch up my beer and suck half of it down.

As there was nothing else on the menu, we ordered seven-way chili, electing all six options. The chili arrived hot, spicy, and rich. The recipe, I noticed, was printed on our paper place mats. I was tempted to snitch mine, but the note at the bottom said "Serves 40," which seemed excessive for someone who usually eats alone standing over the sink. "You never finished telling me about Passages and Beck's participation," I said.

"Glad you asked. I didn't think you'd pursue the subject."

"Here I am," I said. "Care to fill me in?"

She paused to light a cigarette. "It's simple enough. A developer in Dallas bought the land in 1969 and submitted all the plans. He thought it'd be a cakewalk. The guy was so optimistic, he was already putting up signs: 'Passages Shopping Plaza. Coming in the fall of 1973.' The city planners had a ball, running him ragged with all the codes and requirements. He revised the plans sixteen times, but nothing ever seemed to suit. Twelve years later, when the developer still hadn't managed to get approval, he put the word out on the street and someone introduced him to Beck. That was 1981. The project was finished in '85, a speedy three years after construction began."

I waited for the rest.

"I can tell by the look on your face you're not getting it," she said.

"Just tell me, okay? Guessing slows us down and makes me cranky."

"Well, think about it. How do you think Beck got all those approvals and permits? Because he's nice?"

I stared, feeling dense.

Reba rubbed her thumb against her fingers in the universal gesture denoting money changing hands.

"Payoffs?"

"Exactly. That's where the money went—the three hundred and fifty thou I was accused of snitching. I delivered most of it myself, though I didn't realize what it was until later. All I knew was he had me driving to hell and gone with these bulky manila envelopes. Granted, some of it was earmarked for the boys in Sacramento—Beck is forever greasing palms on behalf of pending legislation—but most was for local guys who had the power to say no. Once they pocketed the dough, they were more than happy to be of help."

"But that's political money laundering."

"Wow, you are *quick*," she said, rolling her eyes. "Isn't

that why you're setting up this meeting with the feds, to get the goods on him?"

"I wasn't sure how far you meant to go."

"Right to the bitter end."

"But when we first talked, didn't you say he was depositing the money offshore so he could hide it from his wife?"

"That's the story he gave me. I didn't figure out what he was really doing until the audit came up. I'm sure he's still funneling cash out of the country as fast as he can, but at least I get it now; his efforts were never meant to benefit me."

"I'm sorry. I know that's tough on you."

"Tough, but true," she said, her tone matter-of-fact.

At 9:00, just about on the dot, Marty Blumberg appeared. Reba had been watching for him, and she gave him a big wave and motioned him over the minute he walked in. He paused at the bar to light a cigarette. The bartender was already setting up his usual drink, whiskey so dark it looked like Coke. Glass in hand, he ambled over to our table. He was probably in his fifties, a good-looking guy once upon a time. Now he was overweight by a good hundred pounds, his wardrobe lagging one size behind. His trouser pockets bulged open like a set of ears and the buttons on his shirt were straining against his bulk. He was baby-faced and florid, with sorrowful-looking blue eyes, a pug nose, and a full head of dark frizzy hair. He seemed genuinely glad to see her. Reba invited him to join us, hooking a thumb in my direction by way of introduction. "This is Kinsey Millhone. Marty Blumberg," she said.

I said, "Hi, Marty. Nice to meet you," and the two of us shook hands.

Marty gave Reba a quick visual appraisal. "You're none the worse for wear. When'd you get back?"

"Monday. Kinsey drove down and brought me back. The whole experience was an education . . . in what, I don't know."

"I'll bet."

"I hear you're in the new offices. Nice to be so close. Dale's was always your favorite."

Marty smiled. "I've only been coming in the past four-teen years. I could be part owner with all the money I've spent."

Reba took out a cigarette and Marty picked up her Dun-hill and extended a light. Reba tucked a strand of hair be-hind one ear as she bent to the flame, her hand resting casually on his. She inhaled, her eyes closing briefly. Smok-ing was like prayer, something you approached with rever-ence. "Beck says the offices are awesome."

"Pretty slick," he said.

"Coming from you, that's high praise. How about a tour? Beck said he'd show me around, but he's in Panama."

"A tour? Sure, why not? Give me a call and we'll set it up."

"How about tonight? As long as we're down here, it would be a hoot."

He hesitated. "I could do that, I guess. I need to pick up my briefcase anyway and clean off my desk."

"You're cleaning your desk on a Friday night? That's de-votion."

"Beck's new dictum—no files or papers on any of the surfaces overnight. Place looks like a showroom. I'm mostly playing catch-up, taking care of stuff I've let slide. I'll probably work tomorrow, too."

"The guy's a workaholic," she said to me as an aside and then turned back to him. "Kinsey's a PI . . . a pri-vate de-tec-tive," she said, separating each syllable for emphasis. She turned to me. "You have a business card on you?"

"Let me look," I said. I fumbled in my shoulder bag un-til I found my wallet, where I kept a stash of cards. Reba had her hand out so I passed one to her and she handed it on to Marty, who studied it, pretending it mattered when he couldn't have cared less.

He tucked it in his shirt pocket. "Guess I better watch my backside."

Reba smiled. "That is so so true. You have no idea."

He shook a cigarette from the pack, placing it directly between his lips. Smoking didn't seem like a good idea as he was already wheezing.

Reba said, "Allow me," as she picked up her Dunhill, flicked it, and offered him a light.

"Such service."

"You bet. Tit for tat," she said. She propped her chin on one hand. "Aren't you curious what she's doing here?"

Marty looked from Reba to me. "A drug bust?"

"Don't be dumb," she said, giving him a smack on the arm. She leaned forward flirtatiously and murmured, "She's part of a task force—federal and local dicks—looking into Beck's finances. All very hush-hush. Promise you won't tell." She put a finger to her lips and I could feel myself blanch. I couldn't believe she'd laid it out like that, without a word to me. Not that I'd have agreed. I checked his reaction.

His smile was tentative as he waited for the punch line. "No, seriously."

"Seriously," she said. I could see she enjoyed doling it out to him bit by bit.

"I don't get it."

"What's to get? I'm telling you the truth."

"Why tell me?"

"Fair warning. I like you. You're right in the line of fire."

He must have been one of those men who operated with his body thermostat cranked up into the red zone because his face now bore a sheen of perspiration. Without seeming to be aware of it, he took the flap of his tie and blotted the beads of sweat from his cheek. "What do you mean, I'm right in the line of fire? How do you figure that?"

"Well, A: You know what he's been up to, and B: Beck won't go down for this any more than he'd accept blame for the missing three hundred and fifty thou."

"I thought you volunteered."

"Stupnagel that I am, I made it easy for him. I'd like to think you're smarter than me, but maybe not."

"He can't do anything to me. I'm covered."

"You really think so? All he has to do is point. You've got your fingerprints on everything. You're the one who set up the accounts. Same with the offshore banks and the IBC."

"Exactly. I've got leverage on him. I'm the last guy on earth he ought to fuck with."

"I don't know," she said, with skepticism. "You've been with him a long time . . ."

"Ten years."

"Right. Which means you know a lot more than I do."

"So?"

"So if he stuck it to me, he can stick it to you as well. Believe me, the trap's there. You just can't see it at this point any more than I saw what he was doing to me until it was too late."

"I got no beef with Beck. The guy takes good care of me. Ten years, you know how much money I've managed to sock away? I could retire anytime I want, walk out tomorrow and still be living like a king."

"It may feel cushy, but it's a trap all the same."

Marty was shaking his head. "No. Uhn-uhn. I'm not buying it."

"What if they lean on you?"

"They, who?"

"The feds. What do you think I just got done telling you. The FBI, IRS, what's the other one?" she asked me, snapping her fingers impatiently.

"Department of Justice," I said.

She turned to me and frowned. "I thought you mentioned a couple more."

I cleared my throat. "Customs and Treasury. And the DEA."

"See?" she said to him as though that explained that.

"Why lean on me? Based on what?"

"Based on all the shit they've picked up so far."

"From who?"

"You think they don't have agents in place?"

He laughed, albeit uneasily. "What 'agents'? That's bull."

"Sorry. I misspoke myself. I said 'agents' in the plural. There's really only one."

"Who?"

"See if you can guess. Here, I'll give you a hint. Who in the company has gotten close to Beck in the last umpty-many months? Hmmm." She put a finger against her cheek, deep in mock thought. "Starts with O."

"Onni?"

"There you go," she said. "Talk about a break. I get sent to prison and that gives her the chance to slide right in."

"She works for the feds?"

Reba nodded. "Oh yeah, for *years,* and trust me, Little Miss Onni wants his ass on a plate."

"I don't believe it."

"Marty, this is her golden opportunity. You know how it is with women in these shit government jobs. Sure, they get hired. The guys let 'em do all the grunt work, but forget about promotion. There's no upward mobility without a coup of some kind. She doesn't pull this off, she'll be stuck where she is."

"Doesn't sound right. Are you sure? This makes no sense at all. The girl's dumb as a post."

"That's the *impression* she gives, but she's wily as they come. I'm telling you, she's good. You watch. This lady can write her own ticket, provided she nails Beck first. I mean, look at it this way. Does anybody in the company suspect? You sure as shit didn't and Beck doesn't have a clue. If he knew what was going on, he'd be out the door like a shot. Wouldn't he?"

"Well, yeah."

"You better believe it," she said. "Meanwhile, there she is with a finger in every pie, access to everything. What a sweet deal for her."

Marty seemed to be getting annoyed, though I noticed

two blotches on the front of his shirt where the sweat was soaking through. "Look, Reb. I know you're pissed at him and I don't blame you—"

"Sure, I'm pissed at him, but I'm not pissed at you, which is why I'm here. I'm trusting you to keep your mouth shut. I haven't breathed a word of this to anyone else. She's after his balls. She's so gung-ho she's willing to screw the guy to get the drop on him."

Marty was silent. I could hear him breathing as though he'd just finished running six blocks. "You can't just make claims—"

"I know. You're a man of common sense and you're hard to convince, which is why I brought these." She slid the black-and-white photos from the envelope and passed them over to him.

Marty leafed through them. "Jesus."

"See what I mean?"

"What's he *thinking?*"

"He's not thinking. He's got his brain between his legs. Really, you hadn't guessed he was screwing her? You knew he was doing me."

"Yeah, but you made no secret you had the hots for him. This, I don't know. Shouldn't somebody tell him what's going on?"

Reba raised her brows and gave him the big eyes. "You want to do that? Because I sure as hell don't."

"Poor guy."

" 'Poor guy,' my butt. Are you kidding? If he was willing to work me over, why not you? Thing is, the stakes are bigger this time. You tell him about Onni, the only effect is giving him more time to cover his tracks."

Marty held up his glass and rattled the ice. The bartender caught the gesture and began to make him another drink. "Onni. I can't believe it. Beck must have walked right into it."

"Of course. Minute she makes her move, he'll turn right around and lay it off on you. He'll claim you acted on your own. He never authorized you to do anything. You took it on yourself."

"But it's his signature. Loan aps, incorporation papers—"

"Marty, get *serious*. He'll say he's never had a head for the financial end of things. That's how I was able to get away with the money I stole. Gosh. Guess he should have wised up, but some guys never learn. You told him to sign so he signed. He trusted you and this is what he gets for it. Shamey-shame on him. Meanwhile, you're under federal indictment."

Marty shook his head. "I don't know. This is freaking me out." The bartender brought his drink. Marty took out his wallet and extracted two twenties. "Keep that," he said. As the bartender left, he was well on his way to draining his glass.

During the brief interchange between the two, Reba shot me a look. It's your show, I thought, before she glanced away.

She patted Marty's arm, her tone brisk. "Anyway, ponder the implications. That's really all I ask. Even if you decide I'm making it up, it wouldn't hurt to cover your ass. Once the subpoenas are issued and all the warrants are in place, you'll be shit out of luck. In the meantime, if you're on your way upstairs, how about the two of us tagging along?"

19

I'd passed the entrance to Beck's office building half a dozen
times without ever taking in the sight. The façade was thickly
overgrown with ivy, integrated seamlessly into the architectural conceit of an ancient Spanish town. Flowering trees had
been planted along the front. To the left of the entrance were
side-by-side stairs and escalators, giving access to the additional parking structure at the corner of the mall. A high-end
luggage shop occupied a portion of the ground floor, presumably paying Beck a big whack of high-end rent.

We pushed through glass doors that swung closed
soundlessly as we entered. Windows stretched upward the
full four stories to a slanting glass roof. The interior atrium
was oblong, done in a mottled rosy granite, floors and walls
forming a hard canvas on which natural and artificial light
played according to the time of day. High on the wall, there
was a clock with long brass minute and hour hands and six-
inch-diameter brass dots representing the hours. A curtain

of dark green ivy and philodendron hung from a miniature oasis above the clock.

There were two elevators on the wall dead ahead. To the right of these, in an alcove, there were two more elevators, facing each other, one with a much wider door, which I assumed was designed to accommodate freight. A digital readout next to each elevator showed that all were at lobby level.

In the center of the lobby, a perfect circle of granite was sunk in the floor, sloping sides washed with a constant Niagara of water spilling from a six-inch channel around its rim. The sound was soothing, but the look, I fear, was closer to toiletlike than the restful pool it was meant to suggest.

A uniformed guard sat at a high polished-onyx desk. A lean man in his sixties, he had salt-and-pepper hair and a blank handsome face. Briefly I wondered what curious set of circumstances had landed him here. Surely there was little to guard and less to secure. Did he simply sit for the whole of his eight-hour shift? I saw no indication he had a book in his lap discreetly shielded from view. No radio or pint-size television set. No sketch pad or crossword puzzle book. His eyes tracked us, his face turning slowly as we clattered across the cold expanse of polished granite floor.

Marty lifted his hand and received an unblinking stare in response. Reba smiled at the guy, giving him the full benefit of those big dark eyes of hers. She was rewarded with a tentative smile. She caught up with Marty outside the elevator doors. "What's *his* name? He's cute."

"Willard. He's on nights and weekends. Can't remember who's been covering days."

We entered the elevator and Marty pushed the button for four. "You made a conquest. First time I've ever seen him smile," he said.

"Getting along with guards turns out to be a specialty of mine," she said. "Although, in my case, 'correctional officer' is the appropriate term."

Since Beck's offices took up the entire fourth floor, the elevator doors opened directly into the reception area, hushed with thick pale green carpet. Lights blazed everywhere, but it was clear there was no one on the premises but us. Modern furniture and contemporary art were mixed with antiques. Etched-glass partitions separated the reception area from an airy conference room beyond. From our perspective, corridors opened on four sides like the spokes of a wheel. The hallways appeared to stretch on at length with wide bands of color forming sweeping loops along the wall.

"Oh, Marty. This is gorgeous. Beck said it was spectacular, but this is really over the top. Mind if we look around?"

"Just don't take long. I want to get home."

"I promise we'll make it quick. Think of it this way, if it weren't for that stint in prison, I'd be working here myself. Isn't there a roof garden?"

"The stairs are back that way. You can't miss 'em. I'll be in my office down that hall."

"You could get lost in this place," Reba said.

"Well, don't. Beck's not going to like it if he hears you've been here."

"Mum's the word," she said, producing her dimples for him.

Reba circled the reception area with me following in her wake. As long as Marty was present, she was almost childlike in her hand-clapping enthusiasm, popping her head into offices here and there along the way, oohing and aahing. He watched us briefly and then went off in the opposite direction.

The minute he was out of sight, Reba dropped all pretense of touring and got down to business. I kept pace with her as she checked the names posted on the wall outside each office. When she reached Onni's, she shot a look down the hall to make sure Marty wasn't there. She moved to Onni's desk, grabbed a tissue from the box, and used it as she started opening drawers. "Keep a lookout, okay?"

I checked the corridor behind me. Searching is my all-
time favorite sport (except for time spent with Cheney
Phillips of late). The edgy thrill of invading someone's private space is heightened by the possibility of getting
caught in the act. I wasn't sure what she was looking for or
I'd have joined her in the game. As it was, somebody had to
stand guard.

Still opening and shutting drawers, Reba said, "God, I
can't believe Marty's so paranoid. Must be off his meds.
Ah." She held up a chunky ring of keys that she jingled
midair.

"You can't take those."

"Poo. Onni won't be in until Monday. I can put 'em back
by then."

"Reba, don't. You're going to ruin everything."

"No, I won't. This is scientific research. I'm testing my
hypothesis."

"What hypothesis?"

"I'll tell you later. Quit worrying."

She left Onni's office, trailing a hand along the wall as
she returned to the reception area, scanning the lines of the
ceiling. When she reached the elevators, she circled the
central core, measuring with her eyes. Large abstract paintings dominated the walls and the lighting was such that
one's attention was irresistibly drawn from one artwork to
the next.

"It would help if I knew what you were looking for," I
said.

"I know how his mind works. There's something here he
doesn't want us to see. Let's try his office."

I wanted to protest but knew she wasn't listening.

Beck's corner location was prime—spacious, with clear
cherry paneling and the same footstep-muffling green carpeting. The room was furnished with low-slung chrome-
and-leather chairs of the sort that require winch and pulley
action to remove yourself once you've been foolish enough
to sit. His desktop was black slate, a curious surface unless

he favored doing his long division in chalk along the length. Reba used the same tissue to avoid leaving latent prints on his desk drawers. I loitered uneasily in the doorway.

Dissatisfied, she pivoted. She studied every aspect of the room and finally crossed to the paneled wall, where she tapped her way across, listening for evidence of a hollow space behind. At one point, she activated a touch latch and a door sprang open, but the only treasure revealed was his liquor supply, complete with cut glass decanters and assorted glasses. She said, "Shit." She pushed the door shut and returned to his desk. She sat in his swivel chair and did a second survey from that vantage point.

"Would you hurry up?" I hissed. "Marty could show up any minute, wondering where we went."

She pushed the chair back and leaned down so she could examine the underside of his desk. She extended her hand, almost to the length of her arm. I wasn't sure what she'd discovered and I didn't care to be a witness. I stepped out into the hall and looked toward the reception area. So far no Marty. Idly I noted the fact that the paintings were graduated in size with the largest near the elevators and the smaller ones, in diminishing proportions back here. From the viewpoint of a visitor, the effect would be to create the illusion of corridors much longer than they were—an amusing trompe l'oeil effect.

Reba emerged from Beck's office and grabbed me by the elbow, steering me toward the wide stairs that led up to the roof.

"What's up there besides the roof garden?"

"That's why we're going up—because we don't know," she said. She took the steps two at a time and I kept pace with her. A glass door at the top opened into a fully landscaped garden: trees, shrubs, and flower beds separated by gravel paths that meandered out of sight. Landscape lighting made the whole of it glow. Chairs and umbrella-shaded tables were placed in assorted patios that were dotted throughout. A four-foot wall encircled the perimeter with dazzling city views in all directions.

Central to the garden was what looked like a gardener's cottage, the exterior encompassed by trellises on which gaudy passionflower vines wound up and across, thick with purple blossoms. There was a sign half-concealed in the profusion of greenery. Curious, I pulled the foliage aside.

"What is it?" she asked.

" 'Danger. High Voltage.' There's a phone number for the building supervisor if work needs to be done. Must be a transformer or maybe part of the electrical service. Who knows? I guess it could be housing for the elevators, along with central heating and air conditioning. You have to put stuff like that somewhere." The little building seemed to hum in a way that suggested you'd be fried to a crisp if you made one wrong move.

From the stairway, Marty called up to us. "Hey, Reba?"

"Up here."

"I don't mean to rush you, but we ought to get going. Beck doesn't like strangers on the premises."

"I'm hardly a stranger, Marty. I'm his favorite screw."

"Yeah, well, he'll be pissed anyway and take it out on me."

"No problem. We're ready anytime you are," she said, and then to me: "Take your car keys and wallet out of your shoulder bag and leave it behind that thing."

"My bag? I'm not going to leave my shoulder bag. Are you nuts?"

"Do it."

Marty appeared at the top of the stairs, apparently not trusting us to come down the stairs on our own. He leaned against the stair rail, his breathing stertorous from the climb. Reba crossed to the landing and linked her arm into his, turning to admire the mountains visible in the distance. "What a view! Perfect setting for an office party."

Marty took out a handkerchief and wiped his face, which was glistening with perspiration. "We haven't done that so far. Good weather, the gals eat their lunch out here and grab a little sun. Bad days, they use the break room like they did at the old place, only this one's fancier."

"The break room? I didn't see that."

"I can show you on the way out."

Reba turned to me. "Everything okay?"

"Right behind you," I said.

The two started down the stairs. Grousing to myself, I'd done as she'd instructed, removing my keys and wallet from my bag, which I shoved behind a big potted ficus tree. I hoped she knew what she was doing because I sure as shit didn't. Looking back wistfully, I moved toward the stairs.

I caught up with them in what looked like a midsize kitchen. Sink, dishwasher, two microwaves, a side-by-side refrigerator-freezer, and two vending machines, one with soft drinks, the other with candy bars, potato chips, peanut butter crackers, cookies, packages of nuts, and other fatty snacks. There was a large table in the center of the room surrounded by chairs.

"Is this great?" she said.

I said, "Swell."

"You ready?" Marty asked me.

"Sure. I'm fine. It's been fun."

"Good. Let me get my briefcase and I can lock up."

The three of us proceeded down the hall toward the elevators. As Marty passed his office, he ducked out of sight and reappeared with his briefcase. Reba leaned around the door frame. "Nice office. Did you do this yourself?"

"Oh god, no. Beck hired a design firm to handle everything, except the plants. We have another company for those."

"Pretty highfalutin," she remarked.

We watched as Marty pushed the elevator button, calling the car from down below. While we waited, Reba pointed to a third elevator on the far side of the reception desk. "What's that one for?"

"Service elevator. It's mostly for hauling cartons up and down, file cabinets, furniture, stuff like that. We have fifteen, twenty firms on these three upper floors. That's a lot of office supplies and copy machines. Plus, the cleaning crew uses it when they come in."

"Bart and his brother still work weekends?"

"Fridays, same as ever. They'll be coming in at midnight," he said.

"Nice to know some things don't change. The rest is a major upgrade. Might know Beck would do that as soon as I'm out the door."

The elevator arrived and the doors slid open. Marty reached around and pressed the Door Open button while he entered the alarm system code on the keypad to the right. Reba displayed only cursory interest. Once the three of us got on, Marty released the button and pressed 1 for the first floor. We descended without saying much, all three of us watching the digital floor numbers flash from 4 to 3 to 2 to 1.

As we emerged, the doors to one of the two elevators in the alcove opened and a two-man cleaning crew emerged with their cart and loaded a vacuum cleaner, assorted brooms and mops, industrial-size bottles of cleaning solutions, and packets of paper toweling to resupply the restrooms. Both wore coveralls with a company logo stitched across the back. One gave Willard a nod and he returned a one-finger salute. Reba watched the two men cross the alcove and enter the service elevator.

"What are they up to?"

Marty shrugged. "Beats me. I think they work on two."

The doors closed behind them and the three of us continued to the entrance while Willard made a note of our departure time with the same blank stare he'd given us before. Marty didn't bother to nod his good-byes, but Reba gave Willard a merry finger wave. "Thanks, Willie. Nighty-night."

He hesitated and then lifted a hand.

"Did you see that? True love," she said.

We went down to the lower-level parking garage. At the foot of the stairs, Marty said, "I'm parked over here. Where're you guys?"

"That way," I said, pointing in the opposite direction.

Reba shoved her hands in her jacket pockets and watched him walk toward his car. "Hey, Marty?"

He paused and looked back.

"Think about what I said. You don't act soon, Beck's gonna have your nuts in a vise."

Marty nearly spoke, and then seemed to change his mind. He shook his head, his expression withdrawn, and turned on his heel.

She watched until he was out of sight and then the two of us walked the length of the garage.

"I didn't like the look of those cleaning guys," she said.

"Would you give it a rest?"

"I'm going on record. There's something bogus about them."

"Thanks for telling me. I'll put a note in the file."

When we reached the VW, I unlocked the door on my side, slid behind the wheel, and then leaned over and unlocked the passenger-side door for her. She got in and pulled the door shut, but when I went to insert the key in the ignition, she put her hand out. "Hang on a minute."

"Why?"

"Because we're not done yet. Soon as Marty pulls out, we can have another go."

"You can't go back up there. How're you going to pull that off?"

"We can tell Willie you left your shoulder bag upstairs and you have to have it back."

"Reba! You gotta quit this. You're going to screw up the government's case."

"It's the government that screws up. Look at the state we're in. The country's a mess."

"That's not the point. You can't violate the law."

"Listen to you, Miss Prissy Ass. What law?"

"Shall we start with breaking and entering?"

"That wasn't breaking and entering. We went up with Marty. He let us in of his own free will."

"And then you stole the keys."

"I didn't *steal* them. I borrowed them. I intend to put 'em back."

"It doesn't matter. I'm telling you, I'm through with this," I said. I turned the key in the ignition, shifted gears, and backed out of the space.

"Don't you want your bag?"

"Not now. I'm taking you home."

"Tomorrow morning, then, and I swear that'll be the end of it, okay? I'll pick you up at eight."

"Why so early? It's Saturday. The mall doesn't open until ten."

"We'll be long gone by then."

"Having done what?"

"You'll see."

"Uhn-uhn. No way. You can count me out."

"You don't come with me, I'll do it on my own. No telling what kind of trouble I'll get into."

I would have closed my eyes in despair, but I was already pulling up the exit ramp and didn't want to crash in my haste to get us out of there.

I turned right on Chapel. Out of the corner of my eye, I saw Reba pull something from her jacket pocket, saying, "Well, this is cool."

"What."

"Looks like I stole something after all. Naughty me."

"You didn't."

"Yes, I did. These are Beck's. I found 'em in his desk in that Mickey Mouse secret drawer. Must be planning to skip town, the little so-and-so." She was holding up a passport, a driver's license, and assorted documents.

Abruptly I pulled over to the curb, greatly annoying the

driver of the car behind me, who leaned on his horn and made a rude hand gesture. "Give me those," I said, grabbing for them.

She held the documents out of my reach. "Hang on. This is the real deal here. A passport, birth certificate, driver's license, credit cards. 'Garrison Randell' with Beck's photograph. Must have cost a mint."

"Reba, what do you think's going to happen when he realizes that stuff's gone?"

"How's he going to know?"

"How about he looks in his drawer the minute he gets back? That's his means of escape. He probably checks the docs twice a day."

"You're right," she said. "On the other hand, why would he suspect me?"

"He doesn't have to suspect you. All he has to do is figure out who's been in. Once he gets a bead on Marty, it's over. Marty's not going to risk his neck on your account. You'll end up back in the clink."

She thought about that. "Well, okay. I'll put 'em back in his desk when I return Onni's keys."

"Thank you," I said, but I knew I couldn't take her at her word.

I dropped her at her place and rolled into my apartment at 11:15. The red message light was blinking on my answering machine. Cheney, I thought. There was something erotic in the very idea, and like one of Pavlov's dogs, I nearly whimpered in response. I pressed the button and heard his voice. Eight words. "Hey, babe. Call me when you get in."

I punched in his number and when he picked up, I said, "Hey yourself. Did I wake you?"

"I don't mind. Where you been?"

"Out with Reba. I have tons to report."

"Good. Come on over and spend the night," he said. "I'll make you French toast in the morning if you're good."

"Can't. She's picking me up here at eight."

"How come?"

"Long story. I'll tell you when I see you."

"So how about I come get you and take you home in the morning in time to meet her?"

"Cheney, I can handle the drive. You're only two miles away."

"I know, but I don't want you rattling around the streets at this hour. The world's a dangerous place."

I laughed. "Is that how it's going to be? You're all protective and I'm docile as a lamb."

"You have a better idea?"

"No."

"Great. I'll pick you up in ten," he said.

20

I waited for him outside, sitting on the curb, wearing a black turtleneck T-shirt and one of my new skirts. This was the third night in a row I'd be seeing him. Like a winning streak at the craps table, the roll was bound to come to an end. I couldn't decide if I was being cynical or sensible in acknowledging the fact. I knew how the night was going to go. In the first moments of seeing him, I'd feel neutral—glad to be in his company, but not irresistibly drawn to him. We'd chat about nothing in particular and gradually, I'd become aware of him: the smell of his skin, his face in profile, the shape of his hands as he gripped the steering wheel. He'd sense my attention and turn to look at me. The minute we made eye contact, that low distant humming would start up again, vibrating through my body like the first rumbles of an earthquake.

Curiously, I didn't feel I was in danger with him. Having blundered so often in relationships with men, I tended to be cautious, remote, keeping my options open in case things didn't work out. Inevitably, things turned sour, which only served to reinforce my wariness. In retrospect, I could see that Dietz played the game exactly the way I did, which meant I was also safe with him, but for all the wrong reasons: safe because he was always off somewhere, safe because he probably wasn't capable of coming through for me, and safe, most of all, because his detachment was a mirror of my own.

I heard Cheney's car long before he turned the corner from Bay onto Albanil. His headlights flashed into view and I got to my feet, silently cursing the loss of my shoulder bag. I'd been forced to pack—if you want to call it that—a few things in a paper sack, like a kid's brown-bag lunch: clean underwear, a toothbrush, my wallet, and keys. Cheney was driving with the top down again, but when I got in the car I realized the heater was turned on full blast, which meant that half of me would be warm.

He spotted the sack. "That your overnight case?"

I held up the brown bag. "It's part of a matching set. I have another forty-nine just like it in my kitchen drawer."

"Nice skirt."

"Thanks to Reba. I wasn't going to buy it, but she insisted."

"Good deal." He waited until I'd fastened my seat belt and then he pulled away.

I said, "I can't believe we're doing this. Don't you ever sleep?"

"I promised you a house tour. Last time, all you saw was the bedroom ceiling."

I held up a finger. "I have a question."

"What's that?"

"Is this how you ended up married so fast? You meet old What's-Her-Face and spend every night with her for the first three weeks. Week four, she moves in. Week five, you're engaged, and by week six, you're married and off on your honeymoon. Is that the way it went?"

"Not quite, but close. Why, does that bother you?"

"Well, no. I just wondered how much time I had to get the invitations out."

Cheney conducted a tour, starting with the downstairs rooms. The house was more than a hundred years old and reflected a way of life long past. Most of the original mahogany fireplaces, doors, window trim, and baseboards were still intact. Tall, narrow windows, high ceilings, transoms above the doors to aid the circulation of air. There were five working fireplaces on the first floor and four more in the bedrooms upstairs. The parlor (a concept that has since gone the way of the dodo bird) continued into the morning room, which in turn opened onto a gracious screened-in porch. In the adjacent laundry room, the old double tubs existed side-by-side with a wood-fueled stove for heating water.

Cheney was in the process of redoing the living room where the hardwood floor was covered in canvas drop cloths. Wallpaper had been steamed off and lay in discouraged-looking clumps. The plaster had been patched and the windowpanes had been taped in preparation for painting. He'd taken off one of the doors, which he'd laid across two sawhorses and covered with canvas to provide a surface for any tools not in use. The brass hardware—doorknobs, lock plates, window latches, and pulls—were jumbled into cardboard boxes in one corner of the room.

"How long have you had the house?"

"Little over a year."

Additional drop cloths extended through a set of glass-paned pocket doors into the dining room, which was in marginally better shape. Here the ladder, paint cans, brushes, rollers, paint trays, and liners—not to mention the smell—attested to his having primed and painted, though he hadn't yet replaced the fixtures or the incidental hardware, which littered every sill.

"This the dining room?"

"Right, though the couple who owned the place were using it as a bedroom for her aged mother. They converted the butler's pantry into a makeshift bathroom, so the first thing I did was tear out the toilet, shower, and sink and restore the built-in china cupboards and silverware drawers."

Through the bay of dining room windows, I found myself looking into Neil and Vera's kitchen next door. Cheney's driveway and theirs ran parallel with a modest strip of grass separating the two. I could see Vera standing at the sink, rinsing dishes before she put them in the machine. Neil was perched on a stool at the counter with his back to me, the two chatting as she worked. No sign of the children so they must have been in bed. I seldom witnessed even the briefest moments of a marriage in progress. Occasionally I'd be struck by the sight of one of those couples in restaurants who spend the meal not looking at each other and not exchanging a word. Now that's a scary proposition: all the minor day-to-day frictions with none of the companionship.

Cheney put his arms around me from behind and laid his face against my hair, following my gaze. "One of the few happy couples I know."

"Or so it would appear."

He kissed my ear. "Don't be a cynic."

"I *am* a cynic. So are you."

"Yes, but we both have a streak of optimism way down deep."

"Speak for yourself," I said. "Where's the kitchen?"

"Through here."

The previous owners had done extensive remodeling in the kitchen, which was now a streamlined vision of granite counters, stainless-steel appliances, and high-tech lighting. Far from detracting from the overall Victorian feel of the house, there was a wonderful sense of hope and efficiency at work. I was exploring a walk-in pantry the size of my loft when the telephone rang. Cheney caught the call and his end of it was brief. He replaced the handset on the wall-mounted phone. "That was Jonah. There's been a shoot-out in a parking garage on Floresta. One of my hookers got caught in the crossfire. I said I'd drop you at your place and meet him at the scene."

"Sure thing," I said, thinking, *Great . . . now that Jonah knows we're an item, the entire STPD will be informed by midday tomorrow.* Men are worse gossips than women when it comes right down to it.

I crawled into bed at midnight and found myself tossing and turning, possibly because of the lengthy nap I'd taken in the afternoon. I don't remember the moment when I sank into a leaden sleep, but vaguely, I became aware of a pounding on my door. I opened my eyes and checked the clock. 8:02. Who the heck was it? Oh, shit. Reba was down there.

I pushed the covers back and swung my feet out on the floor, yelling, "Just a minute!" . . . like she could actually hear me. I dry-washed my face, pressing my fingers into my eyes until light sparks appeared on the inside of my lids. I went downstairs and let her in, saying, "Sorry, sorry, sorry. I overslept. I'll be with you in a sec."

I left her to make herself at home while I went upstairs, though in the interest of good manners, I leaned over the loft rail and called down to her. "You can put on a pot of coffee if you can figure out how."

"Don't worry about it. We can stop off at McDonald's."

"You got a deal."

I did an abbreviated bathroom tour and then pulled on jeans, a T-shirt, and tennis shoes. I retrieved my wallet and car keys from the brown-paper bag and in six minutes flat, I was ready to go out the door.

We ordered from the take-out window and then sat in the parking lot with two enormous coffees and four Egg Mc-Muffins with extra packets of salt. Like me, Reba ate like she was competing for the land speed record. "They don't call this fast food for nuttin'," she remarked, her mouth full. There were a scant few minutes when we sank into quiet, focused on our food.

Having finished, we bundled up our trash and shoved it in the bag, which Reba pitched into the container on the sidewalk nearby. She said, "Two points. Hot damn."

While I sipped my coffee, she reached over to the rear seat and picked up three rolled cylinders of architectural plans, bound with a rubber band. She slipped the band on her wrist for safekeeping, then unfurled the first oversize sheet, which she spread across the dashboard. The paper itself was a whitish blue, with the two-dimensional rooms laid out in blue ink. The legend along the bottom read: THE BECKWITH BUILDING, 3-25-81.

Reba said, "These are the old blue-line drawings. I'm hoping they'll tell us what Beck's hiding and where he's hiding it."

"Where'd you get these?"

"We had multiples at the office—everything from framing plans to plumbing plans, heating and air conditioning, fixture requirements, you name it. Every time the architect made changes, he'd print out a new set of drawings for all the principals. Beck told me to toss 'em."

"And you had the foresight to hang on to them? I'm impressed."

"I wouldn't call it foresight. I just love the information. It's like looking at X-rays—all those cracks and bone spurs where you least expect them. Here, take a look at these and we'll compare notes. I realized last night we were going about this all wrong."

She passed me the second batch of drawings on sheets of paper that must have measured eighteen inches by twenty-four. I wrestled the first sheet into a reasonably flat position and studied the particulars. As nearly as I could tell, this had something to do with the service entrance and electrical rooms, showing the location of the meter, the transformer vault, the switchgear, electrical closets, and individual circuits. The wiring diagrams were made up of circles and wavy lines, showing the relationship of outlets to controls.

The next sheet was more interesting. It looked like a cutaway of one corner of the building from the rooftop down. According to the legend at the bottom of the page, every eighth of an inch represented one linear foot. The architect had labeled every aspect of the drawing in that freehand block lettering students must be taught the very first day at architectural school. Reba glanced over, saying, "What they're using there for stablization is a rigid core that runs down the center of the building—a structural tower that contains the restrooms, stairs, and elevators. I remember them talking about diagonal bracing and shear panels, whatever that means."

I could see the concrete columns, the location of precast concrete spandrel panels, the slab on grade and concrete pile foundation, which was backed up by a steel-stud and drywall assembly. I was hoping to spot the correlation between the lines on the page and the spaces I'd seen. The detailed drawing of the rooftop, for instance, did show the mechanicals of the elevator equipment in roughly the same position as the fakey-looking gardener's cottage. Reba put a finger on the page. "I don't like it. That other drawing shows the elevators on the far side, not this, So which is it?"

"Maybe we should take another look," I said. "I don't get how anybody figures this shit out. I wouldn't know where to begin."

Reba unfurled another floor plan, this one dated August of '81. We studied a couple of the drawings next to one another. Having seen the offices firsthand, I had a fair idea what I was looking at, with certain notable exceptions. Where the employee break room was located in reality, the floor plan indicated a conference room, which had been moved closer to reception. "How many sets do you have?"

"Tons, but these seemed the most relevant. From March to August, there's not that much difference. It's the changes that show up in October that looked interesting to me." She wrestled a fourth sheet open and placed it atop the third. Much crackling of paper as the two of us examined the specifics of employee restrooms, wheelchair clearances, metal decks, and rigid insulation—the whole of Beck's fifteen-office suite visible in one sweep.

"Are we looking for anything in particular?" I asked.

She pointed to an oblong area on my sheet adjacent to fire stairs and the elevator envelopes. "See that? The location of the elevators shifted from there to there," she said, moving her finger from my drawing to hers.

"Break room moved, too, but so what?"

"Well, look at it. I mean, I understand they made changes, but there's space unaccounted for. Here it's called storage, but in this drawing, the space is still there with no reference to it at all."

"I still don't see the significance."

"I just think it's odd. I'm telling you, there was a room there on one of the early floor plans. I asked Beck what it was and he blew me off, like I didn't need to know. On the initial blue-line drawings, the architect labeled it a gun vault, which is totally ridiculous. Beck's a pussy about firearms. He doesn't even own one gun, let alone a collection of the damn things. At the time, I figured maybe it was a panic room or whatever you call them . . ."

"A safe room?"

"Like that. Something he didn't want anyone else to know about. Later I wondered if he intended to use it as a love nest, a hidey-hole where he could take his lady friends. I mean, what could be better? In the same building but out of the public eye. Think how easy it'd be to get a little ass on the side."

"Maybe the architect vetoed the idea."

"Nobody vetoes him. He knows exactly what he wants

and he gets it." She laid a finger on an unmarked area just off reception. "Couldn't there be space behind this wall?"

I went back in my mind and pictured the gallery of paintings and the trompe l'oeil effect created by the diminishing sizes of objects as the eye traced them down the hall. I looked back at the floor plan. "I don't think so. If there's a room there, how the heck do you get in? There aren't any doors in that wall that I remember."

"My recollection, too. Because I counted off five offices and Onni's was in the middle. After Jude's office—you know the one with all the black-and-white photographs?"

"Right, right."

"Yeah, well, the gallery picked up from there and that wall had to be a good twenty-five feet long."

"What about that room where they kept office supplies?"

"That's right there. I went around this part twice and there weren't any doors there either, so if it's a room, it's been sealed."

"Maybe it's something to do with the building infrastructure. All the nuts-and-bolts stuff. Don't you have plans any later than this?"

Reba shook her head. "I was in prison by then."

We were both silent for a moment. Then I said, "Too bad we don't have plans for the offices below his. You're just assuming that's a room, but it could be a mechanical chase or something that goes all the way down."

She curled the plans together and made a cylinder of them, replacing the rubber band. She tossed them into the backseat and turned the key in the ignition. "Only one way to find out."

Reba drove around the block, slowly circling Passages Shopping Plaza, peering across me through the passenger-side window as she scanned the exterior. On the south side of the mall she pulled over to the curb, her attention taken up by an entrance marked "Deliveries." A steep ramp led down into the shadows and out of sight.

"Hang on. I gotta see this," she said. She killed the engine and got out on her side of the car while I got out on mine. We walked down the ramp, which descended two levels to what must have been a subbasement. At the foot of the ramp was a portcullis secured with a big handsome padlock. Through the grillwork, we could see ten parking spaces, a blank double door at the end of a cul-de-sac, and a single metal door to the right. I said, "You think this is the only way in?"

"Can't be. When merchandise is delivered, there has to be some way to distribute goods to the individual stores."

We retraced our steps, huffing and puffing slightly as we made the climb. When we reached the sidewalk, she backed up a few steps, her gaze tracking the length of the building. At street level, along this aspect of the fortresslike structure, there were no shop windows and no access to retail establishments. "Second ramp just like this down the block," she remarked. "Oh, wait a minute. I got it. Let's just see if I'm correct."

I looked at her. "Are you going to tell me or not?"

"If I'm right, of course. If I'm wrong, you don't need to know."

"You're very tedious."

She smiled, unfazed.

We returned to the car. She started the engine and glanced over her left shoulder to check for oncoming cars. She pulled out and continued her circuit of the mall, passing the twin of the entrance we'd just seen. She turned right at the corner and headed north on Chapel.

At Passages there was no charge for parking on weekends, probably to encourage spending. The gate to the underground parking lot was up. Reba turned in and eased her car down the ramp. At the bottom she hung a right and drove the length of the garage, parking in a space near the darkened glass doors that marked the lower-level entrance to Macy's. The store at this hour was still closed and wouldn't open until 10:00.

Reba pointed. Ten car lengths to our right there was a nondescript door marked "Service. No Admittance." Beyond that, the ramp for second-, third-, and fourth-level parking spiraled up and out of sight.

"Won't that be locked?" I asked, feeling that queasy sense of excitement at the notion of going where we weren't supposed to be.

"For sure. I told you I did some reconnoitering before, but I couldn't get in. Now I have these." She held up the chunky ring of keys she'd snitched from Onni's desk. She sorted through the keys one by one, smiling at the sight. "My, oh my. I'm sorry for every mean thing I ever said about the girl. Catch this."

Onni, Little Miss Compulsive, had labeled every key with a strip of neatly embossed tape: OFFICE, BECK'S, CNFRCE ROOM, SRVICE COR, WRHSE, S.ELE., S.DEPOSIT MID-CITY, S. DEPOSIT, ST SV'GS & LO. Reba pinched the two safe-deposit keys together and jangled the rest. "Bet these contain a shitload of information. Safe-deposit box is where Beck keeps his second set of books."

"A second set? That's not smart."

"Not real books. The information's all on disks. He's over there every couple of days, dropping off the updates. What's he going to do? He's a businessman. Even if what he's doing is illegal, he still has to keep records. You think he doesn't have to provide a full accounting to Salustio?"

"Sure, but it still seems risky."

"Beck adores taking risks. He's addicted to the rush."

"I can relate to that."

Reba continued to finger the safe-deposit keys. "Wonder if there's any way to get into these boxes . . ."

"Reba . . ."

"I didn't say I'd *do* it. He changed banks the minute I went to prison, so I wouldn't be a signatory in any event. It's probably Marty now."

"Swear you're going to put those back."

"I told you I would. As soon as I've made dupes."

"Goddamn it, Reba. Are you totally out of your mind?"

"Pretty much." She glanced back over her shoulder at the vast empty garage. "We better get going before someone else shows up."

We got out of the car and walked to the service door, our footsteps echoing against the bare concrete walls. Reba tried the knob, locked as anticipated, and then used the key Onni had so thoughtfully designated. The door opened into a stairwell. We walked down a flight and discovered two additional doors about ten feet apart. Reba said, "The lady or the tiger? You pick."

I pointed to the left. She shrugged and handed me the keys. I had to do a bit of experimenting to find the right one. Onni's paucity of imagination had resulted in her labeling some of the keys numerically. I tried three before I came to the one that worked. I unlocked the door and opened it. We found ourselves in the same ten-parking-space cul-de-sac we'd seen from the street.

Reba said, "Aha!"

We closed the first door and moved to the second. "Your turn," I said. "I'd go for the key marked number four."

"No sweat. I already know what's behind this one." She eased the key into the lock, turned it, and pushed the door open. We stood looking into a long windowless corridor. Flats of fluorescent lights affixed to the ceiling lent a bluish cast to the air. At regular intervals, oversize metal doors on either side of the hall opened into the shipping and receiving departments of the various shops along the mall, some of which fronted on Chapel Street and some on the mall's interior esplanade. Signs above the doors indicated the respective retailers: the luggage shop, a children's clothing store, an Italian pottery outlet, the jewelry store, and so on down the line.

I studied the layout. There was no sign of the two elevators I'd seen in the lobby above, but a solid wall of concrete suggested the bottom of the shaft that housed them. A short distance away, a mirror located in the upper right-hand corner was tilted to reveal the alcove, reflecting an image of the service elevator and the second elevator I'd noticed on the lobby level. I started to move forward, but Reba extended her arm, effectively blocking me like the gate at a railroad crossing. She put a finger to her lips and pointed up and to the right.

I spotted a corner-mounted security camera, its aperture focused squarely on the far end of the hall. There was a telephone attached to the wall, presumably to facilitate communication between the front desk and deliverymen. We backed up and eased the door shut. Even so, she dropped her voice to an almost inaudible murmur. "After you dropped me off last night, I picked up my car and came back so I could chat with Willie. He's nice, not as tight-assed as you'd think. Big chess buff. Plays duplicate bridge, and I swear to god, he bakes sourdough bread. Says he's had the same starter for nine years. Whole time we're yakking, I'm checking out the monitors—all ten of 'em—so I'll know what he sees. I was catching flashes of this view, but I didn't know where it was until we opened the door down here. Upstairs, he's got line of sight in both directions on all the hallways, but nothing in the elevators and nothing on the roof."

"What about Beck's offices?"

"Oh, please. Beck wouldn't put up with that Big Brother shit. He doesn't mind Willie spying on his tenants, but not on him."

"Seems like heavy security for a building this size."

"Interesting, isn't it? I thought so myself."

"So where'd the elevators disappear to?"

"The public elevators stop at lobby level. Clearly, Beck doesn't want anyone to have access to his offices from down here," she said. "One elevator does a short loop between the parking garage and the lobby. Anybody who needs to reach floors two, three, or four has to exit into the lobby and cross to the public elevators. That way, Willie can intercept them and quiz them. You better have a pretty good reason for being in the building or you're out of luck. If you need to take an elevator down this far, you have to have a key. There isn't any button you can push."

"But if the service elevator originates down here, can't someone hop on down here and bypass Willard altogether?" I asked. "I mean, even with the cameras rolling he can't be watching all ten monitors at once."

"In theory, you're right, but it'd be tricky. For one thing, all these passageways are kept locked—"

"Which didn't keep us out."

"And for another," she said, plowing right on, "there's a security code for every floor. You *could* risk the service elevator—assuming Willie didn't spot you in the corridor down here—but you couldn't get off unless you knew the code for the alarm panel on any given floor. Mess up the numbers and all hell breaks loose."

"Which means what to us, exactly?"

"Which means we better impose on Willie's good nature and retrieve your purse before the end of his shift."

21

We retraced our steps, emerging from the service corridor in the parking garage near Macy's. We crossed to the escalator and went up one level to the esplanade. When we reached the front entrance to the Beckwith Building, Reba pushed the door and discovered that it was locked. She cupped her hands to the plate glass. "Hey, Willie. Over here."

She tapped on the glass to get the security guard's attention. The minute he looked up, she gave him an enthusiastic wave and pantomimed his unlocking of the door. Willard shook her off, like a pitcher shaking off a sign. Reba motioned him over with an exaggerated rolling of her arm. He stared at her, unmoved, and she clasped her hands together earnestly as though in prayer. Reluctantly he left his perch at the desk and crossed to the door, where he said, "Building's closed!" from his side of the glass.

"Come onnn. Open up," she said.

He considered the request, his ambivalence clearly evident.

She put her mouth against the glass and made a big sucky kiss. She gave him the big eyes and produced the dimples for effect. "Please, please, please?"

He wasn't happy, but he did pick up the keys attached to the chain on his belt. He unlocked the door and opened it a cautious three inches. "What do you want? I can't be doing this unless you're one of the tenants."

"I know, but Kinsey left her bag upstairs and she needs her car keys and wallet."

Unimpressed, Willard flicked a look at me. "She can come back on Monday. Building opens at seven."

"How's she going to do that? Without her car keys, she can't even drive. I had to pick her up at her house and bring her over here myself. This is her *handbag,* Will. Do you know what it's like when a woman's separated from her purse? She's going berserk. She's a private detective. She has her *license* in there. Plus her address book, makeup, credit cards, checkbook, every nickel she owns. Even her birth control pills. She gets pregnant, the burden's on you, so get ready to raise a kid."

"Okay, okay. Tell me where it is and I'll bring it down to her."

"She doesn't *know* where it is. That's the *point.* All she knows is she had it when we went up with Marty last night. Now it's gone and that's the only place she went. It has to be there somewhere. Come on. Be a peach. It won't take five minutes and we'll be out of your hair."

"Can't. The alarm system's on."

"Marty gave me the code. Honest. He said it's fine with him as long as we cleared it with you first."

The long-suffering Willard opened the door and allowed us in. I thought he'd insist on coming upstairs with us, but he was serious about his monitoring duties and didn't want to leave his post. Reba and I took one of the two public elevators, which made the four-floor journey at an agonizingly slow pace.

"You sure you know the code?" I asked.

"I watched Marty do it. Same code we had before when I was working for Beck."

"How come he's such a nut about security and so careless about his codes? Sounds like anybody who ever worked for him could get in."

Reba waved the observation away. "We used to change 'em all the time—once a month—but with twenty-five employees, somebody was always messing up. The alarm would go off three and four times a week. The cops came out so many times, they started charging fifty bucks a pop."

The doors slid open and Reba hit the Stop Run button while she stepped out of the elevator. I leaned around and watched as she punched in the seven-digit code: 4-19-1949. "Beck's birthday," she said. "For a while he used Tracy's, but he was the one who kept forgetting that date so he switched to his own."

The status light on the keypad shifted from red to green. She left the elevator on Stop Run, awaiting our return. I followed her into the reception area.

The offices were dead quiet. There were numerous lights on, which oddly contributed to the overall feeling of abandonment. "Bart and Bret, the cleaning twins, were in last night. Check the vacuum cleaner tracks. We better hope whoever comes in here first thing Monday morning doesn't wonder about our footprints running up and down the halls."

"How do you know the vacuuming was done by Bart and Bret and not the guys with the cleaning cart?"

"I'm so glad you asked. Because I'll tell you why. They weren't real cleaning guys, which is something I figured out in the dead of night. Know what bugged me about them?" She paused for effect. "Wrong shoes. What guy mops the floors wearing four-hundred-dollar shiny Italian loafers?"

"You are Sherlock Holmes."

"You're damn straight. You grab your shoulder bag while I satisfy my curiosity. This shouldn't take long."

I made a beeline for the roof, heading down the corridor closest to the stairs. Given Beck's edict about clean surfaces, every desk I spotted en route looked as barren and untouched as an ad for office furniture. I took the steps two at a time and pushed through the big glass door that opened onto the roof. The morning sky was immense, the perfect shade of blue. I slowed and crossed to the parapet, drawn by a desire to see downtown Santa Teresa from this vantage point. The sun had warmed the air in the rooftop garden, coaxing fragrance from the flowering shrubs while a light breeze rustled through the foliage. In the distance, light spilled like pancake syrup across the mountain peaks. I leaned over and looked at the street, which was largely empty at this hour. I tilted my face to the light and took a deep breath before I righted myself and turned back to the task at hand. I retrieved my bag from behind the big potted ficus tree and went downstairs. Reba had been right about my birth control pills. I pulled out my packet and popped two like after-dinner mints.

When I got downstairs, she'd taken out a tape measure and was busy checking the length and breadth of the corridor, one foot on the metal ribbon while she extended the tape to the full. She released the button and I could hear the metal tape sing as she brought it zinging back to her hand. The tip-end whipped against her finger and dealt her a nasty blow. "Shit. Son of a bitch!" She sucked on her knuckle.

"You need a medic?"

"Look at that. I'm bleeding to death."

The nick on her index finger was a quarter of an inch long and she studied it with a frown. "Anyway, bet you dollars to donuts the friggin' room is right there. Press your ear to the wall and see if you can hear anything. Minute ago I heard a humming. Like machinery."

"Reba, that's the elevator shaft. You probably caught the sound of the service elevator going down."

"Not from this floor. We're the only ones up here."

"But we can't be the only people in the building. The elevator equipment is right above us. Of course you'd hear it."

"You think?"

"Let's try the obvious and check it out," I said.

She followed me around the corner where the service elevator was located. From the digital readout on the wall, we could track the car going down, the number changing from 1 to G.

"Told you," I said, and then glanced at my watch. "Shit. We better get out of here before Willard gets anxious and comes looking for us. I can't believe the nonsense you laid on him. Talk about maneuvering."

"I thought I did great . . . though that begging and pleading shit is only good for limited use. The next time we want in, I'll have to screw the guy for sure."

"You're making a joke, right?"

"Don't be such a prude. Screw one guy, you've screwed 'em all. You're only a virgin once, and after that, you might as well reap the benefits. Besides, I wouldn't mind. I think he's cute." Her gaze was raking the wall again and I could tell she was still speculating about the missing space. She said, "Maybe you get in by way of the roof. Through that little building that looks like a gardener's shack."

"Skip it. We don't have time. Let's get out of here."

"You're such a worrywart," she said, taking out Onni's key ring. "Just give me a second to return these, okay? I'm trying to be a good citizen."

"What about Beck's phony docs."

"Right. I got 'em right here," she said, patting her jacket pocket. She took the hem of her shirt and began cleaning fingerprints from the keys. "Wiping off the prints," she said. "In case they ever dust."

"Just get on with it."

She walked down the hall to Onni's office—not nearly fast enough for my taste—and disappeared from sight. I checked my watch again. We'd been up here twelve minutes. How long was it supposed to take us to find my shoulder bag? By now Willard would be out from behind his desk and on his way up. Reba took her time returning and when she finally appeared, hands shoved in her jacket pockets, instead of getting on the elevator as anticipated, she returned to the alcove where the service elevator was located and stood there staring at it.

"What are you *doing?*"

"I just figured it out. Hot damn." She reached out and pressed the button, calling the service elevator to the fourth floor. As we watched the digital readout, the elevator began its slow and dutiful climb. Eventually the doors opened. She reached in and pressed Stop Run, then entered the service elevator with me close behind her. The space was twice the width and half again as long as an ordinary elevator, apparently to accommodate moving boxes, file cabinets, and oversize office equipment. The walls were hung with quilted gray fabric like the blankets movers use to protect furniture.

Reba moved to the wall opposite the elevator doors and pulled the padding aside to reveal a second set of elevator doors. On a wall-mounted panel to the right of them, there was a nine-digit keypad. She studied it for a moment and then raised a tentative hand.

"You know the code?"

"Maybe. I'll tell you in a minute."

"Guess wrong and won't you set off the alarm?"

"Oh, come on. It's like a fairy tale—you get three tries before the thing goes berserk. If I blow it, we'll tell Willie we made a wee mistake."

"Just leave it for now. You're really pushing your luck."

She ignored me, of course. "I know it's not going to be his birth date—even Beck wouldn't be dumb enough to use that again. But it might be a variation. He's a narcissist. Everything he does relates to him."

"Reba . . ."

She flashed a look at me. "If you'd quit whining and help me out we can get on with it and be on our way. I can't pass this up. It may be the only chance we have."

I rolled my eyes, trying to control my panic, which was already accelerating. She wasn't going to budge until we figured it out or got caught. I said, "Shit. Try the same date backwards."

"Not bad. I like it. That'd be what?"

"9-4-9-1-9-1-4."

She thought about it briefly and then made a face. "Don't think so. Too tough for him to rattle the number off the top of his head. Let's try this . . ."

She punched in 1949-19-4.

No deal.

She punched in 19-4-1949.

I could feel my heart thud. "That's two."

"Would you get off it? I know it's two. I'm the one punching in numbers. Let's just think about it for a second. What's another possibility?"

"What about Onni's birthday?"

"Let's hope not. I know it's November 11, but I'm not sure what year. Anyway, Beck hasn't been boffing her long so he probably doesn't have a clue himself."

I said, "11-11 any year would be eight digits, not seven."

She pointed at me, apparently impressed with my ability to count.

"What's his wife's birthday?" I asked.

"3-17-1952. But he's blown that one so many times he's probably spooked by now. Besides, he prefers numbers with internal connections or sequences. Know what I mean? Repeats or patterns."

"I thought you said he used your birthday at one point."

"True. That'd be 5-15-1955."

"Hey, mine's 5-5-1950," I chirped, sounding like a lunatic.

"Great. We'll do a joint celebration when the dates roll around next year. So what should I try? His birth date backwards or mine straight ahead?"

"Well, his birth date backwards has an internal logic if you group the numbers. 949-191-4. Would he break it down that way?"

"Might."

"Just do one or the other before I have a heart attack."

She punched in 5-15-1955. A moment of silence and then the doors slid open. "My birthday. Sweet. You think he still cares?"

I pushed the Stop Run button and watched her wipe her prints off the keypad, taking care not to trigger the alarm. "Wouldn't want anyone to know we were here," she said, happily.

Meanwhile, I was staring straight ahead. The room was probably six feet by eight—not much bigger than a closet. The cleaning cart we'd seen was shoved up against the left wall. A U-shaped counter took up much of the remaining floor space. I looked up. The room seemed to be well ventilated, the walls heavily padded. A smoke detector and a heat detector had been installed in the shadowy upper reaches of the ceiling, where I could see sprinkler heads as well. Rungs embedded in the wall formed a ladder that went straight up. Around the perimeter of the ceiling, I could see rectangles of daylight roughly corresponding to the vents in the fake gardener's cottage on the roof. Reba was right. In a pinch, you could probably gain entry to the room from the roof. Or escape that way.

There were three currency-counting machines on one arm of the counter and four currency-bundling machines on the adjacent counter. Open suitcases were lined up on the third section, packed with tightly wrapped bundles of hundred-dollar bills. Under the counter, ten cardboard cartons were lined up, their top flaps open, packed with additional bundles of hundreds, fifties, and twenties in U.S. currency. Each bundle was shrink-wrapped, with paper adding-machine tape circling packets of five. There were two styrofoam coffee cups visible and a pile of empty cups in a wastebasket, which also contained wads of discarded plastic wrappers. Several silver-dollar-size plastic disks with small blades were being used to slit the wrappers.

Reba said, "Geez. I've never seen so much money."

"Me neither. It looks like they're pulling bundles from these boxes, removing the wrappers, running the bills through the currency counter, and then rewrapping them for transport."

She advanced a few steps and checked the total on one of the currency counters. "Take a peek at this puppy. They've run a million bucks through this." She picked up a bundle and weighed it in her hand. "Wonder how much this is. Wouldn't you love to know?" She sniffed it. "You'd think it would smell good, but it doesn't smell like anything."

"Would you keep your hands to yourself?"

"I'm just looking. I'm not *doing* anything. How much do you figure is in one of these, twenty grand? Fifty?"

"I have no idea. Don't mess with that. I'm serious."

"Aren't you curious what it feels like? It doesn't weigh all that much," she said. She wiped her prints from the wrapper and put the bundle back, surveying the space. "How many guys you think work here besides the two we saw?"

"There's not room for three. They probably come in weekends when the activity's less conspicuous," I said. I reached out and put my hand on one of the styrofoam cups and nearly moaned in fear. "This is still warm. Suppose they come back?"

"No one can get to us. The elevator's on hold."

"But if they find the elevator on hold, won't they know something's wrong? We have to get out of here. I'm begging you."

"Okay, okay. But I knew I was right about the room. This is incredible, isn't it?"

"Absolutely. Who gives a shit? Let's go."

I backed out of the room and into the service elevator. The other set of doors was still open and I stuck my head out into the corridor to assure myself that no one had entered the premises while we were in the room. Reba was having trouble dragging herself away. I said, "Reba, come on!" sounding every bit as tense and impatient as I felt.

She moved into the elevator as though mesmerized and entered the seven-digit code. The doors on that side of the elevator slid closed. She replaced the wall padding and adjusted the quilted matting to conceal the second set of doors.

"What took you so long?"

"It's all so beautiful. Can you imagine having even half the bundles in there? You'd never have to lift another finger as long as you lived."

"No problem. Your life wouldn't last that long."

We exited through the elevator doors that opened into Beck's offices and Reba released the Stop Run button. We waited until the service elevator doors closed, and then went around the corner and got back on the public elevator.

She released the hold button, the doors closed, and we began our leisurely descent. I was nearly sick with anxiety, but she didn't seem affected. The woman had nerves of steel.

When we reached the lobby level and stepped off, Willard looked up from his desk with a smile. "You find it?"

I held up my shoulder bag to show our mission had been accomplished. My hands were shaking so badly I thought he'd spot the trembling from across the lobby. I was doing what I could to maintain a semblance of normality until we could ease out the front door and be on our way.

Reba, true to form, made a point of crossing to his desk, where she stretched up on tiptoe and rested her arms on the counter, holding her injured finger close to his face. "You got a first-aid kit? Look at this. I about crippled myself."

Willard peered at her knuckle, inspecting the wound that was no bigger than a hyphen. "How'd you do that?"

"I must have snagged it on something. Sucker hurts. You can kiss it and make it better if you want."

He shook his head, smiling indulgently, and started opening his desk drawers. While he rummaged around in search of a Band-Aid, I noticed Reba's gaze flicking across the monitors, taking in all ten views.

Willard held up a bandage. "Think you can manage this yourself?"

"Don't be mean. After all I've done for you?" She held out her finger and he pulled the red thread that opened the paper packaging. He removed the Band-Aid and applied it.

She said, "Thanks. You're a doll. I'll recommend a raise." She made a kissing noise at him as we headed for the door.

Behind us, Willard left his perch and followed, taking out his jumble of keys so he could unlock the front door. "Don't you be coming back. This is the last of it."

"I won't, but you'll miss me," she said as we scooted through the door.

"I doubt that," he said, and Reba blew him another kiss. I thought she was laying it on a bit thick, but Willard didn't seem to mind. He turned the keys in the lock and we were safe.

22

Reba slowed her BMW to a stop in front of my apartment. As I got out and shut the car door behind me, I saw that Cheney's little red Mercedes was parked at the curb. I felt a surge of anxiety. I'd intended to fill him in on my adventures with Reba over the past couple of days, but Jonah's call had intervened and he'd gone off to the shooting scene without my having spoken a word. The omission made me uneasy, as though I were deliberately holding out on him. Even referring to our activities as "adventures" sounded like an attempt to minimize the fact that what we'd done could jeopardize the investigation. Last night's incursion into Beck's offices had been risky enough. In a pinch, an argument could be made that Marty had invited us to tour the premises, but his offer hadn't extended to our rifling through desk drawers and stealing Onni's keys. He'd certainly never given us permission to return in his absence and enjoy the run of the place. I wanted to tell Cheney about the bundles of cash being counted, repackaged, and packed into suitcases, but I knew the discovery encompassed a little matter of criminal trespass, which tainted the knowledge. Nonetheless, I needed to unload before my withholding the information became an issue in itself.

I went through the gate and around the side of my studio, as burdened with guilt as though I'd slept with another man. I could make excuses for my conduct, but I was accountable all the same. Cheney was sitting on my front step, still in the clothes he'd been wearing the night before. He smiled when he saw me, looking exhausted, but good. Confessing was bound to impact our relationship. I dreaded the consequences, but I had to speak up.

I sat down on the step and slipped my hand into his. "How'd it go? You look beat."

"Big mess. Two gangbangers dead. Hooker got caught in the crossfire and she's dead, too. Jonah sent me home to shower and change clothes. I'm due back at one. How's by you?"

"Not that good. We need to talk."

He focused on my face, his eyes searching. "Can it wait?"

"I don't think so. This is about Reba. We've got a problem."

"Meaning what?"

"You're not going to like this."

"Just spit it out," he said.

"She and I connected up for dinner last night. She wanted to introduce me to Marty Blumberg, Beck's company comptroller, and I couldn't see the harm. He has dinner at Dale's every Friday night so that's where we went. He comes in and the three of us are schmoozing away. Next thing I know, she tells him how the feds are mounting a case against Beck and he—Marty—is going to end up taking the blame if he doesn't do something quick. I had no idea what she thought she was doing, but there it was."

Cheney closed his eyes and hung his head. "Geez. I don't believe it. What the hell's wrong with her?"

"It gets worse. She tells him Onni's a federal agent and she's screwing Beck's brains out as a way of getting the goods on him. At first, Marty resists. He really doesn't want to believe it, but Reba shows him the photos and reels him in. Then she gets us invited up to the offices—ostensibly for a tour—but she uses the opportunity to scour the place for anything she can lay her hands on, which turns out to be Onni's keys."

I continued the rundown, giving him an unvarnished account of what had happened over the course of the past two days. I could tell he was getting pissed before I was even halfway through. He was tired. He'd had a long night and this was the last thing he needed. At the same time, I felt compelled to tell him the truth. Either I revealed the whole of it—of myself—or what was the point?

I moved on to events of the morning and when I'd finished, Cheney blew. "You gotta be out of your head! Aside from the issue of unlawful entry, if Beck gets wind of it, he'll know something's off and that's the end of it for us."

"How's he going to find out?"

"Suppose Marty spills the beans or the security guy has second thoughts about letting you in. He knows both of you by name. All it'd take is one offhand remark from either of those guys. Doesn't matter how solid the government's case is, defense attorney puts you on the stand and he'll take you apart. Not that he'll have the chance. Long before it comes to that, the feds will slap you with charges of obstruction of justice, tampering with evidence, and god knows what else. Perjury for sure the minute you try to cover your ass. Reba's got no credibility. Convicted felon, woman scorned. Anything she says is automatically suspect."

"Then why'd you bring her into it? If she's so useless, why recruit her in the first place?"

"Because we needed a confidential informant, not a friggin' one-man posse. You're a pro. You know better—or I assumed you did. The feds play for keeps. Compromise an operation like this and you're the one who pays. What's it to her? She's got nothing to lose."

"Cheney, I hear you. I know I should have stopped her,

but I couldn't see a way to do it. Once she told Marty what was going down, events just started to escalate—"

"Bullshit. You were a willing participant. What you did was illegal—"

"Got it. I know. I'm aware of it," I said. "On the other hand, how could I walk away? She's in this because of us—because of me to be specific. I feel *some* responsibility for what's happening to her."

"Well, you better start taking responsibility for your own behavior. If this sting goes down the shitter, you'll be in more trouble than you can shake a stick at."

"Wait a minute. Wait. I don't mean to sound defensive, but I got backed into this. When the deal first came up, I told you I didn't want to do it, but you talked me into it, smutty photographs and all. Fade out, fade in. I'm sitting there at Dale's and she opens her mouth and blows the deal wide open. What was I supposed to do? If I'd gotten up and left, there was no way of guessing what the hell she'd do next. Believe it or not, I was trying for damage control. I'll admit the situation snowballed—"

"Just do me a favor and stay the hell away from her, okay? She calls you, hang up and leave the rest of it to us. I'll get Vince on the horn and bring him up to speed. We'll see what he can salvage, if anything."

"I'm sorry. I didn't mean to screw things up."

"Well, you can't do anything about it now. What's done is done. Just keep your distance from Reba. Promise."

I held a hand up like I was taking an oath.

"I'll call you later," he said brusquely. He got up and headed around the corner to his car. I heard him fire up his engine and peel away from the curb with a chirp of rubber on pavement. I could feel my face burning for an hour afterward.

I locked myself in my apartment and tidied my underwear drawer. I needed to do something small and useful. I had to get a handle on life in a risk-free arena where I could feel competent again. Maybe folding underpants didn't amount to much, but it was the best I could do. I moved on to the chest of drawers and refolded my shirts. Then I tackled the junk drawer downstairs. I hated the idea of being prosecuted. Obstruction of justice was serious damn shit. I pictured myself in jail garb, legs shackled, hands manacled in front, doing the traditional inmate two-step while shuffling to and from court. That began to seem a bit melodramatic and I decided there was no point in going overboard on the self-flagellation. So I'd goofed. Big deal. I hadn't *killed* anyone.

After an hour, I became aware of voices outside my door, one being Henry's. I glanced out the kitchen window, but the angle was too extreme for me to see who else was there. I went to the front door, popped the locks, and opened it a crack. Henry, Lewis, and William were standing together in the driveway. Lewis and William were both in three-piece suits while Henry wore his usual shorts, T-shirt, and flip-flops. He'd backed the station wagon out of the garage and Lewis was loading his bags in the rear. As I looked on, I heard a soft ping, and William removed his pocket watch from his vest and checked the time. He took out a small packet of trail mix and made a production of opening the sealed cellophane, which generated copious crackling noises. Henry flicked him a look of annoyance but continued the conversation with Lewis, which seemed to be about nothing in particular. I eased the door shut, gratified that one conflict had been peacefully resolved, or so I hoped. The truth about strong emotion is that it's difficult to sustain. Despite how victimized we feel, it's hard work hanging on to anger, even when it's tinged with righteousness. Holding a grudge against someone is (sometimes) more trouble than it's worth.

Reba called at 2:00. As I'm constitutionally unable to resist a ringing phone, I was on the verge of snatching up the handset. I hesitated, curbing the impulse, and let the machine pick up. She said, "Oh, poo. I was hoping you'd be there. I just had this big ol' stinkin' fight with Lucinda and I'm dying to tell you about it. I practically threw her out on her ass only not really, but you know, figuratively speaking. Anyway, call me when you can and I'll fill you in. Also, there's something else we need to talk about. Bye-bye."

She called again at 3:36. "Hey, Kinsey, me again. Don't you check messages these days? I'm going stir-crazy up here. We really need to talk so give me a buzz when you get in, okay? Otherwise, I can't be responsible for what I do. Ha ha ha. That's a joke . . . sort of."

At 5:30, she left only her name with a request that I call.

I went into the office Monday morning and buried myself in the work I'd neglected the previous week. I'd read about the parking-lot shootout in the morning paper, and I knew the STPD vice and homicide detectives were working with the gang detail, interviewing witnesses and running down leads. The Santa Teresa gang population tends to be stable, their activities carefully monitored. Periodically, however, gang members from Olvidado, Perdido, and Los Angeles will swing through town, especially on holiday weekends when the homeboys, like everyone else, are hoping for a change of scene. Happily police officers from those communities make the same swing through town so that unbeknownst to the gangbangers, they're still under the watchful eye of the law.

I didn't hear from Reba again until late Monday afternoon, after I arrived home from work. Mercifully she hadn't called the office, where good business practice dictates that I answer the phone. She'd called my apartment twice, leaving a message at noon and then another one at 2:00. She sounded cheerful at the outset but increasingly plaintive as the day wore on. "Kinsey? Yoo hoo! Did you tell me you were going out of town or something? Don't think so, but I really can't remember for sure. I'm sorry to be such a pest, but Beck's back in town and I'm antsy as hell. I really don't know how much longer I can hold out. I'm on my way to Holloway's to pee in a jar and shoot the shit with her. Then I'm supposed to go to an AA meeting, but I'm thinking I might skip. Too depressing, you know? Anyway, call me when you get this. Hope everything's okay. Bye."

It was hard to leave her hanging when I'd been so available to her the week before. I felt like a mother cow separated from her calf—I could hear Reba's bleating cries, but I wasn't free to respond. I'd been serious when I promised Cheney I'd keep my distance, at least until the situation was under control. Once she'd talked to Vince and his pals, I could reassess. By then, of course, she might well have severed our relationship.

In the meantime, I heard nothing from Cheney, a silence I ascribed to his being up to his ears in work. To avoid the silence, I left the apartment and headed over to see Henry. I tapped on the frame and he motioned me in. He had his heavy-duty mixer on the counter, a ten-pound sack of bread flour, yeast packets, sugar, salt, and water at the ready.

"Can you put up with company?"

He smiled. "If you can put up with the racket my mixer makes. I'm about to throw together a batch of bread, which I'll let rise overnight and bake first thing tomorrow morning. Grab a stool."

I watched him measure ingredients, which he dumped in the big stainless-steel mixing bowl. Once he turned on the machine, we put our conversation on hold until he was done. We chatted while I watched him remove the sticky mass of dough, kneading and adding flour until the whole of it was smooth and elastic. He oiled a big wash pan, turned the dough in it until its surface glistened, and then covered it with a towel. He put the pan in the oven where the pilot light would generate the warmth necessary for the bread to rise.

"How much are you making?" I asked, looking at the quantity of dough.

"Four big loaves and two batches of dinner rolls, all for Rosie," he said. "I may do up a pan of sticky buns if you're interested."

"Always. I take it Lewis went home?"

"I dropped him at the airport Saturday. And speaking of him, he did apologize for butting in, which may be a first. I guess it never occurred to him that his flying out would have that effect. I told him there was no point worrying. What's done is done."

"Someone said the same thing to me yesterday under different circumstances," I said. "At any rate, I'm glad the two of you are back on solid ground."

"Never any doubt of that," he said. "What about you? I didn't see much of you this weekend. How's your new fellow?"

"Good question," I said. I told Henry the sorry saga of my bad behavior, risks taken, laws broken, gains, losses, and tension-filled escapes. He enjoyed the tale a lot more than Cheney had and for that I was grateful.

A little after six, I returned to my place and fixed myself a hot hard-boiled-egg sandwich, with more mayo and salt than your internist would recommend. I was wadding up my paper towel when the phone rang. I tossed the wad and waited until the caller began to speak. Marty Blumberg identified himself and I picked up. "Hey, Marty. It's me. I just now walked in."

"I hope you don't mind me calling you at home. Something weird's come up and I'd be curious what you think."

"Sure." I picked up traffic noises in the background and pictured him calling from a pay phone.

"You want the long version or the short?"

"Long stories are always better."

"Right," he said. "So here's how this goes." I could hear that momentary lull as he inhaled and released a mouthful of smoke. "I get home from work today and my house-keeper's wringing her hands. She's upset about something, but won't say what. I press because I can tell she needs to unburden herself. She says, don't get mad. I say, fine. She tells me she arrived at the house at nine, like always, and she sees this phone company truck parked in the drive and a couple of guys on the porch. She goes ahead and lets herself in the back and then answers the front door. This one guy says the phone company's received a number of calls complaining the service is out and they're going through the neighborhood checking all the lines. They want to know is my phone working, so she asks 'em to wait, tries the line, and sure enough it's dead. Well, she's paranoid—comes from watching way too many cop shows on TV—so she asks 'em to show some ID. Both have these pinch-on plastic picture dealies that say California Bell. Huerta writes down their names and employee numbers. Second guy has a clipboard and he shows her the work order, typed up as neat as you please. She figures it's legit so she lets 'em in. You with me so far?"

"Yes, but I don't like the sound of it."

"Me neither," he said. "She's telling me this shit and I can feel the rocks piling up in my gut. The guys are in my study fifteen, twenty minutes, and then they come out and tell her everything's hunky-dory. She asks what it was and they say the roof rats must've chewed through the outside wires, but now all's well. Afterwards, she's thinking none of this makes sense and she's worried she did wrong. I act like no big deal and tell her I'll handle it from here. So what I'm thinking is somebody's either bugged my house or put a tap on my phone."

"Or both," I supplied.

"Shit, yes. Why else would I be calling from a fuckin' minimart parking lot? I feel like an idiot, but I can't take the chance. My phone's tapped; I don't want whoever's doing it to realize I figured it out. That way I can feed 'em any bullshit I want. You think it's the feds?" I could hear him take another puff on his cigarette.

"I have no clue, but I think you're right to worry."

"How can they do that? I mean, assuming they planted a bug, or, like, a listening device, wouldn't that be illegal?"

"Without a court order, sure."

"Trouble is, if it's not them, it might be someone a whole lot worse."

"Like who?" I was thinking Salustio Castillo, but wanted to hear him say it.

"Never mind who. Either way, I don't like it. Friday night, when Reba laid out that shit about Beck, I figured she was yanking my chain. More I think about it, the more I'm thinkin' maybe she was telling the truth. Beck always made a point of keeping me in the thick of it. Like she says, could be he's setting me up."

"Who else is in on it?"

"On what?"

"The money laundering."

"Who says anyone? I never said that."

"Oh come on, Marty. You can't launder that much money without help."

"I'm not a snitch," he said, his tone indignant.

"But other people are involved, right?"

"I don't know, maybe. A few, but you're never going to get me to name names."

"Fair enough. So what's in it for you?"

"Same as everyone else. We're paid to keep our mouths shut. We help Beck now and he'll see that we're set up for life."

"Life in a federal pen. That'll be a treat," I said.

Marty ignored that, saying, "Truth is, I got plenty and I'd skedaddle right now if I could figure out how. If Customs is in on the deal, I can't leave the country without getting my ass nailed. They flag my name in the computer, minute I check in for my flight, boom, I'm done for."

"I'm telling you, you better throw in your lot with the guys who count. Beck isn't looking after you. He's got himself to protect."

"Yeah, I'm getting that. I mean, sure he may need us, but how far is he willing to go? Beck's about Beck. Comes right down to it, he'd throw us to the wolves."

"Probably so." I nearly confided the rumor I'd heard, that Beck was on the move and likely to disappear within the next few days, but the likelihood hadn't been confirmed and the information wasn't mine to pass on. "Of course, it's always possible the phone company story is on the up and up . . ."

"Nuh-uhn. Don't think so."

"Well, I'm sorry I can't help."

"What about Reba? I've been trying to reach her all day."

"Probably at the house. She had a meeting with her parole officer earlier so you might try her again."

"You talk to her, tell her to give me a call. This is making my stomach hurt. I'm anxious as hell."

"Look, let me talk to a friend of mine and see what I can find out."

"I'd appreciate that. You call back, you be careful what you say. Meantime, you hear from Reba, tell her the two of us gotta talk. I don't like workin' with a noose around my neck."

"Hang in there," I said, and then winced at my choice of words.

Once he disconnected, I dialed both Cheney's home and work numbers and left messages. I tried his pager, punching in my home number in hopes he'd call back. Marty was moving into panic mode, which made him as unpredictable as Reba, though more vulnerable.

I spent the evening stretched out on the couch, book propped in front of me pretending to read while I waited for Cheney's call. I wondered where he was and whether he was still pissed off at me. I needed to talk to him about Marty, but more than that, I craved the physical contact. My body was remembering his with a low-level yearning disruptive to concentration. Before he arrived on the scene, I'd lived in a dead zone—not exactly buzzing with joy, but certainly not discontent. Now I felt like a pup just coming into heat.

One of the problems with being celibate is that once sexual feelings resurface, they're almost impossible to repress. I found myself remembering what had happened between us and fantasizing about what might come next. Cheney had a laziness about him, a natural tempo half the speed of mine. I was beginning to see that operating in high gear was a means of protecting myself. Living at an accelerated pace allowed me to feel only half as much because there wasn't time to feel more. I made love the same way I ate—eager to satisfy the immediate hunger without acknowledging the deeper desire, which was to feel connected at the core. Avoiding the truth was easier if I was on the run. With quick sex, as with fast food, there was no savoring the moment. There was only the headlong rush to be done with it and move on.

At 10:00, when the phone rang, I knew it was him. I turned my head, listening until the machine began recording the sound of his voice. I reached over and picked up, saying, "Hey."

"Hey, yourself. You called."

"Hours ago. I thought you were ignoring me. Are you still mad?"

"About what?"

"Good."

"How about you? Are you pissed off?"

"Not my nature," I said. "Not with you at any rate. Listen, we need to talk about Marty. Where are you?"

"Rosie's. Come join me."

"You trust me to walk half a block by myself? It's pitchy dark outside."

"I was going to meet you halfway."

"Why don't you go the whole distance and meet me here."

"We can do that later. For now, I think we should sit and stare into each other's eyes while I put a hand up your skirt."

"Give me five minutes. I'll step out of my underwear."

"Make it three. I've missed you."

"I've missed you, too."

By the time I locked the door behind me and reached the front gate, he was waiting on the other side of Henry's wrought-iron fence. The sidewalk on his side was one step lower than the walk on mine, which made me feel tall. The night air was chill and the dark settled over us like a veil. I slid my arms around his neck. He tilted his head and ran his mouth down along my throat and across my collarbone. The fence pales were cold, blunt-tipped spears that pressed against my ribs. He rubbed his hands up and down my arms. "You're cold. You should have a jacket on."

"Don't need one. I have you."

"That you do," he said, smiling. He eased a hand between the fence pales, ran his fingers under my skirt and up between my legs. I heard him catch his breath and then he made a sound low in his throat.

"Told you."

"I thought it was a metaphor."

"What do either of us know about metaphors?" I said, laying my face against his hair.

"I know this."

My turn to hum. "We should go to Rosie's," I whispered.

"We should go in and lie down before impaling ourselves on this fence."

At midnight we made grilled cheese sandwiches—the only instance in life when Velveeta isn't such a terrible idea. I found myself sidetracked by the crust, which was crisp, fully saturated with butter. Still munching, I said, "Hate to ask, but what'd Vince say when you told him about Reba and me?"

"He stuck his fingers in his ears and hummed. Actually, he loved the information about the counting room. Said he'd put a note in the file and attribute the tip to an anonymous call. He's scheduling the meeting with Reba for Thursday."

"Can't he make it any sooner than that? He's the one telling us Beck's about to take off. Reba's worried she'll run into him."

"I can mention it to Vince, but I wouldn't hold out much hope. That's the downside of an operation like this, it's unwieldy as hell. All she has to do is lay low."

"You give her the news. I'm not allowed to talk to her."

"That's right. Because I'm looking after you."

"What about Marty? He's the one you ought to be worried about. He's really feeling the squeeze, convinced his phone's tapped or he's got a bug planted in his house."

"Could well be. Tell him to give us a call and we can talk about a deal."

"He's not ready for that. He's still looking for a way out of the bind he's in."

"What do these guys think? They're so smart they're never going to get caught?"

"They haven't been caught so far."

23

Tuesday morning passed in a great big boring blur. Given the egocentric nature of the world, I imagined that since nothing in particular was happening to me, there was nothing in particular happening to anyone else. In truth, events were transpiring that I would hear about only when it was too late to alter either cause or effect. My phone rang at 11:00—Cheney asking me to sit tight for the next half-hour as there was something he wanted me to hear. "You have a tape recorder?" he asked.

"An old one, but it takes a regular-size cassette."

"That'll do."

Fifteen minutes later he walked in the door. While I was waiting for him, I searched through my closet until I found the tape recorder. I opened a fresh package of AA batteries and by the time Cheney arrived, the tape recorder was set up and ready to go. "What is it?"

He slipped the cassette in the machine. "Something the FBI picked up this morning. Some of it sounds garbled, but

the techs have taken it as far as they can." He pressed the
Play button, triggering a generalized hissing and the ringing of a phone. A man on the other end picked up without
identifying himself. "Yes?"

The calling party said, "Problem."

The minute I heard the voice, I shot a look at Cheney.
"Beck?"

He pressed the Pause button. "The guy he's talking to is
Salustio Castillo. This was the first call he placed when he
got to the office." He pressed Play again.

On the tape, Castillo was saying, "What?"

"When I took delivery on that shipment, the inventory
was off."

Silence. Hissing. "Impossible. 'Off' meaning what?"

"Short."

"By how much?"

"A pack."

"Large or small?"

"Large. We're talking twenty-five."

Salustio was silent. "I supervised the count myself.
What about the invoices?"

"Not a match. I checked three times and the numbers
don't tally."

Salustio said, "I told you I wanted someone supervising
your end—"

"This wasn't on my end."

"Or so you say."

Silence from Beck. "You know I wouldn't do this."

"Do I? You've argued for a bigger cut of the action,
which I can't . . . there's no way I can justify from my end.
Now you say . . . missing, all I have is your word."

"You think I'd lie?"

"Let's call it inventory shrinkage. It's been known to happen. From my perspective, you're adequately compen-
sated . . . don't see it that way. So maybe you siphon off a
percentage of the goods and that satisfies your need for a pay
increase. What better cover than claiming I shorted you?"

"I never said that."

"Then what?"

"I said the total's off. Might be the . . . mistake . . ."

"Yours. Not mine."

". . ."

"Fix it."

Silence. There was a stretch of pure hissing on the tape.

Tightly Beck said, "Tell me what you want me to do and I'll do it."

"Make up the shortfall out of your end, which is where the loss occurred. My total's correct and I want full payment deposited to my account. In the meantime, not to worry. I know you're good for it. Pleasure doing business," Salustio said, and clicked off.

Beck said, "Fuck!" as he banged down the phone.

Cheney turned off the tape.

I thought the conversation was interesting, but I wasn't clear why he wanted me to hear it. I was on the verge of making a comment when Cheney said, "A tightly packed bundle of hundred-dollar bills is one inch thick," he said. "That's twenty-five thousand dollars. I know because I asked the Treasury boys. Beck's been back a day. If a currency delivery came in while he was gone, it makes sense he'd double-check the totals first thing."

"Okay," I said. And then I shut my mouth because I could hear the penny drop. He knew Reba and I had ventured into the counting room on Saturday when the currency was being unwrapped and run through the machines. All either of us had to do was clip a pack of hundreds and who'd be the wiser? Beck didn't know we'd been there and all Salustio cared about was having the right total credited to his account. "You think she took it?"

"Sure. Vince was apoplectic. I thought he'd pop a vein. Beck doesn't know she was up there, but he'll rip the place apart looking for that dough. Once he pulls the security tapes, he's got her. You, too, for that matter."

"She has to be nuts. Why take the risk?"

"Because Beck can't report the loss. He calls the cops and he'll generate the kind of scrutiny he can't afford. Not when he's on the verge of skipping out."

I could feel myself flush, overtaken by alternating surges of denial and guilt. I suddenly understood what she'd been doing in the counting room for those few beats after I'd entered the elevator. I'd felt anxious, impatient to be gone while she'd been smitten with the sight of all that cash. Meanwhile, I was preoccupied, intent on checking the corridor to make sure we were in the clear. It wouldn't have taken any time—two seconds?—to stuff a packet of cash down her shirt or in her jacket pocket. I'd been thinking "nerves of steel," amazed at her nonchalance while I was wetting my drawers. Then, of course, there was her exuberance with Willard once we got downstairs. She'd flirted and I'd assumed she was hyper because we'd discovered Beck's counting room. Must have been the feel of all that money next to her skin. Crazy. Reba wiping down her fingerprints. Cheney verbally boxing my ears when I'd confessed our misdeeds. And I'd defended her. Shit! My palms were damp and I rubbed them against my jeans. "What now?"

"Vince wants her in as soon as possible. The meeting with the IRS and Customs has been moved up to tomorrow afternoon at four in the FBI offices. Vince wants to talk to her first, like at one o'clock, and see if he can iron this out. Otherwise, the shit's really going to hit the fan."

"Can't he help her?"

"Sure, if she's willing to put herself in his hands."

"Fat chance. She's never even met the man."

"Why don't you talk to her?"

"If you think it'd do any good. I've been ducking her for days, but I can give it a try."

"Do that. Worst-case scenario, he'll put her in a safe house until he can figure out what's what."

Cheney checked his watch, popped the Eject button on the tape recorder, and removed the tape. "I gotta get this back. You have Vince's number?"

"You better give it to me again."

He snagged a pen and a scratch pad and made a note, tearing off the top sheet, which he handed to me. "Let me know what she says. If you can't reach me, you can talk directly to him."

"Will do."

After he left, I sat at my desk, trying to figure out what to say to Reba. There was really no point in pussyfooting around. She'd dug herself a hole and the sooner she climbed out of it, the better off she'd be. As long as Beck got the money back, he might not inquire too closely how it had disappeared. I picked up the handset and punched in the number for the Lafferty estate. I went through a preliminary round of conversation with the housekeeper, Freddy, who told me Reba was still in bed. "Shall I wake her?"

"I think you better."

"One moment. I'll put you on hold and have her take the call in her room."

"Great. Thanks."

I pictured Freddy in her crepe-soled shoes, padding down the hall and up the stairs, holding on to the rail. The silence went on for a bit, but I imagined her knocking on Reba's door and then a groggy interval before she picked up, which was sure enough how she sounded when she came on the line. "'Lo?"

"Hi, Reeb. It's Kinsey. I'm sorry to wake you."

"That's okay. I should probably be getting up anyway. What d'you want?"

"I need to ask you about something and you have to swear to tell the truth."

"Sure." She was already sounding more alert, so I thought she had a fair idea what was coming.

"Remember when we were together Saturday morning on that little voyage of discovery?"

Silence.

"Did you lift a packet of hundred-dollar bills?"

Silence.

"Never mind admitting it. The point is, Beck knows."

"So what? Serves him right. It's like I told him at Bubbles, he owes me, big time."

"Only one tiny problem. The money wasn't his. It was Salustio's."

"No."

"Yes."

"Shit. Are you sure? I thought it was Beck's, like he was packing it to take with him when he left."

"Nuhn-uhn. He was verifying Salustio's total before making a deposit to his account. Now he's twenty-five grand short."

I could hear her lighting a cigarette. I said, "What made you think you could get away with it?"

"It was a *whim*, like an impulse. Haven't you ever done anything like that? Spur of the moment. I just did it, that's all."

"Well, you better put it back before Beck figures it out."

"How'm I supposed to do that?"

"How would I know? Stick it in an envelope and leave it at Willard's desk. He can pass it on to Marty or take it up himself—"

"But why do I have to do anything? Beck can't prove it, can he? I mean, how can he prove it when I didn't leave fingerprints?"

"For one thing, he's got security tapes that show you going in and out of the building. Beyond that, he doesn't have to prove a thing. All he has to do is tell Salustio and you're screwed."

"He wouldn't do that to me, would he? I mean, I know he's a shit, but he wouldn't tell Salustio. You think?"

"Of course he would! Salustio expects him to cough up the missing twenty-five grand."

"Shit. Shit, shit, shit."

"Look, Reeb. I'll say this again. Vince Turner can probably help if you'll turn around and help him."

"What good does that do me with Salustio?"

"Maybe Vince can put you somewhere safe until it's all ironed out."

"Oh, man. This is bad. You think I should call Beck?"

"You'd be smarter to keep away from him and talk to Vince instead. He wants to see you anyway before you meet with the feds."

"What feds? I don't have a meeting with the feds. The guy dropped the ball."

"He did not. The meeting's been changed to tomorrow afternoon at four. I'll pick you up at twelve-thirty and you can spend a couple of hours with him first."

"About bloody time."

"I told you it would take time."

"Yeah, well, it's too late *now*."

"Meaning what?"

"Meaning, I gotta think how to handle this. I'll call you back." The line went dead.

So much for my powers of persuasion.

That night, Cheney was busy with softball practice, so I was on my own. I had dinner at Rosie's, after which I retired to my apartment and spent the evening with a book.

Twelve-fifteen on Wednesday, I headed south on the 101, relieved to be in motion again. Once I delivered Reba to Vince's office, he could take charge of her and I'd be off the hook. The drive up Bella Sera was exactly as it had been on prior occasions, right down to the scent of bay laurel and the smell of dry grass. It had been thirteen days since I'd taken this route on my way to meet Nord Lafferty, wondering what he could possibly want with me. Escort his daughter home from prison. How complicated was that? In the days since we'd returned, her life had slowly come unraveled. The crazy part was that I liked her. Despite the differences between us, I responded to her out of the outrageous elements in my own nature. Watching her operate was like seeing a distorted version of myself, only larger than life and much more dangerous.

When I reached the property, the gates were standing

open. As I rounded the bend in the drive, I saw the same Lincoln Continental and Mercedes sedan. Now a third vehicle sat beside the other two—this one a Jaguar convertible, a handsome dark green with a caramel interior that looked good enough to eat. I parked, leaving my car unlocked as I moved up the walk to the house. Reba's massive long-haired orange cat, Rags, sauntered out to greet me, looking at me with startling blue eyes. I extended my hand and he sniffed at my fingers. He allowed me to scratch his head, nudging me repeatedly to keep the action afloat.

I rang the bell and waited while he circled my legs, leaving long orange hairs on the legs of my jeans. From inside, I heard the muffled tap of high heels on hard marble tile. The door was opened by a woman I immediately pegged as the legendary Lucinda. She appeared to be in her midforties, thanks to the work of a first-rate plastic surgeon. I knew this because her neck and hands were fifteen years older than her face. Her hair was short, streaked with varying shades of blond as though bleached by the sun. She was slim and beautifully dressed in a designer outfit I recognized, though I'd forgotten the name. The two-piece black knit was banded in white and the jacket had brass buttons running down the front. The knee-length skirt revealed a knotty set of calves. "Yes?"

"I'm Kinsey Millhone. Could you tell Reba I'm here?"

She studied me carefully with eyes as dark as tar. "She's not home. Is this something I can help you with?"

"Ah, no. Don't think so. I'll just wait for her."

"You must be the private investigator Nord's spoken of. I'm Lucinda Cunningham. I'm a friend of the family," she said, extending her hand.

"Nice meeting you," I said, shaking hands with her. "Did Reba say when she'd be home?"

"I'm afraid not. It might help if you told me what this was about."

Pushy woman, I thought. "She has a meeting this afternoon. I told her I'd give her a lift."

Her smile was not entirely warm, but she stepped out onto the porch and pulled the door shut behind her. "I don't mean to pry, but this . . . um . . . appointment, is it important?"

"Very. I called her myself to let her know."

"Well, this may present a problem. We haven't seen Reba since dinnertime last evening."

"She was gone all night?"

"And this morning as well. There's been no note and no call. Her father hasn't said as much, but I know he's concerned. When I saw you at the door, I assumed you had news of her, though I was almost afraid to ask."

"That's weird. I wonder where she went?"

"We have no idea. As I understand it she was out late the night before. She slept until noon and then she had a phone call—"

"That was probably me."

"Oh. Well, we wondered about that. She seemed upset afterwards. I believe she had a visitor. She was gone much of the afternoon and finally put in an appearance while her father was in the midst of his evening meal. He eats early most days, but this was closer to normal—shortly after six, I'd say. The cook had prepared chicken soup and his appetite seemed good. Reba wanted to chat with him and I decided to leave so the two could be alone."

"And she didn't mention anything to him?"

"He says not."

"I better talk to him myself. This is worrisome."

"I understand your concern, but he's resting right now. He's been working with his respiratory therapist and he's exhausted. I'd prefer not to disturb him. Why don't you come back later this afternoon? He should be up and about by four."

"I can't do that. This meeting is urgent, and if she's not going to make it, I need to know right now."

Her gaze dropped from mine and I could almost see her calculate the extent of her authority. "I'll see if he's awake and if he's up to it. You'd have to keep it brief."

"Fine."

She reached behind and opened the door, gesturing me inside. I noticed she put a foot out to prevent the cat from coming in. Rags was offended, shooting her a look. I stepped into the foyer, waiting for directions.

"This way."

She crossed toward the stairs and I followed in her wake. As she climbed the stairs, one hand trailing along the bannister, she delivered a comment over her shoulder to me. "I'm not sure what Reba's told you, but the two of us have never really gotten along."

"I wasn't aware of that. I'm sorry to hear."

"I'm afraid there's been a misunderstanding. She was under the impression I had designs on her father, which couldn't be further from the truth. I don't deny I'm protective. I'm also outspoken when it comes to her behavior. Nord seems to think if he's 'supportive' and gives her everything she wants, eventually she'll straighten out. He's never understood what good parenting is about. Children have to take responsibility for what they've done. Only my opinion . . . not that anybody's asked."

I let that one slide. I knew little of their history and didn't feel a response would be appropriate.

We traversed the wide landing, moving down a carpeted corridor with bedrooms on both sides. The door to the master bedroom was closed. Lucinda tapped softly, then opened the door and looked in on him. "Kinsey's here about Reba. May I show her in?"

I didn't hear his response, but she stepped aside, allowing me to enter. "Five minutes," she said firmly.

24

Nord Lafferty lay propped up against a pile of pillows, his oxygen tank close by. His frail white hands trembled on the crocheted coverlet. I knew his fingers would be icy to the touch, as though his energy and warmth were retreating from his extremities to his core. It wouldn't be long until the last bright spark would be snuffed out. I moved to the side of his bed. He turned to look at me and a smile brought color to his face. "Just the person I was thinking of."

"And here I am. Are you feeling up to this? Lucinda says you had a session with the respiratory therapist. She doesn't want me wearing you out."

"No, no. I've rested a bit and I'm fine. I'm sorry to have to waste so much time in bed, but some days I'm not capable of anything else. I trust you received my check."

"I did. The bonus wasn't necessary, but I appreciate the thought."

"You deserve every penny. Reba enjoys her time with you and I'm grateful for that."

"Lucinda tells me she's been gone since dinnertime last night. Do you happen to know where?"

He shook his head. "She sat with me through supper and helped me into the library afterwards. I heard her making a call. A cab arrived thirty minutes later. She said not to worry, gave me a kiss, and that was the last time we spoke."

"She has a meeting at one o'clock today and then a second meeting at four. I can't imagine her a no-show. She knows how critical this is."

"She made no mention of it. I take it she hasn't been in touch with you."

"We talked briefly yesterday. She said she'd get back to me, but then she never called."

"She did have a visitor. Fellow she used to work with."

"Marty Blumberg?"

"That's him. He came up to the house and the two had their heads together for quite some time. She went out afterwards."

"Lucinda mentioned she was out late the night before."

"She didn't arrive home until two-thirty in the morning. I was still awake when she finally pulled in the drive. I saw the headlights flash across the ceiling and I knew she was safe. Old habits die hard. The months she was in prison— those were the only nights I didn't lie awake waiting for her. I imagine I'll die with an eye on the clock, frightened something's happened."

"Why'd she call a cab? Is something wrong with her car?"

He hesitated. "My guess is she was leaving town and didn't want her car sitting in a parking lot somewhere."

"But where would she go?"

Helplessly, Nord shook his head.

"Did she take any luggage?"

"I asked Freddy myself and she says she did. Mercifully, Lucinda'd left by then, or I'd never hear the end of it. She knows something's happened, but so far I've kept her in the dark. Lucinda's relentless, so do be careful or she'll wheedle it out of you."

"I gathered as much. Which cab company?"

"Freddy might remember if you want to talk to her."

"I'll do that."

A soft tap at the door and Lucinda appeared, holding up two fingers. "Two more minutes," she said, with a smile to indicate her good intent.

Nord said, "Fine," but I saw a flash of irritation cross his face. As soon as she closed the door, he said, "Lock that. And lock the door to the connecting bath while you're about it."

I gave him a momentary look and then crossed to the door and turned the thumb lock. A large white-tiled bathroom opened off to the right, apparently joining his bedroom with the one next to it. I locked the far bathroom door, leaving the near one ajar, and then returned to my seat.

He pulled himself up against the pillows. "Thank you. I suppose she means well, but there are times when she takes too much on herself. To date, I haven't appointed her my guardian. As for Reba, what do you propose?"

"I'm not really sure. I need to find her as soon as possible."

"Is she in trouble?"

"I'd say so. Shall I fill you in?"

"It's best I don't know. Whatever it is, I trust you to take care of it and bill me afterwards."

"I'll do what I can. Couple of government agencies are interested in talking to her about Beck's financial dealings. This is going to get sticky and my position's precarious as it is. When it comes to the feds, I don't want to end up on the wrong side of the fence. If I'm working for you, no privilege attaches to our relationship in any event, so hiring me won't serve as protection for either one of us."

"I understand completely. I wouldn't ask you to compromise yourself in the eyes of the law. That said, I'd be grateful for any help you can give her."

"Is her car still here?"

He nodded. "It's parked in the garage, which is unlocked as far as I know. You're welcome to take a look."

There was a tapping at the door and the handle turned. Lucinda rattled the knob impatiently, her voice muffled. "Nord, what's wrong? Are you in there?"

He gestured toward the door. I crossed and unlocked it. Lucinda turned the knob abruptly and pushed her way in, almost banging me in the face. She stared at me, apparently assuming I'd locked the door on my own. "What's this about?"

Nord strained to raise his voice. "I told her to lock it. I didn't want any further interruptions."

Her body language shifted from suspicion to injury. "You might have mentioned it. If you and Miss Millhone have private business to discuss, I wouldn't dream of interfering."

"Thank you, Lucinda. We appreciate that."

"Perhaps I've overstepped my bounds." Her tone was frosty, the content designed to generate apologies or reassurances.

Nord offered neither. He lifted a hand, almost a gesture of dismissal. "She'd like to see Reba's room."

"What for?"

Nord turned to me. "Down the hall to your right—"

Lucinda cut in. "I'll be happy to show her. We don't want her wandering around on her own."

I glanced at Nord. "I'll get back to you," I said.

I followed Lucinda down the hall, noting her stiff posture and her refusal to look at me. When we reached Reba's room, she opened the door and then stood in my path forcing me to squeeze by her. Her eyes trailed after me. "I hope you're satisfied. You think you're so helpful, but you're killing him," she said.

I locked eyes with her, but she was far more practiced than I at delivering the withering glance. I waited. Her smile was set, and I knew she was the sort who'd find ways to get even. Lucinda, the bitch indeed. She stepped into the hall. I shut the door and locked it, knowing she'd get the point.

I turned and leaned against the door, making a visual survey, taking in the whole of the room before starting my search. The bed was made, a few personal mementos neatly arranged on the bedside table: a framed photo of her father, a book, a scratch pad, and a pen. No clutter. No clothing on the floor. Nothing under the bed. A phone, but no personal address book. I went through the desk drawers, uncovering items that must have been there for years: school papers, exam books, unopened boxes of stationery, which were probably gifts—certainly not her taste, unless she favored kitty-cat cards with cute sayings on the front. No personal correspondence. Dresser drawers were neat.

I checked the closet, where several empty hangers suggested the number of garments missing—six by my count. Among the articles she'd left behind were a navy blue blazer and a leather bomber jacket, askew on its hanger. I had no way of knowing what she'd packed. I wasn't even sure the size or the number of suitcases she owned. I sorted through idly, thinking back to the clothes I'd seen her in. I didn't spot her boots or either of the sweaters I remembered—the one red cotton, the other dark blue with a cowl neck. She'd worn both within the first few days of being home, which meant they might well be her favorites, garments she'd want with her on the road.

I went into the bathroom, which was close to barren: tawny marble floor tile and countertop, spotless mirrors, and the smell of soap. The medicine cabinet had been emptied of items. No deodorant, cologne, or toothpaste. No prescription drugs. I could see a whitish spot on the marble counter where her toothbrush had lain. The hamper had been stuffed with blue jeans, T-shirts, and underwear; a bath towel, still faintly damp, crowded in on top. The shower pan was dry. Nothing in the trash.

I went back to the closet and studied the clothes. I took the bomber jacket off its hanger and checked the pockets. I found some loose change and a slip from a generic order pad that showed she'd paid for a cheeseburger, chili fries, and a Coke. No date and the restaurant wasn't mentioned by name. I slipped the receipt into my jeans pocket and returned the jacket to its hanger. I let myself out of the room and retraced my steps. As I passed Nord's room, I paused and leaned my head close to the door. I could hear the murmur of voices, primarily Lucinda's, and she sounded aggrieved. Any further conversation with him would have to wait. I went downstairs and found my way to the back part of the house.

The housekeeper was sitting at the kitchen table. She'd spread newspapers across the surface, on which she'd laid twelve place settings of sterling silver, two silver water pitchers, and a series of silver beakers. Some of the more ornate pieces had been sprayed with an aerosol polish that was drying to a strange shade of pink. The cloth she used on the flatware was black from the tarnish she'd removed. Her gray hair was wispy, curled and back-combed into a dandelion-like aureole with patches of scalp showing through.

I said, "Hi, Freddy. I've been chatting with Mr. Lafferty. He says you saw Reba last night before she left."

"Going out the door," she said, addressing her remark to the spoon.

"She took a suitcase?"

"Two—a black canvas overnight case and a hard-sided gray suitcase on wheels. She was wearing jeans and boots and a leather hat, but no jacket."

"Did you have a conversation?"

"She put a finger to her lips, like this was our little secret. I was having none of that. I've worked for Mr. Lafferty forty-six years. We don't keep secrets from one another. I went straight into the library and spoke to him, but before I managed to get him up from his chair, she was gone."

"Did she say anything about her intentions? Any talk of a trip?"

Freddy shook her head. "There were calls going back

and forth, but she was quick to catch the phone so I never heard who it was. I couldn't even tell if the caller was a man or woman."

"You know it's a parole violation if she leaves the state," I said. "She could be sent back to prison."

"Miss Millhone, as fond as I am of her, I wouldn't withhold information or cover for her in any way. She's breaking her father's heart and the shame's on her."

"Well, if it makes any difference, I know she adores him, which doesn't change anything, of course." I took out a card with my home number scribbled on the back. "If you should hear from her, would you call me?"

She took my card and slipped it into her apron pocket. "I hope you find her. He doesn't have much time."

"I know," I said. "He told me her car's still parked in the garage."

"Use this back door. It's closer than going out the front. There's a set of keys on the hook," she said, indicating the service porch and mud room visible through the open doorway behind her.

"Thanks."

I snagged the keys and then took a diagonal path across a large brick apron, approaching what must have been the original carriage house, converted now to a four-car garage. Rags appeared from around the corner of the house. Clearly, his job was to oversee arrivals, departures, and all activities involving the property. Above the garage, I could see a stretch of dormer windows with curtains drawn across the glass, which suggested servants' quarters or an apartment, possibly Freddy's. One garage was empty, the retractable door standing open. I used it as ingress and quickly spotted Reba's BMW parked against the far wall. I felt obliged to explain myself to Rags as he followed in my tracks. I got in on the driver's side and slid under the wheel. I put the key in the ignition and checked the gas gauge. The arrow jumped to the top, indicating a full tank of gas.

I leaned over and popped the door to the glove

compartment and then spent a few minutes sorting through the accumulation of gasoline receipts, outdated registration slips, and an owner's manual. In the side pocket to my left, I found another handful of gasoline receipts. Most were dated three to four months before Reba went to prison. The single exception was a receipt dated July 27, 1987—Monday. She'd bought gas at a Chevron station on Main Street in Perdido, twenty miles to the south. I added the receipt to the other one in my pocket. I checked under the front seats, the backseat, the floorboards, and the trunk, but found nothing else of interest. I left the garage and returned the keys to the hook in the mud room, then collected my car. Last I saw of Rags, he was sitting on the porch, calmly grooming himself.

I returned to the 101 and made a speedy round-trip to my apartment, stopping off long enough to pick up the photograph of Reba her father had given me. I folded it and eased it into my shoulder bag before I headed for Perdido. The four-lane highway follows the coastal contours with the foothills on one side and the Pacific Ocean on the other. The concrete seawall all but disappears in places, and waves crack up along the rocks in an impressive display of power. Surfers park their cars on the berm and tote their surfboards down to the beach, looking as sleek as seals in their form-fitting black wetsuits. I counted eight of them in the water, straddling their boards, faces turned toward the waves as they waited for the surf to mount the next assault on the shore.

To my left, the steeply rising foothills were bare of trees and thick with chaparral. Paddle-shaped cactus had taken over large patches of eroding soil. The lush green, encouraged by the winter rains, had given way to spring wildflowers, and then died back to this tinderbox of vegetation, ripe for the autumn fires. The railroad tracks ran sometimes on the mountain side of the road and sometimes crossed under the highway and tracked the surf.

On the outskirts of Perdido, I took the first off-ramp and

proceeded toward town on Main, checking addresses along the way. I spotted the Chevron station on a narrow spit of land that bordered the Perdido Avenue off-ramp. I pulled in and parked on the side of the station nearest the restrooms. A uniformed attendant was standing at the rear of a station wagon, topping off the tank. He spotted me, eyes lingering briefly before returning to his task. I waited until the customer had signed the credit card slip and the wagon had pulled away before I crossed to the pumps. I pulled out the photograph of Reba, intending to inquire if he'd worked on Monday and if so, if he remembered her. As I approached, however, something else occurred to me. I said, "Hi. I need directions. I'm looking for a poker parlor called the Double Down."

He turned and pointed. "Two blocks down on the right. If you get to the stoplight, you've gone too far."

It was close to two in the afternoon when I pulled into the one remaining space in the parking lot behind a low cinder-block building painted an unprepossessing beige. The sign in front flashed a red neon spade, a heart, a diamond, and a club in succession. The Double Down was written out in blue neon script across the face of the building. In lieu of stairs, a wheelchair ramp angled up to a windowless entrance, approximately four feet above ground. I climbed the ramp to the heavy wooden door with its rustic wrought iron hinges. A sign indicated that the hours ran from 10:00 A.M. until 2:00 A.M. I pushed my way in.

There were four large tables, covered in green felt, each with eight to ten poker players seated in wooden captain's chairs. Many turned and looked at me, though no one questioned my presence. Along the rear wall there was a galley-style kitchen with a menu posted above the service window. The selections were listed in removable black letters mounted in white slots: breakfast dishes, sandwiches, and a few dinner items. I was already partial to the scrambled egg and sausage breakfast burrito. I checked the receipt I'd found in Reba's jacket pocket—cheeseburger, chili fries, and Coke. The same items were listed on the board and all the prices matched.

The walls were paneled in pine. Along the acoustical-tile ceiling, a picture rail was festooned with strands of fake ivy and hung with framed reproductions of sports art, football dominant. The lighting was flat. All the players were men except for a woman at the back who was probably in her sixties. A chalkboard mounted on the side wall bore a list of names, presumably guys waiting for an open seat. To my surprise, there was no cigarette smoke and no alcohol in sight. Two color television sets mounted in opposing corners flickered silently with two different baseball games. There was scarcely any conversation, only the sound of plastic chips clicking together softly as the dealer paid off the winners and pulled in the losing bets. As I looked on, the dealers changed tables and three guys took advantage of the break to order something to eat.

There was a counter to my left and behind it, in a cubbyhole, a fellow was sitting on a stool. "I'm looking for the manager," I said. I was wondering, of course, if poker parlors had managers, but it seemed like a safe bet, so to speak. The guy said, "Yo," raising his hand without lifting his gaze from his book.

"What's the book?"

He held it up, turning the cover into view as though wondering himself. "This? Poetry. Kenneth Rexroth. You know his work?"

"I don't."

"The guy's awesome. I'd lend you this, but it's the only copy I have." He put his finger between the pages, marking his place. "You want chips?"

"Sorry, but I'm not here to play." I took Reba's picture from my bag, unfolded it, and held it out to him. "Look familiar?"

"Reba Lafferty," he said, as though the answer was self-evident.

"You remember when you saw her last?"

"Sure. Monday. Night before last. She sat at that table. Came in about five and stayed until we closed the place at two. Played Hold 'Em most of the night and then switched to Omaha, for which she has no feel whatever. Had a roll of bills about like this," he said, making a circle of his thumb and middle finger. "Chick's been out of prison a week, or that's the scuttlebutt. You her parole officer?"

I shook my head. "A personal friend. I was the one who went down to Corona and drove her home."

"Should have saved yourself the trip. Before you know it, she'll be on the sheriff's bus, heading the other way. Too bad. She's cute. About the way a raccoon's cute before it bites the shit out of you."

I said, "Yeah, well, there you have it. She took off last night and we're trying to track her down. I don't suppose you know where she went."

"Off the top of my head? I'd say Vegas. She dropped a bundle in here, but you could tell she was on a roll. She had that look in her eye. Bad luck or good, she's the kind who keeps going till all the money's gone."

"I don't get it."

"You don't gamble?"

"Not at all."

"My theory? Chick runs on empty. She gambles for the hype, thinking she can use that to fill herself up. Ain't never gonna happen. She needs help."

"Don't we all," I said. "By the way, why the Double Down? I thought the term was blackjack."

"We used to have blackjack until the owner phased it out. The locals prefer poker—skill over luck, I guess."

As soon as I reached my office, I grabbed a pencil and notepad, hauled out the phone book, and chose a travel agent at random. I dialed and when she answered, I told her I needed information about a trip to Las Vegas.

"What day?"

"Don't know yet. I work until five and I'm not sure what day I want to go. What flights do you show for weekdays after six P.M.?"

"I can check," she said. I heard *tappity-tap-tap* in the background and after a silence, "I see two. USAir at 7:55 P.M. by way of San Francisco, arriving Las Vegas at 11:16, or United Airlines 8:30 through Los Angeles, arriving LV at 11:17 P.M."

"Where else would I find poker parlors?"

"Say again?"

"Card parlors. Poker."

"I thought you wanted to go to Las Vegas."

"I'm looking at all the options. Anything closer to home?"

"Gardena or Garden Grove. You'd have to fly to LAX and find ground transport."

"That sounds doable. What flights do you have to Los Angeles after six P.M.? I know about the United flight at 8:30. Is there anything else?"

"I show a United at 6:57, arriving in Los Angeles at 7:45."

I was taking notes as she spoke. "Oh wow, thanks. This is great."

Somewhat testily, the travel agent said, "You want to book one of these or not?"

"I'm not sure. Let's try this. Say I had a few bucks in my hot little hand. Where else could I go?"

"After six P.M. weekdays?" she said, drily.

"Exactly."

"You could try Laughlin, Nevada, though there aren't any flights into Laughlin-Bullhead unless you want to fly charter."

"Don't think so," I said.

"There's always Reno–Lake Tahoe. The same airport services both."

"Could you . . ."

"I'm doing it," she sang, and again I could hear her tap-

ping her computer keys. "United Airlines departing Santa
Teresa at 7:55, arrives San Fran 9:07 P.M., departs 10:20, arriving in Reno at 11:16. That's all there is."

"I'll call you back," I said, and hung up. I circled the
word "Reno," thinking about Reba's former cellmate, Misty
Raine, allegedly living up there. If Reba were on the run, it
might make sense to try connecting with a friend. Of
course, consorting with a known felon was a parole violation, but she was already racking them up, so what was one
more to her?

I dialed directory assistance in Reno, the 702 area code,
and asked the operator for a listing under the last name
Raine. There was one: first initial M, but with no address
listed. I thanked her and hung up. I drew a second circle
around the word "Raine," wondering if Reba had been in
touch with Misty since her release. I picked up the phone
again and dialed the number I'd been given for M. Raine.
After four rings, a mechanical male voice said, "No one is
home. Please leave a number." So uninformative. I really
hate that guy.

At 4:30, I drove back to the Lafferty estate. As I pulled
into the parking pad, I was happy to note Lucinda's car was
gone. Rags was asleep in a wicker chair, but he roused himself to greet me, sitting at my feet politely while I rang the
bell. When Freddy let me in, Rags took the opportunity to
slip inside. He followed as Freddy led me to the library
where Nord was entrenched on the sofa, propped up against
a mass of bed pillows and covered with a throw. He said, "I
had Freddy bring me down. I couldn't stand another minute
upstairs." Rags jumped up on the sofa, walked the length of
Nord's body, and sniffed at his breath.

I said, "You look better. You have some color in your
cheeks."

"It's temporary, but I'll take what I can get. I'm assuming you've learned something or you wouldn't be back so
soon."

I told him about the gasoline receipt and my drive to Perdido, where I'd been directed to the card parlor. I related the report I'd had about her poker losses Monday night. I couldn't see any point in plaguing him with the suspicion that she'd stolen twenty-five thousand dollars so I left that part out. "Reba mentioned a stripper named Misty Raine, a former cellmate of hers. Apparently, Misty moved to Reno after she got off parole. I'm thinking if Reba's caught up in gambling, it'd be smart to scout out a place where she could also lay low—"

"In which case she might try hooking up with this friend," Nord said, idly stroking the cat.

"Right. That way, instead of laying out money for a room, she could drop it all at the tables and hope for some return. According to directory assistance, there is an 'M. Raine' in Reno, with no published address."

"But wouldn't traveling to Reno be a violation of her parole?"

"So's the gambling," I said. "There's always the possibility she'll come back before she's missed, but I hate to see her take the chance. Has she been to Reno before?"

"Often," Nord said. "But how can you be sure she's there? Her friend isn't likely to admit to it."

"That's my thought, too. Reba didn't mention Reno?"

"She never said a word."

"What about the phone company? I've been wondering if you could ask about any long-distance calls in the past seven days. A match on Misty's number would at least suggest the two have been in touch."

"I can try."

I rounded up the phone book and dialed the number for him, taking him as far as the billing department before I handed him the phone. He identified himself by name and phone number and explained what he wanted. In the most glib and convincing manner imaginable, he spun a tale of an out-of-town visitor who'd made some long-distance calls but neglected to ask for time and charges. After chatting with the woman, he jotted a number in the 702 area code to which three calls had been made. He thanked her for her help, hung up, and handed me the slip. "I'm afraid this still doesn't give you an address."

"I have a police pal and I'm hoping he can help."

25

By the time I left Nord's it was close to 5:00. There was no point returning to the office so I headed for home. I let myself into my place and tossed my bag on a chair. Cheney had left two cranky messages wanting to know where the hell Reba was as she'd missed her 1:00 appointment with Vince and her 4:00 meeting with the FBI. I called Cheney's pager, punched in my number, and waited for the phone to ring, which it did ten minutes later.

"You called?"

"I need a favor. Can you check a phone number in Reno and get me an address?"

"Who for?"

"A friend of a friend."

"Is this about Reba?"

"Who else?"

He thought about it briefly. "She's already in more trouble than she knows. If she's up there, the best thing for all of us is to have Reno PD pick her up."

"That's one approach," I said. "On the other hand, you still need her cooperation. I'm thinking about driving up to Reno and talking her into coming back—assuming I can find her."

"Does Holloway know she's gone?"

"I doubt it, but Reba doesn't see her until Monday, which means we have five days before she'll be missed. I'd hate to do anything behind Priscilla's back so you can tell her if you like. Or . . ."

"Or what?"

"You can run it by your IRS buddies and see what they have to say. Maybe her value to them takes precedence and they can square it with her PO. There's plenty of time to tell Priscilla once Reba's been debriefed."

"Give me the number in Reno and I'll get back to you."

"Why don't you talk to Vince first and then I'll give you the number. We can work it out from there."

"You don't trust me?"

"Of course I trust *you*. He's the one I'm worried about."

"What about tonight? You want to meet me at Rosie's? I've got a couple of reports to write, but it shouldn't take me long."

"Sounds good."

"I'll be there in a bit."

I left my front door ajar and crossed the patio to Henry's. His kitchen door was open and I knocked on the frame. "Henry? It's me."

"Come on in. I'll be right there," he said.

He had a pot of homemade soup simmering on a back burner and I took that as a good sign. Henry seldom cooks or bakes when he's feeling down. His glass of Black Jack over ice was sitting on the kitchen table, the newspaper neatly folded and waiting in his rocking chair. A newly opened bottle of Chardonnay was sitting in a cooler on the counter. He appeared from the hallway with a stack of clean towels. "You should have poured yourself some wine. I opened that for you. Something I want to talk to you about. You have a few minutes?" He put the towels in a kitchen drawer and took a wineglass out of the kitchen cabinet and filled it halfway.

"Thanks. I have all the time you need. I've been feeling out of touch. How are you?"

"I'm fine, thanks. What about you?" He resumed his seat in the rocking chair and took a sip of his drink.

"I'm good," I said. "Now that we've cleared that pithy matter, you want to tell me what's on your mind?"

He smiled. "Here's what I've been considering. I don't think there's any remedy for my relationship with Mattie. At the moment, she's calling the shots and I don't feel I can impose if she's not interested. That's the way of the world. We didn't know each other long and there are all kinds of reasons it couldn't work—age, geography—the particulars aren't relevant. What I realize is I enjoyed having someone in my life. It put a spring in my step, even at the age of eighty-seven. So I've been thinking it wouldn't be such a terrible idea to make a phone call or two. There were several women on the cruise who seemed lively and nice. Mattie may be one of a kind, but that's beside the point." He paused. "That's as far as I got, but I'd be interested in your thoughts on the matter."

"I think it sounds great. I remember after you got home, you had all kinds of women leaving messages on your machine."

"Embarrassed me."

"Why?"

"I'm old-fashioned. I was taught men should be the pursuers, not the other way around."

"Times have changed."

"For the better?"

"Perhaps. You meet someone you like, why not make an effort? There's nothing wrong with that. If it works, it works, and if it doesn't, oh well."

"That's what I've been thinking. There's a woman named Isabelle, who lives here in town. She's eighty, which is a little closer to my age. She loves to dance, which I haven't done for ages. And another woman, Charlotte. She's seventy-eight and still active in real estate. She lives in Olvidado, close enough," he said. "You think one at a time might be good?"

"Nothing wrong with both. Get your feet wet. The more the merrier."

"Good. Then that's what I'll do." He clicked his glass against mine. "Wish me luck."

"All the luck in the world." I leaned forward and gave him a quick kiss on the cheek.

I sat in my favorite booth in Rosie's, the one in the rear where I can sip a glass of wine while I keep a close eye on the place. I've been a regular at the tavern for seven years and I still can't tell you the names of the day-drinkers or the other steady customers like me. Rosie's the only common thread, and I suspect if the other patrons and I compared notes, we all have the same complaint. We'd grouse at how she bullies us, but we'd all feel smug, seeing her mistreatment as a sign of just how special we are to her. William was working behind the bar. I'd stopped off on the way in and picked up the wine he poured when he saw me enter. He was busy, otherwise, I was certain, he'd have given me the latest in his medical reports.

Once settled, I took a sip of white wine so close to vinegar it was almost enough to make me swear off the stuff. Cheney had called back within minutes to tell me Vince was favoring the personal approach. He offered his blessings as long as he was given the contact number as well. I gave Cheney the number I'd picked up from Nord's telephone bill. I assumed Vince Turner would keep the information to himself, but I worried the FBI would get wind of what was going on and make trouble.

I put in another call to Nord to tell him I'd be taking off in the morning. He'd offered to underwrite the trip and I'd accepted, any charitable impulse quickly overridden by the need to pay my bills. I'd brought along a pocket atlas and I was flipping back and forth between Southern California and the western border of Nevada, considering my route. The obvious choice was to take Highway 101 to the 126, travel east as far as Highway 5, and then north to Sacramento, where I'd connect to the 80 on a north-to-east trajectory that would take me straight into Reno. If Cheney couldn't manage to get me Misty's address, I'd revert to the old-fashioned method—check the public library for the criss-cross directory where phone numbers are listed in numerical order and matched with the corresponding address.

Before I hit the road, I'd make a stop at the auto club and get a proper series of strip maps. I really didn't need them, but I like the white spiral binding and that arrow penned in orange that marches up the page. Makes me feel like I'm getting my money's worth for the cost of my annual membership. I moved on, making a mental list of clothing and toiletries I'd need to pack. I felt a hand on my shoulder and looked up with a smile, anticipating Cheney.

Beck slid into the booth across from me. "You seem happy to see me."

"I thought you were someone else." I took in the sight of him: chinos, dress shirt, with a windbreaker over it.

He laughed, thinking I was making a joke. Casually I closed the atlas and laid it on the seat beside me, then leaned to the right as though scanning the entrance. "Reba's not with you?"

"Not at all. That's why I stopped in. I'm trying to track her down." His eyes strayed to the atlas. "Are you taking a trip?"

"Just indulging in fantasy. I've got too much work piled up to go anywhere."

"Oh, that's right. You're a private detective. What are you working on?"

I knew he couldn't care less about my caseload unless it

involved him. I figured he was fishing, wondering if I was part of the government conspiracy to reel him in. I said, "The usual. A skip-trace, a couple of employee background checks for the Bank of Santa Teresa. Stuff like that." I droned on for a bit, making it up as I went along. I could see his eyes glaze over and I hoped sincerely that I was boring him to death.

I looked up in time to see Rosie appear through the swinging kitchen doors. Her eyes lighted on Beck like a terrier spotting a rat. She made a beeline for the booth, barely able to suppress her happiness. Beck collected himself and rose to his feet. He extended a hand to her, then leaned forward and bussed her on the cheek. "Rosie, you look beautiful. You've had your hair done."

"I did myself. Is home permanent," she said.

As far as I could see, her hair looked the way it always did—badly dyed, badly cut.

She dropped her gaze modestly. "I'm remember what you want. Scotch. Double wit ice and water back. The twenty-fours year, not the twelve."

"Very good. No wonder your customers are loyal."

I thought she'd see through the flattery, but she lapped it up, nearly dropping a little curtsy before she scurried off to get his drink. He sat down again, watching her departure with a fond smile as though he really gave a shit. His gaze drifted back to mine. He was a cold, cold man. The missing twenty-five thousand had put him on red alert. He was out hunting to see who his enemies were.

I crossed my arms and leaned forward, resting my elbows on the table. There was something restful about being in the company of someone I disliked so much. I didn't have to worry about impressing him, which allowed me to focus on the game at hand. "How was Panama City?"

"Fine. Good. The problems started as soon as I came home. A little birdie tells me you and Reba got into trouble while I was gone."

"Me? Well, dang. What'd I do now?"

"You don't know what I'm referring to?"

"We went shopping at the mall if that counts for anything."

"The pow-wow with Marty. What was that about?"

I blinked at him twice as though drawing a blank and then allowed the light to dawn. "Friday night? We ran into him at the mall. Once the stores closed down, we stopped in at Dale's and ordered a couple of bowls of that chili guaranteed to give you the runs. Geez, Louise. Have you ever eaten that crap? Completely gross—"

"Enough already. Just get on with it."

"Sorry. So anyway, about that time Marty came in. He was happy to see Reba. She introduced us and we chatted for a bit. End of story."

He seemed to watch me from a distance, not yet satisfied. "What'd you chat about?"

"Nothing in particular. I meet the guy. I'm nice. That's all it amounted to. Why do you care?"

"You didn't talk about me?"

"You? Not at all. Your name never came up."

"Then what?"

"What do you mean, 'Then what'?"

"Where'd you go from there?"

I shrugged. "The office. Marty was bragging about the new digs and said he'd show us around, so we ended up doing a quick tour. He said you'd be pissed if you heard. Is that what this is about?"

"I don't believe you've finished. Isn't there something else?"

"Well, let's see now. Oh. Now this is earth shattering. I left my purse on the roof and we had to pop back the next day and go in search of it. What a pain in the ass *that* was."

Rosie approached with Beck's scotch on a tray. We dropped the topic of conversation and smiled at her blandly while she set down a ceremonial doily and put his drink on it. Beck murmured his thanks without engaging her in further conversation.

She hesitated, hoping for another round of fawning and

compliments, but he was intent on me. I was wishing she'd sit down and talk to us the rest of the night. Instead she flicked me a look, suspicious that this was romance a-brewing. Little did she know I was sitting there frantically assessing the situation, trying to guess how much Beck knew and how he'd acquired the information. If he'd seen security tapes, I had to make sure I accounted for all our comings and goings. I was aware my being a wiseass was getting on his nerves, but I couldn't help myself. Rosie manufactured a bit of small talk and then departed. I looked at Beck, waiting for his next move.

He picked up his scotch and took a sip, watching me over the rim of his glass. "Clever. You explain it all so nicely, but somehow I'd swear you're lying through your pearly whites."

"My reputation must precede me. I'm good at lying," I said.

He set his drink on the table, making a circular pattern with the moisture from the bottom of the glass. "So where is she?"

"Reba? Beats me. We're not joined at the hip."

"Really. You've been with her constantly and now suddenly you have no idea? She must have said something."

"Beck, I think you've gotten the wrong impression. We're not friends. Her father paid me to go get her. That's the kind of pal I am. I took her to the parole office and the DMV. She was lonesome. We had dinner—"

"Don't forget Bubbles."

"Big deal. We went to Bubbles. I was feeling sorry for her. She doesn't have any friends, except Onni, who treats her like a piece of shit."

He thought about that briefly and shifted gears. "What's she told you about me?"

I tried to make the big eyes like Reba did when she was feigning innocence. "About *you*? Well, gosh now. She told me you screwed her brains out in the car the other night. She was going to give me all the nitty-gritty details about the size of your dick, but I begged off. No offense, but I don't find you nearly as fascinating as she does. Except for the current conversation. What are you fishing for?"

"Nothing. Maybe I misjudged you."

"Well, I doubt that, but so what? Sounds like you're the one in trouble and projecting it on us." I might have pushed the line too far because I wasn't that crazy about the look he turned on me.

"Why do you say that?"

"Because you're laying out all this bullshit and I don't have a clue what you want. You've peppered me with questions from the minute you sat down."

He was dead silent for about fifteen seconds—a long time in the middle of a conversation of this type. Then he said, "I believe she stole money from me when she was in the office that night."

"Ah. Got it. That's a serious accusation."

"Yes, it is."

"Why not turn the matter over to the cops?"

"I can't prove she did it."

I shook my head. "Doesn't sound right to me. I was with her when we toured the office and she never touched a thing. Me neither, for that matter. I hope you don't think I'm involved, because I swear I'm not."

"It's not you I'm worried about. It's her."

"You're worried?"

"I think she's in trouble. I'd hate to see her hurt."

"Why didn't you just say so up front?"

"You're right. I'm sorry. I went about this all wrong and I apologize. Truce?"

"We don't need a truce. I'm worried about her, too. She's back to smoking a pack a day and god knows what else. This morning, she was talking about booze and poker parlors. Scared the crap out of me."

"I didn't realize you'd seen her."

"Oh sure. I thought I mentioned that."

"You didn't, but that's good. I haven't heard a word from her since I got back. She's usually on the phone first thing, tugging at my sleeve. You know Reeb. She tends to cling."

"I'll say. Look, she talked about us having lunch tomorrow. Why don't I tell her to give you a call?"

He smiled tentatively, wanting to believe me. At the same time, I could sense his scrutiny, testing my comments for any false notes. Happily, since I'm a thoroughly accomplished liar, I could pass a polygraph, disavowing murder with blood still dripping from my fingers. He reached out and tapped my hand, something I'd seen him do with her. I wondered what the gesture meant, a sort of tag . . . you're it. "I hope I wasn't out of line. You're a good egg," he said.

"Thanks. You are, too." I reached out and tapped his hand in return.

He pushed up from the booth. "Better to let you go. I've taken up enough of your time as it is. Sorry if I was rude. I didn't mean to grill you."

"Hey, I understand. Stay and have another drink if you like."

"Nah, I gotta hit the road. Just tell Reba I'm looking for her."

"What's your schedule like tomorrow? Are you at the office all day?"

"You bet. I'll be waiting for her call."

Good luck, I thought. I watched him crossing the room, trying to see him as I had at first. I'd thought he was sexy and good-looking, but those qualities had vanished. Now I saw him for what he was, a guy accustomed to having his own way. The world centered on him and others were simply there to service his whims. I wondered if he were capable of killing. Possible, I thought. Maybe not with his own hands, but he could have it done. Belatedly, a warm drop of sweat trickled down the middle of my back. I allowed myself a deep breath, and by the time Cheney showed up, I was feeling calm again and slightly bemused.

He slid in next to me and pushed a folded slip of paper in my direction. "Don't say I never did you one. Address is a rental. Misty's been in residence the past thirteen months."

"Thanks." I glanced at the address and put the paper into my pocket.

He said, "What's the smile about? You're looking pleased with yourself."

"How long have I known you? A couple of years, right?"

"More or less. You haven't *really* known me until this past week."

"Know what I realized? I've never lied to you."

"I should hope not."

"I'm serious. I'm a natural-born liar, but so far I haven't lied to you. That puts you in a category all by yourself . . . well, except for Henry. I can't remember ever lying to him. About anything important."

"Good news. I love the part where you say 'so far.' You're the only person I know who could say something like that and think it was a compliment."

Rosie reappeared and when she caught sight of Cheney, she shot me a quizzical look. She seldom saw me with one man, let alone two on the same night. Cheney ordered a beer. Once she was gone, I rested my chin on my fist so I could look at him. His face was smooth and there was the faintest web of lines at the outer corners of his eyes. Dark suede sport coat the color of coffee grounds. Beige shirt, brown silk tie hanging slightly askew. I reached out and straightened it. He caught my hand and kissed my index finger.

I smiled. "Have you ever dated an older woman?"

"Talking about yourself? I got news for you, kiddo. I'm older than you."

"You are *not*."

"I'm thirty-nine. April 1948." He took out his wallet, flipped it open, removed his driver's license, and held it up.

"Get serious. You were born in 1948?"

"How old did you think I was?"

"Somebody told me you were thirty-four."

"Lies. All lies. You can't believe a word you hear on the street." He put his license in his wallet, which he flipped shut and returned to his hip pocket.

"In that case, your body's even better than I thought. Tell me the day and month again. I wasn't paying attention."

"April 28. I'm a Taurus, like you. That's why we get along so well."

"Is that true?"

"Sure. Look at us. We're Earth signs, the Bull. We're the Boy Scouts of the Zodiac. Determined, practical, reliable, fair-minded, stable—in other words, boring as hell. On the downside, we're jealous, possessive, opinionated, and self-righteous—so what's not to like? We hate change. We hate interruptions. We hate being rushed."

"You really believe all that stuff?"

"No, but you have to admit there's a certain ring of truth to it."

Rosie returned to the table with Cheney's beer. I could tell she was tempted to loiter, hoping to catch a snippet of conversation. Both of us sank into silence until she left again.

Then I said, "Beck was here."

"You're changing the subject. I'd rather talk about us."

"Premature."

"Then why don't we talk about you?"

"Absolutely not."

"For instance, I like it that you don't wear makeup."

"I've worn it twice. That first day at lunch and then again the other night."

"I know. That's how I figured I could get you between the sheets."

"Cheney, we need to talk about Reba. I leave for Reno first thing tomorrow morning. We have to be operating off the same page."

His expression sobered to some extent, and I could see him shift into business mode. "Okay, but don't be dragging it out. We have better things to do."

"Business first."

"Yes, ma'am."

We spent the next ten minutes talking about Reba and Beck—what he'd said, what I'd said, and what, if anything, it meant. Cheney intended to call Priscilla Holloway in the morning and bring her up to speed. He thought the straightforward approach was preferable to taking the risk that she'd find out anyway. He'd refer her to Vince Turner and let the two of them work out their arrangements. If Holloway wanted Reba picked up, then all the better for him. Vince would be thrilled to have her under lock and key.

Finally, Cheney said, "Can we go now? All this talk about criminals is turning me on."

26

The drive from Santa Teresa to Reno took nine hours, including two potty stops and a fifteen-minute lunch break. The first seven hours got me as far as Sacramento, where Highway 80 intersects the 5 and begins its slow climb toward the Donner Summit, 7,240 feet above sea level. Smoke from a series of brush fires in the Tahoe National Forest had saturated the air with a pale brown haze that followed me across the Nevada state line. I reached the Reno city limits at suppertime and cruised through town just to get a feel for the place.

Most of the buildings were two and three stories tall, dwarfed by the occasional chunky hotel. Aside from the casinos, businesses seemed to be devoted to making cash readily available. The working theme was cheap food and pawnshops, with the word "GUNS" writ large on two out of every seven signs.

I chose an unprepossessing two-story motel in the heart of town, its prime attraction being that it sat on a lot adjacent to a McDonald's. I checked in, found my second-floor room, and put my duffel bag on the bed. Before I left again, I picked up the Reno phone book I found in my bed-table drawer. I went downstairs, left the phone book in my car, and then proceeded to McDonald's, where I sat in a window seat and treated myself to a couple of QPs with Cheese.

According to the strip maps I'd picked up at the auto club, Carson City—the last known domicile of the erst-while Robert Dietz—was only thirty miles away. Because of Cheney, I thought about Dietz without bitterness, but without much interest. While I munched fries doused in ketchup, I opened the Reno city map and looked for the street where Misty Raine was supposedly living these days. Wasn't far away and I thought my next order of business was to pay a visit to the place.

I dumped my trash and returned to my car. With the map propped against the steering wheel, I sketched out my course. The route took me through spartan neighborhoods of pines, chain-link fences, and ranch houses faced in stucco or brick. Even at seven in the evening, the light was good. The air was hot and dry and smelled of pine pitch and charred oak from the California fires. I knew the tem-peratures would drop as soon as the sun went down. The lawns I passed were parched, the grasses scorched to a soft yellow-brown. The trees, on the other hand, were surpris-ingly green, dense healthy foliage a relief in the relentless washed-out beige of the surrounding landscape. Maybe the whole of it was designed to keep all the gamblers indoors where gaudy colors dazzled the eye, the air temperature was constant, and lights were ablaze twenty-four hours a day.

I spotted the house I was looking for—a one-story yel-low wood-frame bungalow with three stingy windows across the front. The trim was brown and the door to the single-car garage was decorated with three vertical rows of triangles, yellow paint on brown. Shaggy evergreens marked the corners of the house, and the flower beds along the drive were filled with desiccated plant stalks. I parked on the far side of the street about four houses down with a clear view of the drive. When sitting surveillance, there's always a concern that a neighbor will call the cops to complain about a suspicious vehicle parked out front. To create a diversion, I removed two orange plastic construction cones from the well of my car and then went around to the rear, where I opened the engine compartment. I set up the cones nearby, signaling engine trouble in case anyone got curious.

I stood near the car and scanned the surrounding houses. I saw no one. I crossed the street to Misty's front door and rang the bell. Three minutes passed and then I knocked. No response. I leaned my head against the door. Silence. I walked down the drive and scrutinized the padlocked garage, which was connected to the house by a short enclosed breezeway. Both garage windows were locked and the glass had been painted over. I headed around the front of the house. A wooden fence on the far side opened into a backyard that was depressingly bare. No sign of pets, no children's toys, no lawn furniture, and no barbecue. The windows that overlooked the patio were dark. I cupped my hands to the glass and found myself staring at a home office equipped with the usual desk and swivel chair, a computer, phone, and copier. No sign of Misty or Reba. I was disappointed, having persuaded myself that Reba was staying with her. Now what?

I returned to the car and settled in to wait, amusing myself by browsing the yellow pages of the borrowed phone book. Bored with that, I picked up the first one of three paperbacks I'd brought for this purpose. It was comforting that most of the nearby houses remained dark, suggestive of occupants at work. At 8:10, I saw a Ford Fairlane slow on approach and ease into Misty's drive. In the fading daylight, primer paint on the driver's side of the car glowed as though luminescent. A woman emerged, wearing a white halter, tight jeans, and high heels without hose. She reached into the backseat for two cumbersome plastic grocery bags, crossed to the front door, and let herself in. I could see interior lights go on as she moved through the house. This had to be the very Misty Raine that I was looking for.

So far no one had questioned my presence on the block. I got out, retrieved the orange plastic cones, and returned them to my car—this by way of being prepared for whatever might come next. I resumed my reading with the help of a penlight I dug out of my bag. At intervals I glanced up, but the house remained quiet and nobody entered or left. At 9:40, prison-strength exterior spots came on, flooding the driveway with harsh white light. Misty emerged from the house, leaving lights on behind her as she got in her tank-size Ford and backed out of the drive. I waited fifteen seconds, fired up the VW, and followed.

Once we reached the first intersection, there was sufficient traffic to provide cover, though I didn't think she had any reason to suspect she was being tailed. She drove sedately, refraining from any abrupt or tricky moves that would indicate a concern about the thirteen-year-old pale blue VW traveling three car lengths behind.

We proceeded into town. She took a right on East 4th and after half a block turned into a small city parking lot that sat between an Asian restaurant and a minimarket with a marquee that read: GROCERIES * BEER * SLOTS. I slowed and pulled over to the curb. I left the engine running while I spread out my Reno map and studied the layout. I don't know why I went to such trouble to disguise my purposes. Misty didn't seem to be aware of me and certainly no one else in Reno cared if I was lost. I watched her enter the minimarket and took advantage of her absence to pull into the same lot. I parked as close to the entrance as I could manage. Each space was numbered in paint, and a board

posted on the brick wall of the market indicated that fees
were paid on the honor system. Dutifully, I searched out the
requisite window and inserted the number of dollar bills I
thought would cover my stay. I was so engrossed in this display of municipal virtue that I didn't spot Misty until she
was halfway across the street, munching a candy bar. She
had a carton of cigarettes under one arm.

Her destination lay dead ahead, an adult-entertainment
establishment called the Flesh Emporium. Under the double row of lightbulbs spelling out the name of the place, a
blinking neon sign flashed: GIRLS, GIRLS, GIRLS . . . NUDE,
LEWD, AND CRUDE. And in smaller letters: TATTOOS AND
PIERCING DONE WHILE YOU WAIT. And smaller still: BOOKS,
VIDEOS, LIVE REVUES. The bouncer waved her in. I waited a
decent interval and then crossed the street. There was a
twenty-dollar cover charge that it grieved me to pay, but I
ponied up the cash. I made a note to myself to add it to my
expense account in a manner that didn't suggest play-for-
pay sex.

Inside the entrance, a modest-size casino was hazy with
cigarette smoke, the air aglow with the ambient light from
a hundred slot machines lined up back-to-back. In passing,
I picked up the soft, goofy flute-and-bell music that accom-
panies play. The acoustical-tile ceiling was low, dotted with
can lights, cameras, smoke alarms, and sprinkler heads.
Scarcely anyone was seated at the slots, but farther in, beyond the blackjack tables, I could see a darkened bar with a
wide apron built along one side. On three hotly lighted plat-
forms nude dancers undulated, strutted, and otherwise exhibited body parts. Nothing they did seemed particularly
lewd or crude. I found a table toward the rear, feeling ill at
ease. Most of the customers were men. All were drinking
and most paid little or no attention to the breasts and but-
tocks on parade in front of them.

There was no sign of Misty, but a waitress named Joy arrived at my table and placed a cocktail napkin in front of

me. Sequined pasties the size of dinner mints chastely shielded her nipples from public scrutiny, and she wore a glittering fig leaf over what my aunt Gin would call her "privates." I ordered a bottle of Bass ale, theorizing there was no way the management could water it down. When Joy returned with my beer and a basket of tinted yellow popcorn, I paid the fifteen-dollar tab and tipped her an extra five bucks. "I'm looking for Misty. Is she here?"

"She just went to change. She'll be out in a bit. You're a friend of hers?"

"Not quite, but close enough," I said.

"Give me your name and I'll tell her you're here."

"She won't know me by name. A friend of a friend said I should look her up if I was ever passing through."

"What's the friend's name?"

"Reba Lafferty."

"Lafferty. I'll tell her."

I sipped my beer and picked at the cold, chewy popcorn, glad for the distraction as I didn't really favor watching nude women shaking their booties at me even from a distance. I'd imagined voluptuous, showgirl-style bodies, but only one of the three had the requisite football-size knockers. I figured the other two were saving up.

As it turned out, Misty hadn't gone to change clothes so much as to strip off the garments she was wearing when she got to work. Her legs were bare and only a thong and her high heels remained. She was tall and lanky, with pitch-black hair, a prominent collarbone, and long, thin arms. By way of contrast, she had breasts of burdensome dimensions, the kind that give you back problems and require a bra with straps so fierce they create permanent tracks across your shoulder blades like ruts worn in rock. Not that I've ever suffered from such a fate, but I've heard women complain. I couldn't imagine *choosing* to haul those things around. Her eyes were large and green with dark circles underneath that even heavy makeup couldn't hide. I placed her in her forties though I wasn't sure quite where.

"Joy says you're a friend of Reba's."

I didn't know stripper-greeting etiquette, but I stood and shook her hand. "Kinsey Millhone. I'm from Santa Teresa."

"Same as Reba," she remarked. "How's she doing these days?"

"I was hoping you'd tell me."

"Can't help you there. I haven't seen her in years. Are you in town on vacation or what's the deal?"

"I'm here looking for her."

One of Misty's shoulders went up in what passed for a shrug. "Last I heard she's in prison. California Institution for Women."

"Not anymore. She was released on the twentieth of this month."

"No fooling. Well, good for her! I'll have to drop her a line. The real world's a shock when you're not used to it," she said. "Hope she makes it."

"The prospects of that are dim. She did well at first, but lately things haven't been so hot."

"Sorry to hear that, but why come to me?"

"Just a long shot," I said.

"Must have been awful long. I've worked here a week. I don't get how you managed to track me down."

"Process of elimination. Reba told me you worked as an exotic dancer. With a name like yours, it wasn't difficult."

"Get off it. You know how many strip joints there are in this town?"

"Thirty-five. This is the thirteenth I've tried. Must be my lucky number. Can we chat?"

"About what? I start work in two minutes. I need time to get centered. Gig like this is tough unless you have your head on straight."

"I won't keep you long."

Gingerly she perched and I wondered if the wooden chair seat felt cold on her bare butt. The sensation couldn't be that keen, but she didn't yelp or otherwise vocalize dismay. She said, "Is this a fishing expedition or did you want something in particular?"

"Why do you ask?"

"I just thought if I heard from her, I could pass the message along—provided it's not obscene."

"I've heard she's in town. I'm hoping to talk her into coming back to California before she blows the terms of her parole."

"It's no skin off my nose what she blows. Or who, for that matter."

"I understand you were cellmates."

"Six months or so. I got out before she did—obviously."

"She told me you kept in touch."

"Why not? She's a nice kid and she's fun to be around."

"When was the last time you heard from her?"

Mock thought. "Must have been last Christmas. I sent her a card and she sent one back." She glanced over her shoulder. "Sorry to cut this short, but that music is my cue."

"If she happens to get in touch, tell her I'm in Reno. We really need to talk." I'd written the name of the motel, the telephone number, and my room number on a slip of paper that I handed her as she stood.

She took the note, though she had no place to put it unless she stuck it up her bum. "So who's paying you?"

"Her dad."

"Nice job. Like a bounty hunter, huh."

"It's more than a job. I'm a friend and I'm concerned about her welfare."

"I wouldn't lose any sleep over it. One thing about Reba, she can take care of herself."

I watched her head for the bar. The matching moons of her ass scarcely wobbled as she walked, and I could see the muscles in her thighs flex and relax with every step she took. Bumping and grinding must be better than Jazzercise, plus she didn't have to pay the weekly freight. I made a stop in the ladies' room, where I availed myself of the facilities before returning to my car.

Once there, I fired up the engine and sat with the windows rolled down, listening to the radio to pass the time. An hour later I began to worry about (1) running out of gas, or (2) asphyxiating myself with my own exhaust fumes. I cut the radio, killed the engine, and stared at the brick wall in front of me. This was the perfect screen on which to project recent memories of Cheney Phillips, probably not such a hot idea as he was many miles away.

Unwittingly, I dozed. Lights from a passing car flashed across my windshield and I woke with a start. I looked to my right as Misty's car passed behind me and slowed. She exited the parking lot and turned right. I started my car, backed out of the space with a quick chirp of tires, and pulled out shortly after she did. A glance at my watch showed it was 4:00 A.M. Apparently she did a six-hour shift instead of the usual eight put in by the ordinary working bloke. Then again, it was hard to imagine prancing around in high heels for more than a couple of hours at a stretch.

I kept the Ford Fairlane in view, allowing as big a lead as I could give her without losing sight of her altogether. There were fewer cars on the road now and many of the storefronts were dark. The big casinos were still doing a lively business. Misty pulled up to the front entrance to the Silverado Hotel. The wide overhang that stretched across the eight-lane drive was so densely studded with lightbulbs that the air seemed to shimmer with artificial heat. Misty got out of the car and handed the keys to a valet. The big glass doors opened and closed automatically as she approached and disappeared inside.

There were two vehicles in line between her car and mine. I leaped out and tossed my keys to an irritated-looking valet who'd been chatting with a pal. "Could you keep the car close? There's a twenty in it for you. I shouldn't be long."

Without waiting for a reply I trotted toward the front doors and entered the vast lobby, which was sparsely populated at that hour. I did a quick survey. There was no sign of

Misty. She could have slipped into a waiting elevator, into the ladies' room to my right, or into the casino dead ahead. Pick one, I thought. As I moved into the casino, smoke settled around me like a delicate mantilla. The silvery pings and grace notes from the slots were like a series of falling coins, the chirping of money as it trickled down the drain. Aisles ran in grids between the slot machines, the faces of which glowed bright red, green, yellow, and a saturated blue. I was struck by the patience of the few late-night players—like ants tending aphids on the underside of a leaf.

As I walked, I was glancing right and left, looking for Misty, whose height and black hair would surely set her apart. Toward the rear there were restaurants. I could see a coffee shop, a sushi bar, a pizza parlor, and an "authentic" Italian bistro offering six kinds of pasta and a variety of sauces, complete with Caesar salad, for $2.99. I spotted Misty in the lounge, though my gaze slid right past her at first and touched on the man who sat across the table from her. He was red-haired and gaunt, his complexion ruddy and pitted with acne scars. Neither saw me. I eased into the lounge, which was open on two sides. I sat at the bar some distance away, watching as the two conferred. The bartender ambled over and I ordered a glass of Chardonnay. There were not many patrons present at that hour, and I worried I'd be conspicuous sitting alone.

Out on the casino floor a great whooping and hollering went up, and shortly thereafter a party of five women came in, drunk and triumphant. One flourished a bucket of quarters, having won a five-hundred-dollar jackpot. My line of vision was obscured by their boisterous presence, but they provided me cover. I watched Misty engaged in a lengthy discussion with the man, leaning forward intently as the two examined something on the table in front of them. Finally, satisfied, she passed him a fat white number 10 envelope that I was betting contained a wad of cash. In exchange, he returned the item to a manila mailing pouch and handed it to her. I watched as she shoved it in her oversize purse. I tossed a five-dollar bill next to my empty glass and got up, leaving the bar in anticipation of her departure. I paused near the elevators, sliding a glance in her direction as she passed me and hurried toward the door. I followed in her wake.

She gave the valet parker her ticket, and while she waited for her car, I angled left, keeping my head turned and my back to her. My car was parked near the entrance. I reclaimed my keys, tipped the valet, and slid under the wheel. Two minutes later, her car rolled into view and the valet hopped out. She handed him a tip and took his place under the wheel. I watched her exit the lot. I eased in behind her, this time with only one car between. Once I was convinced she was on her way home, I took a left and sped along a parallel course. I arrived moments before she did. I killed my lights and slouched in my seat, eyes barely clearing the steering wheel. She turned into her drive as she had before, parked, crossed to her front door, and went in.

The front light went out. I sat there for a minute, sorely tempted to return to my motel and crawl into bed. Surely she was in for the night, or what little was left of it. I was tired, I was bored, and I was hungry again. I pictured breakfast in a twenty-four-hour coffee shop: orange juice, bacon and scrambled eggs, buttered rye toast covered with strawberry jam. Then sleep. There had never been any guarantee that Reba was in Reno. I'd taken the chance because it made sense, given what I knew of her. The two of them had certainly been in touch—why else would her number show up on Nord Lafferty's telephone bill? But that hardly spoke to the issue of her present whereabouts. I sat up, staring at Misty's half-darkened house and the narrow line of light running along the bottom of her garage door.

Why park in the driveway when she had a garage right there in front of her? In one of those unexpected jolts, I was clunked in the noggin by the obvious. If Misty were alone, she probably wouldn't need two bulging bags of groceries or a carton of smokes. The groceries might have represented her weekly run, but the woman didn't smoke. In the time we'd spent chatting, most smokers would have found an excuse to light up. It was actually that thin line of light at the bottom of the garage door that made me curious. I got out of the car and crossed the street.

27

I checked the garage windows first. Nicks in the brown paint that covered the glass revealed a makeshift guest room: a chair, a chest of drawers, a double bed, and a lamp sitting on an end table fashioned from a cardboard box. The disheveled linens suggested current occupancy, as did the red cotton sweater flung at the bottom of the bed, which I recognized as Reba's. A hard-sided gray suitcase lay open on the floor near the chest of drawers. The duffel was unzipped on the chair, clothes spilling out.

I circled the house as I had before. The pull latch on the wooden gate made scarcely a sound as I moved into the backyard and approached the lighted window. I ducked and came up at an angle, peering over the sill. Reba and Misty sat together at the desk with their backs to me. I couldn't see what they were doing and their voices were too muffled to discern the topic of conversation, but it was sufficient for the moment to know that Reba was in range.

Here was the question I asked myself: did I dare go back to my motel without confronting them? I was desperate for sleep, but I worried if I waited until morning, one or both of the women would be gone. Of course, I'd be facing the same dilemma anytime I let Reba out of my sight. For the moment, I was reluctant to give up the only advantage I had, which was that I knew where she was, but she didn't know that I knew.

Blessedly, as I watched, Misty gathered up the items they'd been inspecting and tucked them into the mailing pouch I'd seen earlier. Reba left the room and Misty followed, flicking the light switch as she passed. I made my way to the front of the house and hovered in the shadow of the evergreens. Ten minutes later, the living room light went out. I eased across the front of the house to the drive. Another fifteen minutes passed and then the line of light under the garage door was extinguished as well. I figured my little chickadees were in for the night.

I drove back to my motel through a city that was wide awake but quiet. The sun wouldn't be up for another hour or so, but the sky had already lightened to a pearly gray. I parked, took the stairs to the second floor, and unlocked my door. The room was drab but clean enough, as long as you didn't use a black light or get down on your hands and knees with a magnifying glass. I peeled off my clothes and took a good hot shower, then did what I could to secure the drapes across the window. The fabric was a heavyweight plastic, dark red, and very tastefully flocked. Add to that, vinyl wallpaper with its lightning bolts of silver and black, and you had a most amazing decor. I pulled back the pink chenille spread and settled between the sheets, turned off the lights, and slept like the dead.

At some point, my subconscious gave me a nudge. I remembered Reba telling me what a whiz Misty was at reproducing fake passports and other phony documents. Was that why Misty was meeting the fellow at the Silverado?

Even in my sleep, I felt a whisper of fear. Maybe Reba was planning to make a run for it.

At 10:00 the next morning the phone rang. I lifted the handset and laid it against my ear without moving my head. "What."

"Kinsey, this is Reba. Did I wake you?"

I rolled over on my back. "Don't worry about it. I appreciate the call. How're you doing?"

"Pretty much okay until I heard you were here. How'd you find me?"

"I didn't find you, I found Misty," I said.

"So how'd you do that? I'm just curious."

"Detective work, dear. That's what I do for a living."

"Huh. That surprises me."

"What does?"

"I figured Pop was able to hire you because you weren't any good. Clearly you weren't busy, or why would you agree to such a dumb-ass job? Drive his daughter back from prison? You can't be serious."

"Thanks, Reeb. That's nice."

"I'm saying I was wrong. Truth is, it shocked the hell out of me when Misty said you showed. I still don't get how you did it."

"I have my little ways. I hope you called for something more important than congratulating me for being less incompetent than you thought."

"We need to talk."

"Tell me when and where and I'll be there with bells on."

"We'll be at Misty's until noon."

"Great. Give me the address and I'll be over in a bit."

"I thought you'd already have the address."

"Guess I'm not perfect," I said, though as a matter of fact I was. She recited the address and I pretended to make a note.

Once she hung up, I got out of bed and crossed to the window. I pushed open the drapes and winced at the harsh

desert sun. My room looked out over the backside of another dingy two-story motel, so there wasn't much to see.
By resting my forehead against the glass, I could see the
flashing neon sign on the casino down the street still wink-
ing its invitation. How could anyone drink or gamble at this
hour?

I brushed my teeth and showered again, trying to jump-
start myself. I dressed and then sat down on the edge of the
bed and put a call through to Reba's father. Freddy told him
I was on the line and he took the call in his room, sounding
frail. "Yes, Kinsey. Where are you?"

"At the Paradise. It's a motel in downtown Reno. I
thought I'd give you an update. Reba called a while ago. I'm
on my way over to Misty's to talk to her."

"You found her, then. I'm glad. That didn't take long."

"I cheated. Someone gave me Misty's home address before I left Santa Teresa. I kept an eye on the place for hours,
but I didn't think Reeb was there. Misty has a very promis-
ing career as a nude dancer at a strip joint called the Flesh
Emporium. I followed her to work and chatted with her before she went on. When I asked about Reba, she never bat-
ted an eye. Swore up and down the two of 'em hadn't been
in touch since Christmas. I gave her the number of my motel and lo and behold, Reba called."

"I hope you'll be able to persuade her to come home."

"Hey, me too. Wish me luck."

"Ring me anytime you like. I appreciate your efforts on
her behalf."

"Happy to be of help."

We exchanged a few more remarks and I was preparing
to disconnect, when I heard a small click. I said, "Hello?"

"I'm still here."

I hesitated. "Is Lucinda there?"

"Yes. She's downstairs. Did you want to speak with
her?"

"No, no. I was just curious. I'll call you as soon as I
know where we stand."

After I hung up, I sat for a moment and stared at the phone. I was almost certain Lucinda had been listening in. Freddy would never be guilty of such an offense. Lucinda, on the other hand, was clearly someone who needed to insert herself in the thick of every situation, someone who needed to be informed so she could exercise control. I thought about how she'd pumped me for information, how much she'd resented being locked out of Nord's room when he and I conferred. Under the guise of being oh-so-concerned, she'd wreaked havoc in Reba's life, and she'd do so again if she had the chance. She was the kind of woman you didn't want to turn your back on when leaving a room.

I crossed the motel parking lot to McDonald's, where I ordered three large coffees, three OJs, three hash browns, and three Egg McMuffins to go. According to my calculations, Misty, Reba, and I—assuming we cleaned our plates— would each be supplied with 680 calories, 85 grams of carbohydrate, and 20 grams of fat. I amended my order, adding three cinnamon buns just to round things out.

I drove back to Misty's, this time parking in the driveway. Reba was waiting when I knocked on the door. She was barefoot, in a pair of red shorts and a white tank top without benefit of a brassiere. I held the bag out. "Peace offering."

"What for?"

"Invading your turf. I'm sure I'm the last person in the world you wanted to see."

"Second to last, just ahead of Beck. You might as well come in," she said. She took the bag and moved down the hall toward the kitchen, leaving me to close the door. I did a quick check of the living room in passing. The interior was sparsely furnished: bare linoleum flooring, wood-laminate coffee table, one of those brown tweed couches that can flatten to a bed. Brown tweed chair, end table, lamp with a flouncy shade. The next room on the right was the office I'd seen. There was a modest-size bedroom across the hall.

"Getting an eyeful?" Misty asked. She sat at the kitchen table in a black satin robe that was tied at the waist, boobs close to bulging out of her lapels. I was surprised the weight didn't cause her to lose her balance and flop over in her plate.

Reba had a lighted cigarette on the ashtray in front of her. She was drinking a Bloody Mary.

Oh, perfect, I thought.

"You want one?"

"Why not? It's after ten," I said. I reached into the Mc-Donald's bag and unloaded the goodies while Reba made me a drink and set it at my place. I looked at Misty. "You're not having a drink?"

"I got bourbon in here," she said, pointing to her coffee with a red-lacquered nail.

I sat down and doled out hash browns and Egg Mc-Muffins, leaving the cinnamon buns, orange juice, and coffee in the center of the table. "Sorry if I seem rude, but I'm starving to death." Neither seemed to object as I unwrapped my Egg McMuffin.

There was a blissful few minutes while the three of us munched. I figured business could wait. I didn't have a clue what we were doing anyway.

Reba finished first. She wiped her mouth on a paper napkin she kept wadded in her fist. "How's Pop?"

"Not that well. I'm hoping to talk you into going home."

She took a drag of her cigarette. The house felt chilly and I marveled at her bare arms and legs. I tried a sip of Bloody Mary—largely vodka with a thin mist of Bloody Mary mix on top, like blood in a toilet bowl. I could feel my eyes cross as the burning liquor went down. She said, "Does Holloway know?"

"What? That you left the state? That'd be my guess. Cheney told me he'd be getting in touch with her."

"Lucky I'm having fun."

"Mind if I ask why you left?"

"I got bored being good."

"Must be a record. You lasted ten days."

She smiled. "Actually, I wasn't all that good, but I got bored anyway."

"Is Misty in on this?"

"Meaning, can we talk in front of her? She's my best friend. You can say anything you like."

"You blew all the money, didn't you? Salustio's twenty-five grand."

"Not *all* of it," she said.

"How much?"

She shrugged. "Little over twenty. Well, maybe more like twenty-two. I have a couple of thousand left. I figure there's no point talking to him if I don't have the rest. What am I supposed to do, offer him small monthly payments until I've satisfied the debt?"

"You have to do something. How long do you think you can duck a guy like that?"

"Don't worry about it. I'm working on it. I'll figure it out. Anyway, maybe I'll be back in prison before he catches me."

"That's a happy thought," I said. "I don't understand why you can't go back to Santa Teresa and talk to Vince. There's still a chance the feds can cut you a deal."

"I don't need to make a deal with the feds. I got something in the works."

I turned to Misty. "She's nuts, right? I mean, how nuts is she?"

"Might as well leave her alone. Truth is, you can't save anybody but yourself."

"I'm afraid I'd have to agree with you there," I said, then to Reba, "Look, all I want is to get you back to Santa Teresa before shit comes raining down on your head."

"I get that."

"So why don't we leave it at this? You know where I'm staying. I'll hang out until seven tomorrow morning. If I don't hear from you by then, I'll drive back alone. But I gotta warn you—at that point, I'm calling the Reno PD and telling 'em where you are. Fair enough?"

"Oh, thanks. You think that's fair? Calling the Reno cops?"

"As fair as you're going to get. You'd be wise to spend time with your dad while you can."

"That's the only reason I'd go back, assuming I do."

"I don't care about your motive—just getting you there."

I went back to the motel, where I spent one of the most wickedly enjoyable days I've experienced in some time. I finished one paperback novel and started the next. I napped. At 2:30 I bypassed McDonald's and ate at a rival fast-food place. Afterward, I would have taken a walk, but I really didn't care what was out there. Reno is probably a very keen town, but the day was hotter than blue blazes, and my room, while glum, was at least habitable. I slipped my shoes off and read some more. At supper time, I called Cheney and brought him up to speed.

I went to bed at 10:00 and got up at 6:00 the next morning, showered, dressed, and packed my bag. When I got down to my car, I found Reba perched on her suitcase with her duffel at her feet. She had on the same red shorts and tank top she'd been wearing the morning before. Bare legs. Flip-flops.

I said, "This is a surprise. I didn't think I'd see you."

"Yeah, well, I surprised myself. I'll go with you on one condition."

"There aren't any conditions, Reba. You go or you don't. I'm not going to bargain with you."

"Oh, come on. Hear me out. It's no big deal."

"Okay, what."

"I need to make a stop in Beverly Hills."

"I don't want to make a detour. Why Beverly Hills?"

"I have to drop something off at the Neptune Hotel."

"The one on Sunset?"

"That's right. I swear it won't take any time at all. Will you just do me this one tiny thing. Please, please, please?"

I swallowed my irritation, thankful she'd agreed to come at all. I unlocked the car door on the passenger side, flipped the seat forward, and tossed my duffel in the rear. As Reba added her two bags, I noted that the duffel bore a United Airlines tag and a small green sticker showing the bag had cleared security. I'd been right about the fact she'd flown to Reno.

"We might as well have a decent breakfast before we take off. My treat," she said.

We had the McDonald's to ourselves. We gorged on the usual, though even as I ate, I swore off junk food for life, or at least until lunch. A couple of guys came in after us and then the place began to fill up with people on their way to work. By the time we visited the ladies' room and got into the car, it was 7:05. I gassed up at the nearest Chevron station and we headed out of town. "If you smoke in my car, I will kill you," I said.

"Blow it out your butt."

Reba was in charge of the map, directing me to the 395, which cut straight south to Los Angeles. Somehow I knew the detour would be a pain in the ass, but I was so relieved to have her with me, I decided not to make a fuss. Maybe she'd experienced a change of heart and she was ready to take responsibility for herself. Skittish as she was, I figured the best thing I could do was to keep my observations and opinions to myself.

Conversation was in short supply. The problem in dealing with people who are out of control is that the choices are so few—two being the actual number if you want to know the truth: (1) You can play counselor, thinking that perhaps no one (save yourself) has ever offered the rare tidbit of wisdom that will finally cause the light to dawn. Or (2) You can play persecutor, thinking that a strong dose of reality (also delivered by you) will shame or cajole the person into turning her life around. In both instances, you'll be wrong, but the temptation is so strong to take one role or the other that you'll have to bite your tongue bloody to keep from jumping in with all the lectures and the finger wagging. I kept my mouth shut, though it required an effort on my part. She was mercifully quiet, perhaps sensing my struggle to mind my own business.

28

On the road, Reba fiddled with the radio until she found a station that didn't sound like it was broadcasting from Mars. We listened to country-western tunes while I played bumper tag with the same three cars: a pickup with a camper shell, an RV, and a couple of college students in a U-Haul truck. One would pass me and then the next and then I'd pass one of them, a form of vehicular leapfrog that had us hopping over one another at irregular intervals. At the back of my mind, I wondered if we were being followed, but I couldn't imagine how Beck or Salustio could manage to get a bead on us.

Where the 395 and Highway 14 intersected, the kids in the U-Haul went straight while we stayed on Highway 14, angling south and west. Eventually we connected to the San Diego Freeway and drove south. By then the RV had disappeared and I saw no sign of the pickup with the camper shell. Nervous-making nonetheless.

It was close to 3:00 when I got off the freeway at Sunset Boulevard, took a left, and followed the road east again through Bel Air and into Beverly Hills. Reba played navigator, tracking street addresses though it really wasn't necessary. A few blocks beyond Doheny, the Hotel Neptune loomed into view, an Art Deco wonder that vaguely mimicked the Empire State Building, its shoulders narrowing to a point. I'd read an article about the place in a copy of *Los Angeles Magazine*. The property had recently been expanded to encompass a large parcel of land on each side, which allowed the creation of a sweeping entrance and additional guest parking. A name change and the multimillion-dollar renovation had propelled the old hotel into prominence again. Now it was the hot new destination for rock stars, actors, and wide-eyed tourists hoping to be considered hip.

I pulled into the sweeping semicircular drive, taking my place sixth in line behind two stretch limousines, a Rolls, a Mercedes, and a Bentley. This was clearly check-in time. A car-park valet and two to three uniformed bellhops hovered around each vehicle, assisting the guests as they emerged, unloading bag after bag from open trunks onto rolling brass luggage carts. A doorman in livery and white gloves whistled up a taxicab that cut around me on the left and pulled up in front. Two hotel guests dressed like tramps ducked into the cab and I watched it pull away.

Reba said, "This is nuts. Why don't I just run in?"

"Forget it. I don't want you out of my sight."

"Oh, for heaven's sake," she said. "What do you think, I'm going to duck out the back and leave you here by yourself?"

As that was exactly what I thought, I didn't bother to reply. When our turn came, I handed the keys to the parking valet while Reba dazzled him with a smile and pressed a folded bill against his palm. "Hey, how're you? We'll be back in two minutes."

"We'll have it ready for you."

"Thanks." She moved on into the hotel, boobs jiggling,

her slim legs flashing in her red shorts. The guy was so busy ogling her, he nearly dropped the car keys.

The interior of the hotel was a pastiche of dark green marble and mirrors, wall sconces, torchères, and potted palms. The carpet was done in shades of green and blue, stylized waves, which were part of the nautical motif. Not surprisingly, the Roman god Neptune was depicted in a series of massive gilt-and-stucco bas-relief panels, driving his chariot across the waters, shaking his trident to bring down floods, saving a damsel from a satyr. Artificial light glowed from a five-tiered fountain of glass. The chairs were blond wood, the occasional tables lacquered in black. A wide marble staircase curved up to the mezzanine, where I could see black pedestals set in green fluted niches, each bearing an urn filled with fresh flowers.

The lobby walls were curved, with banquettes covered in a fabric that mimicked undulating sea grasses. Swing tunes playing at almost subliminal levels. Two lines had formed in front of the marble-sheathed reception desk—guests checking in, picking up messages, conversing with the staff.

Reba paused to get her bearings and then said, "Wait here."

I took a seat in a curved-back chair, one of four arranged around an etched-glass coffee table. In the center was a crystal bowl in which gardenias floated. I watched as she crossed to the concierge, a middle-aged man in a tuxedo. His desk was a sinuous curve of inlaid woods, banded in chrome and topped with a green glass counter, subtly lighted from below. She removed a manila mailing pouch from her purse, wrote something on the front, and handed it to him. After a brief conversation, he placed the manila envelope on a credenza against the wall behind his desk. She asked him a question. He consulted his files and extracted a white envelope, which he handed to her. She put it in her purse and then crossed to the house phone and picked up the handset. She had a conversation with someone and then returned. "We're meeting in the cocktail lounge."

"Oh, happy day. Can I join you?"

"Don't be a smartass. Of course."

The cocktail lounge was located on the far side of the lobby, across from the elevators. The bar itself was a streamlined curve, sheathed in glass panels that were etched with coral reefs, sea creatures, and goddesses in various states of undress. The space was large and dark, the indirect lighting augmented by a votive candle in the center of each table. The place was almost empty, but I was guessing that within the hour the bar would start filling up with hotel guests, starlets, hookers, and local business types.

Reba snagged a table close to the door. It was only 3:10, but knowing Reba, she'd be ready for a drink. A cocktail waitress wearing a snug gold satin vest, matching shorts, and gold mesh hose, delivered an order of drinks to a nearby table and then approached ours.

Reba said, "We're expecting someone else."

"You want to order now or wait?"

"Now is fine."

The waitress looked to me.

"I'll have coffee," I said, already focused on the drive ahead. This was Saturday so at least we wouldn't have to deal with rush-hour traffic, but it would still be a hard couple of hours, given the seven and a half we'd done.

"And for you?"

"Vodka martini with three olives and a double whiskey for my friend."

The waitress moved toward the bar.

"I don't get it," I said. "You know drinking's a parole violation. If Holloway finds out, she'll come down on you like a ton of bricks."

"Oh, please. It's not like I'm doing *drugs*."

"But you're doing everything else. Don't you want to hang on to your freedom?"

"Hey, you know what? I was free when I was in. I didn't drink or smoke or do drugs or screw around with any dumb-ass guys. You know what I did? I picked up computer skills. I learned to upholster a chair, which I'll bet you sure as shit can't do. I read books and made the kind of friends who'd give their lives for me. I didn't know how happy I was till I got out in this kiss-ass world. I don't give a shit about Holloway. She can do anything she wants."

"Okay by me. It's your lookout," I said.

Reba's sullen gaze was fixed on the bank of elevators directly across from us. Above each elevator there was an old-fashioned half-moon of brass, with a moving brass arrow indicating the progress of the elevators going up or coming down. I watched as the last elevator in line paused at the eighth floor and then worked its way down. The doors slid open and Marty Blumberg emerged. Reba waved and he headed in our direction. When he reached our table, she tilted her head so he could kiss her cheek. "You're lookin' good," he said.

"Thanks. So are you."

Marty pulled out a chair with a glance at me. "Nice seeing you again," he said. His attention shifted back to her. "Everything okay?"

"We're cool. I left something for you at the desk. Thanks for this," she said, patting her bag.

He reached into the pocket of his sport coat and took out a claim check that he slid across the table.

"What's this for?"

"Surprise. A little something extra," he said.

Reba glanced at the claim check and slipped it in her purse. "I hope it's something good."

"I think you'll like it," he said. "What's your timetable? Can you hang out long enough to have dinner with me?"

I opened my mouth to protest, but Reba surprised me by wrinkling her nose, saying, "Nah, better not. Kinsey's anxious to get home. Maybe some other time."

"God willing and the creek don't rise."

Marty took out a cigarette pack and placed it on the table. Without asking, Reba helped herself to one, which she stuck between her teeth, giving it a waggle to request a light. Marty picked up a packet of hotel matches, struck one, held the flame to her cigarette, and then fired up one for himself.

The waitress returned with our order, placing the bill at Marty's elbow. Reba took a sip of her martini and closed her eyes, savoring the vodka with such reverence that I could almost taste it myself. The two of them launched into an inconsequential conversation. I was peripherally included, but it was all low-key chat, a series of drifting subjects that didn't signify much of anything as far as I could tell. I drank two cups of coffee while they tossed down their drinks and ordered a second round. Neither showed the slightest sign of inebriation. Marty's face was more flushed than I'd seen it, but he was in control of himself. Eventually their cigarette smoke began to get on my nerves. I excused myself and retired to the ladies' room, where I wasted as much time as I dared before returning to the table. I sat down again and sneaked a look at my watch. We'd been in the hotel bar forty-five minutes and I was ready to hit the road.

Reba leaned forward and put a hand on Marty's arm. "We probably ought to get going. I'll make a quick trip to the loo and meet the two of you out there." She tipped her glass and sucked down the rest of her drink, chomping on the olive as she moved toward the ladies' room.

I watched Marty calculate a tip and sign the drinks off to Room 817. "How long have you been here?" I asked.

"Couple of days."

"I take it you won't be driving back with us."

"Don't think so," he said, amused.

I didn't see the humor myself, but whatever he and Reba'd cooked up between them had left him feeling smug.

"What happened with your phone? Was the line tapped or not?"

"Don't know. I decided not to hang around and find out."

He pocketed his copy of the receipt and then got up, holding my chair politely. The two of us moved toward the elevators and stood together saying nothing while we waited for Reba. Across the lobby, I saw her emerge from the ladies' room. Marty's gaze followed mine. I saw his focus shift to the left. Two men in chinos and sport coats were crossing the lobby with purposeful strides. I thought they were heading for the cocktail lounge. I turned and looked behind me, half-expecting to see what was generating such urgency. Marty took a step to one side to get out of their path. One man caught the doors to the nearest elevator before they slid shut. He stepped in and extended his hand again as though to hold the door for his friend. The second man bumped up against Marty, who said, "Hey, watch it!"

The man gripped Marty's arm, his forward motion forcing Marty to walk in lockstep into the waiting elevator. Marty flailed and struggled to free himself. He might have succeeded, but one of the two men knocked his feet out from under him. Marty went down on his back, flinging his arms across his face to ward off the savage kick he could see coming at him. The shoe made contact with a wet, thick sound that opened a split in his cheek. The other man pressed the button. In that moment before the doors slid shut, Marty's gaze caught mine.

I said, "Marty?"

The doors closed and the floor indicator moved up.

Two other people in the lobby turned to see what was wrong, but by then everything appeared to be normal. The entire sequence took no more than fifteen seconds.

Reba reached my side, her eyes enormous, the color draining out of her cheeks. "We gotta get out of here."

I banged on the Up button, transfixed by the sight of the arrow as it inched toward the eighth floor and came to a halt. Fear was bathing my internal organs with sufficient acid to eat through my chest wall. Two elevators down, the doors slid open. I grabbed her arm and turned her toward the lobby. "Go get hotel security and tell 'em we need help."

She pulled at my fingers and then lifted her elbow and swung upward to break my grip. "Bullshit. Get off me. Marty's on his own."

I didn't have time to argue. I pushed her as though I could propel her all the way to the front desk, and then I got on the waiting elevator and pushed the button for 8. I had no faith whatever that she'd do as I said. My heart thumped as adrenaline pushed through my system like a drug rush. I needed a game plan, but I didn't know what I was facing. As the elevator climbed, I searched my shoulder bag, though I already knew there was nothing in it in the way of weapons. No gun, no penknife, no pepper spray.

The elevator doors slid open on 8. I stepped into the hall and trotted to the T intersection where the long and short corridors met. I spotted the sign indicating which grouping of room numbers were located on the left and which were on the right, but I could barely make sense of it. I was talking to myself, a litany of cuss words and instructions. I heard a muffled shout of pain, someone banging into a wall somewhere to my left. I race-walked in that direction, scanning room numbers as I went. The hall had a claustrophobic feel to it, Nile green paint, a low ceiling that consisted of four thick cutaway layers stair-stepped back from a central panel of dull artificial light. Every twenty feet there were fluted niches of the sort I'd seen when looking up from the lobby toward the mezzanine. In each niche, there were two black lacquered wooden chairs arranged on each side of a round, glass-topped table set with an urn of fresh flowers. I picked up a chair and held it in front of me, searching for 817 at a pace that reminded me of dreams I'd had: I couldn't make my body move. I walked but I didn't seem to get anywhere.

The door to Marty's room was ajar. I kicked it inward, but the two guys were already on their way out, dragging Marty between them. I was saying *Pick-one-pick-one-pick-one* to myself, so I chose the guy on my right and thrust hard, hitting him bang-on in the face with the legs of the chair. I made contact, jamming hard. The sound he made was savage but the blow didn't seem to do any harm. He grabbed the chair, wrenching it out of my hands. I saw his fist coming at me, low and fast, smacking into my solar plexus with a paralyzing punch that put me down on my butt. The sour taste of regurgitated coffee rose in my throat in a blinding burst of nausea. I couldn't catch my breath and for a terrifying few minutes I thought I'd suffocate where I sat. I looked up in time to see the chair coming down at me. I felt the bang and registered the jolt, but no pain. I was gone.

29

_____

I was lying on a bed, caught up in a confusion of conversations, which seemed to be about me. It reminded me of car trips as a kid, listening to the low, lazy buzz of adults talking in the front seat while I snoozed in the rear. I experienced the same sweet certainty that if I could just remain still, feigning sleep, others would take responsibility for the journey. Something flat and icy cold was pressed against the side of my head, causing a stinging sensation so sharp that I hissed. Someone put the towel-wrapped ice pack in my hand and encouraged me to hold it myself at a pressure I could tolerate.

The hotel doctor arrived and spent an inordinate amount of time checking my vital signs, making sure I still knew my name, the date, and how many fingers he was holding up—a number he varied in an attempt to trick and deceive. There was talk of paramedics, whose services I declined. Next thing I knew, there were two more guys in the room. One I gathered was the head of hotel security, a hefty gentleman in a business suit with a gaping lapel. I caught a glimpse of leather that I hoped was a shoulder holster and not a back brace. The notion of a man with a gun was comforting. He was in his sixties, balding and beefy-faced with a thick gray mustache. The man with him, I was guessing, was part of the hotel-management team. I turned my head slightly. A third man appeared in the doorway with a walkie-talkie in his hand. He was slim, in his forties, sporting what was surely a toupee. He entered and conferred with the other two.

The beefy-faced guy with the mustache introduced himself, saying, "I'm Mr. Fitzgerald, hotel security. This is my associate, Mr. Preston, and the manager, Mr. Shearson. How do you feel?"

I said, "Fine," which was ridiculous, as I was flat on my back with a very tender lump on my head. Someone had removed my shoes and put a blanket over me that really wasn't warm enough.

The manager leaned close to Fitzgerald and spoke to him as though I wasn't there. "I notified corporate. The attorney suggested we have her sign a waiver, releasing us from any liability . . ." He glanced at me and then lowered his voice.

There was a squawk from the walkie-talkie. Mr. Preston retired to the corridor and conducted his conversation beyond my hearing. When he returned moments later, he chatted with Fitzgerald, but in a tone so subdued I couldn't pick up the content. The manager excused himself and after a brief conference Mr. Preston left as well.

I struggled to get my bearings. They had apparently settled me in an empty guest room, though I didn't remember how I'd arrived. For all I knew, they'd dragged me through the halls by my heels. I could see a desk, sofa, two upholstered chairs, and the Art Deco armoire that housed the minibar and TV. I'd never stayed in such an upscale hotel so it was all a revelation to me. The management at the Paradise in Reno could take a lesson from the Neptune when it came to interior design. I adjusted my ice pack and said, "What happened to Marty?"

Fitzgerald said, "We don't know. They managed to get him out of the building without being seen. I had the parking lot attendant check for his car, but someone had already claimed it and had driven it away. No one remembered the driver so we're not sure if Mr. Blumberg left on his own or in the company of the men who abducted him."

"Poor guy."

"The police are here talking to the woman with you. They'd like to ask you a few questions when you're up to it."

"I don't remember much, but sure," I said. In truth, I didn't feel like conversation. I was cold. The knot on the side of my head throbbed sharply with every beat of my pulse. My midsection was sore. I had no idea what Reba was telling them, but I suspected she'd be less than candid. The whole situation was too complicated to explain, especially since I didn't know how much the feds considered confidential. I was sick about Marty. My last glimpse of him—cheek split, blood running down the side of his face—he'd seemed resigned to his fate, like a man being hauled off to the gas chamber, priest at his side. It was the dread in his eyes I found haunting, as though he knew that something far worse was in store for him. I wanted to rewind the reel of film, let events unfold again so I could find a way to help him.

Fitzgerald said something else, but I wasn't taking it in. I removed the ice pack and checked the soggy terry cloth with its blush of blood in the loops. I rearranged the fold and laid the fresh cold of a new spot against my poor banged-up head. I was shivering, but I couldn't bring myself to ask for another blanket. "Sorry. Could you repeat that?"

"Had you ever seen these men before?"

"Not to my recollection. I thought they were on their way to meet someone else. They were coming right at us, but it's like a stranger waving in your direction. You turn around and look back, assuming it isn't you they mean. Reba might remember more than I do. Can I talk to her?"

He debated, wanting to press for information, trying at the same time to appear compassionate and concerned, hotel liability being what it was. "As soon as the police are finished, I'll have her come in."

"Thanks."

I closed my eyes again. I was tired and I didn't think I'd ever want to get out of this bed. I felt a touch on my arm. Reba now sat in a chair she'd pulled over close to the bed. Fitzgerald wasn't in the room.

"Where'd Fitzgerald disappear to?"

"Who knows. I told the cops to call Cheney and he'd fill 'em in. I didn't want to put my foot in my mouth with the FBI involved. How's your head?"

"Hurts. Help me up and let's see if I can sit up without passing out or puking." She held my outstretched hand and eased me into an upright position. I pushed the blanket aside and placed my other hand on the bed table for stability. It really wasn't as bad as I'd thought.

"You're not planning to go anywhere, I hope."

"Not until I know what kind of shape I'm in. You ever see those guys before?"

She hesitated. "I think so. In the pickup truck on the way down from Reno. They're probably Salustio's goons. Beck must have told him I took his twenty-five grand."

"But why snatch Marty? He had nothing to do with it."

"I don't know what's going on. Shit, I wish I'd never told Marty the feds were closing in. All that did was scare him into running. He'd have been better off if he were under arrest. At least he'd be safe."

"What about the claim check he gave you? What was that about?"

She blinked. "I don't know. I'd forgotten about that." She rooted through her bag, pulled it out, and turned it over in her hand. "Hotel luggage claim. I should talk to the bell captain and see what this is. Will you be okay? It shouldn't take me long."

"Sure. Why don't you wait for me downstairs? As soon as I've talked to the cops, I'll meet you in the lobby."

She said, "Great."

I waited until she was gone and then made my way into the bathroom, where I washed my face and ran my head under the faucet to wash away the dried blood that was matted in my hair. I took a bath towel and blotted gingerly until the strands were dry enough to comb. Really, I was doing better than I'd expected, now that I was on my feet.

By the time the uniformed beat officer arrived, I was sitting in a chair, feeling somewhat restored. He was a clean-cut fellow in his twenties with a serious demeanor and a slight, disarming lisp. I repeated what I knew, watching him scribble in his notebook. We went over the sequence of events until he seemed satisfied that he'd wrung as much from me as I was able to remember. I gave him my Santa Teresa address and my phone number, as well as Cheney's. He gave me a card and said I could request a copy of the crime report if I wrote to the Records Section, though it would take about ten days for processing.

Once the door closed behind him, I slipped on my shoes. Bending down to tie the laces was not a happy occasion, but I managed it. I found my shoulder bag and let myself out into the hall, then located the bank of elevators and went down.

In the lobby, I looked across to the bell captain's desk, expecting to catch sight of Reba. No bell captain and no Reba. I'd been talking to the officer for a good ten minutes, so it didn't surprise me to think she'd already retrieved whatever Marty had left for her. I circled the area, peering into the cocktail lounge, the ladies' room, and the corridor near the public phones. I tried the gift boutique and the newsstand next door. Where the hell had she gone? I kept expecting to spot her, and it annoyed me no end that she'd wandered off without leaving me some word. I sat in the lobby for six or seven minutes and then stepped outside. The bell captain was tagging a set of suitcases. When he finished, I said, "I'm looking for a friend . . . petite, dark hair. She came down a little while ago with a claim check for—"

"Of course. She picked up the rolling bag and then she left."

"Do you know where she went?"

He shook his head. "Sorry. I wish I could help." He excused himself to tend to an incoming guest and left me standing there perplexed. Now what?

A car pulled up, the parking valet delivering the vehicle to a waiting guest. The driver got out and as the valet closed the door, he caught my eye. I realized he was the same kid we'd seen when we first arrived. "You looking for your friend?"

"Yes."

"You just missed her," he said.

"What do you mean, 'missed her'?"

"The doorman whistled her up a cab a few minutes ago."

"You mean she left the hotel? Going where?"

"I didn't hear. She gave the driver instructions and then the taxi pulled away."

"Was she alone?"

"Looked like it. She had her suitcase with her so maybe she was headed for the airport."

"Thanks."

Now what?

I couldn't figure out what she was up to. I was anxious to hit the road, but how could I leave the hotel when I had no idea where she was or if she meant to return? Had she left on an impulse or had she intended to ditch me from the moment we left Reno? Whatever the reality, I felt I had to hang around for a while, at least until I was convinced she was gone for good.

In the meantime, there must be something I could do. I returned to the lobby, where I took a seat in the same chair

I'd occupied when we first arrived. I closed my eyes and went back over the entire sequence of events. I pictured Reba crossing to the desk. She'd removed a mailing pouch from her purse, printed something on the face of it, and left it with the concierge. She'd then asked for and received an envelope. Which suggested what?

I got up and approached the concierge's desk. There was only one man on duty—Carl, according to his name tag—and he was in the process of setting up dinner reservations for a well-dressed older gentleman. I waited. Once the gentleman left, Carl turned a blank look on me, his eyes straying to the side of my head, where I suddenly imagined a bump the size of the Palmdale Bulge. "May I be of assistance?"

"Is the manager available?"

"I can certainly check. Are you a guest of the hotel?"

"Well, no, but I seem to have a little problem and I could use his help."

"I see. And will he know what this is in reference to?"

"Probably not. You can tell him the name is Millhone."

He picked up his desk phone and punched in a number, gaze fixed on me. When the line was picked up on the other end, he turned away from me and conducted his conversation with a hand across his mouth like someone trying to be polite while picking his teeth in public. "He'll be with you in just one moment."

"Thanks."

He smiled and his gaze slid past me as he busied himself. For some minutes he was occupied with a ledger and the phone. I started to speak, but he held up a finger—denoting, *One minute, please*—and then went on with his task. Was I being stonewalled? I remembered the comment the manager had made about the hotel's liability in light of Marty's (alleged) abduction and the assault on me. Perhaps he'd put a call through to corporate and his boss, or his boss's boss, had warned him to avoid any further contact with me. Anything said might be used against the hotel in a court of law. I might as well have had a flashing sign on my forehead: LAWSUIT ∗ LAWSUIT ∗ LAWSUIT. "Excuse me. Sir?"

"If you'd care to have a seat, the manager will be with you." His tone was pleasant, but this time he didn't look at me at all. He picked up a sheaf of papers, rapped them against the counter to align the edges, and moved into the inner office as though on a mission related to national security.

Irritated, I noticed that my bad angel was now perched on my shoulder, pointing mutely. I could see the manila mailing pouch Reba'd left earlier. It was still lying on the credenza less than five feet away. From where I stood, Marty's name was visible, printed in bold black ink. *Here we go* . . . I moved down the counter and caught the attention of an idle desk clerk, a kid about twenty, probably still in training for the job. He said, "Yes, ma'am. May I help you?"

"I hope so. My name is Mrs. Blumberg. My husband and I are guests of the hotel. He said he was leaving a package for me and I believe that's it." I pointed at the pouch.

The clerk picked it up. "You're Marty?"

"Yes, I am."

He handed it over, happy to be of service.

I was happy, too. "Thank you."

I made my way to the ladies' room, where I shut myself in a stall. I perched on the toilet seat despite the fact that it had no lid. In correctional facilities, lids are removed to prevent suicide attempts, though offhand it's hard to imagine the procedure whereby one would hang oneself with a toilet seat, especially with that cunning gap in the middle separating the two halves. In some institutions, there's no toilet seat at all, just a tankless one-piece commode, fashioned out of stainless steel. I propped my feet on the door, worried the clerk would burst in and raise a hue and cry about unlawful possession. The pouch had the bulk and heft of a couple of paperbacks. The flap was self-sealed, but I picked at it until the two lines of adhesive loosened their grip. I peered in.

Now this was the perfect example of why it's so impossible to cure me of the naughty lies I tell. Fibs and related forms of deception often have the most remarkable rewards. Inside I found the following:

A United States passport, issued to one Garrisen Randolph, with a two-by-two photograph of Martin Blumberg.

A California driver's license issued to Garrisen Randolph, with a slightly shrunken version of the same photograph. His residence address was listed in Los Angeles, 90024 zip code, which was actually Westwood. Sex: M HAIR: Brn   EYES: Brn   HT: 5-11   WT: 272   DOB: 08-25-42, this latter printed in red. Above the picture, also in red, was the license expiration date: 08-25-90.

In addition, there was an American Express card, a Visa credit card, and a MasterCard issued to the same Garrisen Randolph, plus a birth certificate from Inyo County, California, detailing the particulars of Garrisen Randolph's birth.

These were, of course, versions of the phony documents Reba'd stolen from the hidden drawer in Alan Beckwith's desk. The name on these documents was a variation on the name Garrison Randell, probably to ensure that a computer search wouldn't pick up a match. Technically, Marty could leave the country anytime he liked and no one would be the wiser. There was no doubt in my mind that Misty Raine had done the work. I remembered Reba's telling me Misty's newly discovered forging talents had netted her the bucks to pay for that bodacious set of tits. The fellow she'd met in the lounge at the Silverado was probably supplying counterfeit paper, seals, or credit card blanks.

But what did it mean?

Phony documents of this caliber cost plenty. Reba was the one who'd made all the arrangements, but in exchange for what? Clearly she and Marty had a deal. I could see what he was getting out of it, but what was the benefit to her? I thought about the envelope she'd received at the desk. Maybe he'd given her the twenty-five thousand dollars she needed to pay Salustio. Which left the issue of the suitcase, which contained god knows what. I glanced at my watch. It was now close to 6:00. I shoved the manila pouch in my shoulder bag and left the ladies' room.

I took the elevator up to 8. As I'd hoped, there were maid's carts parked at intervals along the corridor. Many guests had departed for the evening, on their way to dinner. The maids were now going room by room, emptying the trash, replacing towels, replenishing amenities, and turning down the beds. I waited until the maid had entered Marty's room and then I scurried down the hall. I paused near her cart, where I spotted a box of disposable latex gloves. I slipped a pair in my shoulder bag and rapped on the open door. I wondered if the cop had been through Marty's room. Perhaps not, as there wasn't any crime scene tape.

The maid looked up from the bed where she was folding the heavy quilted spread into something the size and shape of a giant Tootsie Roll.

I said, "Sorry to interrupt, but is there any way you can come back and finish this later? I have a dinner date in twenty minutes and I have to get dressed."

She murmured her apologies, picked up her plastic carrier of supplies, and exited.

I hung the Privacy Please sign on the outside knob, pulled on my gloves, and did a thorough search. Marty must have had his wallet, room key, and other items on his person when his assailants hurried him away. I went through the hard-sided suitcase he'd left open on the luggage rack. Underwear, shirts, socks, a few toiletries he hadn't transferred to the bathroom counter. I opened the closet door and ran a hand into the pockets of the pants he'd left. Empty. I made a systematic search of the hanging garment bag, but there was just what you'd expect: suits, trousers, belts, shoes. Aside from the hotel robe, there was no other clothing in the closet and no sign of the usual hotel safe with its four-digit combination lock.

I searched the bathroom, including the underside of the

toilet tank lid, and found nothing. I opened the dresser drawers and ran a hand around the interiors. Empty. I pulled each drawer all the way out, wondering if there was something secured under or behind. When I reached the bed table, I went through the same routine. I removed the Gideon Bible. Inside the cover there was a Delta Air Lines ticket, first class to Zurich, issued in Garrisen Randolph's name. The booking was one-way and the flight was scheduled to depart at 9:30 the next morning.

I replaced the ticket between the pages, returned the Bible to the drawer, and closed it. I didn't believe Marty was coming back, but on the off-chance he made it, the ticket would be waiting. I removed my gloves, plucked the Privacy Please sign from the outside knob, and hung it on the inside. I took the elevator down. I went into the newsstand and bought three dollars' worth of stamps, which I pasted on the front of the mailing pouch. I penned my home address under Marty's name and then pinched the adhesive to secure the opening. I took a seat within sight of the concierge's desk, watching to see if Carl was still on duty. Ten minutes passed and there was no sign of him. A smartly dressed woman, with a name tag pinned to her lapel, had stepped into the job.

I approached the desk. She appeared to be capable, her smile properly cool and professional. "Yes, ma'am."

I put the mailing pouch on the counter. "I'd like to leave this for Mr. Blumberg in Room 817, but I wonder if you could attach a note. If he hasn't picked it up by tomorrow afternoon, I'd appreciate someone's dropping it in the mail to him."

"Of course."

She wrote the appropriate note and clipped it to the top edge of the pouch. I said, "Oh, and do you happen to have a stapler? This has popped open."

"Not a problem." She reached behind the counter and took out a stapler. I watched while she crunched a succession of staples into the upper edge of the pouch, tightly sealing it. She placed it back on the credenza where it had sat earlier. I thanked her, silently sending up a prayer for Marty's survival.

At 7:15 I shelled out twenty-five bucks to the bell captain and retrieved my VW. I drove west on Sunset as far as the on-ramp to the northbound 405, traveling up the long hill toward the valley and down the other side. Once I connected to the 101, I pointed the car toward home.

30

I reached Santa Teresa at 9:00 that night. The summer temperatures had cooled rapidly as the sun inched its way down toward the horizon. Along Cabana Boulevard, the streetlights had flicked on and the wide stretch of ocean had turned all silvery and white. I stopped by my apartment, where I dropped my bags and wrote a quick note to Henry letting him know I was home. I left a message to the same effect on Cheney's answering machine, saying I'd catch up with him when I could.

By 9:20 I was back in the car, heading south toward Montebello and the Lafferty estate. Gingerly I put a hand to the knot on my head—still sore, and still undiminished in size. Happily the headache was gone and I thought it safe to assume that I was on the mend. I didn't think I'd jog for a day or two, but at least my thinking seemed clear.

The drive up from Los Angeles had given me a chance to reflect. I still had no clue how the two goons had found us in Reno. As odious as Beck was, I didn't picture him

with thugs on his payroll, which meant they were sent by
Salustio Castillo. I was baffled by their snatching Marty.
Reba's theft of Salustio's twenty-five grand made her the
logical target. Unless Marty had done something even
more foolish than she. Such as what? I wondered if he'd
packed the remainder of Salustio's money in the rolling
bag. But to what end? From what he'd said that night at
Dale's, he'd set aside sufficient funds to take care of himself. So why steal more and why pass it on to Reba when all
that would do was place her in greater jeopardy than she
was in? Meanwhile, where was she?

I thought it was entirely possible she'd commissioned
Misty to dummy up a passport and other phony documents
for herself as well as for Marty. If that were the case, she
might be on her way out of the country, though I couldn't
believe she'd go without saying good-bye to her dad. She
might not confide her destination, but surely she'd find a
way to let him know that she was okay. Not for the first
time, I was thinking my relationship with Reba was at an
end. She'd blow off her parole and take her chances as a
fugitive.

When I reached the entrance to the Lafferty estate, the
gates were closed. I pulled up to the keypad, rolled down my
window, and pressed the call button. I could hear the line
ring inside. Once. Twice. Freddy picked up, her voice sounding scratchy over the intercom system.

I stuck my head out the window and raised my voice.
"Freddy? It's Kinsey. Can you let me in, please?"

I heard a series of peeps and then a low humming noise
as the gates swung open to the full. I flipped on my brights
and eased my way down the drive. I could see house lights
twinkling through the trees. As I rounded the last curve, I
saw that the second story was dark but the lights were on in
many of the first-floor rooms along the front. Lucinda's car
was parked in its usual spot and I could feel my eyes cross
at the notion of encountering her. As I got out of the car, I
caught motion to my right. Rags sauntered along the drive

at a pace perfectly calculated to intercept my path. When he reached me, I leaned down and scratched between his ears. His long pumpkin-colored fur was silky, his purr becoming more pronounced as he arched his big head and pushed against my hand. "Listen, Rags. I'd be happy to take you in, but if Lucinda answers the door we got no shot at it."

He trailed up the walk with me, sometimes running around in front to inspire additional stroking and conversation. I could see where owning a cat would render a grownup completely goofy in time. I reached for the bell, but the front door swung open in advance of my ring. Lucinda was framed in the porch light, wearing a crisp-looking yellow coatdress, with pale hose and matching yellow heels. She looked tanned and fit, her streaky blond hair arranged as though permanently swept by wind. She said, "Oh! Freddy said someone rang at the gate, but I didn't realize it was you. I thought you were out of town."

"I was. I just got back and I need to talk to Mr. Lafferty."

She let that sink in. "I suppose you might as well come in." She stepped aside to let me enter, frowning with annoyance when she caught sight of Rags. She barred him with a quick foot and pushed him out of the way. That's the kind of person she was, a cat-kicker. What a bitch. As I stepped into the foyer, I spotted a small overnight case sitting near the door. She'd set her purse on the console table and she paused to check her reflection in the mirror, adjusting an earring and an errant strand of hair. She opened her purse, apparently searching for her keys. "Nord's not here. He collapsed this morning and I had to call the paramedics. He's been admitted to Saint Terry's. I'm on my way over to take him his toiletries and robe."

"What happened?"

"Well, he's desperately ill," she said, as though I'd been stupid to inquire. "All this upset over Reba has taken its toll."

"Is she here?"

"Of course not. She's never here when he needs her. That's a job that falls to Freddy or me." Her smile was self-satisfied and brittle, her manner brisk. "Well now. What can we do for you?"

"Is he allowed to have visitors?"

"You must not have heard me. He's ill. He shouldn't be disturbed."

"That wasn't what I asked. What floor is he on?"

"He's on the cardiac ward. If you insist, I suppose you could speak to his private-duty nurse. What is it you want?"

"He asked me to do a job. I'd like to give him my report."

"I'd prefer you didn't."

"But I don't work for you. I work for him," I said.

"She's in trouble again, isn't she?"

"I guess you could say that."

"You don't understand what this has done to him. He's had to rescue her all his life. Reba keeps putting him in the same position. She sets it up so that if he doesn't step in, she'll be doomed, or so she'd like him to think. I'm sure she'd deny this, but she's really still a child, doing anything she can to get her father's attention. If anything happened to her, he'd forever blame himself."

"He's her father. He gets to help her if he wants."

"Well, I may have put an end to *that*."

"How so?"

"I called Priscilla Holloway, Reba's parole officer. I thought she should be aware of what's been going on. I'm sure Reba's been drinking and probably gambling as well. I told Ms. Holloway Reba left the state, and she was furious."

"You'll get her sent back to prison."

"That's my hope. We'd all be better off, including her."

"Great. That's perfect. Who else did you tattle to?" I meant the question as a piece of sarcasm, but the silence that followed suggested I'd scored an unexpected bull's-eye. I stared at her. "Is that how Beck found out where she was?"

She dropped her gaze. "We had a conversation on the subject."

"You *told* him?"

"That's right. And I'd do it again."

"When was this?"

"Thursday. He came to the house. Nord was sleeping so I spoke to him myself. He'd been looking for her and he was very concerned. He said he didn't want to cause a problem, but he thought she'd taken something. He was quite uncomfortable and I had to work very hard persuading him to tell me what it was. He finally admitted she stole twenty-five thousand dollars. He said he didn't want to make trouble, but I thought that was nonsense and told him where she was."

"How'd you get Misty's address?"

"I didn't have her address, I had yours. Nord scribbled a note to himself the night you called. The Paradise Motel. I saw it written on the pad beside his bed."

"Lucinda, Beck *manipulated* you. Don't you see that?"

"Hardly. He's a lovely man. After what she did to him, I'd have told him even if he hadn't asked."

"Do you have any idea what you've done? A man was kidnapped because of you."

She laughed, tucking her purse under one arm as she picked up the overnight case. "No one was *kidnapped*," she said, as though the notion were absurd. "Really. You're just like her, creating drama where there is none. Everything's a crisis. Everything's the end of the world. It's never anything she's done. She's always the victim, always expecting someone else to pick up after her. Well, this time she'll have to take responsibility. Now, if you'll excuse me, I'd like to get over to the hospital and leave these items for Nord."

She opened the door and snapped it shut behind her. In the face of her conviction, I hadn't managed to challenge her view or express even the first shred of protest. There was an element of truth in what she'd said, but it wasn't the whole truth.

"Miss Millhone?"

I turned to find Freddy standing in the hall behind me. "Did you hear her? The woman's horrible," I said.

"Now that she's gone, I wanted to let you know. Reba was here. She arrived shortly before Miss Cunningham stopped by to pick up Mr. Lafferty's things."

"Where'd she go?"

"I don't know. She came by cab and she was only home long enough to pick up her car and a change of clothes. She said she'd go over to the hospital to see her father, but she'd time it to avoid crossing paths with Miss Cunningham. She's going to call Mr. Lafferty's doctor and have his visitors restricted to family only, including me, of course." Freddy permitted herself a sly smile. "That was my idea."

"Serves Lucinda right. How serious is his condition?"

"The doctor says he'll be fine. He was dehydrated and his electrolytes were out of balance. I believe he's suffering from anemia as well. The doctor intends to keep him for a couple of days."

"Well, good. That's one less thing to worry about, especially if the staff can keep Lucinda at bay. Did Reba say anything at all about where she'd be?"

"Staying with a friend."

"She doesn't have a friend. Here in town?"

"I believe so. This was a fellow, someone she met after she got home."

I thought about that briefly. "Maybe someone from AA . . . though now that I say that, it seems unlikely. I can't see her at a meeting this late in the game. What about reaching her? Did she leave a number?"

Freddy shook her head. "She said she'd call by the house at nine, but she was concerned Mr. Beckwith would find her again."

"I'll bet. Lucinda's been dishing out the information right and left," I said. "Look, if you hear from her, tell her it's important we talk. Did she leave a suitcase by any chance?"

"No, but she did have one with her. She put it in the trunk of her car before she left."

"Well, let's hope she calls in." I glanced at my watch.

"I'll be at my office for the next couple of hours and then I'll head home."

My office always feels odd at night, its flaws and shabbiness exaggerated by the artificial light. As I sat at my desk, all I saw through the window was dinginess reflected back at me, the dust and ancient rain streaks barring any view of the street. On weekends this part of downtown Santa Teresa is dead after 6:00 P.M., city buildings closed for the night, the courthouse and public library dark. The bungalow I occupied was the middle unit of three; identical stucco structures that, at some point, represented modest housing. Since I'd moved in, the bungalows on both sides of mine had remained vacant, which afforded me the quiet I preferred, at the same time creating an unsettling sense of isolation.

I sorted through the mound of mail the carrier had shoved through my slot. Much junk, a few bills, which I sat down and paid. I was restless, eager to get home, but felt I should stay, in the hopes that Reba would call. I did some filing. I straightened out my pencil drawer. It was make-work but gave me something useful to do. I kept glancing at the phone, willing it to ring, so when someone rapped on my side window, I nearly leaped out of my skin.

Reba was outside, concealed in the shadowy space between my bungalow and its twin next door. She'd traded her shorts for jeans and her white T-shirt looked like the one she'd been wearing when she left CIW. I unlocked the window and raised the sash. "What are you *doing?*"

"You have access to those garages out back?"

"Sure, the one for this unit. I've never used it, but the landlord did give me the keys."

"Grab 'em and let's go. I gotta get my car off the street. I've had those goons on my tail ever since I left the house."

"The ones we saw in L.A.?"

"Yeah, only one of 'em now has a black eye, like he walked into a door."

"Oh, dear. Wonder if I did that with my widdle chair," I said. "How'd you get away?"

"Fortunately, I know this town a lot better than they do. I led 'em around for a while, then sped up, doused my lights, turned down a little side road, and then behind a hedge. The minute I saw their car pass, I doubled back and came here."

"Where have you been all this time?"

She seemed agitated. "Don't ask. I've been busy as a little bee. Get a move on. I'm cold."

"I'll meet you out back."

I closed the window and locked it. In my bottom desk drawer I lifted aside the phone book and picked up two silver keys hooked together on a paper clip. I picked up my bag and found my trusty penlight, checking the strength of the batteries as I moved down the hallway and out the rear door. A short patch of stubby grass separated the bungalows from the row of three garages along the alley. Reba'd parked her car in the shadow of a pyracantha bush that had probably scratched the shit out of the paint on the right-hand side. I could see her at the wheel, smoking a cigarette while she waited for me.

There was a light fixture with a forty-watt bulb attached to the wood beam above the middle garage, which was the one assigned to me. The bulb yielded just enough light to see by if your eyes were good. I fumbled with the padlock and finally popped it open. I unhooked it from the hasp and hauled up the overhead door with a labored groaning of wood and rusty hinges. I flashed my penlight across the walls and floor, which were bare, smelling of motor oil and soot. There were cobwebs everywhere.

Reba flipped her cigarette out the window and started her car. I stood back as she pulled into the garage. She got out, locked her car door, and came around to the rear. She popped the trunk lid and hauled out a suitcase of a size appropriate for an airplane carry-on, though you'd have to maneuver it to get it in the overhead bin. The bag had an extendable handle and a set of wheels. She seemed preoccupied, caught up in a mood I couldn't read.

"You okay?" I asked.

"Fine."

"Just for the yucks, are you going to tell me what's in there?"

"Want to see?"

"I do."

She collapsed the handle and laid the suitcase flat, unzipped the top portion and flipped it open.

I found myself looking at a metal box, maybe fifteen inches high, eighteen inches long, and eight inches deep. "What the hell is that?"

"You're joking. You don't know?"

"If I knew, I wouldn't ask, Reeb. I'd exclaim with joy and surprise."

"It's a computer. Marty took his with him when he left. He also stopped by the bank and picked up all the floppy disks from the safe-deposit box. You're looking at Beck's business records—the second set of books. Hook it up to a keyboard and monitor, you've got access to everything: bank accounts, deposits, shell companies, payoffs, every dime he laundered for Salustio."

"You're turning it over to the feds, right?"

"Probably. As soon as I'm done . . . though you know how cranky they get about stolen property."

"But you can't even think about keeping this. That's why those guys went after Marty, to get it back. Isn't it?"

"Exactly. So let's put a call through to Beck and offer him a trade. We get Marty, he gets this."

"I thought you just said you'd turn it over to the feds?"

"You weren't listening. I said 'probably.' I'm not sure their crappy investigation is worth Marty's life."

"You can't handle this yourself. Negotiate with Beck? Are you out of your mind? You have to tell Vince. Bring in the cops or the FBI."

"No way. This is my only chance to get even with that son of a bitch."

"Oh, I get it. This isn't about Marty. It's about you and Beck."

"Of course it's about *Marty*, but it's also about settling the score. It's like a test. Let's see what Beck's made of. I don't think it's such a bad deal—Marty in exchange for this. The fact the feds want it is what makes it so valuable."

"There are more important things in life than revenge," I said.

"Well, that's bullshit. Name one," she said. "Besides, I'm not talking about revenge. I'm talking about getting even. Those are two different things."

"No, they're not."

"Yes, they are. Revenge is you hurt me and I grind you underfoot until you wish you were dead. Getting even restores the balance in the Universe. You kill him, I kill you. Now we're even. What else is capital punishment about? Getting even is just what it sounds like. Tit for tat. You hurt me, I hurt you back. We're square again and all's right with the world."

"Why not get even by turning him over to the IRS?"

"That's business. This is personal, between him and me."

"I don't get what you want."

"I want him to say he's sorry for what he did to me. I gave up two years of my life for him. Now I have something he wants so let him beg for it."

"That's asinine. So he pulls a long face and says sorry. What difference will that make? You know what he's like. You can't ever do business with a guy like him. You'll get screwed."

"You don't know that."

"I do. Reba, would you listen to me? He'll work you over the first chance he gets."

Her face was set. "Why don't you go get your car and bring it around? I'll wait for you here."

I shut my mouth and closed my eyes. Why argue the point when her mind was made up? "You want help with this garage door?"

"I can handle it."

I returned to the office. I locked the back door behind me, then moved down the hall turning off lights as I went. I grabbed my shoulder bag and went out the front door, pausing long enough to lock up. I stood for a moment, scanning the darkened street. All the cars in range belonged to neighbors, vehicles I'd seen before and could identify on sight. I let myself into my car and fired up the engine. I drove around the corner and nosed my VW into the alleyway.

Reba had closed and padlocked the garage. She opened the passenger-side door, put the suitcase in the backseat, and got in. I reached over into the rear and grabbed my denim jacket. "Here. Put this on before you catch cold."

"Thanks." She shrugged into the jacket and locked her seat belt in place.

"Where to?"

"The nearest public phone."

"Why not my office, as long as we're here?"

"I don't want you tied into this in any way."

"Tied into what?"

"Just find a phone," she said.

31

Reba wanted me to make the call to Beck. We found a phone booth outside a supermarket. The store was a bright island, icy fluorescent lights reflected in the shiny paint finish of the dozen or so cars in the parking lot out front. This was the store where I did my weekly shopping, and I longed for nothing so much as to buy milk and eggs and then wend my way home.

Reba put a handful of coins and a slip of paper with Beck's home and office numbers on the metal shelf under the phone. "Try his home phone first. If Tracy answers, maybe she'll think he has a girlfriend," she said.

"He does. Her name is Onni."

"She probably knows about her. I'm talking someone new. Might as well bug the shit out of her while we can."

"That's not nice. I thought women were supposed to be nice."

"I wouldn't bet on it if I were you."

I picked up the handset. "So what am I supposed to say to him?"

"Tell him to meet us at the East Beach parking lot in fifteen minutes. As soon as he hands Marty over, he gets his computer."

I held the handset against my chest. "Please don't do this. I'm begging you. What's to prevent him from snatching the damn thing? You don't even have a gun."

"Of course I don't have a *gun*. I'm a convicted felon. I can't carry," she said, as though offended by the very idea.

"What if Beck has one?"

"He doesn't even own a gun. Besides, we'll be right out in plain sight. Anyone driving along Cabana Boulevard can see us. Here, give me that."

She grabbed the handset and put it against my ear, picked up some coins, and dropped them in the slot. In addition to the dial tone, I could have sworn I heard the buzz of electricity running through my frame. My heart rate was picking up and my insides felt like a fuse box with all the lines shorting out. She punched in Beck's home number just to hurry things along. At the first ring, Reba leaned her head against mine and tilted the handset so she could listen in. I said, "This feels like high school. I hate this."

"Would you shut up?" she hissed.

After three rings, he picked up. "Yes."

My mouth was dry. "Beck, this is Kinsey."

"God damn you! Where's Reba? The fuckin' bitch. I want what's mine and she better make it quick."

Reba grabbed the handset, all sweetness and light now that she had him by the balls. "Hey, baby. How's by you? I'm right here."

Whatever Beck's reply, it must have been tart because she laughed with delight. "Oh my, now. You don't have to be crude. I was thinking we should get together and have a chat."

I waited, staring off across the parking lot, while she

spelled out the proposal and the nature of the trade. Then they argued about the rendezvous, tussling to see which of them was going to come out on top. The East Beach bath-house, at the corner of Cabana and Milagro, was where I did the turnaround on my morning runs. Even at night, the area is exposed and well lighted, the Santa Teresa Inn just across the street from the entrance to the parking lot. There's a small separate lot at the far end of the building, but she'd opted for the more public of the two. This showed a grain of common sense unusual for her. She insisted on meeting in fifteen minutes while he swore he couldn't be there any sooner than half an hour. To this, she finally agreed. Score one for him. I was uneasy. I figured the more time she gave him, the more likely he was to round up some help. This must have occurred to her as well. "And Beck, one more thing. You bring anyone but Marty and you'll eat it, big time. Yeah, well, same to you, you little shit!" She slammed down the phone and then shoved her hands in her jacket pockets. "God, I hate him. What a hairball."

I picked up the handset and reached for some coins. "I'm calling Cheney."

She took the handset and returned it to the cradle. "I don't want Cheney. I don't want anyone but us."

"I can't do this. You and Beck can play all the games you want, but I'm out of it," I said.

"Okay. Fine. Take a hike. Drop me at my car and you're off the hook," she said. She turned and walked off.

I'd hoped to jolt her into getting help, but she was having none of it. I blinked, staring at the pavement. What were my choices? Do it her way or risk . . . what? That she'd die or get hurt? Because Marty'd stolen the computer, she'd assumed Beck was the one who'd ordered the snatch, but what if he hadn't? It might have been Salustio Castillo, who had just as much to lose. Beck might be bluffing. He might not have a clue where Marty was being held, and then what? All he had to do was grab the suitcase and what could she do? If it came right down to it, what could I do? Nothing. At the same time, she knew I wouldn't leave her. There was too much at stake.

Reluctantly, I followed. The car doors were locked and she waited, gaze averted, while I let myself in and tossed my bag on the backseat. I slid under the wheel, leaned over, and opened the door on her side. Reba got in and we sat there. I had my hands on the steering wheel, stalling while I racked my brain for some alternative. "There has to be a better way to do this."

"Great. Spell it out. I'm all yours," she said.

I didn't have an answer. The meeting was scheduled for 11:00 P.M., in roughly twenty-five minutes. Technically we had time enough to drive to my place, where I could pick up my gun. I nearly banged my head on the steering wheel. What was I thinking? A gun was out of the question. I wasn't going to *shoot* anyone. Over a *computer?* How absurd.

On the other hand . . . shit . . . on the *other* hand . . . if Marty's home phone was tapped, the FBI must have a tap on Beck's telephone lines as well. One of their agents must have heard Beck and Reba wrangling, so maybe they'd taken note and the cavalry was already on the way.

Out of the corner of my eye, I saw Reba check her watch, saying, "Tick-tock. Tick-tock. Time's a-wasting."

"So where's Marty all this time?"

"He didn't say. I'm assuming somewhere close."

I shook my head in frustration. "I don't believe I'm doing this." I turned the key in the ignition and backed out of the space. "Let's at least take a minute to scope out the area, or have you done that?"

"Not really. Why bother? I figure you're the expert."

The drive seemed to take forever. I cut over to the freeway, thinking to speed our progress. Big mistake. Traffic was heavy, taillights stacked up, as two lanes of cars amassed in the wake of an accident in one of the northbound lanes. I could see lights flashing where the CHP and the emergency vehicles had converged on the scene. There wasn't actually an obstruction on our side of the road, but we were at a dead stop, anyway, while people paused to gawk.

By the time we reached the off-ramp at Cabana, we had less than a minute to spare. I confess I sped the final mile and a half, hoping a cop would spot us and make a traffic stop. No such luck. The ocean was to our right, separated from the road by the beach, a bike path, and a wide strip of grass that was dotted with palm trees. On our left, we passed a string of motels and restaurants. The sidewalk was populated with tourists, which was oddly comforting somehow.

At Milagro, I turned into the designated parking lot. There were no cars in evidence, which meant (perhaps) that if Beck was bringing goons, at least they hadn't arrived before us. Reba told me to make a U-turn at the far end of the lot and circle back to the entrance. I did as instructed and then backed into a parking space, my car facing the street in case we needed to make a hasty retreat. We got out of the car. She flipped her seat forward and removed the suitcase. She popped the handle, extending it, and then rolled the case to the front of the car. "Might as well let him know we mean business," she said.

Behind us, the waves were drumming on the sand, gathering momentum before they battered the shore and then rolled back again. The water was intensely black with a fine sheen of white where moonlight caught the peaks of each wave. A damp breeze buffeted my hair and pushed against the legs of my jeans. I turned and scanned the beach behind us, hopping from foot to foot to keep warm. So far, to all appearances, we were alone.

Reba leaned on the front fender, lit a cigarette, and smoked. Ten minutes passed. She checked her watch. "What's this about? Does he want the friggin' thing or not?"

Across the street, hotel guests pulled in at the entrance to the Santa Teresa Inn. There were two valet parkers and a smattering of pedestrians. In the restaurant on the second floor, tables were arranged along the big curved front window. Diners were visible, though as dark as it was now, I doubted they could see us. A black-and-white patrol car approached and turned right, speeding up Milagro. I could feel my hopes flare and fade.

"I think we should get out of here. I don't like this," I said.

She looked at her watch again. "Not yet. If he doesn't show by 11:30, we'll bail."

At 11:19 two cars crawled into view and turned into the lot. Reba dropped her cigarette and stepped on it. "That's Marty's car in front. The second one's Beck."

"Is that Marty at the wheel?"

"I can't tell. It looks like him."

"Well, great then. No sweat. Get it over with," I said.

Reba crossed her arms, whether from cold or tension, I couldn't be sure. Once in the lot, Marty's car turned left, circled as we had, and made a slow return. He stopped his car thirty feet away and sat, engine idling, while Beck pulled up fifteen feet closer to us. The two sets of headlights formed a line of harsh spots. I raised a hand and shaded my eyes. I could see Beck at the wheel of his car, but I wasn't at all convinced the second driver was Marty.

A minute passed.

Reba shifted restlessly. "What's he doing?"

"Reba, let's go. There's something off about this."

Beck got out of the car. He stood by the open door, his attention fixed on the rolling bag. He wore a dark raincoat, open along its length, sides flapping in the wind. "Is that it?"

"No, Beck, it's not. I've decided to leave town."

"Bring it over here and let's have a look."

"Tell Marty to get out so we can see it's him."

Beck called over his shoulder. "Hey, Marty? Give Reeb a wave. She thinks you're someone else."

The driver in Marty's car waved to us and blinked his headlights, then revved his engine like a stock car driver at the start of a race. I touched Reba's arm, warbling, "Run . . ."

I took off, breaking left, as Marty's car pitched forward, tires chirping, the vehicle gathering speed as it bore down on us. Reba grabbed the handle of the rolling bag and scrambled after me. The suitcase teetered on the uneven surface of the parking lot and then toppled to one side. She headed for the street, dragging it after her. I could hear it scraping along the pavement, as awkward as an anchor if she hoped to escape. I yelled, "Dump that!"

The driver in Marty's car slammed on his brakes and turned the wheel so his rear end swung around, missing my car by inches. Two men jumped out, the driver and a second man who suddenly appeared from the back where he'd been concealed.

Beck stood with his hands in his coat pockets, watching with detachment as Reba abandoned the suitcase and took off at a dead run. The two men were fast. She'd gone no distance at all when one tackled her from behind and the two of them went down.

I reversed myself and headed in her direction. I had no plan. I didn't give a shit about the suitcase, but I wasn't going to leave Reba on her own. She was struggling, kicking at the guy who'd tackled her. He punched her in the face. Her head jerked and banged against the ground. I reached him as he raised his fist to punch her again. I hooked my arms around his right arm and hung on for dear life. Someone grabbed me from behind. He pinned my arms against my sides, lifted me off the ground, and then swung me away from his pal. I craned my neck for sight of Reba, who'd rolled over on her side. I watched as she pulled herself up on her hands and knees. She seemed dazed, blood pouring out of her mouth and nose. The guy who'd punched her turned to me. He lifted my feet and the two hauled me over to Marty's car. I arched my back, trying to free myself, but the guy simply tightened his grip and there was nothing I could do.

Beck crossed to Marty's car and opened one of the rear doors. The guy in whose arms I was locked fell into the backseat and dragged me in on top of him. He flipped me so that I was pinned under him, my face mashed against the upholstery. His weight was so crushing, I couldn't draw a breath. I thought my ribs would collapse, crushing my lungs in the process. I tried a groan, but all I could manage was a huffing sound, barely audible.

"Get the fuck off her," someone snapped.

The guy dug an elbow in my back as he lifted himself off me. At the same time, he took my right wrist and wrenched my arm up behind me while he shoved my head toward the floor. I was staring at the floor mats, my nose six inches away. Someone folded my legs in and slammed the door. Half a second later, I heard Beck's car door slam. He started his engine while the driver of Marty's car slid under the wheel, shut the door, and started the car. He pulled away sedately. We slowed at the exit to the parking lot. No squealing of brakes. No calling attention to ourselves in any way. As far as I knew, Reba was still out there on the asphalt, trying to stanch the blood gushing from her nose. I'd caught a glimpse of my backseat companion, who had a white gauze patch taped across his left eye. Two harsh red and purple bruises ran along his cheek like streaks of paint. The chair leg must have come close to taking that eye out, which is probably why he'd so relished mauling me. I focused on the drive. I assumed we were forming a two-car motorcade. I thought about the kidnappings I'd seen in movies, how the heroine later identified the final destination by the sound of the tires crossing railroad tracks or the bleat of a foghorn in the distance. Most of what I heard was my companion's labored breathing. Neither of the two guys was in as good a shape as they appeared. Or perhaps, more flattering to us, Reba and I had put up more of a fight than they'd expected.

We turned left onto Cabana Boulevard and proceeded at an easy pace for less than a minute before we slowed to a stop. I was guessing this was the light at the intersection of

State and Cabana. The driver turned on the radio and music filled the car, a male vocalist singing, *"I want your sex . . ."*

My new best friend said, "Turn that shit off."

The driver said, "I like George Michael." But the radio did go off.

"Roll your window down and see what Beck wants."

I could picture Beck's car in the lane next to ours, him making that rolling gesture, leaning across the front seat of his car to converse. Annoyed, our driver said, "Okay, okay. Got it. I'm doing that!" And to the fellow in the backseat, "He has the key card, so we're supposed to follow. How many times he tell us that?"

Faintly, in the distance, I heard sirens approaching. The wailing grew louder, the sound splitting in two. Two cop cars, oh please.

I tried turning my head, hoping for a glimpse of something out the window, but all that netted me was a searing jerk to my arm. The sirens were almost on top of us. I caught the strobe of lights from two patrol cars that passed in rapid succession. The sirens trailed down Cabana Boulevard, volume diminishing until it faded altogether. So much for help being on the way.

We turned right on what I was guessing was Castle. When we slowed to a second stop, I imagined the light at Montebello Street. We started up again, proceeding at maybe ten miles an hour. I caught the hollow sound of the road as it went under the freeway. We came up the incline on the other side, which would put us on Granizo. Left on Chapel. We had to be going to Beck's office, which was only a couple of blocks away. I knew the stores along the mall would be closed and the office buildings locked. The "card" the driver had referred to probably triggered the mechanical barrier to the underground garage. Sure enough, I felt us slow and then turn right, easing down a ramp. At this hour, the garage would be empty. We drove the length of the cavernous space and pulled into a spot. Beck must have parked just ahead of us because I heard his car door slam before our driver had a chance to shut his engine down.

I was hauled unceremoniously from the backseat and set on my feet. I'd hoped to catch Beck's eye, establish a connection, thinking I had a better chance of charming him than the goons on each side of me. He avoided my eyes, his face set. We waited while he opened his trunk and extracted the rolling bag. The sides were scraped gray, embedded with the beach sand accumulated from its being dragged across the pavement. The handle had snapped. Beck flipped the suitcase and knelt beside it. He unzipped the compartment and pulled open the flap.

Empty.

I stared as though trying to catch the mechanics of a magic trick. Reba had *showed* me the computer. It had been in there less than an hour ago, but where had it gone? The only time we'd been separated was when I'd left her in the alley while I went to fetch my car. She must have taken advantage of my absence to remove the computer and lock it in the trunk of her car. Which meant she'd anticipated Beck's betrayal and she'd beat him to the punch. By the same token, he must have known she was going to pull a fast one, or why snatch me?

Beck stood up and pushed the bag with his toe, his expression thoughtful. I was expecting fury, but he seemed bemused instead. Maybe he liked Reba's taking the conflict to such extremes, imagining his ultimate victory the sweeter for it. He turned and walked toward the elevators.

The three of us followed, our footsteps clattering like a herd of beasts in the vast empty space. The guy with the injured eye kept a steady pressure on the arm he'd wrenched up behind me. There was no way I could move without ripping my arm out like a cooked chicken wing. The elevator doors opened and the four of us trooped in. Beck pressed the button. The doors closed and the elevator began its ascent.

"Why here?" I asked.

"So Reba will know how to reach me. In case you haven't noticed, we're engaged in a little battle of wits."

"That'd be hard to miss."

Beck sent me a fleeting smile.

The doors opened at shop level. We emerged inside the Beckwith Building and trooped across the marble lobby to the public elevators that would take us to the fourth floor. I turned to look at Willard, who was sitting at his desk. He watched us pass without comment, his face the same handsome blank. I sent him what I hoped was a pleading look, but I got nothing in return. How could such a good-looking guy have so little life in his eyes? Couldn't he see what was going on? Beck was his boss. Maybe he was paid the big bucks to look the other way.

We went up to the fourth floor. The elevator doors opened to reveal offices filled with artificial light, the colors as dazzling as a Disney cartoon. Long sweeps of green carpeting, bright abstract paintings in a line down the hall. Healthy plants, modern furniture. I expected to be marched off to Beck's office, but he steered me around the corner to the freight elevator. He pressed the call button and the doors opened. He moved to the back wall of the elevator and pushed aside the gray quilted padding. He punched the code into the keyboard mounted on the elevator wall. The door to his counting room slid open. Beck pressed the Stop Run button and stepped aside, turning to look at me. He had his hands in his raincoat pockets.

Nobody said a word.

Peripherally, I saw the counting and bundling machines. In the same flash, I saw that all the cardboard boxes had been emptied of loose bills, which were now packaged and stacked on the countertop.

What I had no way to avoid was the sight of Marty. He'd been tied to a chair, beaten almost beyond recognition. His head was slumped on his chest. Even without a full view of his face, I knew he was dead. The curve of his cheek was puffy and dented, dried blood turning black at his hairline.

Blood had oozed from his ears and coagulated along the collar of his shirt. I made a sound and jerked my head, blocking out the sight. Pain shot through me as though I'd been tapped with a taser gun. My palms were instantly damp and a flash of heat swept over me. I felt the blood drain out of my head. My legs buckled. The guy with the eye patch caught me and supported me briefly. Beck pressed a button and the doors to the counting room eased shut.

I was walked, rubber-legged, to Beck's office, where I sank onto the couch and covered my face with my hands. The image of Marty was like a photograph that I saw now in negative, light and dark reversed. There was conversation going on above my head—Beck instructing the two guys to get the body out of there and dispose of it. I knew they'd take him down in the service elevator to the ground floor, where they could drag him through the service corridor and out to the garage. They'd stick him in the trunk of his car and dump his body by the side of the road. Odd, so odd. I'd seen it in his eyes—this ending, this death—but I'd been unable to intervene.

My vision condensed, threatening to shut down. Dark closed in from the periphery and I had that curious sensation in my ears—white noise—that told me how close I was to fainting. I put my head down between my knees. I remembered to breathe. Within a minute, the air seemed to cool and I could feel the darkness recede. When I looked up, the two guys were gone and Beck was sitting at his desk. "Sorry about that. It's not what you think. He had a heart attack."

"He's dead all the same and it's your fault," I said.

"Reba had her share in it."

"How do you figure that?"

"Take a look at what she did. We're supposed to have a deal and she shows up with an empty suitcase? What's she think, she can fuck with me and get away with it?"

"She didn't steal the computer. Marty took it with him when he left."

"I don't give a shit who *took* it. All she had to do was give it back and he might be alive. The stress was what killed him. Couple of harmless punches and he was gone."

I couldn't argue with the man. He was so sure of himself and his thinking was so bent. Where was this going to end? The contest between them had spiraled out of control and matters could only escalate. Beck had the upper hand. It was as simple as that. He had me.

He smiled slightly. "You're hoping she'll call the police, but she won't. You know why? Because it wouldn't be any fun. She's a gambler. She likes betting against the house. Poor girl's not nearly as smart as she thinks she is."

"I don't want to talk about this shit. The two of you can hash it out."

"I'm sure we will."

We sat, the two of us, waiting for the phone to ring. I'd given up trying to predict what either would do. My job was taking care of me. The problem was, I was tired and feeling panicky. The jitters were causing my hands to shake and I was having trouble marshaling my thoughts. Beck rocked back in his swivel chair, fiddling with a paperweight, tossing it from hand to hand.

I noticed a row of cardboard boxes, lined up along the wall, all of them neatly taped and ready to be shipped. His office was a mess—shelves half empty, numerous bulging files on his desk. It looked as if Beck was all packed and ready to go. No wonder he was hell-bent on reclaiming his computer and his floppy disks. The disks and his hard drive contained his entire enterprise, every nickel he owned, all the money he'd salted away, shell corporations, Panamanian bank accounts. He wasn't a man who remembered numbers or dates. He had to have it written down or it was lost to him. He knew as well as I did the data would be his undoing if it fell into the wrong hands.

I said, "I have to go to the ladies' room."

"No."

"Come on, Beck. You can tag along with me and listen at the door while I tinkle."

He shook his head. "Can't do it. I want to be by the phone when she calls."

"What if it takes an hour?"

"Tough."

We waited in silence. I checked my watch. The crystal was smashed, the hands permanently frozen at 11:22. I couldn't see a clock from where I sat. Time dragged on and on. If and when Reba called, I had one more chance to signal the agents recording Beck's calls. I wasn't sure how I'd manage it or what I'd say, but the possibility was there.

The silence went on for so long that when the phone finally rang, I jumped. Beck picked up the handset and held it loosely against his ear. He smiled and leaned forward, resting his elbows on his desk. "Hey, Reeb, good girl. I knew you'd touch base. Are you ready to do business? Oh wait. Hang on a second. I have a friend of yours here and wondered if you wanted a chance to speak to her."

He pressed the speaker function on the phone and the office was filled with the hollow sound of Reba's voice. "Kinsey? Oh, geez . . . are you okay?"

I said, "I could use some help here. Why don't you call Cheney and tell him what's going on?"

"Forget him. Let me talk to Beck," she said, irritated.

Now that his hands were free, Beck opened his desk drawer and took out a gun. He slipped the safety off and pointed it at me. "Hey, Reeb? Sorry to interrupt, but let's cut to the chase. Listen to this."

He pointed at the wall above my head and fired. A sound came out of my throat, half scream and half moan. Tears sprang into my eyes. He said, "Oops. I missed."

She said, "Beck, don't."

"I'm not very good with this thing. Willard tried to show

me, but I can't seem to get the hang of it. Should I try again?"

"Ohmygod, ohmygod. Oh, please, Beck, don't hurt her."

"I didn't hear your answer. You ready to do business?"

"Don't fire again. Don't shoot. Don't do that. I'll bring the thing. I got it. It's in the trunk of my car. I put it in a duffel."

"You said that before. I believed you then, but look what you went and did. You pulled the big switcheroo."

"I swear. I'll do it right this time. I'm not far. Give me two minutes. Just hang on. Please."

His tone was skeptical. "Gee, I don't know, Reeb. I trusted you. I thought you'd play fair. What you did was bad. I'd say very bad indeed."

"This time I'll bring it for sure. No tricks. I swear."

Beck was watching me while she spoke. He winked and smiled, having a wonderful time. "How do I know you won't pull the same old gag? Give me a duffel and there's nothing inside."

I stood up and pointed at the door, mouthing, "I have to pee."

He motioned me to sit again while Reba, sounding desperate, was saying, "I know what we can do. I'll come in through the service corridor. You can go to Willard's desk and watch on the monitor. I'll unzip the bag and show you the computer. You can see it with your own eyes."

I clutched the crotch of my jeans and then clasped my hands, mouthing, *Please* . . . I pointed at the hall again.

Distracted, he waved the gun at me, motioning me to sit down. I was edging out of the room. I held up a finger, whispering, "I'll be right back."

I left the room and walked rapidly down the hall, footsteps soundless on the carpeting. I pulled office doors shut as I passed, letting them *bang, bang, bang.* I could hear him yell, "Hey!" He didn't sound angry so much as annoyed at my disobedience.

I doubled my pace. I reached the vestibule. Mercifully, the service elevator doors stood open. I moved to the back wall and punched in the code for the counting room. 5-15-1955. Reba's birthday. The doors slid open.

Out in the corridor, I could hear Beck shout my name, banging into offices in search of me. He fired a shot that made me jump even at this remove. While I'd known I wouldn't shoot him, I wasn't at all convinced he wouldn't shoot me, accidentally if nothing else. I yanked off one shoe and set it in the path of the open elevator door. The door slid shut, encountered the shoe, and popped open again, a process that repeated like a tic. I turned and pressed the G button on the opposite panel, dispatching the freight elevator to the garage level. The doors were slow to respond, which gave me time enough to cross to the second set of doors. I yanked my shoe from the track and slipped into the counting room as the corridor doors slid shut. The doors to the counting room slid shut half a beat later, and I was safe. Temporarily, at any rate.

Marty's body was still there.

I went on disconnect and blocked any and all emotional responses. Now was the wrong time. I tossed the shoe aside, not daring to take time to slip it on again. I looked at the ladder affixed to the wall, following the sight of it, rung by rung, all the way to the top. I started climbing, one shoe off and one shoe on, diddle-diddle-dumpling, my son John. I knew the trap door at the top opened onto the roof. Once there, I'd hide or hang over the parapet screaming until the cops showed up. Maybe officers were already scrambling— regular Santa Teresa cops, the SWAT team, hostage negotiators—all of them decked out in bulletproof vests.

I flicked a look at Marty, still bound to his chair. Why hadn't the guys done as Beck instructed? They were supposed to get him out of there, but they'd left him where he was. My hands were perspiring, but I ventured a second quick look down, noting what I'd failed to spot earlier. The counting and bundling machines were still sitting on the counter. The currency was gone. Instead of disposing of the body, the goons must have packed up the cash and removed that instead.

I reached the top rung of the ladder and reached for the door directly above my head. I couldn't find a lock or a knob or any means to open it. I ran my hand across the surface, looking for a hook or a handle, any kind of lever that might cause it to spring open. Nothing. I clung to the top rung, hanging on for dear life while I tried to get my fingertips in the crack. I banged on it with the flat of my hand, then pushed as hard as I could.

Below, I heard the elevator door slide open. I laid my head against the ladder and held my breath.

In a conversational tone, Beck said, "That door's locked so you might as well come down. Reba's on her way. Soon as we've settled up, you're free to go."

I looked down at him. He was wearing his raincoat, apparently in preparation for his departure. He had the gun in one hand and it was pointed right at me. He probably didn't have a clue how much pressure it took to pull the trigger. If he inadvertently blew my head off, I'd be dead all the same. He leaned down and picked up my shoe.

He waggled the gun. "Come on. I don't want to hurt you. This is almost over. Wrong time to cut and run when we're down to the wire."

I eased my way down, feeling for each rung with my foot, suddenly fearful of heights. I considered letting go, plunging down on top of him, but I'd only hurt myself and there was no guarantee I'd do him any harm at all. He watched me patiently until I reached the bottom. He probably preferred keeping his eyes on me to looking at Marty. He hadn't seemed to register the fact that the body hadn't been removed.

He smiled slightly. "Good try. You had me goin' there. I thought you ran the other way . . ." He handed me my shoe. I paused, leaning against the wall while I pulled the shoe on.

He took my elbow and urged me through the service elevator to the corridor. He was right. It was almost over so what was the point of risking my neck. In the end, this had nothing to do with me. I hunkered, taking my time while I tied my shoelaces. Beck was getting short on patience, but I didn't like to walk with laces flapping loose. He took me by the elbow again and steered me around the corner to the public elevators. He'd left his briefcase in the hall. He picked it up and used the knuckle of his index finger to push the call button. The elevator must have been sitting right there because the doors opened instantly. The two of us got on. Beck pressed the button for the lobby. Like strangers, we stood silently against the back wall, eyes on the digital readout while the floor numbers dropped from 4 to 3 to 2 to the lobby. I had one brief hope that when the doors opened, I'd see cops, guns drawn, ready to arrest him and put an end to this.

The lobby was empty except for Willard, sitting at his desk. The fountain in the center of the lobby was gushing like a toilet. My bladder was so full I could have drawn a diagram of its shape and size. Outside the plate-glass windows, the walkway was dark, not a soul in sight. The stores across the way were shut down tight. Willard was on his feet, his attention focused on his bank of ten monitors. He held an arm out and snapped his fingers rapidly. Beck and I crossed the lobby and rounded the end of Willard's desk. He pointed. The image on one of the black-and-white screens showed the underground parking lot. Reba, driving my VW, nosed down the ramp and turned right. The car passed from our view. Three minutes later, we saw her enter the service corridor, one floor below. She was using two hands to haul the duffel, which was clearly heavy. She eased it down on the floor and looked up at the corner-mounted security camera. "Hey, Beck?" Her cheek was swollen from the blow she'd taken, lips puffy, one eye black. Her nose looked as though it had been flattened across the bridge.

She waited, looking up at us.

Willard handed Beck the handset from the phone on his desk. He pressed a button and we could hear the wall phone ring in the service corridor. Reba picked up, her gaze fixed on the camera.

Beck said, "Hey, baby. How's by you?" Mocking her earlier greeting.

"Knock it off, Beck. You want this or not?"

"Show me first."

She dropped the handset and it banged against the wall, bouncing on its spiral cord. Beck jerked his head back, murmuring "Shit." Below, Reba leaned over and opened the duffel bag. The computer was clearly visible.

"And the floppy disks?"

She opened a side pocket and extracted a handful of disks, probably twenty by the look. She held them toward the camera, holding them face forward so he could read the sequence of dates he'd probably written himself. "Okay. Good enough," he said.

She slipped them back inside and zipped the duffel shut. "Happy now, you asshole?"

"I am. Thanks for asking. Come on up to the lobby and behave yourself. I've got Kinsey right here in case you want to get cute about this."

Reba flipped him the bird. Attagirl, I thought. That would show him.

I glanced at Willard. "You just going to stand there?"

No response. Maybe Willard had died and no one had remembered to mention it. I wanted to wave a hand in front of his eyes to see if he would blink.

The service elevator reached the lobby level and the doors slid open. Reba stepped forward, struggling with the weight of the duffel. Beck, gun in hand, watched her for any hint of rebellion or treachery. She set the duffel on the floor in front of him.

He motioned with the gun. "Open it."

"Oh, geez. You think it's booby-trapped?"

"I wouldn't put it past you."

She leaned down and unzipped the duffel, exposing the computer for the second time. Without his having to ask, she took out the floppy disks and handed them to him.

"Now step back."

She backed up about ten feet, her hands in the air. "So worried," she remarked.

Beck passed the gun to Willard. "Keep an eye on both."

He knelt and freed the computer case from the duffel. He reached in his coat pocket and took out a small Phillips-head screwdriver, which he used to loosen the screws that held the housing in place. He tossed the screws aside and then took off the back panel. I couldn't figure out what he was up to.

The inner workings of the computer were now exposed. I don't own a computer and I'd never seen the inside of one. What a complex assortment of multicolored connectors, wires, circuits, transistors, or whatever they were called, lots of weensy things at any rate. Willard held the gun steady, barrel pointing first at Reba and then at me, but almost idly I thought. Beck opened his briefcase and took out a glass beaker with a glass stopper wedged in the top. He opened it and dolloped a clear liquid across the circuits like salad dressing. It must have been acid because a hissing went up and the smell of chemical burning filled the air. Insulated wires dissolved, small parts curling as though alive, shriveling and shrinking as the caustic liquid made contact. He took out a second beaker and poured acid over the floppy disks, spreading them out so as not to miss any. Holes appeared instantly, and a sizzling smoke developed as the disks disintegrated.

Reba said, "You won't remember all that stuff."

"Don't worry about it. I have dupes in Panama."

"Well, goody for you." Her voice sounded odd.

I glanced at her. Her mouth had begun to tremble and tears glistened in her eyes as she watched. Hoarsely, she said, "I really loved you. I did. You were everything to me."

I found myself staring at her with interest. Why did I think she was faking?

"Geez, Reeb, you never learn, do you. What's it going to take to get it through that thick head of yours? You're just like a kid. Someone tells you there's a Santa Claus and you believe."

"But you said I could trust you. You said you loved me and you'd take care of me. You said that."

"I know, but I lied."

"About everything?"

"Pretty much," he said, ruefully.

I caught a glimpse of motion on one of the monitors. In the underground garage, two Santa Teresa black-and-whites were coming down the ramp. Two unmarked cars followed.

Meanwhile, Beck was intent on his task. He took the screwdriver and jammed it into the workings of the computer, twisting metal parts, snapping wires, careful to avoid any direct contact between the acid and his hands. He had his back to the big plate-glass windows so he didn't see Cheney step out of the shadows with his gun drawn. Vince Turner appeared along with four agents in FBI vests.

Too late to salvage the data, but I was grateful nonetheless.

Reba caught sight of them. I saw her gaze flick to the window and back to Beck. "Oh, poor Beck. You are *so* screwed," she said.

He stood up and reached for his briefcase. He looked at her, his expression pleasant. "Really? How do you figure that?"

Reba was silent for a beat, a slow smile lighting her battered face. "The minute I got back to town, I put in a call to a man who works for the IRS. I spilled the beans, spelled it all out—names, numbers, dates—everything he needed to get his warrants. He had to call the judge at home, but he was happy to be of help."

Facetiously, Beck said, "Oh, Jesus, Reba, get a grip. I've known for months they were on to me. This is the only thing I was really worried about and now it's taken care of. How much incriminating data you think they'll salvage from this mess?"

"Probably none."

"That's right. Thank you very much."

Beck saw Reba's attention shift. He looked over his shoulder and spotted Cheney, Vince Turner, and assorted cops and federal agents lined up on the walk. His smile might have faltered, but he didn't seem concerned. He signaled to Willard to let them in. Willard set the gun on the floor, raised his hands to show he had no weapons, and used his jumble of keys to unlock the doors.

Reba wasn't finished. "Only one problem."

Beck turned back to her. "Which is?"

"That's not Marty's."

Beck laughed. "You're full of crap."

Reba shook her head. "Nope. Not so. The feds didn't like the fact the computer had been stolen so I swapped it back."

"How'd you get into the building?"

"He let me in," she said, indicating Willard.

"Give it up, baby. The man works for me."

"Maybe so but I'm the one who's been screwing his brains out. We're just like this." She raised her left hand and made a circle with the thumb and index finger. She stuck her right index finger in the hole and pumped it like a piston. Beck winced at the crudity, but Reba laughed.

I shot a quick look at Willard, who dropped his gaze with appropriate modesty. Cops and FBI agents were crowding into the lobby. Cheney picked up Beck's gun and flicked the safety before he handed it to Vince.

Reba was saying, "After Willie let me in, I took Marty's computer up to your office. I disconnected your computer, pulled it out, and put Marty's in its place. Then I put your computer under Marty's desk. That one's Onni's. Nothing much on it but personal correspondence and a bunch of stupid computer games. I can't believe you paid her so well when all she did was waste time."

Beck still wasn't buying it. He shook his head, sliding his tongue across his front teeth while trying to suppress a smile. She might as well have been telling him she'd been abducted by aliens for use in sexual experiments.

She said, "Want to know what else I did? I'm tellin' you, Beck, I've been a busy little girl. After I swapped computers, I drove over to Salustio's and paid him the twenty-five grand I stole. Marty gave me the cash in exchange for documents he never got to use. Truth is, Salustio didn't give a damn where the money came from. Problem is, I pay him and he's still pissed at me. So I figure to compensate him for the inconvenience, I'd warn him about the raid. That gave him *just* enough time to get his money out of here. So now all's forgiven. He and I are square. You're the one who's left standing out in the cold."

Beck's expression was opaque. He was never going to give her the satisfaction of ceding the win, but she knew it was hers.

Epilogue

That wasn't the end of it, of course.

Beck was indicted on charges of murder, assault with a deadly weapon, kidnapping, money laundering, income tax evasion, conspiracy to defraud the United States government, tampering with evidence, obstruction of justice, failure to report currency transactions, and corruption of public officials. At first, Beck was undismayed. After all, he knew he had enough money stashed away to support an army of attorneys for as long as it took. There was just that one small matter Reba had neglected to mention. This was something I guessed at, but couldn't persuade her to confirm. Before she swapped the two computers, she'd tapped into Beck's accounts, consolidated all his funds, and moved the money out of the country, probably to another of Salustio's numbered accounts. I'm sure she'd thought of some way to repay him for holding the money until she could lay claim to it.

The feds suspected this as well because the cranky little

shits refused to cut her a deal. Reba was returned to CIW on the first sheriff's bus. I don't worry about her. In prison, she has good friends, she's fond of the staff, and she knows her only choice is to behave herself. In the meantime, her father's doing fine. He's not going to die as long as Reba needs him.

As for Cheney and me, that's still up in the air, but I'm feeling the teeny-tiniest bit optimistic. I'm about due, don't you think?

So here's what I've learned. In the passing drama of life, I'm usually the heroine, but occasionally I'm simply a minor character in someone else's play.

Respectfully submitted,
Kinsey Millhone